BARBARA HAMBLY

# Dark Hand
# of
# Magic

GraftonBooks
*A Division of* HarperCollins*Publishers*

GraftonBooks
A Division of HarperCollins*Publishers*
77–85 Fulham Palace Road,
Hammersmith, London W6 8JB

Published by GraftonBooks 1991
9 8 7 6 5 4 3 2 1

First published in Great Britain by
Unwin Paperbacks 1990

ISBN 0-586-21470-4

Printed in Great Britain by
HarperCollinsManufacturing Glasgow

Set in Times

A new adventure for Sun Wolf and Star Hawk

After his trials and tribulations with the Ladies of Mandrigyn and the Witches of Wenshar, Sun Wolf felt like a rest. But he wasn't expecting to be taking that rest pegged out over a large and lethal ant-hill . . .

Meanwhile his mercenaries are in deep trouble, too. Having been hired by the King – Council of Kwest Malre to besiege the city of Vorsinge, they haven't had much luck. In fact, they've had a lot of bad luck. Too much for it to be coincidence. Someone has put a curse on them. They need Sun Wolf's help.

Sun Wolf had had enough of dealing with wizards and witches to last him a lifetime. But if it came to a choice between being eaten alive by ants and a battle of magic. Well . . .

By the same author

*The Darwath Trilogy*
*The Ladies of Mandrigyn*
*Dragonsbane*
*The Silent Tower*
*The Silicon Mage*
*The Witches of Wenshar*
*Immortal Blood*

For Sensei

## AUTHOR'S NOTE

It should be noted here that not all of the opinions
expressed in this book are those of the author.

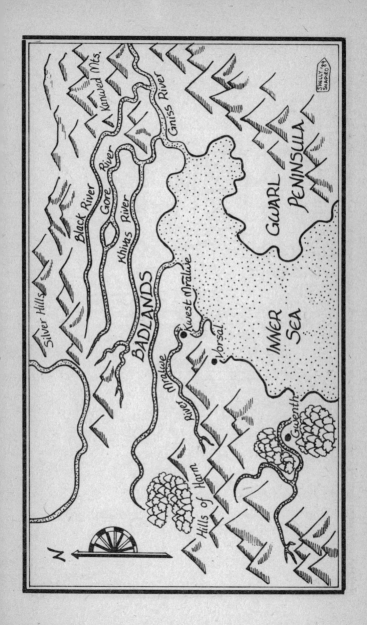

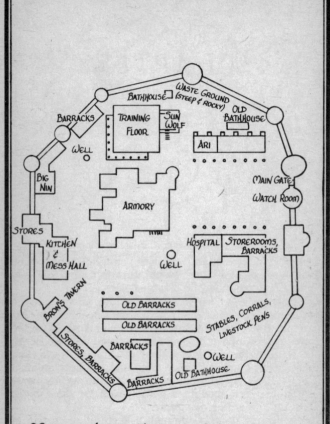

# MERCENARY WINTER CAMP
## (FORMERLY GARRISON QUARTERS OF WRYNDE)

# CHAPTER

—— 1 ——

Sun Wolf's capture, as Sun Wolf himself reflected at his execution, was sheer, stupid ill luck, which Dogbreath of Mallincore would have told him was only to be expected under the circumstances.

The arrow that brought him down took him high in the back from the shelter of a pile of stones he'd have bet his last silver bit—which happened to be in his pocket at the time—couldn't have hidden an emaciated coyote. He hit the sand of the dry arroyo bed in a second's whirling disorientation and sickening pain and the next moment got a gritty faceful of gravel, kicked up as his horse bolted. His first thought was, *So much for the King of Wenshar's guarding our backs.*

His second thought, through a descending curtain of gray weakness, was that, if he blacked out, he was a dead man.

Hooves throbbed in the sand under his unshaven cheek. He made his good eye open and, with odd, tunneled clarity, saw his partner, Starhawk, spur after his escaping horse. It was like her, he thought detachedly, watching her lean from her saddle to grab at the trailing rein, to go after the horse before ascertaining that he still lived. They had been lovers for nearly a year, but she'd been a

mercenary soldier for eight, and knew precisely how long
a ride it was over the black granite mountains of the Dragon's Backbone to safety.

He knew who'd ambushed them, of course, and why.

Lying in the deep sand of the wash with an arrow in
his back, he wondered why he'd been under the impression that this wasn't the sort of thing that people had to
put up with after they became wizards.

Shirdar warriors, the fast-moving cavalry of the deep
desert, were already coming down the canyon wall, their
horses springing down trails for which goats would have
demanded hazard pay. By this time of the afternoon, the
foothill canyons were drowned in dove-colored shadow,
though the rim of sky above was amber-hot. In the bur-
nished light, the warriors' white robes billowed with
dreamy slowness. The Wolf knew he was going into
shock and fought to stay conscious and to keep his
breathing slow and deep. He had to fight, too, not to
spring up and make a run for it. Besides making a target
of him—provided he managed to get on his feet at all—
with the Hawk as far off as she still was, it would only
waste his strength. Long experience of being wounded in
the battles that he'd spent most of his forty years fighting
for other men's pay told him now that he had none to
spare.

*Healing spells*, he thought belatedly. *I'm supposed to
be a wizard, dammit.*

His mind fumbled at the words to call forth power and
to slow the blood welling stickily between the thick muscles of his back and the scuffed sheepskin of his jerkin,
but the pain of the wound itself clouded his mind and
made it difficult to concentrate. It was a very different
thing from healing others, totally leaving aside the fact
that, when he'd worked healing-magic on others, he
hadn't had half a dozen irate warriors getting set to play
cat's cradle with his entrails.

Starhawk was riding back already, the captured horse
on a rein, weaving and ducking the arrows that flashed
around her—a tallish, rangy woman in her late twenties
whom most men were blind and stupid enough to call
plain. She still wore the metal-studded green leather doublet of the King of Wenshar's guards, in which she'd lately
been employed; short-cropped hair the color of old ivory

whipped in strings across a face that was thin, cool, and marked with an old scar down one cheek and a blackly recent bruise the width of a sword blade. Their stay in Wenshar, southernmost of the Middle Kingdoms, had been brief but wildly eventful.

Her distance to him shortened. So did the shirdar's. This was going to be close. There was just time, he thought, if he could mount fast and unaided. With two horses they should be able to hold that slim lead over the lizard-dry mountains to the more settled lands of Dalwirin to the north, where the shirdar dared not hunt.

Gathering his limbs under him, he reflected, with grim detachment, on what a hell of a word "if" was.

It wasn't his wizardry, but thirty years of soldiering that got him on his feet, breathless with pain as the arrow grated in the wound—a massive, tawny, craggy-faced man with a broken nose that jutted like a granite cliff above an unkempt gold mustache and a buckskin patch covering the empty socket of his left eye. His right, under a long brow the same dusty hue as his thinning, shoulder-length hair, was cold and yellow, a wolf's eye, gauging the equidistant approach of rescue and death. He was perfectly well aware that the pain of the arrow in his back was a mosquito bite compared to what the shirdar would do to him if they took him alive.

The horses were still fifty feet away when Starhawk's mount went down. Sudden though it was, Sun Wolf thought the beast hadn't been shot—had only tripped in some unseen pocket of the deep sand. But the result was the same. Starhawk was flung clear as the horse somersaulted, dust and sand flying everywhere in a yellow curtain. The lead horse skidded, balked, head up and eyes white, then veered away like a startled gazelle. The Wolf made two steps of a staggering run to catch Starhawk's fallen mount before it scrambled to its feet and followed, then nearly fell himself. Around him the yells of the shirdar bounced shrilly from the rocks as they drew near. Though he stood in the open, they weren't shooting at him—a very bad sign. They knew he was theirs.

He glimpsed Starhawk's body lying like a broken marionette, twenty feet away, unmoving in the sand.

Vision darkening and legs turning watery, he tried to remember some spell that would get him out of this and failed. Magic was a newfound art to him, an unknown and scarcely comprehended power that had blossomed, late and agonizingly, barely a year ago. For most of his forty years, he had made his living by his sword. As the mounted shirdar closed around him, he groped blindly for his weapon, knowing what they'd do to him and determined, if possible, to get himself killed in the ensuing fray.

But he didn't have any luck with that, either.

"She's coming around . . ."

The voice was directly above her, Starhawk thought. Eyelids shut, she kept her breathing slow, the deep breath of unconsciousness. The speaker was kneeling beside her, at a guess. She could tell she lay on sand, likely still in the arroyo. Dreams of pain and urgency—of the smothering heat of the King of Wenshar's dungeons and the scorch of cherry-red iron inches from her flesh, of splattered blood crawling thickly down the walls of a stone room—all flicked away with the split-second wakefulness of a warrior's training, and Starhawk struck straight up and silent at the man leaning over her, thumbs going for his eyes, knowing this would be her only chance.

There was a yell, an oath, and strong hands grabbed her arms from behind. She was dropping her weight and twisting like a cat at this new assailant—she'd already known by the first man's speaking that there were more than one—when her vision cleared.

She relaxed, then jerked disgustedly free of the suddenly slacked grip.

"If I knew you'd be in hell when I got here, Dogbreath, I'd have tried to be a better person." She scratched the sand out of her hair, and took the waterskin he offered her. The tepid fluid was ambrosia to her dry mouth.

The man who'd first grabbed her, accepting back the vessel and slinging it around his shoulder again, responded gravely, "I always told you you should have given more money to the Church." Then he grinned, bright black, beady eyes sparkling in a tanned face between long, inky hair braided with ribbons, and they embraced, Dogbreath of Mallincore thumping her happily on the back while the others—dim shapes against a luminous channel of twilight sky—grouped in around them.

"Believe me, I'll try it, you damn heretic." He'd been her sergeant in Sun Wolf's mercenary troop when she'd been a squad-leader, later promoted to squad-leader himself. Hugging the sinewy hardness of his rib cage was like hugging a tree.

The fair-haired blond youth whose eyes she'd tried to gouge out upon awakening held out one hand like a beggar. "You can give money to me," he volunteered hopefully. "I was a choirboy in the Church back home."

"If those are your credentials, she's the wrong sex to be interested in you," retorted a stocky little woman named Firecat, getting a general laugh, even from the members of the group who nominally worshiped the Triple God, and a stone flung at her by the youth.

"That's okay, Choirboy, you can sing at my dinners anytime," Starhawk promised, grinning, and the youth drew himself up and made a dignified retreat. She turned back to Dogbreath, still kneeling in the sand beside her, and her gray eyes hardened as she took in the lapis depth of the sky behind his head. "They've got the Chief," she said simply, and in one swift movement was on her feet and heading for the horses. She barely noticed how sore she was from her impact with the ground; in any case it didn't matter. With the shirdar you had to work fast. "Shirdar warriors, six of them . . ."

"We saw the blood." Dogbreath strode at her side, the other two behind. "By the tracks they took him out of here on foot on a lead-line . . ."

Starhawk cursed dispassionately.

"It means they can't be going far," Firecat pointed out.

"Of course they're not going far, they're going to kill him the minute they find an anthill big enough to stake him out on." Starhawk looked around as another man came up—the Little Thurg, stocky and tough, with a round, open face and blue eyes, dragging a couple of saddlebags.

"I found these. By the tracks they took the horses."

"Stuff the horses," Starhawk responded. "It's the books in those bags that the Chief wants."

"Books?" Thurg looked disgusted and dismayed as

Starhawk continued to fire orders, tightening cinches all the while.

"Thurg, Choirboy, you stay here . . ."

"The name is Miris, thank you," retorted the youth with mock dignity. She didn't recognize him—he must have joined the troop after she and the Wolf had left it, almost exactly a year ago. *Had it really been that long?* With them around her, it was as if that year had never been.

"They've got a couple hours' start on us," she went on, gauging the four warriors with a practiced glance, deciding which could best be spared from the upcoming fight. "We have to catch up with them before sunrise . . ."

"You're going to need more than two swords," Choirboy pointed out. "You'll have to steal back the horses anyway, so why take an empty saddle when you can take a fighter?"

"Because I don't want one of my men left here alone, afoot." The words "my men" came easily to her—hers to command and to answer for. "There's still bands of shirdar around, sonny—you won't like what happens when they show up." Past the horses, she could see the dark patches of blood-soaked sand where Sun Wolf had been cornered and she hoped to the Mother that blood wasn't all his. Scuffed tracks led away down the wash toward the desert—hoofprints, stumbling footprints, a dark dribble of gore.

"He's right, Hawk," the Little Thurg said. "I'll manage."

She stood for a moment, reins gathered in her hand, sizing up the pair of them. She knew the Little Thurg well—tough, short, in his early thirties, with ten years of campaigning gouged into his hard little face, and obviously the better man in a fight than the yearling boy. But that cut both ways. If a roving band of vengeful shirdar did show up, Thurg could, as he'd said, "manage." Choirboy—obviously to everyone but Choirboy— couldn't.

"Right." With a curt nod she stepped up into the saddle. "Watch your back, Thurg."

"What do the shirdar want with the Chief, anyway?" Dogbreath demanded as they reined away down the canyon. "You don't get them coming in this close to the Middle Kingdoms on the warpath."

"Long story. I'll tell you that after you tell me what in the name of the Seven Torments you gruts are doing down here." The coarse, vivid slang of the mercenary armies slipped easily back to her tongue, like the ache in her muscles—in her soldiering days she'd seldom been without a bruise or two—and the habit of thinking in terms of many instead of one. Yet in another way these dusty, grimy figures in their iron-plated leather jerkins, their bits of spike and chain glinting coldly in the light of the lemon-colored moon, seemed specters of a dream, called forth from her thoughts by the most casually spoken of words. "I thought the troop would be on the road back to Wrynde by this time of year."

"That," Dogbreath said, "is also a hell of a long story. We been to Pardle Sho on the sniff for you and found the King's Citadel twittering like a cageful of finches—you ever kicked a cageful of finches? Hours of fun. Some pook there said you'd gone to some lost city out in the desert, but halfway there we met the King and he allowed as how you'd lit out north with half the shirdar in the desert on your tails . . ."

"The Chief is supposed to have croaked a shirdar lord." Starhawk bent from her saddle to squint at the ground as they came clear of the canyon's shadows into the heartbreaking, liquid brilliance of the desert moon. The tracks were harder to follow now as the deep sand gave way to coarse gray pebbles that crunched under the hooves. "He's supposed to have summoned demons. They made pemmican of the poor bastard."

Leaning down, scanning the shapeless earth for the scuffy trail of unshod hooves and the occasional dark blood spoor, she still felt the look that passed between them over her head.

"He—he really did turn into a hoodoo, then?" The word Firecat used was merc slang, with all its lower-class connotations of dowsery and love drops and murder in the night. "Not that he offed that grut," she hastened to add. "But I mean—they seem to think he could have."

"Yeah." Starhawk straightened in the saddle, and something within her cringed from speaking of it to these friends who wouldn't understand. "Yeah, he's a wizard."

The silence was awkward, as if she'd admitted he'd suddenly developed a romantic attachment to boys, something they would at least have encountered elsewhere. They'd heard it last spring, when she and the Wolf had returned from Mandrigyn and the horrors of the citadel of the Wizard-King Altiokis, but she knew they hadn't really believed it then. And why should they? For as long as any of them had been alive, no wizard had dared risk murder by the Wizard-King by revealing himself; for at least three generations, fewer and fewer of the mageborn had lived long enough to pass their teachings on.

They knew he had changed. He'd been in their winter camp in Wrynde for a week or so before Ari, the troop's new commander, had led that band of killers south to the newest war, and he'd been very quiet then, still dealing with the fact that he would not, after all, be their commander, their Chief, anymore. Even the most disbelieving of the troop would admit that more had befallen him than the loss of his left eye and the breaking of his voice, of which now little more was left than a scraped, metallic rasp. In his remaining eye, cold amber under the long tufts of brow, was the haunted look of one who has leaned drunk over a ditch to vomit and found himself looking straight down to the bottommost depths of hell.

But knowing that he had changed, and believing what he said he had changed into, were different things.

It was clear to Starhawk from the reactions of her friends in the troop that they did not realize that she, too, had changed. But that, she reflected, was probably just as well.

Choirboy's puzzled voice broke into her thoughts. "If he's a hookum," he asked, "why can't he just make the shirdar all disappear?"

The same thought had crossed Sun Wolf's mind.

How long he'd been walking he didn't know; the moon had set, but through the feverish blur of pain and semiconsciousness he kept a wizard's ability to see in darkness, though some of the things he was beginning to see he knew weren't real. Poison on the arrow, he thought groggily; toadwort or poppy, something that would cloud the mind but not kill.

That, too, was a bad sign.

Other shirdar had joined the men who'd captured him; now and then he seemed to emerge from a black tunnel of hazy agony to find the night freezing on his face, the air burning the wound in his back, and all around him those white-robed riders who never spoke. He'd fainted once, and the shirdar had whipped their horses to a gallop and dragged him a dozen yards before stopping to kick and flog him to his feet; he was fighting hard not to faint again.

*Think!* he ordered himself blurrily. *Yirth of Mandrigyn taught you rope-breaking spells, dammit* . . . But the words of them couldn't rise through the pain and the dull buzzing in his ears; only Yirth's face, dark and ugly, with hook nose and brown birthmark and the glow of those jade-green eyes as she'd taught him spell after spell on the single night he'd spent in her teaching, patterns of power sketched in the air or on the floor; words whose sounds bridged the gap between Nothing and Something; healing, illusion, scrying, weatherspinning . . .

*And how far do you think you'd run if you could remember one?* he demanded grimly. At the moment he was perfectly well aware that the rawhide rope that dragged so excruciatingly at his wrists was the only thing holding him up.

He tried to think like the wizard he now was instead of the warrior he had been for the whole of his life. *Summon fire* . . . *confusion* . . . *steal a horse* . . . And the warrior in him asked cynically, *And which one of these gruts are you going to talk into helping you mount?*

Yirth's image melted, blended in his delirium with that of Kaletha of Wenshar, the only other teacher he'd been able to locate in a year of seeking, coldly beautiful in the dappled shade of the public gardens where he'd seen her first. Then that image, too, darkened, changed before his eyes to blood splattered on a mosaic floor, to screams in darkness, and to the chittering of the demons of Wenshar . . .

He must have fallen. In the drugged black deeps of exhausted unconsciousness, he became aware that he wasn't walking anymore, but lay on his back, stripped to

the waist, flesh cold with the bitter chill of the desert
night and crying out with a hundred abrasions, as if he'd
been beaten with hammers of flint.

In his dreams he could feel the horror in the ground.

He had always dreamed vividly—his father, he remembered, had beaten him when he'd caught him in daytime
reverie, trying to recapture the colors of the previous
night. Since the ordeal of the Great Trial whereby the
magic born into his flesh, the magic he had all his life
denied, had blossomed in a rose of fire, his dreams had
been clearer still.

He lay on the ground, cold sand gritty beneath his
lacerated back and arms, the blood of the arrow wound
still seeping thickly into the earth. His arms and legs
were spread out, and he couldn't move, though whether
this was because he was still unconscious or because he
was tied that way he didn't know. By the utter silence,
he knew it was the hushed hour preceding dawn, before
the hum of insects wakes the desert. The smell of dust
and blood filled his nostrils, and another smell that sent
his mind screaming at him to wake up, _wake up!_ as if
his bound flesh could feel through the earth on which it
lay what was beneath it.

They, too, were waking.

In dreams he saw them, blackish-red clots like dark
raspberries in the winding night of their tunnels, huddled
together and stupid with cold. As big as a man's thumb,
they were like armored horses with their malignant eyes
and dangling mandibles—tunnels, chambers, the caverns
where bloated queens sat dully squeezing out eggs. The
distant sun was already beginning to warm them. He
smelled the acid of their bodies, as he knew they smelled
his flesh.

With desperate effort, he wrenched his mind free of
sleep. The blurry haze of the poison had lessened, which
meant the pain was sharper, and with it the nauseated
weakness of shock. Above him the sky was black opal,
save when he turned his head to see where the blue turned
to violet, the violet to pink, and then amber where it
touched the cool citrine of distant sand. Moving his head
again, he saw his own right arm, stretched from his
shoulder to the rawhide strips that bound his wrist to a
stake in the ground. A foot beyond his fingertips was an

anthill four feet across, its top nearly the height of a man's knee.

He nearly threw up with horror. There were two others visible beyond it; raising his head, a movement which sent renewed shoots of agony down every screaming muscle of his body, he could see another between his spread-eagled feet and others beyond that. It must be the same around on his blind left side.

For an instant shrieking panic swelled in him; then the calm that had gotten him out of a hundred traps and ambushes in his years as a mercenary commander forced the horror away. Calmly he closed his eye, and began sorting in his mind everything Yirth of Mandrigyn had told him, as if he had all the day before him, item by item . . .

And the spell was there. A spell of slipping, of loosening, of the fibers of the uncured leather growing damp, gathering moisture from the air, stretching gradually . . .

The breathless air warmed where it touched his naked belly and chest. He opened his eye to see that the sky had lightened. As he felt the rawhide that cut the flesh of his right wrist loosen a little, his glance went beyond it to the crown of the hideous hillock, and he saw the gritty sand glow suddenly gold. Each pebble, each grain, of the filigreed pit edge of its top was feathered with the long black crescent of a tiny shadow where the first sunlight hit it. The pebbles moved and shifted. Stiffly, an ant crawled forth.

Sun Wolf's concentration failed in a second of horror, and he felt the rope bite again into the bleeding flesh. Like the clenching of a fist, he clamped his mind shut, forcing himself to think only of the spells of undoing, of the dry air turning moist on the leather, of oily knots sliding apart . . . *It'll never work in time* . . .

Other ants were moving about on the mounds now, big soldier ants, bulbous bodies an inch and a half in length, mandibles dangling from heads like shining coffee beans. Sun Wolf fancied he could feel the spiked tickle of their feet on his bare flesh, twisted at his bonds in panic, and felt the rawhide tighten again as the spell's slow working slacked . . . *Not now, pox rot it . . . !*

His mind groped, slid. It would take too long; they'd scent his flesh in moments . . .

But what would it smell like?

It wouldn't work for long—he was too weak, the pain of his wounds too insistent, and if he blacked out again he was dead—but in a split second of clear thought he called to his flesh the searing illusion of heat, poison, fire, burning oil, anything, and threw it around him like a cloak at those tiny, vicious, mindless minds. Dust, smoke . . . that's what they'd smell . . . the crackle of flames where he lay twisting frantically at the ropes that held him pinned over their tunnels . . .

He saw the ants—and there were quite a lot of them—hesitate and draw back.

He knew he couldn't keep it up, couldn't maintain the illusion and work spells on the ropes at the same time. A wave of sick weakness clouded his thoughts, and he fought to keep them clear, fought both the pain and the panic he could sense tearing at the edges of his concentration. Either would kill him; if the ants actually started on him he'd never keep his thoughts clear . . .

*Blood,* he thought; *the juices of sweat and terror; meat sugary-sweet for the tasting* . . . He had never tried a double illusion like this, but it was that or wait for the single spell to outlast his physical ability to remain conscious. Like a smell he twined this new illusion around the ropes that held his outspread hands and feet, and shut his teeth hard on a scream as the ants swarmed greedily forward. *They would eat the rawhide,* he told himself, *they would not touch his flesh—they thought his flesh was fire—his flesh WAS fire—it was the rawhide that was his flesh* . . .

He closed his fists and turned up his hands as much as he could, though the mere effort of that made his arms shake with weakness. Ants clotted the rawhide ropes on the stakes in threshing, glittering blobs. They kept a few inches from the backs of his knuckles, and from his heels, as if his flesh were in fact the fire he projected. If he could keep it up . . .

There was a shrill cry of rage, and the muffled thunder of hooves in the ground. *The shirdar,* he thought, in some floating corner of his awareness. *Of course they'd stayed to watch from a safe distance.* He moved his head, slowly, holding his concentration on the double spell, his whole body drenched now with sweat in the dawn cold.

The riders whirling toward him seemed to come in a slow-motion bellying of white cloaks, shouting with fury, lances raised. He thought detachedly that he probably wouldn't be able to maintain his concentration on either spell with three spears in his belly; death would take almost as long with them as without. But he held to the spells anyway, weirdly fascinated with the mere technique of it, as if these weren't going to be the last few seconds of his life, too taken up with his concentration as the nearest warrior raised his spear . . .

The rider's head snapped back, his body contorting as an arrow appeared suddenly in the middle of his breast, red blossoming over the white of his robe. Sun Wolf thought, *The Hawk must not have been killed.* He couldn't care, couldn't let himself feel joy or fear or anything else which would distract him from a mental exercise he only barely understood. Dizziness swept him. Ants swarmed all around him now, racing back and forth over the pale earth or crawling in heaving swarms on the ropes and stakes, centimeters from the backs of his hands. Other hooves shook the ground under his back, but he dared not break the tunnel of his vision, the wordless images of the spells . . .

*Hurry it up, damn you, Hawk!*

Someone screamed, a death cry of agony, at the same moment the ropes parted. Sun Wolf rolled over, shaking, aware again of the scores of open cuts, the raw flesh of his wrists and the shredded wounds on his knees beneath his torn breeches, aware of the cracked rib he'd gotten in Wenshar, the swollen, dust-clotted hole where the arrow had been pulled out, and the half-healed demon bites—another souvenir of Wenshar—on his hands. He tried to stand and fell immediately, his mind plunging toward unconsciousness. The ants swarmed forward.

*Fire,* he thought blindly, *fire all around my body . . . Just a few seconds more, damn it!*

Starhawk saw the flames roar up in a wall around the Wolf's fallen body and thought, *Illusion.* She hoped to the Mother it was an illusion, anyway. She drove in her spurs and yelled to Choirboy, "It isn't real . . . !"

It looked damn real.

Beside her in the din—the shirdar she'd shot was still partially alive, buried under a shroud of insects and

screaming like a mechanical noisemaker—she heard
Choirboy yell, and from the tail of her eye saw the panic
in his face at the sight of the flames.

"It's not real, dammit!"

But panicky uncertainty had claimed him. The youth
hauled on the reins, dragging his horse to a skidding halt
among the ants. Starhawk felt her own mount veer at the
sight and heat of the blaze and lashed it brutally with the
quirt, driving it straight toward the shimmering wall.
Choirboy's horse reared and twisted as the ants, fully
aroused now and covering the sandy knoll in a seething
blackish-red carpet, poured up over its hooves and began
tearing the flesh of its fetlocks. Choirboy screamed again
as the frenzied animal flung him; then the Hawk saw no
more, her own mount plunging through the pale circle of
flame.

She hauled rein with the Wolf nearly under the hooves.
The heat beat upon her as if she'd ridden into a furnace,
and she didn't dare dismount. The flame seemed to pour
straight up out of the ground, as if the dirt itself were
burning. She screamed, "Get on your feet, you stinking
oaf! You waiting for a goddamned mounting block or
something?!"

Reeling like a drunken man, Sun Wolf half rose. She
grabbed a flailing arm, nails digging hard enough to bring
blood from the bare and filthy flesh—she could only spare
one hand from the dithering horse's rein. She pitched her
voice as she'd pitch a battle yell over the greedy roar of
the flames, the screaming and yells of the shirdar up
among the rocks. "Get your arse in the goddam saddle
or I'll goddam drag it out of here!" Through the bloody
curtain of his ragged hair she could see that his one good
eye was closed, his face white as a dying man's beneath
a layer of grime. Somehow he got a bare foot in the
stirrup and heaved; she hooked her arm under his shoulder and hauled with all her strength, dumping him over
the saddlebow like a killed pig. Then she drove in the
spurs and plunged for the hills, the circle of surrounding
fire sweeping after them like the head of a comet trailing
flame, leaving no burn upon the ground.

Fifty feet farther on, the fire flicked suddenly out of
existence, and she knew Sun Wolf had fainted.

In the rocks Dogbreath and Firecat joined them, leading four shirdar horses in a string. The Hawk glanced back swiftly at the teeming knoll and Dogbreath shook his head and gestured with the bow on the back of his saddle. She shivered, but knew he was right. He and the Cat had been busy in the rocks dealing with the rest of the shirdar. By the time they'd been able to get to Choirboy—running, rolling, tearing frenziedly at the gnawing carpet of ants that had already eaten out his eyes and ears and brain—shooting him was all they could have done.

So the ants, she supposed, if no one else, had done well out of the day. A philosopher might take that as proof that the Mother *did* look out for the humblest of Her creatures, and that it was an ill wind indeed that blew *nobody* good.

That was one reason she'd become a mercenary instead of a philosopher—the other, of course, being that the pay was better.

*This isn't right,* Sun Wolf thought, pulling himself stickily from the darkness of fevered sleep. He'd left the troop with Ari, left them for good . . . He was a mage now. He had to find a teacher, had to find his destiny . . . find what he should have gone looking for twenty years ago . . . Hadn't he?

But they seemed so real—Dogbreath cross-legged by a fist-sized fire built in the shelter of black granite boulders, sharpening a dagger, and Starhawk's silhouette crouched against the blazing desert stars. Somewhere close by a horse whickered, and distant, liquid, unbearably hurtful, coyotes cried in lonely chorus at the moon.

Had he left them? Or was he, in fact, still their commander? Was this that hellish desert summer they'd fought the armies of Shilmarne of Dalwirin back and forth through the passes of the Dragon's Backbone? Had he just been wounded and dreamed it all—the horrors of Altiokis' Citadel, the scorching birth agonies of magic within him . . . Starhawk saying she loved him?

Maybe none of it had ever happened, he thought, sinking again into the fever's shroud of many-colored pain. Maybe he was still commander of these people, fighting small wars for pay and for whatever loot they could steal. Maybe he had never really felt that power kindle deep fire in his flesh.

Starhawk's cool voice said something about it being time to ride on, if they wanted to get over the passes before the shirdar gathered for another attack. He heard the light scrunch of her boots and turned his face away, so that she would not see him weep.

He woke clearheaded, indoors, this time. He heard the groan of dry wind in wooden eaves, the scratchy rattle of pine boughs against the wall by his head, and the petulant bang of a poorly fastened shutter. Musty straw, cooking, and woodsmoke—*an inn*, he thought, opening his eye. Opposite the bed where he lay, he saw an open door and, beyond it, the carved railing of an indoor gallery and high ceiling rafters dyed amber with firelight from a hearth somewhere below. Then he moved his head and saw Starhawk, Firecat, Dogbreath, and the Little Thurg grouped around a crude table across from the foot of his bed.

"Raise you two."

"Come on, I saw you take three cards . . ."

"You gonna see me or sit there whining about it, you sleaze-eating heretic?"

"You should talk about heresy! I'll see you and raise you, you pox-ridden antisubstantiationist tart . . ."

"I bet you say that to all the girls . . ."

"I've got better things to do than throw good money after bad . . ."

"Who dealt this mess?"

Gear was heaped under the table around their feet. He saw his sword, which they must have picked up in the arroyo, his boots, and the battered saddlebags containing the books of the Witches of Wenshar. He waited until Starhawk had gathered up her winnings, then said, "I thought I'd have to be pretty far off my head to hallucinate something that looked that much like Dogbreath."

They crowded around his bed—Starhawk carefully pocketing her money before leaving the table—all talking at once. Over Thurg's head he met the Hawk's eyes, cool and gray and enigmatic as always, but deep in them he read what she'd die before saying in the presence of others, her shy pleasure at seeing him once more himself, if not precisely on his feet. Idiotically, his heart did a little flip in his chest.

"We been hunting you all around St. Gambion's barn, Chief," Thurg was saying.

Firecat added, "Be a hell of a thing to catch up with you just in time to see you get et by bugs."

"Yeah, I thought that myself." He struggled to sit up, shaking the long hair out of his face.

Under a bandaged pad of dressings, the wound in his back hurt like a mother-in-law's bite, but it was the scouring sting of poultices, no longer the burn of poison. From the feel of it, he could tell it wasn't serious. A whore long ago had once given him worse with a pair of scissors.

"But"—Dogbreath grinned, perching tailor-fashion on the end of the bed, his mad eyes sparkling —"odds were damn near even we would."

"What the hell is that supposed to mean?"

Starhawk tossed him a shirt. It was his last spare from the saddlebags, patched, frayed at the cuffs, most of the points missing, and stained faintly with somebody's blood. They'd probably got the innkeeper's wife to patch it—no mercenary he knew, with the exception of himself, had any idea which end of the needle the thread went through. In the past year of traveling with Starhawk it had been he who had mended her shirts—a hell of a thing in a grown woman who'd presumably been raised right. He rubbed his eyepatch, readjusting the set of the leather over the empty socket.

"And what the hell are you doing here anyway? I thought Ari would be halfway back to Wrynde by this time of year."

"Ari sent us, Chief," Dogbreath said, the wicked sparkle fading from his dark eyes. "We're in trouble, all of us—we need your help bad. We can't be certain, but it's looking more and more like some wizard's put a hex on the troop."

# CHAPTER

## —— 2 ——

"*It started with little things.*" Dogbreath shrugged and gestured helplessly with big, knuckly hands. Never a dirty man, Dogbreath was invariably ragged; under the dingy leather of his iron-plated doublet lurked a sweater that looked as if it had been knitted by a wittol on hashish, over which the grimy and horrifically parti-colored dags of a court coat's sleeves hung like rotting kelp. "Stuff happens—it always happens, any campaign, you know that, Chief. But this time . . ."

"Where are they now?"

"Vorsal."

Sun Wolf swore, with considerable variety and feeling.

It wasn't that he felt any shock over the siege of Vorsal. He'd been expecting trouble there since its hereditary Duke had defied the economic leadership of Kwest Mralwe and started weaving and exporting local cloth via Vorsal's own small but excellent harbor, instead of selling the fleeces to the great merchant houses of Kwest Mralwe. When anyone, let alone some two-by-three principality like Vorsal, crossed the richest cloth-trade monopoly in the Middle Kingdoms, war was strictly a matter of the King-Council's earliest convenience. But for Ari and the mercs to still be there this late in the year . . .

"Does he know how close the rains are?" Sun Wolf rasped, appalled. "What the hell's he been doing all summer? God's Grandmother, the Hawk and I between us could take that town in two weeks with a troop of nuns and a performing dog act!"

"It's not that easy, Chief." Dogbreath drew up his knees and wrapped his long arms around them, his simian brow puckered as he tried to marshal thoughts he was uncertain how—or if—to express. "I never believed in all that garf about hoodoos," he continued after a moment. "I mean, yeah, I laid out a dozen summer nights watching for the fairies when I was a kid, and all I ever saw was the older kids canoodling in the woods. But now they say you—you've turned into some kind of hoodoo, and there might be others—wizards, witches—hoodoos who've been on the bunk all these years, coming out now Altiokis the Wizard-King isn't around to snuff 'em. And damn if I know what to believe."

Through the open door, voices drifted up from the common room below the gallery, the innkeeper's wife's raised in exasperation above the chirping giggles of her assorted offspring. This close to the coming of the winter storms, few travelers were on the road. Sun Wolf guessed the woman wouldn't have permitted her children into the common room in the busy season. By their voices, at least one of them was old enough to be made a slave, either as a pit-brat in the Wenshar silver mines, or—if pretty—he knew brothels that took boys and girls as young as eight.

"It's not just the usual bellyaching during a siege, Chief," Dogbreath went on. "It's not just soldiers' luck or that kind of stupid thing. This is different. I can't say how." He slouched back against the wooden wall behind him and seemed to concentrate all his attention on plaiting and unplaiting the last three-inch tuft of hair at the end of his left braid as he spoke.

"It isn't just some of the arrows being warped, or the glue on the fletch rotting—it's every motherless arrow you touch, and especially the one you use to try to pick off the guy who's about to dump molten lead on your buddy. Motherlovin' boxes of 'em that were fine in Wrynde. It isn't just the food's bad—it's either tryin' to climb out of the cask or it's got this back-taste that you

barely notice going down, but you notice it lots when it's
coming back up the other way half an hour before the
sortie at dawn. I never seen so many roaches, chiggers,
and ticks, and all the rats in the Middle Kingdoms have
been living in the catapult ropes. And I'll tell you something else—there's not a cat in the camp anymore.

"That's how it started. Then the sapper tunnels started
flooding. Tunnels where we'd checked the supports and
didn't see a worm or a splinter or so much as an ant—
sorry, Chief, didn't mean to mention ants—would collapse on us. One of 'em *caught fire*, and if you can figure
out how that happened, I'll give you a sweet. Then the
horses would spook—first just in the lines at night, but
these days they'll do it in battle, or even riding back and
forth to town—horses who were damn near foaled on a
battlefield. We lost a dozen men including Gadget—you
remember Gadget, the engineer?—when one of the ballistas collapsed. We still don't know how that happened,
but I was one of the guards on it the night before it packed
in and I swear by the Queen of Hell's corset nobody got
near it.

"There's something going on there, Chief, and the
troops are starting to spook."

Sun Wolf barely heard those last words. *A wizard.*
Something inside him gave a great, excited bound, like
a child who sees his father surreptitiously clearing another stall in the stables a week before his birthday feast.
*A wizard in Vorsal.*

For a year, since being banished from Mandrigyn,
where his only potential teacher lived, he'd been seeking
a master wizard, someone who had been trained in the
use of those terrifying powers, someone who could train
him. For a year he had traced rumors that led nowhere
and run to earth every trail he could think of that might
lead to another wizard, someone who could teach him
what he was and what he could be. The last of those trails
had ended in the dead city of Wenshar, in bloody shreds
of black cloth and red hair and a staggering line of sticky
red handprints leading away into dust-silted gloom.

Across Dogbreath's shoulder he met Starhawk's eyes.
But she said nothing, just sat at the table, silently shuf-
fling and reshuffling the cards.

His one eye flicked back to Dogbreath. "Why doesn't

Ari just pull out? Write it off as a lost cause, take his front money and get his rosy little backside up to Wrynde before the rains turn the badlands into a white-water death trap and strand his arse in the Middle Kingdoms for the winter?'' Firecat and the Little Thurg, who'd scootched their chairs around to his bedside, looked down into their painted clay mugs and said nothing. "He *did* get front money, didn't he?''

"Well—not enough to buy food through the winter.''

Sun Wolf cursed again, a comprehensive and hair-raising execration that included several generations of Ari's descendants and all of his luckless ancestors.

"It was some kind of a deal with the King-Council,'' Dogbreath continued, unperturbed by his former commander's eloquence. "Penpusher said . . .''

"Penpusher should have goddam known better than to get you in a position you couldn't get out of!'' He made a furious gesture and gasped as his wounded shoulder and the cracked ribs he'd acquired in Wenshar added their mite to the discussion.

"That's just it, Chief,'' said Dogbreath. "We *can't* get out of it, not now. Without the money we're gonna starve in Wrynde, if we make it that far and, if we don't break Vorsal soon, we're gonna get hit by the rains anyway and stranded. Yeah, Kwest Mralwe *might* feed us through the winter, or they might turn against us, but either way, by spring, Laedden or Dalwirin is gonna get in the act and send an army against us that we won't be in any shape to fight. And anyhow,'' he added quietly, "if there *is* a hoodoo holed up in Vorsal, we might none of us make it to spring.''

Sun Wolf leaned back against the flattened and rather dirty hay pillow wadded behind him, his big arms folded, his one eyelid drooping low over the chill amber glitter of his eye. The winter storms were late already; the desert sandstorms had started weeks ago. In his bones, in the dim extended senses of wizardry and animal watchfulness, he could feel the weather, hear the moan of distant tempests whispering behind the wind as it shook the heavy window shutters. He studied them all—the thin brown man sitting cross-legged on the foot of his bed in a messy welter of sleeve dags; the sturdy red-haired woman in the chair beside him, sipping her beer and watching his face anxiously; the Little Thurg, looking down at his blunt, folded hands; even the Hawk, seemingly absorbed in getting every card in the two halves of the divided pack to interleave exactly, one to one. He'd spent years with these people and knew them far better than any of the parade of lovely young concubines who had filed through his bed. He'd trained them to fight, crossed swords with them at the school he'd operated for so many years in Wrynde, and drunk with them after battles; he knew their flaws, their jokes, their loves, and the minutest timbres of their voices. The day before yesterday was far from the first time they'd saved his life, at the risk—and sometimes, as in Choirboy's case, at the cost—of their own.

For an instant everything was as it had been, and he understood that, as with Starhawk, he was still their commander in their hearts—and in his own.

But there was magic now in his veins. And the man who could bring it forth, give him what his soul most craved, was in Vorsal, holding it against them.

"You feel okay to sit a horse tomorrow?" Dogbreath went on, glancing up when the weight of the silence became oppressive. "It's a week's ride—five days if we push it . . ."

He was expecting the Wolf to say, as he would have a year ago, *So let's push it*. The Wolf still felt weak and tired, but he'd fought battles in worse shape. It was all so familiar, so easy, that he nearly made that automatic response. But after all, he thought, and said nothing. After a moment he saw that *nothing* change the expression in his friend's face.

"Chief?" It hadn't even occurred to him, Sun Wolf thought, that he might say no.

Because they trusted him. Trusted that he'd be there for them, to the cold gates of hell and beyond, as they were for him.

He sighed. "Yeah. I'll be ready to go in the morning."

Relief sprang into Firecat's face and Thurg's, like children when they can convince themselves after an overheard fight that their parents still love one another, that nothing has changed. Only the doubt lingered in Dogbreath's troubled glance, as they filed out of the room to investigate the smells of roast pig that floated ever more insistently up from the common room below. As for Starhawk, rising last to follow them out the door, it had always been difficult to read her enigmatic gray eyes.

*A wizard in Vorsal.*

As a child, Sun Wolf had crept by night from the loft he'd shared with the household stores to steal through freezing darkness to the house of Many Voices, shaman of the village. The shaman's house had a door which looked out onto the moor; he would crouch in the lichenous shelter of a fallen menhir and watch that dapper little man sorting his herbs, experimenting with smokes and incense, or sketching the Circles of Power in the dirt of the floor. His father had caught him at it and beaten him, more than once. Many Voices was a charlatan, his father had said, a faker whose curses were worthless unless backed with poison. Finally the big warrior, who had wanted a warrior son, had paid Many Voices to illwish a neighbor's goats, and had sat out with his son most of one rainy night until they'd caught the shaman red-handed, mixing jimson with the goats' feed.

Sun Wolf, who'd been seven at the time, had never forgotten the searing blister of shame at his own credulity, nor his father's uproarious laughter at his cheated, helpless rage. It had been the end of his conscious dreams of magic.

Like his father—like most people in the days of Altiokis the Wizard-King's century and a half of dominance—he had come to believe that magic was only sleight of hand or trickery and that the shadows of power and fire that haunted his own dreams were, in fact, nothing but the lurking seeds of madness. He had become what his father had wanted him to be and had been the best.

And then the seeds had blossomed. Untaught magefire had broken forth within him like glowing magma from a shell of black volcanic stone, and with it the craving, the yearning to learn and understand.

A wizard in Vorsal. A week's ride—five days, if they pushed it. The strategist, the fighter, the commander his men knew and trusted, might turn ways and means over coolly in his mind, but the untaught mage—like the born

musician who has never been allowed to lay hands on an
instrument, or the natural artist who has only heard of
paint—breathed faster at the thought. He'd found one,
after all those barren months!

The reflection of the firelight had changed against the
common room's ceiling, visible to him through the half-
open door. The groaning of the wind about the walls
waxed shriller as full darkness fell, and the dry restlessness of the air prickled his skin. Through the door and
down in the commons he heard Dogbreath's flexible bass
voice ranging the hills and valleys of some tale he was
spinning, broken by the braying delight of the Little
Thurg's laugh; closer, he caught the brief scatter of children's voices as the innkeeper's wife herded her brood
up some backstair to the attics where they slept. Sun Wolf
wondered if the inn stores were kept up there, and if
those children woke in the night as he had done in his
childhood to see the red eyes of rats reflecting the glow
of the moon. Then a light creak of floorboards sounded
in the gallery outside the door, a tread he identified as
Starhawk's in the same moment that he reached down
with his unwounded arm to locate the sword he kept habitually by the bed. A dark form against the ruby-dyed
rafters outside, a slip of brightness catching colorless
hair; then she was inside. She disliked standing framed
in doorways as much as she did sitting with her back to
open space.

The ability to see in pitch darkness had been one of
the first things that had come to him with his wizard's
power. He watched her locate her bedroll by touch after
closing the door, and spread the blankets soundlessly
across the threshold. She unbuckled her swordbelt and
laid it on the floor beside her, removed half a dozen daggers and a spiked knuckle-duster from various corners of
her person, then folded herself neatly down to a sitting
position to pull off her boots.

"I'm not hurt that bad, dammit."

Her grin was fleet and shy even in the dark. "I was
afraid of getting stabbed if I startled you awake."

"Come over here and I'll stab you so you'll never forget it."

She laughed softly, collected her weapons, and came
to sit on the bed. Only when she reached down to locate

its edge could he tell that she was almost totally unable to see in the dense gloom. The shutters might be opened an hour a day at this time of year to air the room, but against his shoulder he could feel through the wall that the outer air was freezing. With his good hand, he guided her face down to his, and they kissed, long and deep, in the darkness.

She stripped quickly out of her jerkin and buckskin breeches, and awkwardly he turned back the blankets for her to crowd into the narrow space beside him.

"I was scared for you," she said after a time, her soft voice husky and hesitant. "I couldn't let myself think about it then. I can't ever, really. They're right when they say falling in love is a bad idea. You get scared . . . I don't want to lose you."

"I never did like bugs," he rumbled, and pulled the blanket up to cover them both.

She laughed softly, putting aside the memory of that fear, and said, "Then we've come to the wrong inn."

He was too weary and still in too much pain to feel much desire for her, but it was good only to lie together, to feel the warmth of that long bony body at his side, to hear her cool voice and see the faint shape of her delicate, broken nose outlined in the darkness.

At length she asked him, "You going to kill that wizard in Vorsal?"

*Trust the Hawk,* he thought, and sighed heavily. The question had been cruising, sharklike, beneath the surface of his own thoughts for hours. "I don't know."

"You help the folks who are trying to sack his town and skrag his family and friends, I doubt he'll feel like teaching you much, you know." He could feel the steel in her light voice, like a finely made dagger flexing, and wished sometimes she wouldn't put her finger so unerringly on his own thoughts.

"I didn't say I was going to help them."

"It's what Ari's asking," she pointed out. "For you to use your magic to help them take the town."

"No," he said quietly. "They're asking my help against a wizard, and against a wizard's curse. That's different."

"You feel up to explaining the difference to them when you get there? Or to him?"

She paused, turning her head sharply at the sound of a swift patter of footsteps on the gallery outside the door; then relaxed as a child's treble voice whispered urgently, "Niddy, come back here!" There was the happy giggle of a toddler, and Starhawk smiled in spite of herself, as an older child evidently caught up with its wayward sibling and hustled it, unwillingly, up several flights of creaking backstairs to the attic once again. Earlier the Wolf had seen them scurry past the door of his room, two little towheads in the clumsy white linsey-woolsey smocks of peasant children, and had heard their mother scolding them to stay away from the common room and the guests.

And well she should, he'd reflected. Dogbreath and Firecat looked as if they'd split a baby between them for supper and feed the scraps to the pigs.

Her voice soft in the darkness, Starhawk went on, "The boys aren't going to see it that way, Chief. They're my friends, yeah—I'd say my brothers, if my brothers weren't . . . Well, anyhow. But in the past year I've been friends with the people who live in the towns we used to sack. That's something you can't think about if you're a merc—and maybe that's why mercs only hang around with other mercs. When you torch a house, you can't explain to the woman whose kids are trapped upstairs while she's being raped in the yard by six of your buddies that this is just your job. You do what you think best, Chief, and you know, when you finally make it to the bottommost pit of Hell, I'll be there at your side, but I gave up war. I'm not going back."

"I wouldn't ask you to," he said softly. Then, in a burst of honesty, "Well, not unless I was in trouble real bad," and she chuckled softly, a faint vibration through the bones of his chest that stirred in him an odd, passionate tenderness. She lay on his blind left side; he had to turn his head to look down into her face. "And I need a teacher. You remember those hotshot kids who used to come to the school at Wrynde, the ones who seemed as if they'd been born with a sword in their hands. Those are the dangerous ones, the ones who leave a trail of dead and maimed until they learn what they're doing—learn when to keep the sword sheathed.

"I'm like that, Hawk. It isn't just that I want it, need

it—need someone to show me what this magic is. Most mageborn get *some* kind of teaching before the Trial brings on their full power. I have power and, by all my ancestors, I saw in Wenshar what power without discipline can do. But I owe Ari. I owe my men. I'd be dead now if it wasn't for them. You too, since you couldn't have saved me alone, and you'd probably have tried.''

She said nothing. Pillowed against the scarred muscle and golden fur of his chest, her face remained impassive, gray eyes open in the darkness, thinking. In the eight years of brotherhood which had preceded their becoming lovers, he had gotten to know those silences, the thoughts that hid so stubbornly behind the steely armor she wore locked around her heart. In the last year, he'd occasionally wondered that she had ever emerged from behind that armor to tell him that she loved him.

It was a damn good thing that she had, he reflected. He'd never have had the nerve to say it to her.

"It sounds bad, Hawk," he said gently. "Whatever I decide when I get there, I can't not go.''

"I'm not saying you shouldn't." She didn't turn her face to him, only considered the darkness before her, impassive, as if Ari, Dogbreath, Firecat and the others were not also her friends and not also in danger of their lives. "But it's going to come down to a choice for you sooner or later, Chief—him or them.''

Her hand reached up, long, competent fingers tracing idly the scabbed-over crescents of demon bites on the heavy muscle of his hands. "You always told us in training that the man who knows what he wants in a fight has it all over the man who doesn't quite; it's the robber who's able to kill a man in the five seconds it takes that man to make up his mind whether he'd kill somebody to protect his goods. I just think you'd better figure out what it's going to be soon, because there's a good chance that, when the time comes to make that decision, he's going to be actively trying to kill you.''

She was right, of course. She generally was, but that didn't give him any clue as to what he should do, or make his own indecision any easier to deal with.

Starhawk's breath sank to a nearly soundless whisper of sleep, but Sun Wolf lay awake, his one eye open in the darkness. After a time he heard the brawling laughter

of his troopers as they piled up the narrow wooden stair
to the gallery—why shut up for the benefit of anyone
spoilsport enough to be asleep at this hour? The arrogant
clamor dimmed as they settled into the next-door room
they shared. Then for a time, he listened to the hushed
stirrings downstairs as the innkeeper's wife and servants,
who'd stayed awake to do so, cleaned the empty tankards
and the spilled beer, swept the hearth where battles had
been fought with the kindling from the wood-boxes and
left strewn about the floors, and banked the kitchen fires.
By the dim vibration and creak, he tracked them up the
stairs, across the gallery, and up still further into the high
dark reaches of the upper floors.

Then he heard only the groan of the wind and the gob-
lin pecking of branches against the shutters, felt the faint
sway of the tall wooden building in the heavy gusts; the
slow drift of the inn into slumber was like a great, black
ship riding at anchor in the windy night. He would go to
Vorsal, but what he would do when he got there he did
not know.

Lying in the darkness, he remembered Ari as he'd first
seen him, a puppy-fat child with rainwater streaming
down his long, dark hair, standing on the edge of the
training floor of the winter camp in Wrynde, with his
father's pike and arrows balanced on his shoulder; Sun
Wolf remembered a thousand winter afternoons and evenings on that floor, with the rain pounding the high roof
above the vaulted lattice of the rafters while he put his
men through their paces or ducked and dodged the Big
Thurg or Starhawk in a practice bout. He'd yelled at them,
ragged them, cursed them, and, when necessary, beaten
them black and blue, conditioning them to the instant
obedience of absolute trust—Dogbreath, Penpusher, the
Hawk, the Big and Little Thurgs, Battlesow, the Goddess, that black warrior Ryter who'd been so skilled and
so easy to drink with and who'd died with an arrow in
his eye at some stupid battle in Gwarl . . .

He had made them killers, had led them to their kills—
had forged of them a brotherhood as only war can forge
it. It had been hard enough to leave them and to choose
the solitary search for another art, another need. Now to
choose again, to kill the one person who could give him
what he needed in order to save their lives . . .

*Dammit!* he raged at the spirits of his ancestors, *it isn't fair!*

But the dry howl of the wind outside brought him only the suspicion of cosmic laughter.

*This might be my only chance!*

But he knew already he could not abandon his friends.

He was still trying to make up his mind, to come to some conclusion, when the inn caught fire.


"That scum-sucking smear of lizard dung!" The Wolf was coughing so badly he could barely get the words out; the pain of his cracked rib and his wounded shoulder gouged at him with every spasm of his smoke-clogged lungs. He could barely see, his eye and the empty left socket under its patch burning with the black billows of smoke that rolled up the narrow stairs from below. Starhawk's arm was around him, dragging him; his wounds and exhaustion had left him weaker than he'd suspected. The heat was incredible.

She yelled over the noise of shouts from below, "Who?"

"That codless bastard of a Vorsal hoodoo, that's . . . !" He broke off in another fit of coughing that ripped his lungs like a saw, and for a moment the hot light seemed to darken and the floor to sway. Then he felt the stab of his broken ribs as her arm tightened around him. Lit by a hellish storm of red glare and blackness, the stair plunged down before them like a coal chute to Hell. Memory flooded him and he grabbed at the newel-post. "The books! The Witches' books!"

"I have one set of saddlebags, I'll go back for the other."

He could barely see through the burn of the smoke, but realized what the buckled leather straps were that he felt, draped around her shoulder.

"Hang on. These stairs are a bastard."

He balked, groping for the saddlebag strap. The inn was wood and the wind bone-dry—he'd torched hundreds like it and knew exactly how fast they went up. Below them, all around them in furnace glare and darkness, the roar of the fire was a bass bellow over which unidentifiable screams and shouts floated like whirling flakes of ash.

"Go back for 'em now! Dammit, they're the only books of magic we've got—the only ones we've even *heard* of!" He braced himself against her determined shove, which wasn't easy, considering it was only her shoulder which held him up. "This place'll be a pyre by the time we get downstairs . . ."

"You stubborn old . . ."

"DO IT!" he roared. She stiffened, bristling like an affronted cheetah. But for eight years, when he had yelled at her, with a wooden training sword, to go after men twice her size who were waiting to attack her with clubs, she'd gone, and the training held true. She dumped him unceremoniously at the top of the stairs, threw the saddlebags at him, and strode back down the hall, the veils of smoke closing round her like a suffocating curtain.

Downstairs he heard the roar of something collapsing. Heat heaved up around him, blinding him, sickening him. Below he could see stringers of fire racing along the boards of the common-room floor, tendrils of it crawling up onto the carved rails of the stair. The hair rose on his scalp with primal terror and he had to fight the urge not to throw himself down the stairs, not to stagger, crawl, anything . . . anything not to be trapped abovestairs and burned.

*But we can't lose the books,* he told himself feverishly. *It's only a dozen feet . . .* He clung to the saddlebags, his head swimming with suffocation and smoke, the superheated air scalding his lungs like burning sand, and squinted desperately into the smoke to catch a glimpse of Starhawk returning. More screaming, piercing and shrill, sliced through the roar of the flames with a sense of urgency that he could not place . . . He hoped to his first ancestor they'd gotten the horses out of the stable. According to Dogbreath, they hadn't started out their search with much more money than he had, and it was nearly spent. If they were stranded without horses . . .

Downstairs, outside in the yard, a woman was shrieking . . . Animal fear clawed him, but he wouldn't leave Starhawk alone. They couldn't lose the books, his only link with what he was . . . *Where the hell was the Hawk . . . ?*

* * *

He came to, gasping, coughing, his clothes and the air all around him rank with smoke, wet horse dung and hay pungent beneath him. By the noise and the hot wind that stroked his face, he knew he was outside. He rolled over onto something soft and threw up what little was in him. The smell of burning pine trees came to him, sappy and sweet.

He fought the spasms of his lungs to a standstill; it seemed to take forever. A storming chaos of meaningless noise whirled around him, the fire's greedy bellow, yelling voices, the thin splash of water by the inn-yard well and its cold stony smell, the frenzied whinnying of the horses in the hellstorm of the burning stable. Another piercing shriek, shrill with terror and despair—this time, remembering something Starhawk had said earlier, he identified it. It was coming from the attic where the inn-keeper's children slept.

In horror, he rolled up to his elbow and opened his eye.

Flames swirled thirty feet above the crumbling thatch of the inn roof; the sparks cascaded higher still, an upside-down waterfall pouring at the stars. Beyond it, the sky pulsed with a feverish light, and a bass roaring, like the sea in a narrow place, made him shudder. The trees on the mountainside behind the inn had caught. In a wild chiaroscuro of gold and ink, he made out the faces of the line stretching between wellhead and inn—Dogbreath and Firecat were among them, stripped to their shirts and passing buckets that slopped over and turned the ground around their feet to a processional carpet of glittering mud. He himself was stretched on the wet straw of the stable's muck pile, a safe distance from the buildings, amid a strange assortment of bedding, clothes, bags, silver tankards, and furniture. By the feel of it, the straw had been doused down well.

There was only one pair of saddlebags beside him.

His empty belly turned to lead.

"Starhawk . . ."

He tried to rise, but the weakness of smoke and fatigue made his head swim, and he sank down again, retching. Someone came to stand over him. Looking up, he saw the Little Thurg silhouetted against the flare of the burning stables.

"Starhawk . . ."

The round face creased into a frown. "Was she with you, Chief? We found you at the top of the stairs . . ."

"She went back for the books." *It was only a dozen feet!* his mind protested frantically. *She should have been in and out of there . . . !*

"Damn stupid thing to do!" He glanced over his shoulder—Sun Wolf now saw that the Little Thurg held the halter ropes of three horses, blindfolded with pieces of sacking. His barrel chest gleamed with sweat as if it had been oiled, where it wasn't black with grime. "You were hanging onto those like they were your last hope of dinner," he said, knotting the headstall ropes onto the leg of a huge oak wedding chest on the heap nearby—a monstrosity so garishly carved and painted the Wolf personally would have left it inside to burn. With a quick movement, the little man pulled the blindfolds from the beasts' eyes, wadded them under one hard-muscled arm, then took a deep breath and turned to dash back to the stables once more.

*Hawk, no!* thought Sun Wolf, stunned. *No, please . . . !* He shut his eye, as if that would blot from his mind the image of the Hawk walking away from him, black rolls of smoke closing her in . . .

Then he heard the Little Thurg swear and a woman scream and opened his eye once more.

The shutters of the inn's highest gable were kicked out from within. Smoke rolled forth, its underside catching the glare of flames from below like reflected sunlight on a summer tree against the sullen blackness of the sky. Something dropped from the window, whirling and twisting as it fell—a pair of saddlebags. As they plunged, a book fell free, to splat face-down in the wet muck of the yard. Sun Wolf barely noticed.

Like everyone else in the inn yard, his gaze was riveted to the window as Starhawk emerged, carefully straddling the sill.

A boy of about four was clinging like a monkey to her back, naked but for a rag of shirt, his flesh showing burned beneath it. Starhawk gently reached into the black maw of smoke behind her and helped out a girl of eight or nine, naked but unburned, with a baby tied to her back in the torn remains of her nightshirt. The Hawk pointed at the timbering and beam ends, lit by the flames pouring out of every window of the four storeys which separated them from the ground.

Above the horrified silence, Dogbreath's harsh voice yelled, "Somebody get a blanket, dammit!"

The little girl began to descend.

Only the Hawk, thought Sun Wolf, could have given a child like that confidence to do something most adults he knew would have thought twice about. The smoke in the window behind Starhawk was lit from within by the bloody glare of fire—sparks swirled out and onto the wind. The ochre light showed her scarred face black with a mask of smoke and grime and oily with sweat, but calm, as he had seen it for years in battle. Against the filth her eyes seemed very pale. The thatch overhead was already in flames. It couldn't be very many minutes be-fore the rafters collapsed, taking all the floors in between and very likely the wall with them . . .

She was giving the little girl all the time she could, in case she herself fell.

When the girl had gone down far enough so that the odds were good a fall wouldn't kill her, Starhawk swung herself cautiously out the window and started down. She moved slowly, overweighted by the child on her back—in many places the timbers and beam ends were smoking, the window sills flaming streaks against the soot-blackened plaster of the wall.

There was a shrill scream and the girl beneath her slipped, skidding and falling, grabbing like a little animal at the beam ends of the first floor as they struck her. Nobody in all that chaos in the yard had managed to come up with a blanket and she hit the ground hard. A knot of people swallowed her up at once, one woman's sobbing howls rising above the others. Starhawk, still up on the wall, stopped for a moment, her blackened face pressed to the plaster, the hot wind of the fire flattening her smutched white shirtsleeves and the pale flutter of her hair. Neither she nor the little boy clinging to her back made a sound. Then the baby's crying sliced through the noise, wailing in terror and pain. The firelight splattered the mouthing faces, the line of buckets abandoned in the welter of puddles and mud.

Dogbreath's bass voice boomed, "She's okay, just get her the hell out of the way . . ."

The crowd broke, milling uncertainly. Someone carried the girl, someone else the baby, back away from the wall that was now in flames.

Somehow the Wolf got to his feet. Wobbly-kneed and shedding straw and muck from his patched breeches, he staggered from the midden toward the billowing heat of the blazing inn wall. Dogbreath, Firecat, and a fat woman who must have been the children's mother still stood close enough to the wall to be scorched, but would not run away. As Sun Wolf joined them, the little girl, still naked, ran back out of the crowd to stand with them, looking up. Starhawk edged down another few feet, the wall clearly burning hot to her touch.

A voice yelled, "WATCH OUT!"

And with a roar like the booming of blasting powder, the inn roof collapsed. The wall bulged, cracked, split—fire spewed from the cracks. Men and women fled in all directions, black against torrents of flame. In the slow-motion unreality of horror, Sun Wolf watched the whole building cave in, swallowing Starhawk and the child she carried in a firefall of burning beams.

# CHAPTER

## —— 3 ——

*"I'LL KILL HIM," WHISPERED THE WOLF. "I SWEAR* it by my ancestors."

He set down Starhawk's limp hand, his own fingers shaking with fatigue, leaned against the carved proscenium that framed the cupboard-bed and closed his eye. Behind him, Dogbreath and Firecat exchanged a worried glance. In the doorway of the closetlike second-best bedroom, the woman of the house—the innkeeper's fat wife's sister—stood silent, her hands tucked beneath her apron for warmth, for in the long night and cold morning the fire in the room's tiled hearth had burned low. In spite of it being nearly midday now the house was very still, save for the far-off sounds of a woman crying. The innkeeper's wife's sister bore the tracks of tears on her own thin cheeks. Though the single window was closed, a stench of ashes lingered on the air.

Cautiously, Firecat said, "It looks like it was an accident, Chief." She scratched her tangled red hair, her pointy face grave—she had been drinking buddies with Starhawk for years. "We all saw the potboy knock over the kindling basket early in the evening. When we helped him pick it up we probably missed some, that's all."

The wood-paneled room had been long disused; it felt

damp and cold and smelled faintly of mildew. The light
that came through the thick, yellowish panes of the shut
window had a sickly cast, and through the bumpy glass
could be seen the still-smoldering ruins of the inn and
the blackened acres of pine woods on the mountain behind. Sun Wolf raised his head slowly, the dust-colored
stubble of his beard glittering and his yellow eye gleaming malevolently. "Potboy, hell!" His voice was the grate
of a rusty nail. Though Dogbreath and Firecat had
washed, their clothes looked as if they'd been through
some particularly nasty street fighting; the Wolf's face
was still smeared with soot, against which the thong of
his eyepatch had cut a pale streak, like a scar.

From the bed beside him, a faint voice breathed,
"Chief?"

"Yeah?"

Starhawk's eyes remained shut, sunk in black hollows
in a face chalky beneath its windburn and tan. Bits of her
ivory-colored hair stuck out through the bandages around
her head, strands so fine that they hung limply down like
a child's. Though she hadn't been much burned, he had
found neither breath nor pulse when they'd carried her
here last night; in the darkness of the Invisible Circle,
the deepest spirals of meditation where life begins and
ends, it had taken him hours of seeking to bring her back.
Too scoured to feel either victory or elation, he only
reached out to gather her fingers into his again, to take
comfort from the touch of her living flesh.

Her lips barely moved. "Children?" she asked.

"Baby and the girl are fine," he said softly. "The
little boy's dead."

"Pox."

The child had been dead, his neck broken, when they'd
dug him out of the rubble. It had saved Sun Wolf a decision—
he had been, so far, only able to work healing magic on one
person at a time. He didn't know whether having proper
training would have made a difference or not.

Wearily, he looked around him. The small room faced
north, dim and cold even in daylight, and the fire in its
beehive hearth of blue and yellow tiles did little to warm
it. The sister of the innkeeper's wife—departing now to
look after her kin—had married the town miller, and the
house was commodious, given the size of the village; this

room had a puncheon floor, from which the carpet of rushes had been swept to permit the Wolf to trace the Circles of Power around the bed. Their chalked curves were smudged now, from people walking back and forth across them, but they'd served their purpose. At least the Wolf hoped they had.

Slowly, he said, "That fire was no damn accident."

Firecat came over to him and laid a worried hand on his arm. "Chief . . ."

He pulled irritably away from the blunt little hand with its bitten nails, regarded the woman with an eye blood-shot and gritty with leftover smoke and lack of sleep. "I know it," he said softly. "I was the one who was sup-posed to die in that inn."

How he knew this he wasn't precisely sure. But he had the impression of having seen something, felt something, just before he had smelled the smoke—and when he looked at it now, it made a kind of sense. His death in the inn fire, like his capture by the shirdar, would have been just one more of those stupid, random accidents contributing to the destruction of his troop by someone who didn't care who else got caught in the nimbus of ruin.

Listening to the distant sobbing of that fat woman who'd mended his shirt, the fat woman whose little boy now lay dead in the nursery upstairs, he was surprised at how angry this made him.

"Well," Dogbreath's bass voice broke into his reverie, "you better keep *that* theory to yourself if you don't want us run out of town on a rail."

Though obviously nervous at the prospect of dealing with this savage-looking crew of brigands, the miller—prodded, Sun Wolf had no doubt, by his wife and sister-in-law—offered to let Starhawk remain in his house until she recovered. But, though her breathing was easy by the following morning and she seemed to be recovering, he had seen enough head wounds in his days as a warrior to be leery of leaving her alone. And Starhawk, though shaky, had agreed that they dared not delay.

So he refused, to the miller's patent relief, and Dog-breath, surprisingly, produced a large sum of assorted coinage to purchase the miller's litter and two mules, plus provisions for the journey north. Sun Wolf recalled clearly the squad-leader mentioning at some point in the previous night how little money they had. Watching the Wenshar eagles, Peninsular stallins, and one or two of the silver pieces weight-minted with the mark of the House of Stratus—one of the most reliable coinages of the dozens circulating in the Middle Kingdoms—change hands, he guessed that Dogbreath had had the presence of mind to loot the inn cashbox in the confusion of the fire before joining the bucket brigade in the yard.

The Little Thurg met them in the scrubby pine woods east of the village with a string of eight horses, a guarantee of good speed on the road north. "Those ours?" the Wolf asked, seeing among them the dappled gelding he'd gotten from the King of Wenshar, but not Starhawk's skinny bay.

The Little Thurg shrugged. "They are now."

They took the switchback road along the mountain face, the pines that covered the high country on this side of the Dragon's Backbone rising stiffly around them against a blowing gray overcast. Looking back, Sun Wolf could see the charred blot where the inn had stood beside the Wenshar road above the village, the small dull shapes of men and women moving about it like ants around a carcass, and the lingering columns of smoke lifting to the morning sky.

Vorsal stood two miles inland, where the long, fertile coastline of the Inner Sea drew near to the projecting towers of the Gorn Mountains that split the Middle Kingdoms in two. Twelve miles north, Kwest Mralwe dominated the end of the mountains and the roads to the west and north through the golden Hills of Harm. But Vorsal, the Wolf thought, looking out at it across the brown landscape of autumn, had a fine natural harbor—or had had, until its wharves had been wrecked by the navies of Kwest Mralwe and all the Duke's ships burned to the waterline—plus some excellent croplands, as well as the usual upland sheep pastures. Its walls, of the hard gray local granite, were tall and thick, rising in jostling rings on a small promontory, a final outspur of the distant Gorns; the roofs that could be glimpsed over them were tiled in red and yellow, clustered with turrets and crisscrossed with the fussy little balconies and catwalks typical of this part of the world. There had probably, the Wolf thought, once been a number of trees making rustling glades of the small town gardens of the rich.

Those, of course, were gone. They'd been under siege all summer.

Ari's troops were camped north and west of the town on rising land. The camp was ringed with a trashy gaggle of raw stumps of the oaks common to these golden hills. Coming from the north around the swell of a whaleback ridge, Sun Wolf could see that the armies had stripped and felled every tree for miles to feed their cook fires. On the town's southern side, another mercenary troop was camped—he made out the black-and-yellow banners of Krayth of Kilpithie, a man he'd always gotten on well with—while the main body of the Kwest Mralwe levies occupied what was left of the harbor and stretched in a wide crescent around the east of the town. Smoke hung over all three camps and wreathed the turreted walls of the city like the brooding presence of evil. The day was still, but the close feeling of breeding weather and the sullen, bruised look of the sky over the eastern sea hackled Sun Wolf's nape as he and Dogbreath rode through the silence of the burned-out farms. Thick and stenchy, the smell of the camps reached him—privies, woodsmoke, rotting flesh—and the black shapes of ravens circled like blown leaves against a charcoal sky.

In the camp itself, it was worse.

"It's uncanny, Chief." Ari led the way through the maze of tents and shelters with the unthinking ease of long familiarity, stepping over pegs and ducking guy ropes, fending aside makeshift clotheslines and avoiding clotted puddles of garbage, the gold rings he wore on his ears, on his bare arms, and in his long black hair flashing coldly in the wasted light. "It's weird. It isn't just the bows breaking anymore, or the ballistas collapsing—one of the siege towers caught fire in the assault yesterday, caught fire on the inside as far as we can tell. Gods know how it happened." He still used, the Wolf noted, the old triple/singular case for the Deity, a vestige of childhood as unconscious as putting hand to scabbard in a crowded place. "Twenty men bought it inside, and forty snuffed it on the walls—the damn siege ladders broke when we

tried to go up to back them. God's grandmother, we'd
used those ladders a hundred times! It isn't just that.''

*No,* thought the Wolf, listening to the eerie quiet of
the camp. *It's more than that.*

He knew the sound of camps as a sailor knows the rush
and murmur of the sea, a beloved element that any moment might rise to kill. Behind the sullen hush, dim un-
dercurrents reached him: men shouting at each other, the
passionate rage in their voices speaking of causes deeper
than any immediate quarrel; closer to, a man's voice
cursing; the sound of blows; and a woman's sobs. The
camp smelled of misfortune. Had he been a stranger, the
Wolf would have gotten his horse from the lines and ridden out, rather than spend a night in the place.

''The food's been bad all summer,'' Ari went on, as
they reached more open ground in the middle of the
camp. ''It's making Hog crazy—his bread won't rise, the
salt meat rots, the beer sickens in the barrels. One flour
cask we broke open was literally squirming with red-
worms. There's jimsonweed everywhere in the hills—
we've cut it three times near the horse lines but we always
seem to miss a patch or two, and we've had to put down
almost thirty horses. I swear, even the camp followers
have been coming down with more cases of this-and-that
than I've ever seen! It's nothing you can ever put your
finger on. It's just—things.''

In the shadowless, late-afternoon gloom, the Wolf
could see lines in Ari's face that hadn't been there when
they'd parted in the spring. The young man had lost
flesh—a few inches shorter than Sun Wolf's six feet, he'd
always, behind his panther hardness and grace, carried
the suggestion of the chubby orphan the Wolf had first
taken in. His mustache, thick as the bear's pelt which
draped his shoulders and back, had gray in it, though the
young captain was only twenty-five, and there were faint
smudges of fatigue under his warm gray-brown eyes.

''Take me around,'' said the Wolf. ''Show me what
you can.''

After a week and a half on the road, he was somewhat
recovered from the vicissitudes of his brief stay in Wenshar, though the ribs cracked by the King of Wenshar's
guards still pinched him, if he made an unguarded move,
and he occasionally dreamed about ants. After traveling

by litter for most of the journey north along the stony rim of the Gorn Massif, Starhawk had been well enough yesterday to mount a horse, though, by the time they reached Kwest Mralwe, she'd looked exhausted and sick. He had left her in the Convent of the Mother in that city, though he hadn't felt easy about it—he had never quite trusted the Old Religion. Now he was glad he hadn't brought her here. There was ill in the air of the camp. On a warrior with a head wound, it would stick.

"We've moved the armory four times." Ari held aside the clumsy hide door flap, letting the Wolf duck through ahead of him into the vast, smelly darkness of the tent where the arrows, the spare weapons, and the ropes were stored. As the bar of sickly daylight fell through onto crates and coils, red eyes gleamed furiously from the shadows— then, with an angry scurry, they were gone. The place stank of rat droppings, mildew, and spoiling hides. "Feel the ground." Letting the curtain fall, Ari lifted high the cheap clay lamp he'd lit from the guard's fire. "It's as damp as a spring. It was bone-dry four days ago."

Sun Wolf knelt—Ari was right. "And rats in the daytime," he murmured. Dogbreath had told the truth—he hadn't seen a cat yet.

Ari said nothing. But his eyes, as he glanced over his shoulder at shadows which, now that the door flap was down, seemed oppressively close around the dirty blob of lamplight, said far more than he would ever admit aloud. "Watch out," he warned, as the Wolf reached for the nearest arrow chest. "We got brown dancer spiders hiding in some of the boxes. Three or four people have died."

"Place hasn't been hit by lightning lately, has it?" The Wolf drew his sword and used its tip gently to lever off the lid of the chest. Something the size and color of an apple seed flicked away on long, threadlike legs. "Or the sea risen to flood you out?"

"Believe me," Ari said gloomily, "I'm waiting for it."

Sun Wolf knocked with the pommel on the box a couple of times for good measure, then sheathed the blade and ran his fingers lightly over the warped slats, half shutting his eyes. Nothing showed on the damp-splotched wood but smudges of dirt and the half-obscured stencil of the maker's name, ——LGICUS, K.M., but he felt a queer sensation, not heat, not cold, not yet dampness, but definitely something, a concentration of the miasma that seemed to hang everywhere in the camp. Unconsciously he wiped his hands on the elkskin of his breeches as he turned away.

"As far as I know, a curse like this can't be thrown from a distance," he said as they ducked back under the tent flap and Ari blew out the lamp and returned it to the depressed-looking guard. "It needs a mark of some kind to work through, an Eye." Though there was no mark, no stain, upon them, he wiped his hands again. "Just because I didn't see anything in there doesn't mean it wasn't written. Sometimes a wizard can only see an Eye if he uses salt, or powdered hellebore, or mercury . . . there's probably other things as well, for other kinds of hexes. And the Eye could be anywhere in the camp."

"Mother pus-bucket . . ." Ari muttered, tucking his hands behind the buckle of his sword belt as he walked, an unconscious imitation of Sun Wolf that Starhawk affected as well. "We've had the place guarded . . ."

"Doesn't mean a thing."

"Oh, come on!" Ari protested. "I haven't let the troop go to hell *that* much since you've been gone."

In front of a nearby tent, a camp follower—a slave, by her hopeless face and the steel choke-chain that circled her throat—was kindling a supper fire for whatever soldier was her master. Though the wood was dry, Sun Wolf, without breaking stride, reached out with his mind and called smoke from it as if it were damp and, with a skiff of wind from the motionless air, twitched the stinging gust into Ari's eyes. The young captain coughed and flinched, fanning at the smoke . . .

. . . and when he opened his eyes a split second later Sun Wolf was gone.

"Skill has nothing to do with it."

Ari was going for his sword, even as he turned, but stepping swiftly, soundlessly behind him in that moment of blindness, the Wolf had taken it. In a training class he would have struck him with the flat of it, and both men would have laughed and cursed at the joke. Now, after a long moment of silence, he only turned it hilt-first to hand it back.

But for nearly a minute Ari did not touch it. In his eyes, in his silence, Sun Wolf read uncertainty and fear, and more painful than either, shock—the sense of loss,

of seeing his friend turn before him into a man he wasn't
sure he knew.

Fathers, Sun Wolf knew, sometimes see sons like this,
though his own never had. To Ari he had been a father
for years, and to be a father, he knew, was to be un-
changing . . .

It was a long time before Ari spoke.

"It's true, isn't it." There was no question in his voice.

"I told you that last spring."

"You told me . . ." Ari hesitated, then reached out
and took the sword from his hand. Breeze made silvery
flecks in the black bearskin of his cape, snagged a lock
of his heavy black hair among the old scalps hanging at
his shoulder, then seemed to think better of it and fell
still again.

"You told me you needed to go seek a teacher, if
one could be found. But you'd been elbow-deep in witchery all winter, Chief. It was still on you, then. And I
thought . . ." He sighed, and looked away. "I thought
you might have seen it as a way out. A way to retire, to
give me the troop, to ride away before you ended up
buying some little six-foot daisy farm someplace." The
steady, gray-brown gaze returned to Sun Wolf's face.
"And I was glad, you know? Glad if you wanted out you
could leave instead of die. Because, face it, Chief, you
could put all the fifty-year-old mercs in the world into
one bathtub and still have room for the soap. I didn't
give two cow-pies together whether you found what you
were looking for, really. I just—didn't want to have to
bury you. But you did find it, didn't you?"

Sun Wolf remembered Kaletha of Wenshar, the end
result of his first year of seeking—her vanity, her petti-
ness, her ghastly death. Then he turned to the crowded
spires of Vorsal barely visible above the tangle of canvas,
dirty banners, and woodsmoke. "Yeah," he said softly.
"I found it."

"That's good."

He looked back at Ari, tufted brow rising over his single
eye, and the young captain met the look squarely, not understanding, perhaps, but willing to accept. Just as well, thought
Sun Wolf, that the Vorsal mage had made it obvious by burning the inn just where the lines were drawn.

But his mouth and eyebrows still quirked with irony as

they walked on together to the open ground where the engineering park stood.

The afternoon was fading to eerie, windless twilight against which the siege engines rose up like the monsters of antediluvian tales. Sun Wolf felt a pang of grief and of renewed anger at the Vorsal mage, remembering that Gadget was dead—Gadget who'd built those machines and others, who had fiddled with new inventions during the long winters in Wrynde, and taught the Wolf and anyone else who'd listen about mathematics and engineering and the tensile strengths of steel. His anger—and for that matter his grief—he knew to be unreasonable. They all lived by death. Anyone he knew in the troop could be gone tomorrow. But still, he would miss the little engineer, and the anger made him feel better about destroying the only other mage he'd ever found.

Three men in the steel-chain nooses of slaves were finishing up their work on a broken catapult; a man the Wolf recognized as one of Gadget's former assistants was arguing with Zane the Golden, Ari's chief lieutenant. "Look," Zane was saying in that reasonable tone the Wolf remembered well, "I didn't ask you how much top-quality iron costs. I didn't ask you how the thing broke in the first place. There's tragedy in every life; we all have to endure it and go on. But we're going to attack those guys on that wall over there—you see that wall over there?—four days from now and it'll really help if we have a catapult to shoot at them with."

Ari grinned and strode across the open ground of the park toward them. The Wolf almost followed, then thought again and stayed where he was. It was Ari's troop now. The fact that many of the men, like Dogbreath and the Little Thurg, still regarded him as their commander wouldn't help Ari any, and it was better not even to put himself in a position where someone could turn to him to ask his support instead of the new Captain's.

But watching them at a distance, something in his heart smiled and warmed at Zane gesturing extravagantly, like an actor posing for a statue of himself—vain as a peacock with his shoulder-length golden curls and that small, perfect nose that everyone accused him of wearing an iron nose-guard into battle to protect—and Ari, patiently smoothing the engineer's ruffled temper. Ari, formerly something of a smart-

mouth, had evidently learned tact in the year he'd been in
command. Starhawk had always been the diplomat—it was
good to see that Ari was learning the other things besides
leading men which command involved.

Something in him sighed and settled. It was good to
be home.

Then behind him, in the shadow of one of the siege engines, movement snagged at the corner of his good eye.

Not a rat, though there were far too many of them
about the camp, even in daylight. This was a furtive
shadow, slipping into the vast gloom of the burned siege
tower's charred skeleton. It was growing dark; the park
slaves were setting up torches at a careful distance from
anything remotely combustible, the night-guards coming
in under the command of a pink-faced, muscle-bound
woman called Battlesow.

The spells of diversion he'd used on Ari he drew about
him now. A slave busied himself with a suddenly stubborn lash on a torch-holder; a guard stubbed his toe and
bent down to rub it as Sun Wolf ghosted past and melted
into the tangled darkness of the tower.

Within, it was like an improbable house of cards—
charred beams, broken boards, and burned struts, all
leaning against one another in a crazy rattrap a sharp
wind could bring down. Above him, a portion of the
spiral stair to the top still dangled perilously, like clots
of filth on a spider strand; skeletal black rafters made a
broken lattice against dun sky. It smelled of ashes and
burned flesh, as the inn had done. Only here, more than
just one little boy had died.

A woman was moving around the ruined inner wall, a
branch of something in her hand.

She was cloaked, a hood drawn over her face. Motionless in the fey web of illusion, the Wolf smelled the perfume of her body, mingled scents of autumn flowers and
womanhood, mixed with the dim pungence of what he
recognized as hellebore. Now and then her cloak would
move aside with the sweep of her arm as she passed the
branch along the charred beams, and in its shadow jewels
sparked on velvet. For a few moments he watched her in
silence, big arms folded across his chest, breathing slow
and soundless. Then he moved.

She gasped as his hands seized her arms above the elbows,

dropping the plant she carried as she tried to turn and strike him, but didn't go for a weapon. Her hood fell back, freeing a raven torrent of curls. "No! Let me go! Please!" His hands tightened hard, and she stood still in his grasp.

To say her eyes were brown would have been like describing those deep, volcanic lakes of the Gorn Massif as blue—accurate only up to a point. In the crisscrossed darkness of the siege tower they seemed almost black, enormous in the delicate modeling of the most exquisite face Sun Wolf had ever seen. The ends of her hair tickled his wrists where he held on to her; it would spring back, he thought distractedly, were he to crush it in his hands.

"What are you doing here?" His voice, never melodious and worse since the Great Trial, sounded hoarser than ever in his ears.

She gazed up at him for a moment with scared eyes, wary as a wildcat in the gloom. Around her throat, shining against the dusky skin, lay the thin steel of a gold-plated slip-chain, a slave collar too delicate to discommode a master's caressing hand seriously. She wore another necklace with it, a baroque pearl on a chain. Where the cloak had slipped down, he saw half-bared creamy shoulders above a bodice of blood-colored silk and the froth of chemise lace. Gently he released her and bent to pick up the herbs she'd dropped. "White hellebore," he said softly. "They brew poison from its roots."

Her hand, which had reached out for the branch, drew quickly back. "I didn't know that." Her accent was the soft drawl of the Gwarl Peninsula, on whose western coasts they'd been fighting last year. "They said in the camp the tower was witched. My granny used to tell me hellebore would show a witch's mark."

"Only to another witch." Her brows—butterfly lines of fragile black—puckered slightly, breaking the smooth quizzical beauty of her face with something infinitely more human and tender.

"Oh, damn," she breathed, vexed, and bit her red lower lip with small white teeth as if in thought. Then her frown deepened, and she looked quickly up at him in the gloom. "Oh, double damn! Are *you* the wizard?"

He grinned at the startled disbelief in her voice. "Yeah, but I left my beard and pointy hat back in the tent."

It startled her into a giggle, swiftly suppressed; the

dimples still quivered in the corners of her lips as she dropped her gaze in confusion. He fought the impulse to reach out and touch her. By the chain, she was another man's slave. He wondered whose.

"I'm sorry." She looked up at him again, her eyes filled with rueful self-amusement. "They did say you used to command the troop. Of course you couldn't do that if you were . . ." She bit her lip again, a tiny gesture that didn't disturb the dark stain of rose petals there.

"Were old enough to look like wizards are supposed to look?"

She ducked her head again. "Something like that."

"And you are . . . ?"

"Opium." The delicate brows flexed down again; something changed in her kohl-darkened eyes. As if she felt his gaze, she drew her cloak back up over her shoulders and, with a gesture almost instinctive, tucked up a stray tendril of her tumbled hair and straightened the pearl on its chain. "My man was killed by that fire." There was a note that was not quite defensive, not quite defiant, in her voice. "He was one of the ones trapped on the wall when the tower burned, slaughtered when the others couldn't get to them in time. They said—the ones who got out of the tower alive—that the fire started under the hides. Those hides had been soaked so the fire arrows from the walls wouldn't catch them. I know they've had guards on the camp and on the park, but I thought . . . what if it's somebody in the camp already? A spy or someone working for them? There's been more and more talk about witchery. I just wanted to see . . . I don't know what."

She glanced at the hellebore still in his hand, then warily up at his face, as if trying to read what was now no more than a blurred pattern of light and darkness in the gloom. He turned the branch over, fingering the pale greenish flowers. There seemed no reason to doubt her story; after all, no one could possibly use this tower again.

"You'd better be careful who sees you with things like this," he said softly. "Yeah, there's more and more talk about witchery; if it goes on, things could get damn ugly here in camp. You won't be the only one to think it might be an inside job." He didn't add that the thought had occurred to him the moment he'd seen her enter the tower.

The sky had gone the color of iron beyond the charred

rafters overhead, and crazy slips and patches of yellow torchlight flared erratically through cracks in the wooden wall. "You'd better get on back to your tent." If her man had been killed yesterday, he found himself thinking, she'd be sleeping alone.

She drew her hood up over those crisp curls and settled its folds around her shoulders. For a moment he thought she would say something else to him—fishing, as he found himself mentally fishing, for more words. Even in silence and uncertainty, she radiated an immense vitality, a quality of bright wildness beyond her beauty that defied description but that drew him, as the warmth of fire draws travelers in the cold. Hands tucked thoughtfully behind the buckle of his sword belt, the Wolf turned from her to step out into the wavering lake of the engineering park's torch glare once more.

For a moment he stood watching the slaves putting away their tools. Three or four men and a woman too homely to be prostituted moved briskly about under the barked orders of the engineer. From thinking about the girl, his mind went to what she had said.

A year's search had yielded him only one wizard, but along the way he'd now and then encountered granny magic, primitive and untrained tinkerings with the fringes of power by those who had little understanding of what they did—those who did not even know of the Great Trial which broke the barriers protecting the soul from what it was. As Opium had pointed out, the Vorsal mage might not be in Vorsal at all. There were those in camp who well might wish ill upon their masters, whether they served in one man's bed, or every man's, or mucked out the latrines. Among them, there could be one who knew a curse that would stick.

But in his gut, he didn't believe it. Whatever was in the camp—whatever he had sensed in the armory tent— was greater and deadlier than that.

Ari and Zane came striding over to him, young animals in the gold-and-black light. In contrast to Ari's metal-studded leather doublet and faded shirt, Zane had taken advantage of their presence in the Middle Kingdoms to deck himself in the brilliant colors for which their cloth was famous, a slashed blue doublet, breeches striped with scarlet that sported a codpiece decorated with a tongue-lolling demon face. "Chief!" grinned Zane with delight. "I knew you'd come!"

"You can look around here tomorrow if you want," Ari said softly. "But this is all fakement. We're putting together a major assault—the last one, we hope—in three days' time, and the engines for that are being built in the big engineering park at Kwest Mralwe itself."

The Wolf raised one tawny brow. "Whose idea was that?"

"Mine. They're being guarded day and night, too—it's those you really need to look at, not these."

"Yeah," argued Zane. "But if we're dealing with a hookum, won't he just be able to see them in a crystal ball or something?"

"He might." The Wolf glanced around him, feeling again the tension in the air and hearing it in the guards' voices and in the sharp staccato of an argument somewhere among the dark jumble of tents beyond the park's circle of light. "But there are other ways for curses to be spread. How about the other troops? Krayth's and the City forces? This kind of garf happening to them, too?"

"I think so," Ari said. "Krayth was over here two days ago—he tells me his men have started deserting. He's had to put a guard on the horses and the money box, not that there's much in that. If this assault doesn't do the job, we may come to that here. Krayth's got a longer road home than we do, too, clear the hell to Kilpithie. I'm not sure he'll make it."

"If I don't find and take care of that mage before your assault," the Wolf said quietly, "I'm not sure you will."

Across the warm-lit circle of the open park, Sun Wolf got a glimpse of Opium's cloaked form, heading for the voices and soft-glowing tents of the main camp. Zane turned his head as the velvet dark of her cape stirred the dry weeds with a passing gleam of white petticoat lace. Like a heat, the Wolf felt more than saw the greed and calculation in his eyes.

Her man was dead, the Wolf thought, who had bought her and used her and had held the legal claim to her. There would probably be a lot of men looking at her like that now. He wondered how she'd make her living, once her man's front money ran out, assuming there was any

left of it by this time. It was something he had never
thought about, when he'd bought women for himself.

Full dark had fallen, the night eerily still for this late in
autumn and turning cold. The flare of campfires and
torches ruddied the sky above the camp; on the dark and
shapeless land, ten thousand watchfires sprinkled the darkness, a slave collar of fire around Vorsal's throat. But Vorsal itself was dark, save for the tiny lights of the guards
on its walls, its turrets and balconies and ornamented roof-
trees a dead black filigree on the windless sky.

"Come on over to Bron's tavern," Zane offered, turning his eyes quickly, once Opium had blended with the
darkness. "All his beer blew up a couple weeks ago, but
that old White Death still of his works fine. It'll be just
like old times."

Old times—more nights than he could count in that
shabby ambulatory pothouse with which Bron followed the
troop every summer, night breeze and torchlight filtering
in from the maze of marquees and open walls, the talk
going around of horses, of women, of the art and the technique of war, conclusionless and absorbing until late in
the lamplit nights. He wondered if Opium would be there,
and the thought made him shake his head, remembering
other things. "Tomorrow, maybe," he said. "It was a
rough road up here. The Hawk had a bad time of it, worse
than she said, I think. Something tells me I ought to ride
back to town, and make sure she's all right."

Zane looked startled, puzzled, and a little hurt, but
Ari nodded and said, "Tomorrow, then. You watch your
blind side, Chief."

She'd be asleep when he got there, he knew. Even so,
he rode back to Kwest Mralwe under an evil sky, listening to the dim singing at the camp fade into darkness
behind him.

# CHAPTER

## —— 4 ——

"*A* *WIZARD IN VORSAL?*" *RENAEKA STRATA, LADY* Prince of the largest banking house in Kwest Mralwe, folded her well-groomed hands on the pearl inlay of the council table and considered the matter with narrowed hazel eyes.

"That's what it looks like, my Lady."

The great Guild Hall in Kwest Mralwe was designed to accommodate the Grand Council, a comprehensively representative body whose laboriously elected ward and craft stewards balanced their votes against those of the ancient houses of the local nobility. But whenever matters of actual policy had to be decided, it was the King-Council which met in the small chamber upstairs. Having worked for the King-Council before, the Wolf knew them and the Small Council Chamber well: the heads of the greatest merchant houses plus the Trinitarian Bishop—a cadet member of the House of Stratus himself—assembled in a pastel jewel box of a room, whose wide windows, with their twisted pilasters of pink marble, overlooked the teeming pool of the Mralwe docks. It was a chill day; the crystal-paned windows were shut. Even so, the din of the harbor was faintly audible in the hush—the clamor of stevedores, the braying of pack asses, and the thin mew of circling gulls. This late in the season, the deep-water traders that plied the Inner Sea were long since moored for the winter, but the more foolhardy of the coasting vessels were still in operation, trying to sneak through one last run of timber or wheat before the storms closed the sea lanes for good.

The Lady Prince held her silence a few moments more, and none of the other members of the King-Council, grouped about her like the wings of a particularly inefficient battle array, had the temerity to interrupt. Certainly the King didn't, seated immediately to her left, his stiff, archaic robe of Mandrigyn silk all but hiding the shabby doublet beneath. When he poked his hand out surreptitiously to pick his nose, Sun Wolf could see that his ruffleless cuff was frayed.

"Since the death of Altiokis of Grimscarp, there has been a good deal of talk about wizardry," the Lady said after a time. "He was said to be a wizard—certainly he had some secret to his longevity, if in fact he was the same man to whom my grandfather and great-grandfather lent money."

"He was the same man, my Lady." Sun Wolf tucked his hands behind the buckle of his sword belt. "And he was a wizard. A powerful one, too, before he started drinking himself silly—court wizard of the Thane of Grimscarp, before he put the Thane away and took the power himself. Before he died, he had a century and a half to murder his competition."

The cold light of the windows before which he stood pricked at the tarnished bullion trimming his doublet of dark-red pigskin. With his scuffed eyepatch, thinning shoulder-length hair, and ragged mustache, he had the appearance of a rather mangy and bitten old rogue lion. But if any of the King-Council thought he had come down in the world from the days when he had stood there, armored and with a dozen of his men loitering in the anteroom, they forbore to say so. Even alone, there was something formidable about him.

"As his 'competition,' as you term it," the Bishop said grimly, "consisted of wizards, witches, and other such tools of Hell, one can only comment on the wondrous ways in which God uses Evil against itself."

"Oh, I'm not denying you helped him," rumbled the

Wolf, more to see indignant fire flash in the prelate's lackluster eyes than for any other reason.

The Bishop, a young man whose few strands of limp ecclesiastical beard were totally inadequate to cover what chin he possessed, started to protest, but the Lady Prince silenced him with a lifted finger, the great emerald of her ring flashing like a warning beacon in the steely light.

"Yet Altiokis has been dead little less than a year— surely too short a time for anyone to master the powers with which Captain Ari seems to think he deals."

"It only means this wizard studied magic in secret. I've come across those who have—a woman in Mandri- gyn, whose teacher was snuffed by Altiokis, and another woman in Wenshar, who had access to ancient books." The Bishop looked affronted, but clearly wasn't about to incur the Lady's annoyance by commenting on the spread of Evil down the years.

Sun Wolf went on, "Wizardry is an inborn skill, a calling like art or music. But like perfection in art or music, it needs years of teaching, of discipline, and of technique." What else it needed, it was best not to say. The Lady Prince was a tall, sword-thin woman in her fifties who gave an impression of great beauty without actually possessing any; he could see her thoughts being sorted and shuffled like cards. "The wizards I've met have been incomplete half wizards, trying to piece to- gether what they need out of lore that's been cut to pieces over the years. Maybe this one in Vorsal is the same. Maybe not.

"But wizardry's not something that can be hidden. The people of Vorsal might not have known this person was a mage, but there's a good chance they'll have known *something*. And it's likely that this wizard learned from a master before him. Is there any rumor, any tradition, any gossip, about someone in Vorsal? Maybe someone who's dead already . . ." Turning his head slightly, his one eye caught the expressions of the King-Council—the Bishop almost sputtering with righteous indignation, but the merchants' attention already beginning to wander, like men settling themselves to hear too-familiar quibbles over something that has neither the immediacy nor the importance of real life.

"Personally," sighed the head of the House of Balkus,

a fat man with eyes like locked money boxes, "I have better things to do than listen to the gossip of the marketplace. The simple folk are always accusing some hag or other of witchcraft. It gives them occupation, I suppose, and target practice. Presumably they do so in other towns than this." He folded his hands before him like a round white suet pudding, stuck all over with diamonds. "But I have always wondered why, if those poor deluded old witches truly had power, they live in hovels, dress in rags, and allow brats to throw dung at them in the first place."

"Maybe because their idea of what's important goes beyond their next meal," Sun Wolf retorted, with a pointed glance at the bulging mountain of flesh beneath the well-tailored black doublet and robe.

The flabby jowls reddened, but before Lord Balkus—who controlled most of the wool trade from the inland nobles—could decide what to reply to this, the Bishop inquired silkily, "And have you yourself become a wizard these days, Captain Sun Wolf?"

"Purcell," the King said, leaning toward the elderly head of the House of Cronesme, "you were the agent for your brother's interests in Vorsal before his death. Do you recall anyone in that city who was accused of being—er—unusual in any way?"

"It is difficult to say, Majesty," replied the old man with punctilious politeness somewhat rare in the Council members' dealings with their king. Balkus and the head of the Greambii were already conversing in low voices, like men during the uninteresting scenes of a play, negotiating about next year's fleeces or space on one another's trading ships. "The simple folk always look upon scholars with mistrust and accuse them of evil powers merely because they are literate. Likewise, as Lord Balkus has pointed out, ill-favored or eccentric old women tend to be pointed at as witches, whether their powers extend beyond mere herbalism or not, just as women who . . ." He stopped himself short so suddenly Sun Wolf wondered for an instant if he'd been stabbed, and his nervous glance cut to the head of the table, where the Lady Prince sat with her white hands still folded but her face like a catapult's trigger rope and poison in her pale eyes. "Er—that is—what I meant to say . . ."

"And were there such people in Vorsal?" inquired Sun Wolf, after it became clear that the old man's panicked silence was not going to be broken without help.

Councilor Purcell, who had seemed momentarily hypnotized with terror, fumbled to retrieve his train of thought; a little man of sixty or so, lean and birdlike in the boned black wool doublet and fur-lined over-robe characteristic of the respectable folk of those lands. The white ruffle around his neck was starched linen, not the three-strat-per-foot lace that prickled stiffly under Lord Balkus' bottommost chin; the Lady Renaeka, Sun Wolf thought, was getting ready to swat this little man like a fly. He made a mental note to inquire what that was all about, later.

"Er—As I said, there is always talk . . ."

"About whom?"

Purcell seemed to be trying to make himself the same color as the pink-and-white inlay of the wall behind him. His voice, always soft, faded to a colorless little murmur, as if apologizing for speaking on the unpleasant subject at all. "There was an old scholar named Drosis, who died several years ago; not a wealthy man, you understand, but respectably off. I would put his income at five hundred a year. The street mongers used to threaten their children with his name, and not a child in the town would walk past his house. He was friends with one Moggin Aerbaldus, a philosopher, to whom he left his library when he died. Aerbaldus has never had a word said against him since, though. He is the author of the treatise 'On the Nature of Responsibility' and 'On the Divisions of the Universe'—perfectly respectable and orthodox, as our good bishop will attest. He has an income of approximately . . ."

"And is there a witch?" Sun Wolf cut off this pecuniary information—Purcell looked rather surprised that he wouldn't be interested in a catalogue of the man's investments.

Again Purcell rolled a frightened eye toward the quietly glittering Renaeka. "A—a woman named Skinshab," he said, almost stammering in his haste. "Ugly—very ugly—and vulgar—I'm not even sure she still lives. Goodness knows how she made her living; several mornings I saw

her through my office window picking through the garbage
bins and had to summon my servants to chase her away.''

"Why?" Sun Wolf demanded curiously. "Were you
planning to sell the garbage?"

"Er . . ." Purcell blinked at him, then laughed hesitantly. "You will have your little joke, Captain."

"Yeah," the Wolf muttered and turned his attention
back to the Lady Prince. "Let's understand one another
from the start, my Lady. It's to your advantage to give
me what help I ask for, to pay me at least the cost of my
own keep and that of my friend who's ill. She's staying
at the Convent of the Mother—"

"Since the Sisters take in supplicants," interposed the
Bishop, disapproval of the Old Faith heavy in his voice,
"it hardly behooves *us* to contribute to their cult. Do *they*
know you're a witch?"

The Wolf's breathless, scratchy voice hardened—he
didn't spare the Bishop so much as a glance. "I think a
donation of some kind would be in order. Eight silver
pieces a day isn't too much to . . ."

"My lord Captain," the Lady Prince said suavely. She
seemed to have recovered her poise—heavy lids thick
with gilding drooped lazily over those brilliant eyes. "We
agreed to meet with you today to give you information
regarding the possibility of a magician in Vorsal. It is
Captain Ari who is hiring you to find and destroy this
man—if he indeed exists. It is to him you should apply
for money."

"After paying his men enough to keep them fighting
your damn war, you know he's got little enough of that.
I'll need money when I go into the city to buy information or get myself out of trouble."

She spread her lovely hands helplessly. Among mercs,
the Lady Renaeka was notorious for her parsimony, a
hardfistedness which didn't seem to extend to her
dresses—the pounced green silk that made her stand out
from the soberly dressed Councilors like a peacock among
ravens must have cost seventy gold pieces, several times
what one of the dyers in her employ would have made in
his life. "I absolutely agree with you, Captain. But that
is between yourself and Captain Ari. Personally, I have
no proof that a wizard even exists in Vorsal. The misfortunes that have plagued the army camped before its gates

are nothing much out of the way, after all. If the Captain attributes them to an evil magician, and believes you to be a magician and able to win him victory . . .''

"We're a week and a half past the time the rains started last year, and they were late, then," Sun Wolf cut her off. Several of the Councilors looked scandalized at this *lèse majesté*, but, he reflected, if they refused to pay him they couldn't very well fire him for impudence. "You want Ari to pull up stakes and head north while he can still make it over the Khivas River gorges?"

"To feed his men on what all winter?"

"Is the knowledge they're starving going to cheer you up when Vorsal starts making alliances with your trade rivals, come spring?"

She regarded him for a moment as if determining which herbs to use for seasoning when she braised his liver. "Two silver pieces."

"Six."

"Three."

"*Six*. Three won't leave me enough in hand to buy a dead rat in a city that's been under siege all summer."

Another member of the Council opened his mouth to contribute his mite to the negotiations, and without so much as looking at him the Lady Prince said, "Shut up. Four and a half."

"Five days in advance." She opened her mouth to retort, and he cut in with, "And don't say it."

After a single, venomous instant, her expression changed to the coquette's smile that had kept her enemies running in circles for the eighteen years of her rulership of the Council. "My dear Captain—it's going to take you five days?"

The Councilors tried not to look as if they'd been ready to take refuge under the council table.

He smiled back. "I'll pro-rate your refund—but I'll keep the interest."

"No one in town would give you better interest than the Stratii, Captain." She rose to her feet in a rustling storm of petticoats, signifying that the audience was at an end. "My clerk will prepare the contract."

"Good," said the Wolf. "I'll compare your copy with mine when they're done.

"Not a quarter-bit up front," he grumbled to Dogbreath, who had been lingering inconspicuously in the arches of the Guild Hall's filigreed porch. "May his ancestors help the poor bastard who owes her money."

Admittedly, a single bodyguard would have been little use in case of real trouble, but going into a city that was hiring him without any backing whatsoever set Sun Wolf's teeth on edge. So Dogbreath had stuffed his braids up under a countryman's wide straw hat, donned fustian shirt and slops—all property of a shepherd they'd met in the hills who'd had the misfortune of being roughly his size—and had loafed, chewing a straw and examining with fascination the lingerie on sale from vendors' stalls in the porch, which overlooked the vast chaos of the Wool Market, waiting to see if the Wolf was going to come out.

Stretching in front of the Guild Hall, the Wool Market of Kwest Mralwe was a stone-paved forum larger than many small towns and seething with activity like a beehive in swarming time. Crossing it, Sun Wolf and his bucolic-looking bodyguard jostled shoulders with clerks and staplers, master weavers, merchants, and bankers, among the high-piled ranks of goods—woolpacks and fleeces, aromatic bales of dyewoods, huge baskets of madder and indigo, and netted parcels of shellfish and of the tiny insects from the forests of the south, whose crushed bodies yielded the richest of scarlet dyes. Dealers were there, too, displaying jars and cakes of mordants—potash, tartar, and the precious alum without which the gaudiest dyes would be useless. The air was sharp with the sweetish smell of the alum, the musty odors of wool, with the stinks of smoke and vinegar from the dyeing yards of all the Great Houses that had their headquarters in the neighborhood; the mellow pink sandstone walls flung back a surging chatter of up-country dialects and the sharp-voiced monosyllables of the merchants, quoting prices, credit, and risk. Money-changers and bankers had set up their tables along the walls to finance deals for percentages and futures, little heaps of silver gleaming coldly on their checkered surfaces, and near the gate a fat woman in a widow's elaborate coif was doing a land-office business in meat pasties from a steaming cart.

As they passed beneath the main gate to the even more crowded streets outside, Dogbreath glanced up at the red-

and-blue banners of the House of Stratus, with their gory heraldic device of the Pierced Heart, which rippled over-head, and wondered aloud, ''Why'd they choose that as their symbol?''

Remembering the Lady Prince, Sun Wolf replied dourly, ''I think they're trying to prove you can, too, get blood out of a stone.''

''So are you going in?''

''Not tonight.'' Sun Wolf put one big hand over the Hawk's. She squeezed his fingers lightly, but there was something in the quality of her touch, some lassitude in the way she sat beside him in the stone embrasure of the cloister arch, that he didn't like, and he asked her again, ''You sure you're all right?''

She turned her face away, embarrassed and angry at herself for showing weakness. She'd been sleeping when he had come by the Convent that morning. For the Hawk, who was usually up prowling before dawn, this was un-usual, and to Sun Wolf's eye she didn't look as if she'd got much good from her sleep. The day before yester-day—the last day of their journey—she'd been able to back a horse.

''I've felt better,'' she admitted, looking back at him with only the usual cool irony in her gray gaze. ''Not recently, I'll admit. If we had to fight our way out of here, I could probably manage.''

''I don't know,'' he said, judiciously deadpan. ''Some of those nuns look damn tough.'' And he was rewarded by her grin.

The Convent of St. Dwade perched on the edge of a mountain gorge a mile to the northwest of Kwest Mralwe, which, like all the Middle Kingdoms, was Trinitarian. St. Dwade was one of the few centers of the Mother's worship left in the eastern Middle Kingdoms. By the heavy, old-fashioned architecture of its vine-tangled stone mazes, Sun Wolf guessed it had existed long before the Forty Years' War that had ended the Empire in chaos. He wondered if it still had a Prophetess, through whom the Mother spoke in visions, or whether the Trinitarians had made Delegation one of the conditions for the Con-vent's survival.

In either case the place made him vaguely uneasy, as all strong points of the Old Faith did. Half-deserted, gently crumbling under its shroud of ivy, blending into the rocks of the mountainside, rather than simply clinging, it whispered with secrets beneath the hushed mantle of soul-deep peace.

"I'll have to go in sooner or later," he said, in reply to her earlier question. "I'd rather wait a day and have a look through the books."

On the journey north he'd fully intended to study the books of the Witches of Wenshar for which he'd risked his own and Starhawk's lives, to search in them for lore concerning the magic of ill. But conscious of the danger in which Ari and his men stood, he had pressed on as quickly as he dared over the mossy dolomite uplands west of the mountains. The first three nights he had sat up with Starhawk, who had been little better than comatose after all day in the swaying litter. Prey to the aftereffects of his own ordeals in Wenshar and the desert, it hadn't been easy to stay awake even for that, let alone to engage in the unfamiliar discipline of study.

Starhawk had worried him. One night she had wept in delirium, calling again and again for someone whose name he did not recognize, begging not to be left alone; after that she had struggled in bitter silence with the secrets of her dreams. When she seemed a little better, they had traveled more swiftly, far into the autumn nights. Though he'd meant to read, his body's own need for recovery had caught up with him, and, at each day's end, he'd slept like a dead man.

It had helped him. His shoulder only hurt now when he made an incautious move. He had thought Starhawk looked a little better a few days ago, but now, considering the hollows beneath her scarred cheekbones and the dark circles around her pale eyes, he wondered how much of that had been an act, put on to keep him from delaying and further jeopardizing their friends. Something in her closed quiet now reminded him of her fighting days, the way she'd get when she was badly injured, and would retreat alone to her small rooms in the maze of lofts above the square stone bulk of the camp Armory. He wanted to knock her head against the knobby fieldstone of the archway behind them and tell her to get back to bed.

After a little silence, broken only by the taffeta rustle of ivy leaves and the murmur of distant prayer, she said, "Every day you wait you're giving to him, you know." She turned back to look at him, and he saw clearly then the pain printed in the corners of her eyes. "He's going to know sooner or later there's another wizard working for Kwest Mralwe. If he does have a confederate in the camp he may know it already. Then I don't think there'll be much in those books that'll help you."

"Maybe," he grumbled, unwilling to believe that she was probably right. "But knowledge of any kind is a weapon. I'm not walking into there naked. This Moggin—and of the two Purcell knew about he seems the likelier candidate—has had books to study, he's had training, and I have a feeling he's had the Great Trial as well." She cocked her head at him curiously; he made a vague gesture, not knowing why he had that impression, only knowing that something—the feeling in the armory tent? the half-submerged memory of some dream which had waked him with the smoke of the inn fire stinging his nostrils?—made him almost sure of it. "My first ancestor may know what makes me think that—and what I'll be up against," he said. "I don't."

Two nuns passed, climbing the worn stair up the side of the tiny courtyard, little bigger than a bedroom and rising to the vertical chaos of walls and vegetation hanging above, a tall figure and a short, soundless in their dark-gray robes of ancient cut, their shaven heads bowed. They barely glanced in the direction of the big warrior in his dark-red leather doublet and the woman dressed like him, like a man and a warrior, in travel-stained breeches and doublet and scarred old boots, wisps of fair hair sticking out through the white slash of head bandages. Their silence—like the Hawk's, Sun Wolf realized—was a silence of deep-kept secrets to which no one was party. Had she learned that in her years serving the Mother's altars? he wondered. Or had it been that silence that had drawn her to the decaying convent within sound of the Outer Ocean, where first their paths had crossed?

Starhawk laid her other hand, cold and slightly unsteady, over his. "Only your ancestors know how much of the magic in those books is safe to use. The women who wrote them couldn't have entered the demon cult unless they were corrupt in their souls, Chief. Maybe there are kinds of power it's better not to use. You be careful.''

''I will be,'' he agreed, rising as the gray-robed Sister materialized from the overgrown grotto of the cloister at the bottom of the court to sign him that it was time for him to go. ''If I can figure out what 'careful' is.''

As he picked his way down the uneven path to be guided out—for, like most of the Mother's dwelling places, St. Dwade was a maze within a maze, a tangle of organic spirals growing, like the chambers of a sea-shell or the infinite tiny labyrinths of insect lairs, through the long deeps of the years—Starhawk watched him go from where she sat, observing the width and movement of his shoulders in the velvety pigskin, the burnish of light and shadow on the muscles of his knee, and the cold flick of daylight on the brass hardware of his boots, as if mem-orizing the shape of him against lonely darkness to come. As soon as he had vanished through the dark archway at the bottom of the court she put her hand to her head and lay down on the bench, the close-grained stone still warm from his thighs. The sour sky overhead had darkened perceptibly by the time the garden around her stopped rolling and heaving enough for her to stand and stagger somehow back to her room.

Sun Wolf's father, a great black-haired beast of a man whose glory had been to boast in the long-houses of the women he had raped, had from time to time repeated a piece of advice which his son still recognized as valid, though he was no longer in a position to live up to it as once he had. Never mess with magic, the big warrior had said; never fall in love—and never argue with drunks or religious fanatics. The latter activity would simply waste time which could be better spent doing practically any-thing else, but the former two could get a man killed before he had time to turn around.

He had, of course, been right.

The ten books of the Witches of Wenshar which had been written in the common tongue of Gwenth ranged from herbals and anatomies to grimoires and notebooks, covering topics from the treatment of loose bowels and sore throats to the summoning of the Eater of Heads. No notes, the Wolf reflected, on how either to control or dismiss the Eater of Heads, whatever it was—and he had no desire to find out—once it arrived. He thought he'd skip that one. Some spells and processes were meticulously outlined; others contained only sketchy references to ''make strong the Cyrcle''—presumably a Circle of Protection, but no hint of which of the several Circles Yirth had shown him was appropriate for this case, if indeed the necessary circle hadn't also been beyond his onetime master's limited ken. Some had the key words of power deliberately omitted. A number of the spells in one of the grimoires had been starred in red ink by some later hand, which could have been a personal reference as to source, a reminder that they worked better in the dark of the moon, or a warning never to touch. One, to summon the eldritch magic from the bones of the earth, had been extensively glossed with marginal notes in the shirdar tongue.

*A shortcut to the Cold Hells, no error,* thought the Wolf tiredly, pushing the books from him and rubbing his eye patch. Rather to this surprise, he found the tent around him quite dark.

He had always had sharp eyes in the night and, since passing through the hallucinatory agonies of the Great Trial, he had been able to see as clearly in darkness as in light, though the sight was not the same. Still, something about reading those dark books in darkness made him vaguely uneasy, and he started to rise from the narrow cot where he'd been sitting tailor-fashion to fetch a spill from the brazier, then remembered he was a wizard, and reached out with his mind to the wick of the nearest lamp. This cost him a little mental effort even now, as did the calling of blue witchlight. When he'd first tried it, it had been much easier to use a taper as other men did.

The light danced up behind the bronze vine tendrils embracing the cracked bowl of the lamp, a votive looted from a church somewhere, like much of the other bizarre paraphernalia that dangled from the ridgepole and struts of Dogbreath's closet-sized tent. Ari had offered him his own old tent back, an elegant dwelling of three rooms replete with peacock-colored hangings, looted years ago from a shirdar prince. He had refused; it was the commander's tent, and Ari, not himself, now led the troop. The squad-leader had offered him the loan of his lodgings, which, with their tattered hangings, beribboned totems, and decaying lamps, seemed to echo with the resonances of that erratic personality. As the light brightened, he heard the startled scurry of vermin among the clutter along the wall and cursed. Yirth had taught him a Circle against rats, and he wondered if he remembered its spells well enough to put one around the tent, or whether this would be more trouble than it was worth.

Voices clamored suddenly outside, torchlight smearing the striped rugs of the door curtains with orange light and shadow shapes. A woman laughed, high and sweet, and Zane's voice jeered good-naturedly, "Shove it up your nose, heretic . . ." Then Penpusher's deep, stammering voice: ". . . g-got to welcome the Ch-Chief back. Besides, he may have some money." The curtains were thrust aside to reveal a whole swarm of half-drunk warriors: Ari in the lead, winecup in one hand and arm around his favorite concubine; Penpusher, massive and terrifying in the rotting ruin of black doublet, ruffled collar, and trunk hose that were the uniform of gentlemen in the Middle Kingdoms, his curls brushing the sloping ceiling of the tent; Dogbreath and Firecat, passing a wineskin back and forth between them; Zane like a well-fed cat with the giggling blonde light-skirt who was his current mistress on his arm; and the Big and Little Thurgs like bizarre brothers.

They crowded in, filling the little room with others still jostling in the entrance. Dogbreath, still clad in most of the hapless shepherd's clothes but with his long, beribboned braids hanging down his chest, waved the wineskin and called out, "We're trying to get up a poker game, Chief, but so far we've got two strats, three stallins and twenty-five coppers between us . . ."

"Hey, man, you can't play poker with a hoodoo!" Firecat protested, jabbing Dogbreath in the ribs and taking the wineskin away from him. She winked at the Wolf. As usual, jewels flashed from her ears, her wrists, her tangled hair, and in the throat of her grubby silk shirt.

"There's an idea, if you're ever hungry in a strange town," Opium's sweet, lazy voice crooned as she snaked past the men in the doorway. Her brown eyes were warm, sparkling into his in the erratic lamplight. She'd discarded her cloak, and a creamy paradise of breast surged up against the blood-red silk of her bodice, half-hidden by the scented glory of her hair. "Or do wizards ever end up hungry in strange towns?"

"No more than ladies with jugs like yours!" Zane laughed with joviality too prompt, too hard-edged. Opium's dusky cheeks flared with humiliated color, and she stepped swiftly back.

"Oh, shove it, Zane," Firecast snapped angrily, and the Big Thurg rumbled, "Stop thinking with your codpiece, man."

"C-can you really c-call c-cards?" asked Penpusher, perhaps out of curiosity, perhaps only to gloss past what might have become an argument, since Zane and Firecat were both drunk and both likely to be interested in Opium for the same reasons.

Sun Wolf sighed. It was one of the first things he and the Hawk had tried when they'd hit the road from Mandrigyn. "If I've got something to look in—a candle flame, or a jewel . . ."

"Like the crystal balls wizards have?" Little Thurg asked, perching on the edge of the room's one chair.

Zane hooted. "Yeah, that's why wizards make so much noise when they . . ."

"Would somebody go drown him in the latrine?"

"No, c'mon, Chief, show us," urged Ari, pulling a truly sorry pack of cards from the purse at his belt. "Beats penny-ante . . ."

"So does getting a tooth drawn," Dogbreath reminded him.

"Watch out, man, those are the Captain's special marked cards . . ."

And from behind Dogbreath came the whisper of red silk and dark hair and the low, lazy voice asking, "Pretty-please?"

Sun Wolf laughed, and held out his hand; for a moment it was all the same—the casual camaraderie of a thousand other nights, the taste of beer and muscle, Penpusher's grousing about cheap balladeers putting real minstrels out of work, Dogbreath's outrageous stories—poker, jokes, boasting, rehashes of races or cockfights or what happened at the siege of Saltyre.

But it wasn't. For the wizard in him smelled a change
in the wind, a curious prickling of the hairs at his nape,
like the passage of a ghost. For a moment he considered
disregarding it, and spending the evening as he used to,
drinking and playing cards, maybe with Opium on his
knee . . .

And the smell on the wind, the sense of change, was
indeed gone.

But it troubled him sufficiently that he shook his head
and said, "Gotta be some other night, kids."

"Aw, Daddy, *please* do us a magic trick?" Dogbreath
begged in a schoolboy whine.

"Yeah, I'll make you all disappear, how's that?"

"Oh, too easy," Opium protested with a flashing
laugh. "All it'd take to make Zane disappear is soap and
water." And her eye caught the Wolf's, half-teasing, half-
asking, coffee-warm under kohl-dark lids.

After perhaps too long an instant he shook his head.
"I might catch up with you later," he half promised, his
eyes going to Ari. "There's things I got to do."

Ari looked disappointed; the Little Thurg groused,
"God's toenails, he not only risks his life to save the
lousy books but he *reads* 'em!"

"Watch out, Chief, that'll give you hair on your eyeballs!"

The others craned their necks to look at the books
scattered open across the bed where he'd been sitting.

"Jealous I know the alphabet?" the Wolf shot back,
and they all laughed. "I can count, too."

"How high?" challenged the little man fiercely, drawing himself up to his full five feet of red-and-purple puff-
and-slash.

"Twenty—and *without* taking off my shoes."

The Little Thurg's face fell like an abashed monkey's.
In a hoarse stage whisper, Dogbreath asked Firecat,
"What's twenty?"

"It's the number that comes after 'some more.' "

To the Wolf, she confided, "Everything past twelve is
higher mathematics to him because he needs help getting
his shoes off."

Zane's next—unprintable—contribution to the conversation steered it into other channels; trading increasingly
obscene banter, they jostled their way out of the tent and

into the night in search of more entertaining game. Ari lingered for a moment, as if he would say something; past his shoulder, the Wolf got a glimpse of Opium's dark, regretful gaze. Then they, too, were gone.

In the sudden quiet of the tent the Wolf felt curiously bereft.

But an instant later the faint sibilance of breeze was audible in the silence. Without the heavy stinks of wine and sweaty wool and the women's perfumes the scent of the sea came plain. The weather had turned. The storms were coming in.

Cursing systematically, Sun Wolf thrust aside the cluttered table, pushed the cot back, and dragged up the filthy rugs that formed the floor of the tent. On the earth beneath he scratched with his dagger the Circle of Light, as large as he could make it in the restricted room—the great curves of the powers of air leading into it, the grand and the lesser stars. He worked the pattern from memory, sinking his mind into the runes of power, whispering the words that Yirth of Mandrigyn had given him, drawing the strength of the universe like glittering plasm into the marrow of his bones. In the points of the Great Star he kindled fires with pinches of the herbs he carried these days in his saddlebags, then touched the flame in the green bronze lamp, quenching it to a ribbon of smoke and darkness. He sank down through the darkness, to where the Invisible Circle lay like a coil of shadow and light.

Far below him, he could see the iron-gray crawl of the sea; above and before him, half-veiled with beggar-rags of cloud, was the cold arc of the waxing moon. Around him whispered and cried the voices of the winds, and in the blackness he saw them, dark and light air mixed, warm and cold. He could see the cold front moving in like a blue-gray wall, smell the ozone of the lightning, and hear the driving thunder of its rain. Reaching out toward them, he touched them, the winds flowing at his call into his hands.

In a dream, he thought, he might once have felt this. It was both less and more than ecstasy—wholeness, the sensation of being exactly and perfectly what from the beginning of time he had been meant and longed to be. In a dream, or perhaps on certain nights when training his warriors, he had felt the whole body of them answering like a single blazing weapon forged of souls. The winds streamed through his hands, the colors of them visible through the incense smoke, palpable as rippling bolts of silk that he could weave, braid, and twist to his will. Throughout his life he had lied, claiming to revel most in the joys common to other men, knowing none would understand because he did not understand himself. But in his heart of hearts, nothing—not sex, not love, not wealth or drink or victory, had ever come remotely close to this, for which there was no word but magic.

His soul filled with the bright darkness of it, and he put forth his shadow strength to turn the storm aside. Its power pressed on him, like a wild horse on a breaking line or a sail held in a squall, twisting him, dragging him after it. His magic was insufficient yet, untrained, without technique; he drew against the wind, collecting his strength, trying to remember everything Yirth had taught him . . .

Then he became aware of something in the wind and darkness besides himself.

Blue like clouds, black like the cold of the air, he seemed to see it through curtain after curtain of illusions. It, too, moved beyond and through the Invisible Circle. It, too, gathered the reins of the wind. The shape of it came and went, edges vanishing, melting, yet always there—in his mind, in the clouds, in the winds, he couldn't tell. But it seemed that a dark hand stretched out toward him in a universe of shadow, darkness streaming from its bony fingers.

And in his mind he heard the whisper, *A little wizardling, is it? A fledgling mage to be my slave.*

Frightened, Sun Wolf tried to draw away, but realized he was too deep within the trance he'd entered in working the weather to escape. The shadow hand moved, sketching signs woven of the storms' lightning, runes weaving a shivering net of ice. *Fight!* the Wolf thought, but he had no idea how to do so—it was his soul that was being trapped, through the trance, through his own magic, not his body. The runes merged, blended with one another as on a curtain of silk billowing in the dark air all around him, a shining web drawing closer, while his mind screamed *No! No!* and a thunderclap of voiceless, ecstatic laughter rocked the darkness with triumphant delight.

And as if remembering a dream, it came to him that he'd seen that dark hand before, a dream—just before the fire at the inn?—of the hand reaching toward him . . .

*Wake up!* he screamed at himself. *Break the trance, damn you!* But he had no idea how to do that, either. Trailing the silvery darkness like sticky grave-bands, the hand seemed to grow enormously, the long fingers extending to close him in. Without a body he could not fight. He screamed, *I will not serve you* . . . and laughter again whispered like a chuckle of thunder.

*Wizardling, you will have no choice.*

In the deeps of his trance he could not reach the refuge of his own body, but, like a fragment of a forgotten dream, he conjured a vision to himself, a vision he'd had first as a child, and later in the hallucinatory agonies of the Great Trial: the vision of his own right hand with the flesh seared off it from grasping the fires at the core of his mind. The fire-core, the magic, rose up like a sword in his grip, and with it he slashed at the tangling runes, cleaving them through in a swirling tatter of sparks, flame pouring out the back of his hand through the interstices of the bones. He strode forward to cut at the hand of darkness itself, but he heard—felt—the blazing explosion of an oath, of rage, of pain, and the hand was gone, and he was falling, plunging toward the sea like a black meteor . . .

He cried out, and like the snapping of a twig felt something strike his face—his real face, flesh and skull and stubble. A woman's voice cried "Captain!" and he was struck again, and this time he opened his eyes.

He was kneeling on the dirt floor of Dogbreath's tent. The pinpricks of the herb fires had all gone out, and the air was cloying with smoke. In the dim glow of a clay lamp, Opium crouched before him.

He swayed and almost fell, shaking as if with ague and soaked through with perspiration despite the night's cold. The sea scent, the rain scent, of the air was gone, replaced once more by the prickling weight of sullen stillness.

"Captain?" she said again.

Agony seared his right hand; he had to look at it to

make sure the bones were still clothed in flesh, and felt
almost surprised to see the heavy fingers intact, the curly
gold hair on their backs not even singed. For a moment,
it seemed to him that were the flesh peeled back the bones
would be charred within. "Water," he managed to say.
"Or tea—something . . ."

Long used to the ways of mercenaries, Opium rose
with the leggy grace of an animal and went straight to
Dogbreath's cache of two-bit gin. He pushed it away, the
mere smell of the alcohol nauseating him. She stood ir-
resolutely for a moment, then rummaged around in the
mess and found the water jar. She dipped a cup full,
opened Dogbreath's travel chest and brought out two
painted tin boxes, dumping half a handful of coarse
brown sugar from one and a pinch of salt from the other
into the water.

The draught cleared his head a little. He was shaking
all over from the shock, but, as if he were in battle, as
if he had fought with his body instead of in spirit, he was
already thinking ahead.

"What hour is it?"

"Fourth or fifth." She knelt on the floor before him
again, hair a cloak of magical darkness over the silk gown
of the deep crimson which had made Kwest Mralwe's
fortune. In the single lamp's wavering shadows, the
golden slave-chain shone at her throat. "The others are
still over at Ari's. I came back."

Remembering the lust in Zane's eyes—whether he had
another woman with him or not—Sun Wolf didn't have
to ask her why. In the smoke-scented gloom her lips
seemed almost purple against the creamy dusk of her
skin, darkened with the lees of wine. Earrings hung with
dozens of tiny gold flowers twinkled in the endless night
of her hair. When she touched his hand, her soft fingers
felt warm, soothing.

"What were you doing?"

He was aware of her as he had been in the siege tower
yesterday evening, aware of wanting her, and he looked
away from her and got unsteadily to his feet.

"Working the weather." He knew now what he'd half
seen, half sensed, half dreamed before the fire at the
inn—the dark hand reaching toward them, the curse's
darkness trailing from its fingers . . .

Her dark brows quirked down. "I thought—earlier tonight I thought . . . But then the wind changed."

"Yeah." He pushed aside the hangings over the tent door and let the night's chill burn his face and the thin soaked strings of his hair. His shirt, his elkskin breeches, and his doublet were damp, the flesh within them cold, as after a fight. Behind him the lamp flickered, and all the crazy shadows of the random hangings, the ribbon-decked bones of saints and bits of chain and straw dangling from the ridgepole, totems, dried vegetables, old embroidered gloves and hanging fragments of glass that Dogbreath collected, all seemed to stir with restless life. The memory of the web of silver runes that had seemed more real to him than his own body and the memory of the strength of that shadow hand lingered like the after-taste of nightmare.

But the battle had been real. The attempt to enslave him had been real. And as a fighter, he knew what should be his next, logical move.

Against the tarry black of the night sky, only his wizard's eye could make out the lampless spires and steeples of Vorsal.

A touch of warmth, a breathing softness of perfume, brushed his back, and a slim hand rested from behind on his sleeve. "May I stay?"

"If you want," he said. He turned his head, to look down into her eyes. "I won't be here, though. There's someplace I have to go."

# CHAPTER

## —— 5 ——

*I*T TOOK THE WOLF TEN MINUTES TO SOBER PENPUSHER
up enough to borrow his least tatty black doublet and
breeches, the bookkeeper owlishly insisting that hose and
short trunks were the proper wear for evening visits. Ari,
too ingrained in the habit of command now ever to get
completely drunk on campaign, watched this interchange
in silence, but when Penpusher reeled out into the night,
still muttering about the decay in sartorial standards, the
captain made his way across the tent to the Wolf. Behind
them, against a tarnished jewel box of filthy peacock tent
hangings, the poker game continued. Under cover of
Dogbreath's extravagantly voiced offers of sacrifice to all
the saints of chaos Ari asked softly, "Why?"

Sun Wolf glanced sharply at him.

"You ought to look at yourself." Ari's broad shoulders
bulked dark against the dirty glow of the grease lamps as
he folded his arms. "You look as if you just went five
rounds with an earthquake and lost. What happened?
Why go into the city now?"

"Because he won't be expecting it." The Wolf pushed
back the sweaty strings of his hair and rubbed his unshaven chin. "I hurt him some—I don't know how bad.
I can't afford to give him a chance to recover. He knows

he hurt me and he'll be off his guard. If I go after him cold, head to head, power against power, he'll make sauerkraut of me.''

"Yeah, well, your resemblance to what my mother used to spoon over the sausages is pretty strong right now.''

Sun Wolf growled, knowing Ari was right. But he knew, too, that a day's rest wouldn't make him any more able to defeat Moggin Aerbaldus—and that now, Moggin knew there was another wizard working against him. A wizard, he reflected uneasily, whom it was to his advantage—and within his power—to enslave.

The memory of that dark hand closing around him and of that sticky net of silver runes turned his flesh cold. To cover his fear he went on roughly, "He'll be ready for more magic tomorrow, but it's my guess he won't be ready for an assassin tonight.''

"You garlic-eating heretic . . . !" Little Thurg's voice rose from within the tent.

"Aaah, better we eat garlic than perform ritual acts with canteloupes and tender little piggies the way you people do . . .''

The voices were good-natured; Sun Wolf glanced back over his shoulder to see Zane dozing like a disheveled orchid on the divan while Dogbreath, the two concubines, and the Big and Little Thurgs pushed the same twelve coppers dispiritedly back and forth among themselves. Nobody seemed to be winning much—Sun Wolf wondered if the hex had extended itself to the cards.

Ari pointed out doggedly, "It was your guess that Laedden's armies would be able to cope with the invasion from Ambersith without falling back on the city, remember? That time we ended up trapped in the siege? And it was your guess nobody would join the K'Chin coalition twelve years ago when we invaded . . .''

"Everybody's entitled to a few mistakes," the Wolf retorted defensively. "And I don't need some smart-mouthed kid to tell me . . .''

"Chief." Ari's hand stayed him as he let the door's filthy brocade curtain fall to shut out the night. "You watch your back in there. You need backup?''

He said it as an afterthought, a courtesy, like the offer of a bed for the night to a guest already bent upon returning home. The Wolf gestured it aside. Entering the besieged city would be difficult enough for a lone assassin who had the power to turn aside the eyes of the watchers on the walls; companions would only increase his risk of detection without adding much to his chances of escape, and they both knew it.

"Captain?" The Wolf had been aware of the dry crunch of approaching footfalls outside; Battlesow poked a helmeted head through the curtains. "Some grut here to see the Chief." There was disbelief in her incongruous, little-girl voice. "*Claims* to be the King of Kwest Mralwe."

"He does, does he?"

Dogbreath looked up from his cards. "He wearing a crown?"

"Rot the crown," the Little Thurg chipped in. "Find out if he's wearing a purse."

"How much ransom you figure they'd pay?"

"If he's really the King of Kwest Mralwe," the Wolf rumbled, "you'd better not count on much."

"You want to see him, Chief?" Ari asked quietly. "We can get rid of him . . ."

He shook his head, though part of him wanted to start at once for Vorsal, to strike quickly while surprise would still be a weapon—to start before he had time to get cold feet. "I better see what he wants. I asked them for information—he may have some he didn't want the others to hear." Privately, having seen the King of Kwest Mralwe on a dozen occasions over the years—whenever Renaeka Strata had permitted the rightful monarch to attend Council meetings—he didn't think that any too likely. But he'd dealt with peril too many years to disregard even the most unlikely help.

The poker players left, one of the women and the Little Thurg toting the snoring Zane between them, and Dogbreath thoughtfully collecting the wine jar and all the remaining coppers on the table. Ari left last, holding up the tent curtain for Raven Girl. As he went out he said, "I'll get Penpusher to leave the black clothes in your tent. Good luck, Chief."

"If that's your idea of humor," Sun Wolf grumbled back, slouching into Ari's favorite chair—once his own—

of gold-bound staghorns and ebony, "I don't think it's very funny."

Ari laughed, and left him. Curious, the Wolf turned over the cards that scattered the table amid the shell and ebony winecups, and saw he'd guessed right about the extent of the curse.

Then the tent flap opened. Derisively, Battlesow announced, "His Royal Majesty King Hontus III of Kwest Mralwe."

He knew the gawkish shape and the peering squint, even before the King pushed his cheap corduroy hood back from his face and removed the black domino mask. "Captain Sun Wolf?"

"Nobody's been impersonating me since this afternoon, so I guess it still is."

The King laughed nervously, as if uncertain that it really was a joke. Though in his mid-thirties, the King of Kwest Mralwe had the unwrinkled countenance of a child who has never bothered himself with learning the right and wrong of matters to which he lent his name. This, the Wolf supposed from his years of dealing with the King-Council, might have to do with the fact that those hardfisted bankers and merchants weren't about to let a mere hereditary ruler have anything to do with the running of a complex mercantile economy. But studying the weak chin and petulant lips, the jittery restlessness of those big-boned hands, and the aimless gaze of the squinting eyes, he concluded that there were other, better reasons for this exclusion. In reigns gone by, the King-Council's power, he knew, had been more equitably divided. He himself wouldn't have divided the running of a two-cow farmstead with this gam-handed dolt.

"I've come to ask you—there were things said in the council this afternoon, you know . . . Oh, of course you know, you were there, haha . . . That is, I realize it's all supposed to be superstition, and of course wild rumors are always circulated . . . You see . . ."

The King coughed, laughed again as a sort of punctuation to his own remarks, then unconsciously picked his long nose and wiped his fingers on the threadbare panes of his trunk hose. Uninvited, he took the chair Dogbreath had recently vacated, changing position almost continually as he talked, like a restive child. "Well,

I'm not quite sure how to put this—not wishing to give offense . . . But at the Council today, the Bishop said something about—well, about you being a wizard. Is that true? I mean, is it true that you're a wizard—of course we both know that it's true that the Bishop said it, hahaha . . ."

Sun Wolf leaned back in his own chair, his solitary eye narrowing. "Why do you ask?"

"Well . . ." The King put his feet on the floor and sat forward, clasping his hands; he wore some of the cheapest rings Sun Wolf had ever seen, as well as a flat, worn gold signet carved from an opal the color of ice. Pulled back in a sandy pigtail, his hair was unwashed. "Your men did call you back out of retirement to deal with a magician in Vorsal, didn't they? And I've heard rumors, you know. Sometimes I go about the marketplace in disguise . . ."

Sun Wolf shuddered at the mental picture *that* conjured up.

"You are going to destroy this wizard in Vorsal, aren't you? To let my men take the city?"

Though this was exactly what Sun Wolf proposed to do, the way it was phrased, in that eager, whining voice, set his teeth on edge. "Yes," he said, and added pointedly, "that is, as soon as I'm free to do so."

"Oh, you have my permission, of course." The King gave a magnanimous wave, the sarcasm zipping over his head like a badly aimed catapult bolt. "The man is obviously a threat to my realm. But I want to speak to you about what you will do . . ." He paused, wriggled, and dropped his voice portentously. ". . . Afterwards."

"Afterwards." As if he had kicked a carpet and seen its entire pattern unroll before his feet, Sun Wolf saw the King's proposal open up in his mind in a blinding panorama of the obvious. He barely restrained himself from sighing as the King, with numerous circumlocutions, nervous giggles, and absentminded peeps into the few winecups which remained on the table—all of them empty, and Sun Wolf was sure he would have helped himself to them if they hadn't been—laboriously unfolded his proposition as if he were the first man in the history of the world to have ever had the idea of hiring a wizard to put him into the position of power he felt he deserved.

"You see," the King went on, "it's all the fault of that witch's bastard Renaeka. That's why she glared at old Purcell today. Her mother *was* a witch, who used her powers to get the Prince of the House of Stratus to fall in love with her. Of course he'd married a land baron's daughter—that's how the House of Stratus got control of the alum mines in Tilth and, through it, control of the whole cloth trade, since there isn't another source of alum closer than the Gwarl Peninsula, and that one's tied up tight by Ciselfarge. The old prince put his true wife aside for his paramour, and when it looked as if her family was going to give trouble and take the diggings back, the witch Renaeka's mother tried to poison Lord Stratus' true wife. But of course in spite of everything—her mother was burned in the end, when Lord Stratus turned against her—That Woman is now the head of the House of Stratus, and controls the only source of alum for cloth dyeing in the whole of the Middle Kingdoms. She can charge what she pleases, call the tune for them all. They all toady and crawl to her, the painted whore! But if I had a wizard on my side . . ."

". . . that wizard would run the risk of getting the ax from the House of Stratus the same way this alleged witch did," Sun Wolf finished. "In case it's slipped your mind, the Bishop is Renaeka's cousin, and the Triple God takes a damn dim view of hookum."

"Oh, don't worry about that," the King said. "I'll protect you."

Sun Wolf sighed and pushed with one blunt forefinger at the pitiful collection of Dogbreath's cards. "Your Majesty, I doubt you could protect your own head in a rainstorm." He stood up; the King, who'd been peering inquiringly into a rejected cup to see how much wine was left, raised his head in hurt surprise. "And I've got plenty of better things to do with what powers I have than waste them rigging ward elections in a snake pit like the Middle Kingdoms, always supposing you didn't start distrusting me and slip something into my drink."

"Never!" The King leaped melodramatically to his feet, knocking over his own chair, then the winecup as he grabbed unsuccessfully to catch it. Mopping at the

spilled dregs, he straightened up and squinted shortsight-
edly into Sun Wolf's face. "We would make a pact! Together we would rule . . ."

Patiently, Sun Wolf caught the fragile cup just before
it rolled off the edge of the table. He set it upright with
a small click on the inlaid ebony tabletop. "And what
would be the first act of this pact?" he demanded quietly.
"To poison Renaeka?"

Their eyes held for an instant; then the King's shifted
away. "Well—I thought something more subtle than
that."

"You mean something less easy for the Church to
trace? To ill-wish her, to mark her with an Eye, so one
day her horse would stumble, or a fish bone would lodge
in her throat, or one of her lovers would strangle her with
her own pearls?"

"She deserves it," the King pointed out righteously.
"She's the daughter of a witch—she's probably a witch
herself. If we had a true bishop in this town and not one
of the Stratus lapdogs he'd say the same. He'd be on my
side. They all would be, if they weren't afraid of her, but
she controls the alum mines, and all the money—she really does deserve to die. They're usurpers, all of them,
thieves of what belongs to others . . ."

"Like the power in this kingdom?"

"Yes!"

"Your Majesty," the Wolf said, tipping his head a little on one side to study with his good eye the stringy
figure before him, "the Kings of Kwest Mralwe haven't
held power since the wars of your great-grandfather's day.
And from what I've heard of the slaughters they perpe-
trated, quarreling over the crown and over how many
gods constitute God and what sex they are, it's no wonder
the merchants and bankers took the power away from
them and their land barons, so they could make money
without it being confiscated every time the ruler had a
religious experience and everybody could raise their children in peace. Now why don't you get your backside back
to Kwest Mralwe, if you can remember the way there,
and let me do the job I came here for."

"But I'll make you wealthy beyond your wildest
dreams!" protested the King, as if he hadn't reiterated
this point a number of times in his opening narration.

"Together we'll rule Kwest Mralwe! We'll go on to conquer all the Middle Kingdoms . . ."

Wearily, Sun Wolf took him by one bony elbow and pushed him toward the tent flap. The King, never a man to give up easily, clutched his sleeve.

"You don't understand! I'm offering you money, power—all the women you want . . ."

Sun Wolf stopped, and turned to face the King, close enough to get a noseful of the man's rancid breath. "There's only one woman I want," he said softly. "And it's for her sake, not for yours or anyone else's, that I'm going into Vorsal tonight. Now air yourself."

"But I'll make you rich . . ."

At this point Sun Wolf committed an act of the grossest sort of *lèse majesté*.

Dogbreath materialized as if by magic at the sound of the body hitting the dirt. "Got a problem?"

Sun Wolf flexed his hand. "The whole Middle Kingdoms are going to have a problem if this grut ever comes to power around here," he remarked. "But I don't think they need to worry much. Get somebody to take him back to Kwest Mralwe."

The squad-leader gave him a grin and a cockeyed salute, and bent to pick up the monarch's recumbent form. "Wake up, your Majesty—you and I are going to take a little ride . . ." The King's arm slung across his shoulders, he paused, regarding the Wolf with bright, demented eyes oddly sober for once. "You going to be all right?"

"Yeah."

"You need backup as far as the walls?"

The Wolf hesitated, considering the matter. From Bron's makeshift tavern, a bard's voice lifted in a ballad of some more ancient war, singing of sacked towers and crumbled walls as if they had nothing to do with men killed, lives twisted askew, or children sold as slaves to the stews and the mines. The camp's ill luck seemed to extend to bards; this was the worst Sun Wolf had heard in his life. Across the small open space between the tents he watched Hog the Cook's dog Helmpiddle waddle deliberately over to a pile of battle armor someone had left outside his tent to let the sweat-soaked lining dry and lift one short leg solemnly at the helmet. Damp as the lining already was, Sun Wolf guessed the owner would not be aware it had been baptized until the next time he went into combat. He sighed and shook his head.

"No," he said at last. "It's not likely I'll be seen, and you might be—in fact with the way luck's going, it's damn sure you *would* be."

"Same goes for you, Chief," the squad-leader pointed out, renewing his grip on the sagging King with one hand and relieving him of his purse with the other. Then his eyes returned to Sun Wolf's face. "What do I tell the Hawk?"

*What indeed?* He wondered what Moggin Aerbaldus would have done with him, once his soul had been drawn into that softly shining web.

*I escaped him,* he reminded himself doggedly, pushing the cold terror aside. *I did get away.*

"Tell her to send the books to Princess Taswind at Mandrigyn," he said, knowing he could not speak to any but the Hawk herself of his deepest fear. "And tell her to keep a mirror handy."

Opium was still at his tent when he returned there to change into Penpusher's black clothing. She lay curled on Dogbreath's disorderly cot beneath the cloak of her hair, watching him with onyx eyes. He was burningly aware of wanting her—aware, too, for the first time in his life, of not being able freely to take a woman he desired. He knew perfectly well that the desire had nothing to do with love; unquestioningly, to the bottom of his soul, he knew that Starhawk was the only woman he would ever love. He was barely acquainted with Opium, didn't know what kind of person she was and, so far as wanting to bed her was concerned, didn't really care. But knowing this didn't lessen his desire, and the fact that he knew it was mere lust was like terming a week's starvation "mere" hunger. Love might conquer many things, he reflected, changing clothes self-consciously under that silent, beautiful gaze, but evidently there were elements of his nature impervious to its effects.

He was heartily glad to leave the tent and melt into the anonymous dark of the night.

The noises of the camp had subsided, though somewhere he could hear men still quarreling: "I told you to go through them and throw all the rotten ones away!'' ''I *did* throw them away, pox-rot your muck-picking eyes!'' ''Then what do you call this, you festering whoreson . . .'' ''Are you calling me a liar?'' The smell of burnt flesh and ashes stung his nose as he passed the engineering park on his way out of camp, reminding him of the men who had died in that inexplicable fire.

In the distance, beyond the lightless towers, thunderheads rose like a black wall. Eerily, he felt neither wind nor cold from that direction—only darkness waiting, and the cold rain emptying itself into the sea.

*I did hurt him,* he told himself again, and conjured to mind the dim echo of the pain where the fire-sword of his power had seared his hand. *Physically he'll be off his guard.* Yirth had said wizards couldn't call the images of other wizards to crystal, fire, water. *He knows there's a wizard, but not a trained warrior. He'll be expecting magic, not a knife.*

But he knew it had better be a clean kill. If Moggin escaped, and survived, that shadow hand would always be there, reaching out for him.

What had once been the crop lands, the small farms and market gardens whose richness in the dry lands of the eastern Middle Kingdoms had made Vorsal a target of Kwest Mralwe's greed, had long since been trampled and burned. Raw stumps showed where orchards had been felled for firewood and to make siege engines after the houses themselves had been plundered of their beams; rotting corpses dangled from the few trees that remained, seven and ten men all hanged together and now swollen and black. The battlefield stench of carrion lay over the place like ground-mist.

His wizard's sight caught the scurry of fat, insolent rats among the gutted farmhouses. A patrol passed him in the dark, steel back-and-breasts and turbaned helms proclaiming them Kwest Mralwe's troops. He faded into the shadows of a half-ruined dovecote until they were gone, then moved on toward rising ground strewn with broken arrow shafts, fouled rags, and here and there a severed hand or finger that the rats hadn't got. Though still some distance away, he could see the dim topaz

specks of the watch fires along the town walls, now and
then blotted by the movement of weary sentinels.

Another skitter caught his ear, away to his right. *More
rats*, he guessed. Another reason not to become a wizard—it made one think about things, like what battlefield
rats fed on, something he'd been pretty much inured to
in the days when he was one of the chief suppliers of rat
food in the West.

Before him stretched the open ground most towns kept
around their walls, crisscrossed with trenches to slow
down the big siege engines and lines of sharpened stakes
to break massed charges. Here and there, like suppurating sores, rucked patches of light and shadow marked
the places where clay jars had been buried, an old defender's trick that would bear the weight of men but would
collapse and strand a turtle or a ram. Ground water had
collected in the bottom of the trenches, and Sun Wolf
turned away from the thought that the torn land had the
unsettling appearance of the dead body of the victim of
torture.

The open ground had probably once been much
wider—wide enough to have permitted the digging of defense emplacements out of bowshot of potential enemy
cover—but had been whittled down through the years by
men who wanted villas more spacious than could be had
within the city walls, but close enough to town to be
convenient. A line of ruins ran right up to the main gates,
flattened now by the battles that had swept over them all
summer, but still offering cover to the attackers. Sun Wolf
wondered how many city councilmen had been bribed by
merchants and home owners to permit that.

As he advanced along that line of ruined walls, the
smell was worse, for his own archers and Krayth of Kilpithie's had a habit of shooting at those who tried to collect the enemy dead—mostly to keep them from gathering
up the slain horses for food—but the cover was good. He
was glad of this, for his struggle with the shadow hand
had left him depleted and weak, and he was putting off
using a cloaking-spell for as long as possible. Once under the ramparts, he'd be able to scout a low place to toss
a grapple. He was ragingly hungry, too.

*Fine*, he thought, with dour humor. *I'll just buy fritters
from a street vendor in the city when I get there.* And

then, *Just my luck to be looking around for a snack in a city under siege . . .*

Again movement caught his eye, on his left, his blind side—he turned quickly to look.

Nothing. Only a whisper of wind turning a strand of his hair against the ragged black linen of his shirt collar, and a half-heard flitter, like blown leaves.

*Must have been rats.*

*Mustn't it?*

In the black overcast another man would have been groping with his hands. To the Wolf's odd, colorless night vision the ruins round him were clear, shadowless, black within black within black—walls and shattered beams, furniture and siege equipment, weapons and dishes, all pulped together into a barely recognizable mass, all stinking, all rotted, all swarming with vermin. This close, he could smell the smoke and carrion of the city, the overwhelming stench of night soil dumped from the walls. Even the pools and puddles of standing water did not gleam, but looked like flat patches of blackness on black ground. Without light to reflect, the eyes of the rats did not flash.

So he saw no glint, no slip of light along metal . . . he didn't know what it was that caught his eye. Perhaps a sound, metal scraping on stone, soft and vicious—perhaps the faint, sudden mustiness of oil.

Then it moved again, and he saw the thing clearly.

For one single, shocked second, he knew why some women screamed.

The thing was as big as the biggest dog he'd ever seen, almost the size of a man. But its body was slung low, round and flat to the ground like a monster cockroach, the knees of its four angular legs rising high above the oily black metal of its back, its arms protruding in bars of jointed metal, slipping cable, and razor-tipped, articulated claws. It resembled nothing so much as a giant spider, headless, eyeless, like a vast metal puppet frozen for a suspended instant at the lip of a defensive trench.

Then it moved.

With a yell of terror Sun Wolf sprang back over the wall behind him, fumbling for his sword even as the logical portion of his mind asked what target he should strike for on that steel carapace. The thing flung itself at him

over the trampled ground of no-man's-land, moving with
blinding speed, leg cables scissoring, razored claws
snatching, all its metal joints whispering with an oily
hiss. He ran back toward the higher ruins at the edge of
the battlefield, and it scooted after him, oblivious alike
to trenches and spikes, the articulated claws of its feet
cutting little crescents in the rucked earth. *Don't be stupid,* he thought, *it can outrun you, it'll never tire and
you will* . . . The low ruins around him offered no cover—
the taller shapes of the burned-out houses seemed impossibly far away.

The thing was only a dozen yards behind him when he
plunged into the first of the standing ruins. He tripped
over something soft that stank and rolled in the shadow
pools of a shattered kitchen, flung himself toward the
crazy ruins of what had been the stair to the skeleton of
the upper floor. The thing sprang after him, long legs
twisting nimbly over the nameless muck on the floor.
The Wolf knew he had to be fast, deadly fast, for the
thing was faster than he . . . if it caught him he was a
dead man, and he had only seconds . . .

The crazy stair lurched under his weight, scorched
beams reeling drunkenly down from the darkness at him.
The creature swarmed up after him like a roach up a
wall, jointed metal knees pistoning faster than his own
flesh and bone. Seconds . . .

A razor claw ripped his back, cold metal, colder air,
the steaming heat of his own blood. He grabbed a beam
and threw himself over the side of the stair, swinging his
weight full into the supporting struts, praying he hadn't
miscalculated and wouldn't break his leg when he hit the
floor. His body crashed into the fire-weakened joists that
held the stairway up, a hundred and ninety pounds of
whipping muscle and bone. The burned-out wood collapsed like a house of cards, bringing a torrent of seared
timbers, rotted thatch, and startled rats down with it.

The creature—spider, monster, killing machine—fell
in the midst of the tangle, landing on its back, half-buried
in debris. A metal arm snatched and claws whined as
Sun Wolf ducked, grabbed the heaviest rafter he could
find and heaved it on top of the waving legs. Broken
timbers bucked with the thing's struggling strength and
he sprang back and ran, heart pounding, all weariness

forgotten. He barely heard the shouts of the guards on the wall, the zing of the arrows they sent flying after him—the most viciously barbed warhead now no more terrifying than a flea bite. He stumbled, fell, muck and water and worse things splattering him, and scrambled to his feet faster than he'd ever have thought possible, running on, running for his life as he'd never run before.

He reached the camp sick, nauseated with exertion and terror, lungs splitting and pulse hammering. Ari, Dog-breath, and the Little Thurg—the only poker players still futilely pushing the same twelve coppers back and forth among a musky frowst of sleeping concubines and empty winecups—didn't even ask what pursued him, but at his gasped command seized whatever pole arms were handy and grouped around him, waiting . . .

And waiting.

Still standing around him, they listened over their shoulders while he told what had attacked him in the ruins of the houses. After half an hour they relaxed enough to produce some food—the bread had not risen and the beans were crunchy—and after an hour, they re-turned, watchfully and with one guard always posted, to the poker game. Though he was exhausted, and, by this time, they were tired as well, Sun Wolf stayed awake, playing poker in Penpusher's wet and filthy black clothes, until dawn.

Nobody ever got more than two of a kind.

And the creature, whatever it was, made no appear-ance at the camp.

For a long while after she woke Starhawk lay in dark-ness, wondering where she was.

Her woozy disorientation frightened her—the knowl-edge that if trouble came she was in no shape either to fight or run. Her head hurt her, as it had since . . . since something that for a moment eluded her . . . but the pain focused and intensified itself until she was almost nau-seated, and her battered limbs felt weak. And there was something else, some sense of terrible danger, something that had wakened her in this darkness . . .

*Where?*

*The convent?* In her dreams she'd heard the small silver voice of the bells speaking the holy hours, calling the

nuns to their reverences. For a moment she felt a flash
of guilt that she lay still abed. Mother Vorannis would
miss her at the chapel . . . though she felt sick, she had
never missed the deep-night vigils . . .

No, she thought. If this was the convent where she'd
grown from girl to woman, she'd be able to hear the throb
of the sea mauling at the cliffs below, see the moonlight
where it lanced cold and patchy through the smoke hole
of her stone beehive cell. The night would smell of the
rock barrens and ocean, not be thick with the scent of a
hundred thousand hearths and privies, nor weighted with
this dreadful, louring closeness.

Then the bells chimed again, near and sweet. She
sensed somewhere the soundless pat of feet in stone pas-
sageways and the murmur of nuns chanting the Mother's
ancient names. Beyond the darkness she felt the Circle
that turned, eternal and invisible, through the Being that
was both Life and Death.

It was a convent, then . . .

Mother Vorannis' face returned to her as her eyelids
slipped shut again. In a gray frame of her shabby veils,
the long nose, the V-shaped, agile lips, and the bright
green eyes seemed overlaid with the spin of the years, at
once young and middle-aged, like ivory slowly turning
color. She realized she didn't even know whether Mother
Vorannis still lived.

The pain hit her, making her head throb so that she
wanted to wrench it off her spine and throw it away. Very
clearly, she saw Mother Vorannis, standing in the cor-
roded limestone arch between two cells, like a too-thin
standing stone herself in the wan daylight, talking to a
man . . .

And Starhawk—though that had not been her name
then—had been walking across the mossed stone and
heather of the overgrown court, her colorless habit
smudged all over with dirt and a pruning knife in her
hand. The smell of the sky that day filled her, wet and
cold with the coming of the storms, the salt pungence of
the ocean, and the musky reek of damp earth. She'd been
cutting the convent rose trees. Alien to the north, they
were her particular care; she'd looked after them for ten
bitter winters, wrapping them against the cold, begging
dead fish from the kitchens to bury in the stony soil at

their roots, caring for them as she'd once cared for her mother's gardens. And it struck her, as she gazed back into the past at that tiny crystal scene, that she hadn't so much as asked anyone to take care of her roses when she left.

Or to take care of Mother Vorannis.

Because the man Vorannis was talking to had turned and stepped into the watery glitter of the pale day, red-blond hair a flaring halo around the craggy, broken-nosed face. His beer-colored eyes had met hers, eyes she felt she had known—should have known, would know—all her life.

She had said nothing. Never in her life had she known what to say. But when he'd ridden on the next day, scrounging food from the villages and farms of the cold northwest, she'd been with him. At the time she had never thought to ask someone else to tend the roses and not to let them die, had never asked how badly it had hurt Mother Vorannis to have the gawky, inarticulate Sister she had taught and cared for since girlhood turn her back upon her with no more words than a muttered "I have to go."

But as the nuns all said, one may run for years along the track of the Invisible Circle, and the Invisible Circle will always lead home.

Then she heard it again, in the night's deep silence, and remembered what had happened to her, why she was here, and what it was that had waked her with sweat standing cold on her face.

It was the creak of a leather strap and the faint, ringing brush of steel armor against the arch that led onto the balcony outside her cell.

The pound of her pulse for a moment threatened to sicken her, crushing like a nutcracker on her brain. Then it steadied—she made it steady—and she listened again. Earlier in the night, she could have sworn it was going to rain, but the wind slept once more. The night was still, overcast and dark as if a blanket had been thrown over her head, but she remembered the layout of the tiny room. The thick archway with its squat pilasters was to her left; the doorway into the corridor, to her right.

Without a sound her hand slid under her pillow, and came up empty. It didn't even occur to her to curse, for whatever was happening might limit her time to seconds, and she was already turning, with the soft murmur of sleep, to slip her hand under the mattress. The Chief, may the Mother bless his balding head, hadn't forgotten where she habitually stowed her weapons. The Sisters had probably insisted on putting her sword and larger dagger away, but he'd managed to leave her with one of her hideouts, a six-inch blade with barely a ripple of a tang to the grip.

That in hand, she muttered again and turned once more, humping the covers over her and sliding like an eel to the floor. The room was a box of night. Even the night rail she wore, the bleached homespun woven in all the Mother's convents—including those in the greatest cloth-making city in the west—would be invisible. As she bellied soundlessly over the tiles, she wondered if she'd be able to stand. Her legs felt weaker than they had even this afternoon. Odds on there'd be men in the corridor . . . Did this mean the Chief was in trouble, too?

Somehow she groped her way to her feet, breathless with the exertion, found the door in the dark and pressed her ear to it. An oiled lantern slide hissed. Yellow light struck her, blinding her in a momentary explosion of pain that seemed to blast to the back of her skull as she swung around, knife in hand. For a disorienting second she thought there were a dozen men in an endless colonnade of window arches. Then they solidified into three men, one arch, and one smaller figure whose white hand on the lantern slide flashed with gems.

"Don't go out that way, Warlady," said a voice she recognized from years gone by as that of Renaeka Strata. "My men are in the corridor. I think you'd probably be safer in my house than you would be here."

# CHAPTER

## —— 6 ——

"'K IDNAP' IS A HARD WORD, CAPTAIN." AGAINST the queer, dead dun of the morning sky visible through the trefoiled points of the study windows, Renaeka Strata had the appearance of an exotic flower in her gown of pink and white. Entirely apart from the pearls which covered it, the gown itself was an advertisement for her wealth. Kwest Mralwe's silks, the Wolf knew, with their vivid delicacy of coloring, cost a fortune on the market, and there had to be thirty yards of the stuff hung around that skinny frame.

He growled, "So's 'extort' and 'assassinate,' words which rumor also attribute to the Lady Prince."

She raised her ostrich-plume fan modestly, like a woman who simpers "Oh, this old rag," of a dress which cost some poor grut the price of a good farm and everything on it. "Well," she purred deprecatingly, "we all do what we must." The fan retreated, and the hazel eyes lost their coquettishness, becoming again the eyes of a king. "I spoke only the truth, Commander. She is safer here than she would be among the Sisters."

Sun Wolf opened his mouth to retort, then remembered his conversation with the King, and shut it again. His eye narrowed as he studied this thin, erect woman, in her pearl-crusted gown and preposterous maquillage, and he wondered how far she could be trusted. "May I see her?"

"But of course." She rang a bell, the note of it silver and small among the plaster arabesques of the study's pendant ceiling, and a girl page appeared. "See if the Lady Starhawk is able to receive visitors," she instructed coolly, and the girl bowed and hurried away in a dragonfly flash of green and gold. "She may even leave here with you, if you both insist. I don't advise it and I won't permit you to take her out of here against her will. My physicians tell me she isn't well." Those cool dappled eyes raked him, taking in the deepening of the lines that bracketed mustache and mouth, the bruise of sleeplessness that turned his one eye pale as yellow wine, and the scabbing-over abrasions on his high forehead he hadn't even felt last night. "You look less than rampant yourself."

"A touch of the vapors."

Her thin mouth flexed with amusement, and she offered him her smelling salts in the bottle of cut rose crystal half the size of his fist. With a grin he waved them away, the wizard in him wondering what spices had gone to scent that aromatic vinegar while the mercenary priced the bottle at nearly two gold pieces—three, if your buyer was honest. He was interested to note how the Lady Prince's smile etched a whole new network of lines in her face under the heavy plaster of cosmetics, the wrinkles of ready humor eradicating for that fleeting instant the deep gravings of sleeplessness, stress, and cruelty. It was the first time he'd seen her truly at ease.

At least a mercenary didn't have to fight all year round, he thought abstractly, stroking the corner of his mustache. There were no winter quarters for the rulers of trading cities, no off season for banker-queens. He wondered how long it had been since she'd allowed herself to trust one of the young men whom Wool Market tittle-tattle ascribed as her numerous lovers.

"What about the land barons?" he inquired, curious. "They going to sit down under it when you annex all Vorsal's land? The Duke of Farkash has a claim on that town from his aunt's marriage—so do the Counts of Sal-.

tyre. It's damn near the only decent crop land left in this part of the world.''

She smiled, the easy playfulness slipping back into her usual catlike malice; the pendant pearls on her vast lace collar quivered like dew on a monstrous rose as she shrugged. "It was Vorsal who first attacked us,'' she pointed out. "Their troops started the war . . .''

"In a tavern brawl here that I'll bet you gold to garlic bulbs *you* set up.''

"Nonsense.'' Again the coquette's sliding intonation, denying she'd dropped a handkerchief on purpose while four swains battled for the honor of returning it. "The Duke of Vorsal is a proud man, but he could have stopped the proceedings at any time with an apology and the smallest of reparations. And in any case, what's done is done. By the laws of the Middle Kingdoms, Vorsal is the proved aggressor. Any land baron, or any city, dispatching troops to its assistance is liable to attack by me or my allies.''

He noticed the unconscious use of the word "me.'' The King had used it, too. Needless to say, should Saltyre, Skathcrow, or Farkash decide to jump into the fray on behalf of the beleaguered town, it was also gold to garlic bulbs that their ancestral enemies—Dalwirin, heretical Mallincore, Grodas, or any of a dozen other Kingdoms—would fall over themselves in their speed to dig up an ancient alliance with Kwest Mralwe to attack their foes' armies were away. At this time of the year it was far too late for one of the cities of the Gwarl Peninsula to send an ally's help to Vorsal before the storms hit. And by spring, of course, it would all be over.

At least, the Wolf knew Renaeka Strata and the other members of the King-Council were fervently hoping it would all be over.

As for the land barons, and the Duke of Vorsal was nominally one of in spite of his connections with the trading houses, the Wolf knew that, powerful as those rulers were in their own territory, none of them would risk getting on the bad side of Kwest Mralwe. Some of them had formidable private armies, but they also had investments. Even if they found another market for their wool, the risk of boycott in other goods was too great.

And Renaeka Strata, bastard, slut, and witch's daugh-

ter, was notorious not only for her wealth, but for the
length of her memory and the coldhearted implacability
of her revenges.

He admired her as a woman and a ruler, but the thought
of Starhawk, ill and helpless in this delicate pink fortress, made him profoundly uneasy.

The page returned. A pair of the Lady Prince's body-
guards—picked, uncharitable hearsay ran, for their good
looks and amorous abilities as much as for their skill with
arms—escorted them down pillared breezeways and
across cool salons whose every arch and vault clustered
thick with the filigreed stalactites fashionable in these
warm lands. The room Starhawk had been given looked
onto the gardens at the rear of the house, far from the
noise of business carried on closer to the street. He saw
her from the shadows of the pillared breezeway that separated forecourt from gardens, seated on a bench of
honey-colored sandstone on the broad terrace, watching
water trickle down a stair-step fountain among the brown
mazes of topiary below. She was dressed as a young gen-
tleman of the Middle Kingdoms, and the stiffly boned
black doublet, frilled ruff, black hose and paned trunks
made her face seem more white and haggard by contrast.
She looked around at the swift scrunch of his boots on
the gravel, but didn't rise. The hand she held out to him
and the mouth he bent quickly to kiss felt cold.

Her gray gaze had lost none of its shrewd quickness
as it took in the bruises and cuts. "You all right, Chief?"

"Compared to what I might have been, yeah, I'm
fine." He flung a glance back at the Lady Prince and her
brace of stallions, and lowered his voice to a faint, scraping rasp as he bent toward her. "I'll tell you later. You?"

She nodded, and turned her hip a little to show the
long dagger there. Her low court shoes couldn't conceal
a blade, and her doublet sleeves fit closely with their little
frills of white shirt, but he'd have bet his family jewels
she had at least two other knives somewhere on her person, plus something innocuous-looking which could double as a garrote. *Probably the bandages on her head,* he
decided, looking down at her. The pale hair stuck up
through them like a child's, and he was seized by an
embarrassing tenderness at the sight of it, a desire to
touch. Instead he hooked his hands through the buckle

of his sword belt and said, "She says you're free to go if you want."

Starhawk glanced past him at that gorgeous pink rose of a woman, both of them remembering the land baron who'd tried to set up competition against Kwest Mralwe's silk monopoly by smuggling in his own silkworms from the East. There was still a shade of ruby crimson ironically named after him, to commemorate the grotesque "accident" which had claimed his life. She lifted her voice a little. "That true?"

The Lady Prince inclined her golden-wigged head. "I shall give you a horse, clothes, money, whatever you feel you need. But I repeat, I do not advise it."

"How much money?"

The Lady Prince looked nonplussed, but said, "Twenty silver pieces, Stratus weight," in the voice of one who expects to have to fight for that ridiculously low figure.

"Forty," the Hawk said promptly.

"My dear Warlady . . ."

"I'll think about it." With a gesture she forestalled further haggling, and, graciously though with a slightly militant glint in her old eye, Renaeka and her guards departed. "I think the offer's genuine. She'd have said fifty if she didn't intend really to pay up."

"Grasping old witch . . ."

"Now what happened?"

The Wolf settled himself beside her on the bench and related last night's events: his attempt to turn back the storms; the King's offer; the hand full of darkness; and the creature that had attacked him below Vorsal's walls. "This morning I had a look through the books of the Witches," he went on quietly, his big fingers clasped lightly through hers. "They talk about something called a *djerkas* in the shirdane tongue. It's a kind of *golem*— an animate statue controlled by a wizard's will."

"I always wondered about *golems*." The lines printed in the fragile flesh around her eyes deepened as she considered the thread of the fountain among its allegorical bronze nymphs. "I mean, suppose you *did* breathe life into a statue. It wouldn't do you a damn bit of good unless you gave it some joints as well. The *djerkas* sounds as if it were constructed specifically for the purpose of killing."

"Wonder why we haven't heard about it before?" The Wolf turned his head a little to consider her with his single eye—as usual, she was sitting on his blind side. "If Moggin's got that thing out patrolling the walls . . ."

"The obvious answer is that he doesn't," the Hawk replied calmly. "Metal or not, it's not a war machine. One swat with a battering ram or dump a load from the ballista on it and you've got scrap iron. Same story if he uses it as a killer-scout. Once our boys know it's out there, all it'll take is six or seven gruts with long pikes and a big sack of sand to grit up its joints."

Sun Wolf laughed, Starhawk's deadly insouciance lifting the fear of the thing from him like a cloud shifted from the sun.

She shrugged. "And why should it patrol outside, when they've got guards on the walls? If I were Moggin and had only one of those metal bugs—and with fuel and iron as short as they are in that city you can bet they're not going to tinker up another—I'd put it patrolling the *inside* of the wall, to mince up anything that gets past the guards. If, that is, I wanted the people in the town to know I was a wizard, which is a piece of news I'd think real carefully about advertising in a town under siege."

Sun Wolf nodded, remembering the siege of Laedden—the lynchings, the hysterical accusations, the neurotic confessions and impossible charges that had turned its later weeks into a bizarre hell of paranoia and death.

After dawn he'd gone back to Dogbreath's tent and slept for a few hours, exhaustion imprisoning him in nightmares he was too tired to escape, while Dogbreath, Firecat, and the Little Thurg traded off lackadaisical guard. He didn't seriously think the *djerkas* would come near the camp in daylight, but the thought of lying alone in the tent didn't appeal to him much either. He had drawn the Runes of Ward around his cot, but had dreamed again and again that he hadn't done it properly—that he had forgotten something, or there was some spell he had not known—and the shadow of a dark hand could be seen upon the tent wall, weaving its silvery net.

Awakening after two hours' sleep, ghastly as it was, had been an improvement.

Then he had ridden to the Convent of St. Dwade, to

hear from the Sisters that Starhawk had been taken away in the night.

"They want me to ride out and look over the new siege machines for the day after tomorrow's assault," he said after a time. "Her Ladyship's sent to every apothecary in town for mercury and powdered hellebore, but that doesn't mean we'll find squat. There's something called auligar powder used in hexes—that isn't all it's good for, but it'll bring up an Eye—but it takes about a week to make, even after you've got all the ingredients."

"What's in it?" inquired the Hawk curiously.

"Not much—staghorn and dried violets and mistletoe and a little silver. Yirth told me how to make it. Kaletha mentioned it, too. Silver alone can be used to read some kinds of marks as well . . ."

"Bet me Renaeka'll make you use your own."

"Or count it real good when she gets it back from me," he grunted. "Something in one of the Witch books makes me think you can use blood as well."

"She'd probably make you use your own for that, too."

"More likely find some perfectly legal reason to volunteer the man who's been underselling her prices on ammoniated salts. The woman doesn't miss a trick, Hawk."

"If she did she'd be dead." Starhawk shrugged, her long fingers stroking at her wrist ruffles. "The Sisters told me about her rivalry with the Cronesmae when Purcell's brother was alive. That nearly came to a trade war over the alum diggings. He ended up falling down a flight of stairs one night and breaking his neck. To this day, nobody can figure out how she managed it, because, by all witnesses, the house was absolutely empty and the stairs weren't high, but there's nobody in the town who thought it was an accident. Poor old Purcell might be one of the richest traders in the Middle Kingdoms these days, but if she says 'Jump' he's the first man on his feet asking 'How high?' "

Sun Wolf nodded, remembering other things he'd been told about the intricate, bloody machinations of Middle Kingdoms politics. He thought about it later, when he was met at the engineering park to the northeast of the city by Purcell himself, thin, gray, elderly, and self-effacing to the point of invisibility, huddled in the wind-ruffled fur collar of his black velvet gown as if, like a turtle, he felt safer within its shell.

"I've been asked to accompany you, to send for whatever you might need," he said in his apologetic voice.

*To keep an eye on me, you mean,* the Wolf thought. Despite Purcell's air of being Renaeka Strata's footstool, the man was the head of one of the fastest-rising trading houses in the Middle Kingdoms; the guards who followed a few paces behind them wore the yellow livery of the Cronesmae, not the green and gold of the Stratii. Sun Wolf wondered, as he crossed the trampled grass of the hilltop on which the park stood, how much of the man's timid diffidence was natural and how much had been adopted as protective coloration in dealing with the redoubtable mistress of the Council. If there was no respite for banker-queens, still less was there a respite *from* them for the poor bastards they ruled.

Wind snagged at his hair, flattening his dull crimson doublet sleeves, rippling Purcell's black gown and the brown hackle feathers which tufted the guards' turbaned helms. The engineering park overlooked the marshy estuary where the Mralwe River flowed into the sea. Unlike Vorsal, Kwest Mralwe had no separate harbor, but was built where the Mralwe River bent around the jutting granite promontory upon which the city had originally been built. Oceangoing vessels could sail inland as far as its ancient bridge, its great pool with its massive stone quays, perhaps seven miles from the open sea. It was valuable shelter during the winter storms, but, the Wolf observed cynically, nothing compared to Vorsal's cupshaped bay. Gazing at Kwest Mralwe, the cluster of ancient citadels on the hillside and the newer suburbs spread downward in a succession of pillars, turrets, and protective walls over the hill's feet like petticoats of pink and white, he wondered how much that had to do with the final decision to provoke Vorsal to war. Something certainly had been involved; the two cities had existed in a state of uneasy truce for years. Someone on the Council had clearly wanted something, but what it was impossible to know.

From this trampled hilltop, by turning, the Wolf could see across the slaty river to the rolling brown lands on the other side, the gaggle of fishing villages along the estuary, the thin stringers of bare trees marking stony farmlands beyond. Far out over the ocean wavered the slanted purplish curtains of rain squalls; the sea itself was green, running high to meal-colored hills. The air felt very still.

Like sleeping ruminants, the siege engines towered all around them, as they did in the smaller park by the camp. Local flurries of rain had darkened their raw yellow wood and the burnt orange of hastily cured hides. In the strange calm, the whole place reeked of sawdust, carrion, and the latrine trenches of the slaves. The smoke of the forge on the lee side of the hill rose straight in the leaden sky. The metal clink of hammers punctuated the thud of mallets, the rasp of saws, and the clamor of men stretching ropes. Artisans in leather aprons and slaves in coarse canvas smocks swarmed everywhere over those five monstrous constructions: the ram like an ambulatory longhouse; a turtle, ridiculously like its namesake under a heavy shell of hides; two towers, their flying bridges extended like blunt tongues protruding rudely against the cold sky; and a half-built ballista. Guards were everywhere, the red and blue of the City Troops an incongruous garland ringing the hill's dull brow. The rise of the ground to the south just hid this hill from where Vorsal's poppy-bright turrets would be.

"You needn't have bothered building the machines out here, you know," he grunted to Purcell as they ducked to enter the close, smelly shadows of the ram. The Councillor, gingerly holding up the hem of his gown, seemed to be trying to walk without touching the ground with his expensive kid-leather shoes. "If there's a wizard in Vorsal, he could conjure the image of this place in a crystal."

The elderly man's eyes flared with alarm, then vexation. "Oh, dear," he fussed, and Sun Wolf laughed.

Patiently, thoroughly, Sun Wolf went over the ram, running his hands along the great hanging beam, the ropes that held it and its iron head. As Yirth had taught him, he squinted sidelong at them, conjured the words of power from the half-forgotten tangle of remembered spells, hoping he remembered aright. It had been a year—he'd periodically repeated everything he'd learned that night to refresh his memory, but there had never been

anything against which to check it, and he had been, he
knew, slack about it when other matters demanded his
time.

He touched the ropes, and then all around the engine's
hide and canvas walls, inside and out, up as far as his
arm could reach, then untied and removed the leather
sleeves of his doublet, rolled his shirt sleeves to his biceps, and went over it all again, first with his hands
smeared with powdered hellebore, then with a flour-sifter
in which he'd put a powder of mercury cut with flour to
make it go farther.

"Must you just dump it on that way?" twittered Purcell, shifting anxiously from foot to foot. "Mercury's
over a silver piece an ounce! It's getting all over the
ground . . ." He pulled off his silk skullcap and held it
ineffectually under the beam, the gray dust falling over
it like a film of ash. In the chill, shadowy light his thin
pink face and almost-naked scalp, covered with its fluff
of gray wisps, looked like an anxious bird's.

Sun Wolf swung lightly down from his perch among
the struts and handed him the shaker. "You want to save
money, fine. I won't use it."

The little man dithered a moment, cap in one hand,
sifter clutched inexpertly in the other, as the Wolf started
to stalk out of the ram. "Wait . . . no . . . Do—do as
you think best. Please."

In other years Sun Wolf had seen Renaeka Strata's famous tantrums when she thought one of her generals had
been wasting her money—which wasn't hers at all, but
the King-Council's. He understood Purcell's concern.

After that he went over all the other machines, one by
one. It was his own troop—now Ari's troop, but still his
friends, men he had trained and had led into a hundred
battles—who'd be spearheading this assault. They were
the best, the toughest, the shock troops. It was for that
he'd trained them, and for that they'd been hired—for that
they could command the highest prices, *when*, he reflected irritably, *they could pry the money out of certain
tightfisted employers*. If the siege towers went down, if
those flying bridges that stuck out over the dizzying gulfs
of nothing collapsed, it was Ari, Dogbreath, Penpusher,
and Zane who'd be on them when they did. The forced,
extended concentration wearied him, coupled with his

lack of sleep; his mind stumbled on the endless repetitions, and he forced himself not to wonder whether he was doing it right. Between spells, between muttered incantations to focus himself into the floating state of half meditation where the Eyes could be read, he cursed Moggin Aerbaldus for a gutter-festering bastard hoodoo.

Moggin Aerbaldus.

Kneeling on the end of the extended bridge with the faintest of chill breezes flicking at the ends of his hair, with hand, knees, and rolled-up sleeves smeared with mercury and hellebore and the goose fat with which the machines were greased, it occurred to him that if the supporting ropes broke *now* or if the planks of the bridge gave beneath *him* and he plunged sixty feet to the stony ground below, that, too, would be a "misfortune," an "unavoidable accident" in the bad luck of the troop.

He finished his work and came down as quickly as he could.

It was nearly dark when he completed his task. As he smeared salt and silver in the last siege tower he could hear the clatter of hooves outside and the voices of men exclaiming. The overpowering sweetness of torches made up with incense stung his nose. *Renaeka Strata, without a doubt.* He grinned, picturing Purcell's panicked discomfiture. Wiping his fouled hands on his thighs as he emerged from the darkness of the tower, he found he'd guessed right on all counts. The Lady Prince stood before its narrow door in a refulgent golden gown which put the torches of her guards to shame. Nervous and looking colder than ever with a drip on his narrow nose, Purcell hovered a few paces behind. "Did you find aught?" the Lady inquired, and Sun Wolf shook his head.

"But that doesn't necessarily mean there isn't anything there."

And as he gave her the same little lecture he'd given Ari—of which he was beginning to become extremely tired—on Eyes and auligar, he wondered what other substances might raise marks, substances that the Witches of Wenshar had not written down or that Yirth of Mandrigyn's teacher had been murdered before she could pass along.

Renaeka Strata listened, her head tipped a little to one side, the jewels in her pink wig flashing in the cresset's juddering light, eyes narrowed and long, white, impossibly graceful hands fingering the luminous ropes of her pearls. When he was done she said, "The attack is set for an hour before dawn, the morning after tomorrow. If our wicked magician—should he exist at all—is to put the Eye on these engines, he must do so tonight."

"He exists, my Lady." Sun Wolf sighed.

"Indeed?" She studied him from beneath hennaed lashes, seeing a big, grimy lion of a man, with his heavy forearms furred with gold beneath the stained linen of his rolled-back sleeves and his hands scarred by the teeth of demons. "How fortunate, then, that you are working for us. Will you watch tonight?"

He thought, *I should try to get into the city again*, but the thought of the *djerkas* raised gooseflesh on his back. Sooner or later they'd have to meet, that he knew—and better sooner, before worse harm could befall his friends. And yet, there was a good chance that the Lady Prince was right—that Moggin would come to him, here. If not, there was tomorrow, and no one else he knew could expect to catch the mage if he did come.

Slowly he nodded. "All right." And if Moggin came, he found himself thinking, at least there'd be help within call.

Her voice got brisk. "It would also assist matters if, on the night preceding the attack, we might count upon a good, heavy fog to cover the advance of the siege engines along the road from here to the walls of Vorsal. As a wizard I'm sure you could arrange . . ."

"No."

She didn't shift an eye at the bald finality in his voice. "You would be paid extra, and not, I assure you, ungenerously."

"No."

Though she was far too controlled to redden, even supposing any blush could penetrate the stucco of her cosmetics, there was an edged quality to her laugh. "Captain, really . . ."

"I may be a killer but I'm not a whore," he said quietly. "I don't use power for other peoples' convenience. What I'm doing in Vorsal is for my men and because Moggin's damn hex killed innocent people and nearly killed someone I love." The phrase echoed strangely on his tongue; he realized it was the first time he'd publicly admitted to caring for anyone. "My quarrel is with him, not with the people of Vorsal."

By her eyes, he saw she understood, but she tried anyway, laughing through her thin nose. "Your quarrel may not be with them, but they'll certainly suffer along with him when he dies. If you kill this man, his city will fall. And when his city falls, we'll give you your chance to kill him or kill him for you if you prefer, in any manner you want. You can't kill him without dooming those 'innocent people' in the town, you know."

"I know."

"And it is, after all, the object of the siege," Purcell pointed out, hastening to back up anything the Lady might say. "Believe me, you will be well paid . . ."

"Pay isn't the reason I'm doing this!" He swung around upon the little man, stung with the knowledge of his own evil, and saw the affronted surprise in that collapsed pinkish face. "God's grandmother, don't you people ever think about anything but money?"

"Of what use is your power, if not to give you a good living?" the Councillor inquired, with very real puzzlement. "I should think that now that you are too old to lead a mercenary troop, you would welcome another way of making an even better living without effort, something which will guarantee you a comfortable old age. Isn't that what we all do?"

"NO!" Anger filled him, stung by the words "too old," but with it a curious cold sickness, a disgust with them and with himself. When he had been a mercenary, he realized, there had never been a wrong course—only inept, inefficient, or erroneous ones. He had been paid, and that was that. It was different now.

"No," he said again, softly now. "That's what a bandit does."

The banker's thin little mouth hardened, and he tucked his hands into the fur muff he carried. "Well, *really* . . ."

*Or a merchant*, he thought belatedly.

"It isn't—It's different with power," he said clumsily, groping for what he meant and knowing they would not understand, for he did not understand it himself. It was another reason, he realized, that he needed training with an experienced wizard, not only to learn to put that rationale into words, but to have someone else who understood that it was needed. "I can't sell it . . . I can't use it without knowing in myself that what I'm doing is . . . is right . . ." It wasn't exactly what he meant and he knew he'd lost them by the cool glint in the Lady Prince's eye.

"And does the distinction you make mean that a thing will be right when it is done for one reason, and wrong if done for another? Particularly when the results are exactly the same?"

"I suppose you mean," Purcell put in, tilting his skullcapped head to one side, "that you feel there's a taboo of some kind on the use of your powers. But if so, wherein lies the difference between wizards using power for what they think is worthwhile and using it for what another thinks is worthwhile, especially if that other is able to take a wider view?"

"I don't know!" Sun Wolf said, backed into a corner now, angry, outmaneuvered, and wondering why he hadn't simply stuck to killing people for his living.

"But that's nonsense! Really, you're like an artist refusing to buy bread by taking commissions or a skilled accountant refusing to use his skills for his own benefit by working for a wealthy man . . ."

Renaeka gestured impatiently. Purcell, though more earnest than the Wolf had ever seen him, pinched shut his mouth and looked at her protestingly, truly not understanding, as quarreling lovers say, "what the fuss is about." Awkward silence hovered for a moment, broken only by the crackle of the scented torches and the dull background of overseers' voices as they counted the slaves for the night. Then, with a kind of prim self-satisfaction and a glance at his ruler, Purcell began, "And in any case you really have no choice. We have . . . "

*"Be silent!"* Renaeka Strata didn't raise her voice—though she could do so with hair-raising effect if it would get her what she wanted—but the venom of her tone was even worse. Purcell flinched and seemed to look around for a small hole in the ground into which to crawl, and Sun Wolf, knowing Starhawk's name had been on his lips, balled his fists hard on a red surge of anger. Just for an instant, he caught the glance Purcell gave his mistress,

a glance of protest, of resentment, in which, like a hidden glass splinter, gleamed hate.

But if she was aware of this, she said nothing. With her usual smooth graciousness she turned back to the Wolf. "I will not ask it of you, then. But you will watch?"

He turned his face away from them, looking past the ring of torches set up in the open space of the park, past the dull knees of the hills to the south, as if beyond them he could see the black walls, the lightless towers of Vorsal against the unnatural sky. It stood to reason that the hex marks—if the hex marks were in fact made on the machines and not somewhere else in the camp—couldn't be made by a confederate, that Moggin had to be coming into the camps himself—didn't it?

He didn't know and cursed his ignorance, his lack of training that put not only himself but all his friends in peril of their lives. As had been the case in trying to explain magic to these two grasping and money-loving merchants, he felt helpless, awash in a sea of things he simply did not know, and anger stirred in him again, like a goaded beast's, undirected and dull.

"Yeah," he said softly, to the hills, to the torches, to the night. "Yeah, I'll watch."

"And *was* your mother a witch?"

Renaeka Strata, standing at the half-opened curtain of the window of the small dining room, moved her head a little, her cold white profile thin and hook-nosed and suddenly very old against the dark. She had taken off her wig, covering the thin, lackluster hair of an ageing woman with a close-fitting velvet cap like a man's. Instead of the gorgeous dresses she changed into and out of all day, she wore a loose robe of equal gorgeousness, voided velvet colored as only the velvets of Kwest Mralwe could be colored, the luminous violet of sunset with a collar of shagged silk soft as fur. Only her hands were the same, incredibly long, incredibly narrow, white as a spirit's hands and thick with a lifetime's ransom of jewels.

"I don't think so, no."

She turned slowly and came back to the table, where Starhawk still sat like a well-mannered young boy in her petaled neck ruff and head bandages. The servants had

cleared away the remains of the meal which the Lady
Prince had asked her guest to share with her in privacy;
the musicians who had played softly in a corner of the
chamber had departed. A lute, a psaltry, and a painted
porcelain flute still lay on the bright-blue cushions of
their ivory stools; the candlelight that warmed the room
picked out the gold spider strands of strings, the hard
flicks of the bright tuning keys, softening where it cast
shadows like mottled water on the molded plaster of the
wall behind.

Wine gleamed like liquid rubies in goblets of gold-
mounted nacre and nautilus shell. The smell of meats
was in the air, with that of the patchouli in an ornate
table jar of enamel and gold. Voices and the noise of
traffic jangled faintly from the street outside, for this
room was close to the front of the house. In a pierced
bronze brazier close by charcoal flickered, warming the
room; as the Lady Prince held her hands out toward it,
the amber glow edged her long fingers in rose and called
secret colors from the hidden hearts of her jewels.

Her voice, with its veined sweetness of silver and rust,
was low. "Had she been a witch, she would not have
staked her power, her very life, upon the lust of a man.
Had she been a witch, she would not have had to. My
mother was a greedy woman, wanting money, wanting
power, and wanting to control men—wanting especially
to control my father, and through him all that the wealth
of the House could buy. With the alum mines that were
his first wife's dowry, he'd become truly the ruler of
Kwest Mralwe, and she wanted that. But had she been
truly a witch, she'd have been able to control him with
more than his lust—an evanescent bridle at best, particularly in my father's case. And had she been truly a witch,
she'd have been able to keep him from learning of her
infidelities far longer than she did."

She turned her hands over, above the jewel bed of the
glowing coals. "They burned her," she said after a time.
"Publicly, in the square, clothed only in a rag of a white
shift—though the servants who told me about it when I
was four said she was naked—and in her hair, which was
black and reached her knees. They do that to the mageborn in the Middle Kingdoms, you know. She'd lost most
of her beauty by then, I'm told—she lost it when she

miscarried my brother—and my father repudiated her, but it was noticed he didn't take his old wife back, nor return her dowry. In many ways I'm more like him than her.''

"I'm sorry," Starhawk said softly. Sun Wolf had not told her that.

Renaeka Strata shrugged. "It was a long time ago," she said. "And she was far too vain and taken up with fascinating every young man in the city to have much time for me, in any case. I don't think, even had she had power, she'd have known what to do with it, how to make it work for her—always provided such power exists, as your friend seems to think.''

"It exists," Starhawk said, unconsciously echoing the Wolf's assertion.

The older woman smiled, her eyes suddenly warm. "If it does, I've never seen it. And with Church law on the subject as it is, I'll hold to that disbelief for everyone's sake. Ill luck is ill luck, and someone is always bound to benefit from it, as Purcell did when old Greambus's dye lots all turned the year of the King of Dalwirin's coronation, or as I did, when that dreadful brother of his fell down the stairs.''

"Perhaps," the Hawk said softly, "your mother merely chose to use her powers for other things—to bring her a man she wanted beyond sense or reason—and didn't look beyond that.''

That sharp face, so old in its narrow frame of colorless hair and dull purple velvet, turned toward her with a wry expression, the flames picking out all the intricate tracery of lip and eye wrinkles that cosmetics usually hid. "It scarcely explains why she'd stand by and let them burn her.''

"Maybe she wasn't a very good witch and didn't know how to escape," the Hawk pointed out, folding her bony hands together in the elongated linen flowers of her cuffs. "Maybe the miscarriage you spoke about wearied her, drained her, to the point where she couldn't summon the power. And maybe," she added more softly, "when the man she loved repudiated her, she simply didn't care.''

She winced suddenly, the fine muscles of her jaw twisting into flame-touched relief as a stab of pain in her head left her breathless. She opened her eyes and, for a moment, saw two figures, columns of damson shadow blazing in a firestorm of jewels, bending toward her, white hands reaching . . .

Then they resolved themselves into the Lady Prince.

"Are you all right, child?"

Starhawk managed to nod, cursing herself for showing weakness. "Fine," she whispered, wanting more than anything to lie down and not certain that she could negotiate the marble corridors as far as her room. If she were attacked now, she thought giddily, she wouldn't stand a chance. She could barely remember where she'd put her hideout knives.

The crystal tone of the Lady's bell was like another spear going through her brain. "I just need rest," Starhawk said haltingly, and forced herself to rise. The room doubled, reeled, then stabilized again; embarrassed and feeling ridiculously shy, she started for the door. Another pain struck her, buckling her knees, and Renaeka, who had been walking close beside her, waiting for that, caught her in arms surprisingly strong, and lowered her to the floor.

# CHAPTER

—— 7 ——

*I*N THE DEAD, WAITING CALM OF THE NIGHT *S*UN *W*OLF watched, listening to the darkness.

All day and evening the wind had been still. He had dozed for an hour after Renaeka Strata had left, and had shared the guards' rations, but always, it seemed, with one ear cocked toward the east. When he slept, his uneasy dreams had been a confusion of cloud and storm. Later, sitting in the pooled-ink shadow of a siege tower, facing out into the night, he had cautiously conjured winds.

Though unable to summon them against a natural inclination without sinking into the moving trance of deep magic—something he feared to do, now—he was able to herd and coax a kind of gentle push of land breezes eastward, to thrust against the cold masses over the sea. It was the most he could do, though his hands, his spirit, ached with holding back from more, and he cursed his ignorance again—his ignorance of weather; his ignorance of the healing that he was coming more and more to sense that Starhawk needed; his fatal ignorance of the magic of ill.

He knew he shouldn't have to track down the ill-wisher like an assassin and kill him with his hands. There had to be other ways to finesse around a lack of power. His methods of healing were inefficient, he only bulled his way through on strength when he should have used skill. As a warrior and a teacher of warriors he knew that only worked until you met someone stronger.

Worry clawed him like a rat chewing in a wall. In thirty years' experience with physical mayhem, he had seen thousands of head wounds, and he hadn't liked Starhawk's pallor that morning, or the lines of strain around her eyes. Glad as he'd been to see her out of bed, there was a part of him that had wanted to order her down again. She shouldn't have been up, shouldn't have been sitting with him . . .

But, by his ancestors, it had been good to talk to her again!

The warm land breeze stirred his tawny hair, and he watched its footprint pass him in the nodding weeds. Far down the dark line of the coast he could see the lights of the City Troops, camped in the ruins of Vorsal's little port. By this time next year, those ruins would be replaced by warehouses, ropewalks, and the barracoons of slaves; the wharves would bristle with mastheads bearing the red-and-blue banners of the Pierced Heart.

On the way out to the engineering park to meet Purcell, he had ridden past the decaying walls of the ancient Royal Palace. Through unguarded gates rusted open, the Wolf had glimpsed unswept courtyards and a weed-choked portico, empty of life save for one laundress taking a shortcut with a basket of washing on her arm. The contrast with the city's markets, with the lively chaos of money and fine clothes around any of the great merchant houses—the Stratii, the Cronesmae, the Balkii—was glaring. No wonder the King wanted a tame wizard, to win him back power in this land.

Feet soughed the long grass in the windless silence, too light and furtive for the measured swish of the patrolling guard. Catlike the Wolf rose and slid into the shelter of one of the tower's wheel housings. *Not Moggin already,* he thought, following the dry breath with his ears. In any case he refused to believe that the master wizard's coming would be detected so easily. *A confederate after all?*

Then the breeze that flowed along the side of the hill

threw wide the corner of a cloak, and brought, above the stinks of raw wood and hides and smoke, a strand of dark perfume. Edging the hood as blown snow edges a drift crest, he glimpsed the unraveling tangle of hair. The dim phosphor of reflected torchlight from within the circle of the engines picked from the dense shadows a thread of golden chain.

*Or a distraction?*

He said, "Opium?" softly, and she spun, catching her breath at finding him so near.

He stepped from the shadow.

"They said you were here." Black hair spilled forth as she put back her hood; again he had to remind himself not to touch. "Do you mind if I walk with you for a while?"

"We've got to be fifteen miles from the camp," he pointed out, starting to move widdershins along the outer edge of the park, his one eye scanning the formless land where the blocky shadows of the towers and rams blurred into the darkness. "Don't walk on my right," he added, and wondered, for a brief splinter of a moment, how much he could trust this woman to walk in the darkness on his blind side. He ought, he supposed, to send her away.

"Not if you come straight overland," Opium's voice replied, husky and a little high above the continuous soft rustle of her skirts on the grass. In Ari's company last night, he'd seen her wear her company face, bright and saucy and quick. Now, as he'd seen her first among the ruined siege engines of the camp, she was more subdued, with a kind of shy thoughtfulness behind her soft chatter. "I can go back that way. I was in the city this evening." She nodded toward the fairy-tale glitter of Kwest Mralwe's domes and turrets, spilling down the shape of its invisible hillside to throw a broken carpet of reflections on the lamp-sewn river below. "Sorry—I look a mess, I know—I barely had a moment to comb my hair . . ."

The thick braids hanging at her temples smelled of sweetgrass and herbs; kohl deepened the subtle colors of her eyes. "You look fine," he murmured.

"I just didn't want to go back just yet."

"You can leave, you know," the Wolf said quietly after a time. "Leave the troop, I mean, if Zane's really giving you hardship."

"And do what? Dance in taverns where I'd have to sleep with the customers and pay the innkeeper for the privilege? I've got money in Wrynde, all Geldark's—my man's—savings, and a little I saved, dancing at Bron's tavern during the winter. If I can get back there and get it, I can come south again in the spring." With a quick, wild gesture, she scooped aside the dark cloud of her hair where it snagged her cloak collar, shook it out, and with practiced fingers adjusted its delicate tendrils around her face. Sun Wolf found himself wanting very much to see her dance. "But for a woman by herself, it takes a lot of money to stay free, you know? I've seen them. Even the highest-paid women in town have keepers."

She moved closer to him as they walked, and he forced himself to be ready for an attack from that direction, though he didn't seriously think she was Moggin's confederate—if there was such a thing—inside the camp. And that, he added to himself, was probably fortunate. It was difficult enough to watch, not only the empty lands on three sides of the engineering park but the park itself, with only one eye, without having her soft, inconsequential chatter covering possible sounds and soothing his mind with the warm pleasure of her presence. But he was loath to send her away. And he could manage, he told himself.

At one point in their circuit of the park he said, "Look, Opium, if I tell you to run, you RUN—run screaming back to the middle of the park where the fires are and get the guards. Even if it looks like I need help, you *don't* help, you *get* help, as much of it as you can and as fast as you can. All right?"

"But if that—that thing that attacked you last night—comes back, by the time I get guards you could be dead." She moved anxiously, to get into the line of his sight, but his face was turned away from her, watching the dark. On guard duty it was fatal to have anything block his view.

"And so could you."

"I'd throw my cloak over it . . ."

Her eyes were dark and wide and anxious, and she was young and very beautiful and genuinely concerned about him, so he didn't make the remark that he wasn't about to trust both their lives to her ability to hurl ten pounds of velvet accurately in an emergency. Instead he said, quite truthfully, "Opium, if that thing shows up, it isn't going to be the way you think. It isn't what *anybody* thinks. Our best chance is if you do what I say, all right?"

She nodded willingly. "All right. It's just that I'd feel treacherous, running away. I don't run when my friends are in danger." And she bent her head to readjust the jewel-tipped points of her bodice.

"You run when I tell you to," he said gruffly, "and run damn fast."

They moved on through the shadows, slipping cautiously through the spaces between them, where the light of the torches and fires inside the ring shone through, the Wolf showing Opium how to do this most quickly, most efficiently, without arousing the suspicion of someone watching the camp. Sometimes she walked quietly on his blind side, the musk of her perfume faint to his nostrils; other times she talked in her soft, drawling voice—camp gossip, the events of the siege, all the horrendous details of Ari's earlier efforts to sap and mine the walls, and of the last battle in which the mine tunnels had collapsed, the siege tower had burned, and the man who had bought her last summer from a brothel keeper in Kedwyr had been killed.

"He was good to me," she said, folding her cloak close around her for warmth, her breath a luminous haze as they passed close to the lights of the park. "I'd been sold there when I was fourteen, when Father couldn't pay his debts; Geldark looted some rich pook's house when they sacked Melplith, else he couldn't have bought me. It was the first time—I don't know. It wasn't that I could say no, but it was better, you know? I was still his slave, but . . ." Her hand strayed to the thin gold chain around her throat.

The Wolf stopped in the shadows of the siege tower where they had begun their circuit, and put his hands to her throat in the velvet shadows of the cloak. "This is all there is to being a slave." Twisting both hands in the delicate chain, he snapped it. It was a lot stronger than it looked, but he was damned if, after those words, he'd give up and exerted all his strength. The metal cut into

his flesh, drawing blood as it parted. He cursed, and
started to draw his hands out of the warmed shadows of
her hair. She caught his wrists and drew his mouth down
to hers.

A shudder passed through his body; pulling a barbed
war arrow from his flesh would have been easier than
thinking about drawing back. "I can't," he whispered,
even as his arms shut closer around her, her hand tangling in his long hair, digging into the curly fur at the
back of his neck. The scent of her, the warmth and
strength of her embrace, clouded his senses and blurred
his thoughts; dark, uncaring madness loomed suddenly
in his mind, uncaring of what happened now or later . . .

He pulled up his head against the unexpected strength
of her arms. "I have a lady of my own." His voice was
thickened, his mouth so dry he could barely speak, and
it was hard to remember that he wanted to.

"Does she need to know?"

*No,* he thought, as his head was drawn down again to
meet those moist silken lips, *she didn't.* And if she did
she'd understand. He hadn't had a woman in weeks, and
the soft urgency of Opium's body against his kindled dev-
astating heat in his flesh. It was, pure and simple, a case
of eating to satisfy ravenous hunger . . . if she ever found
out, Starhawk would know that . . .

But that knowledge wouldn't change what it would do
to her.

As surely as he knew his name, knew the flesh and
bone and magic within his own hide, he knew he would
lose something which could never be replaced, and the
loss would taint the days that had been and demolish all
those long, bright future joys. To take this woman, as he
had casually taken so many in his life, would mean, literally, absolutely nothing to him, except for the momentary release of his aching flesh. But to Starhawk it would
be betrayal.

She would understand, of course. She probably
wouldn't even be surprised.

That was the worst—that she wouldn't be surprised if
he betrayed her.

That she wouldn't be surprised if anyone betrayed her.

His hands shaking—for while his mind raced, his body

had thought for itself—he pushed Opium from him, first gently and then, when she clung, more forcefully.

She breathed, "No. I want you . . ." and the touch of her hands was torment.

"No." He was panting, every atom of his flesh needing her, trying not to be aware of his hands on her waist where he held her away from him.

Her smooth brow, curtained with the veils of her hair that his clutching fingers had loosed, puckered as she read the desperate sincerity in his hoarse voice.

"I won't."

She lowered her hands from his shoulders to his arms, the warmth of them still maddening through the leather and lawn of his sleeves. Her eyes were pools of desire—everything he was and had always been screamed to him *To hell with Starhawk . . . this only comes once . . .*

But even as he thought it, he knew that what he had with the Hawk only came once—to many men, not at all—and was fragile as glass in his clumsy hands. *I can't let that go,* he told himself blindly. *I can't . . .* But he no more knew the words to say it than he'd known how to explain to Purcell that he couldn't make a whore of his magic.

He could only push her away from him and turn aside, folding his arms now as if for protection across his chest, still shuddering all over with passion. Having never broken off such an encounter before in his life, he had no idea how to do it with any kind of grace.

"You afraid she'll find out?" Beneath the vicious spite her voice trembled, but through the blinding smoke of his own need he didn't hear.

The men would laugh themselves sick if *this* got back to them—it suddenly occurred to him to wonder how discreet this woman was. Trying to think of that, of his men, and of his own conflict between manhood and magic and his love for Starhawk, of Starhawk's own feelings, confused and stalled him. He managed to stammer, "I won't do it to her," but he wasn't sure Opium heard. She drew breath to say something, but at that instant another sound came, the soft brush of a foot in the weeds nearby, far too near . . .

His head snapped up. Opium stepped swiftly away as Purcell appeared around the side of the siege tower with

a horn cup of wine in his hand. Startled, the little Councillor dropped the cup, the wine dumping down his front,
his hands fumbling nervously. "I—er—I . . ." He
gulped, and then his eyes went to Opium and his narrow,
delicate mouth pinched.

*"Well . . . !"* Even in the darkness, Sun Wolf was
aware of what the reflected torchlight would show Purcell—the Wolf's shirt and doublet parted by those probing
fingers, the tender disarray of the girl's hair and dress. A
white square of handkerchief billowed into view as Purcell began dabbing ineffectually at the spilled wine on
his gown. *"Really*, Captain, I *do* apologize . . ." He
stiffly turned to go, and the Wolf reached him in two
strides, blocking his way, massive and dark against the
torchlight.

But what, he wondered, embarrassed, flustered, and
furious even as he extended his arm like a barrier to the
tower's wooden corner, could he say without making
himself look even worse? *Don't tell anyone* would sound
absolutely ridiculous. Other phrases flashed through his
mind, the stock-in-trade of bawdy theater . . . *It isn't the
way it looks . . . Nothing really happened . . . SHE was
the one who tried to rape ME . . .*

He was aware that he was blushing furiously.

He settled for the simplest. "You say one word of this
to anyone and I'll break your neck."

Cringe and whimper as he might around Renaeka
Strata, Purcell drew himself up to his fullest height—his
dark cap reached just above Sun Wolf's shoulder—and
said with dignity, "What you do when you are off duty,
Captain, is no concern of mine. Or even," he added
frostily, "when you are *on* duty—as you are tonight. But
as Treasurer of the Council I feel obliged to dock your
pay."

"You can stuff my pay up your . . . Aah, get a guard
or somebody with a horse and take this girl back to the
camp." He turned to gesture to Opium, but she had vanished like a shadow in the night.

He stood for a moment feeling overwhelmingly stupid,
anger and frustrated lust eating at his soul, while Purcell
gave him a coldly formal bow and walked back toward
the lights of the inner ring where the slaves' voices could
be heard quarreling wearily over a supper of corn bread

and gruel. The cup Purcell had dropped lay half in the bar of light that streamed from around the corner of the siege tower, an ordinary horn cup from the engineer's cookshack. The reek of cheap wine lay heavy on the air.

*Now why . . . ?* thought the Wolf, and after a moment's thought strode after that prim, retreating form.

Purcell was climbing into his litter, assisted by one of his half-dozen personal guards while another one, resplendent in the daffodil tabard of the House of Cronesme, held an armload of furs to be tucked about his lap.

The Wolf strode through the group of them, peripherally aware that two were watching him, hands ready on their swords. "Why were you coming to see me?" he demanded. "Did you have information of some kind?"

Purcell's cold gray eye traveled over him, taking in with slow distaste every untied lace and shirt point, the bared tangle of chest hair and the stains of grease and powders that still blotched his clothes. "No. Good night . . . Captain." He settled back into the litter, pulled the lap robes up to his narrow chin, and jerked the yellow curtains shut. One of the guards mounted the fore horse, and reined it toward the hard-beaten track that led back to the city.

"And I hope your privy collapses," growled the Wolf after the retreating cavalcade.

Later, alone once again and walking patrol in the dark, he reflected dourly that neither love nor magic was turning out to be something easily dealt with, no matter how desperately he might want them. He was beginning to have the mortifying suspicion that he was not particularly good at either.

"I should have stuck to breaking heads," he muttered, shoving his hands behind the buckle of his sword belt and scanning the queer stillness of the dark hills beneath the hanging black of the clouds. "At least I was good at that."

It was not until the following afternoon that news reached him that Starhawk was dying.

He left the engineering park shortly after sunup, and took the shorter way through the brown morning hills to Vorsal and the siege camps that surrounded it. The air was clear, but felt ominous and strange. Ground-mist hugged the stream beds with their shrunken gurgles of water, but on the hilltops the wind brought him alien smells of sea and wind and sky. He hoped the storm fronts wouldn't turn today, but it was odds on they would. Moggin had had twenty-four hours in which to rest and regather his forces. He would know about the mobilization, and guess the attack would be soon. Sun Wolf shivered at the thought of trying to work the weather again, exposing his soul once more to the strength of that shadow hand. The books might contain some clue of how to strengthen his defenses, but, when he reached the siege camp, his eyes felt gummed and his head heavy from two nights with almost no sleep. He ordered the Little Thurg, who was the first person he met, to wake him at once if the weather looked to be changing, and fell into Dogbreath's cot in all his clothes, rolled up, and slept.

And dreamed of Opium.

"Chief?" The voice was blurred with dreams. "Chief?" But he recognized the touch of something cold and hard on his arm.

His reaction, slamming up out of sleep, was hard and instinctive—grab, twist, slash with the dagger under his pillow. It whipped through nothingness, and as his eyes cleared he saw that Dogbreath, very wisely, had poked him with the butt end of a spear from a distance of six feet.

He slapped the heavy oak shaft aside in disgust. He'd had four hours' sleep, and felt infinitely worse than he had when he'd stumbled into bed. "What the pox-festering eyeless hell do you want?"

"Message from Renaeka Strata." The squad-leader's thin face was more serious than he'd seen it, at odds with his coat of rags and scrap and the gaudy ribbons in his hair. "It's Starhawk."

He had ridden like a man driven by demons, scoured by guilt and fear. *She can't be dying,* he though desperately. *Not now. Not like this.*

It was only last night that he had fully realized how desperately he needed her—what he was willing to do, or not do, to keep what they had for the rest of their lives. The thought of living without her was more than he could bear. With manlike illogic, he cursed Opium for a lascivious slut to ease the guilt he felt, as the thudding rhythm of the horse's muscles worked its way through his thighs and trunk, and the white road dust stung his nose.

*Not Starhawk. Not her.*

But years as an expert in death would not permit him to think anything else when he saw the gray, sunken face against the exquisite linen of Renaeka Strata's pillows and felt the cold, weak flutter of her pulse.

"Curse him," he whispered blindly, sinking to his knees on the honey-colored tiles of the floor. "Curse him, curse him, curse him . . ."

"My personal physician bled her last night," the Lady Prince said softly, close enough behind him that he could feel the black velvet of her bejeweled skirts against his back. "He wanted to do so again this morning, but I ordered him to wait until you could be reached."

"What about trephining?" he asked softly. "Boring the skull—it sometimes works . . ."

"Good heavens!" The Lady Prince drew back, startled and appalled. "I've never heard of such a thing! Nor, I may add, has my physician, who's the best in this city. I didn't hear that Purcell had not told you until the third hour this morning. I sent a messenger to the engineering park at once but you'd gone . . ."

Her words floated past him, meaningless as the distant clamor of the Wool Market that at this hour murmured even through the tightly closed and curtained windows. He sent one of her messengers back to the camp to fetch Butcher, the troop surgeon, then sank into the healing trance once more, seeking deeper and deeper for Starhawk's spirit, trying desperately to piece together some means of holding it until somehow her flesh could be healed enough to contain it once again.

*Just that,* he prayed—to the Mother, to the coldly clever Triple God, to the Valhalla tableful of his drunken, bearded, hairy ancestors . . . *Just give me time.*

But he'd had time, his first ancestor would have said to him, with the ironic wisdom of those who have seen their own time feasted, fought, and fornicated away to nothing. He'd had a year.

*I never had training, pox rot you! I can't do this! I
don't know how!*

But he stilled his mind again, as Yirth had showed
him, and searched the darkness for Starhawk's spirit,
holding the cold flesh of her hand in his, softly calling
her name. When Yirth had taught him these spells, she
had said that the spirit most frequently responded to the
name it had known as a child. He'd long ago forgotten
Starhawk's convent name, if he'd ever known it; she had
never told him what her parents and brothers had called
her in the shabby little village by the western cliffs. So
he called her by the name he'd always known, as pupil,
friend, brother-in-arms, and lover, and in time she answered, as she had said she would, from the Cold Hells
and beyond.

But when he came out of his healing trance, exhausted,
cold, and cramped from kneeling beside her bed, he knew
he had very little time left. Whatever was wrong with
her, whatever damage the falling beam had done her,
would claim her in the end. He felt as if he had piled in
a little heap the detached petals of a white almond blos-
som in the mist of an empty plain, knowing that the wind
would rise soon.

Butcher was there when he came out of his trance, a
plump, clever little woman with biceps like a wrestler's
and close-cropped, grayish-yellow hair framing one of
the most beautiful faces the Wolf had ever seen. She read
Starhawk's pulse, gently felt around the ragged, crescent-
shaped wound where the falling beam had struck her, and
shook her head. "Trephining only works if you know
where to drill," she told him, folding big, tattooed arms
over her massive breasts. "That's the trick of it. Hell,
you've helped me do it enough to know there's nothing
but lightness of touch needed in the drilling itself. But I
don't feel anything amiss near the wound. It could mean
blood's leaking into the brain somewhere else, or it could
mean there's something else wrong. The medical faculties
of the University here are the worst in the world—with the
Trinitarians running them that's no surprise—but nobody
knows much about head wounds, Chief, and that's a fact."

There was regret in her bright-blue eyes. The Wolf
remembered she had been one of Starhawk's particular

friends during their days with the troop, part of the small squad of fighting women drawn together in the largely masculine camp. But Butcher had seen many of her friends die, some of them hideously, and had somehow adjusted her philosophy to let her live with it.

Sun Wolf wondered what had happened to his own philosophy that had let him carry on after the deaths of more friends than he cared to think about.

But none like the Hawk.

Outside, the gray sky was losing its color. By the waterclock on the terrace it was the tenth hour of the day. Quietly, deliberately, he steadied himself, putting aside his fear of what life would be like without that cool voice and wicked grin, putting aside his guilt over Opium's scented kisses. "Can you stay with her?"

Butcher hesitated. "How long? The assault hits the road an hour before dawn, so I need to leave for the camp by midnight." And, seeing the hard glint of the Wolf's yellow eye, she went on quietly, "I can save those lives, Chief. I can't save hers. And we're talking hundreds against one."

He sighed, and bent his head, leaning one heavy-muscled, shaggy arm on the soft tangle of sheets at Starhawk's side. "I know," he said, ashamed of that thoroughly selfish reaction. "You probably want to get some sleep tonight as well."

She shrugged as he got to his feet, shoving her hands into the pockets of the man's breeches she wore. "Hell, I've gone into battle after staying up drinking all night, that doesn't matter. Riding back at midnight won't kill me, unless this curse decides that me falling off my horse and breaking my neck in a ditch is *the* thing needed to further bollix up the assault. If you have something to do, I'll wait till then. But only till then—you understand?"

"I understand," the Wolf said softly. "And yeah—I have something to do."

He looked down at Starhawk, seeing with hideous clarity the sunken lavender flesh around her eyes, the pinched look of her nose and lips. *The curse,* he thought. *Like the bread not rising or those damn poker hands, like the arrows that won't hit their targets or the rats that eat the catapult ropes; one misfortune in a chain of misfortunes*

*that will keep me here at her side through the night and
in the morning when I might be helping them survive the
assault—or that'll get me killed by dawn.*

And he knew that *djerkas* or no *djerkas*, silver runes
or no silver runes, he'd have to kill Moggin Aerbaldus
tonight.

Moggin Aerbaldus' house stood in the patrician quarter of Vorsal, next to the hubristic granite palace of some
merchant prince, which these days, due to its fortresslike
construction, served as the city grain store. The filth here
was less than it was in the poor quarters at the base of
Vorsal's hill, where skeletal women sifted patiently
through the night soil heaped in the streets for something
edible that the rats might have missed, but the stench of
decay was the same. The city had long ago run out of
fuel to burn the corpses of the dead or space to bury
them. They were dumping them over the wall in places,
and the reek was a hellish miasma through which all
things seemed to move as through palpable fog. On his
way up the hill, the Wolf had seen all the commonplaces
of siege: the dim-lit taverns where hysterical laughter vied
with the drunken ranting of voices screaming about the
rich who'd started this war, and dreamsugar addicts sat
giggling quietly, for drugs were easier to come by than
food and these days one could get drunk on very little;
the rail-thin children selling themselves or their siblings
to soldiers of the watch for the flesh of rats; and the rats
themselves, sleek and fearless as they always were once
all the cats and dogs had been eaten, too quick and strong
to catch and watching passersby with businesslike in-
tentness.

The city had been under siege for six months. Even if
the rains came before the walls were broken, the Wolf
guessed most of these people would not survive winter.

Though it was barely the third hour of the night, the
line outside the grain store for tomorrow's ration stretched
out of sight down the cobbled street. Men and women
and here and there an adolescent boy—the heads of
households, Sun Wolf knew from the few sieges he'd had
the misfortune to be caught in—bearing horn or metal
cups in their hands. Wrapped in the spell of nonvisibility, he drifted like a ghost along the other side of the

street. If they saw him at all, they'd be under the impression that he was a rat or someone they knew, but it wasn't likely they did. Apart from the fact that none had brought a lamp—oil being for eating these days, not burning—he knew that starving men did not see so clearly in darkness. The cold was sharp. He saw one of the men sitting against the grain-store wall turn to speak to another, drawing his several coats closer around his shoulders, his breath a drift of steam. The man spoken to did not reply, and when his neighbor touched him, fell forward stiffly. Those on either side merely pushed the body a little out of the way with their feet, unwilling to surrender their places in line even for an instant.

Sun Wolf circled the block and found the alley that backed both the grain store and the house of the Aerbaldi. Even in these black streets he felt reasonably safe from the *djerkas*, knowing the hysterical paranoia bred by sieges. Within Moggin's grounds it might be another matter. On the little rear gate where night soil and garbage were carried away, he sought in vain for the marks of protection and warning which his common sense told him must be there. He found nothing. But, he reflected wryly, as he had told Renaeka Strata, Ari, Purcell, and Starhawk—and it seemed every other interested party in the eastern half of the Middle Kingdoms—that didn't mean they weren't there. And again he cursed his ignorance.

There was no way of telling, but it didn't pay to take chances. He found a corner where the seven-foot sandstone wall of the garden ran into the granite side of the grain store, and flung the grapple that he'd brought to get him over the city wall up to one of the small windows of the grain store's second floor. By scaling that wall he was able to edge himself sidelong over Moggin's garden wall without touching it, a tricky and annoying process which made him curse the length of the siege. Of course every tree in Moggin's garden had been felled, the fruit trees last, when the final crop had been plucked. The garden was a small one, and had been stripped bare, its shrubs pulled up, its vines torn down, lying baled on the brick terrace that stretched across the back of the pale sandstone bulk of the house itself, ready to be burned for fuel. In the midst of the bare ground with its crossing paths, the fountain was dry; the Kwest Mralwe troops had wrecked the city aqueducts. Though the hill springs over which Vorsal was built could support the populace even this late in the year, there was no water left over to spill, merely for the pleasure of its sound.

Near where he had come over the wall, a bare circle of ground marked where a gazebo had been pulled down for firewood, and, as he approached the house, he saw that even the tool and potting sheds had been dismantled, their contents stacked with a kind of pathetic neatness along the edge of terrace. The muted orange light delineating the rounded arches of windows flickered over the blades of shovels and hoes, the tines of pitchforks and those great implements' miniature brothers, and the Wolf felt an odd pang as he realized that Moggin, too, might like himself be a gardener.

But the utter barrenness of the garden did, at least, insure that the *djerkas* couldn't sneak up on him unawares. It left him no cover either, of course, and he glided swiftly along the wall, avoiding the line of sight from the lighted windows, checking his weapons as he moved—knife, sword, and the small, deadly throwing ax that could bring a man down thirty feet away.

The house was small, as such town palaces went, old and elegant, the house of antique town nobility rather than merchants new-rich on cloth or spice. The windows were glass, barred with iron, the curtains within only half-closed. Tilting his head a little to angle his vision, the Wolf could see into the warm, firelit room.

His first impression was one of comfortable shabbiness, of an old-fashioned frescoed ceiling, of walls lined with books and shelves and curio cabinets crammed to overflowing with tiny statues, painted eggs, ornate mechanical clocks, and astrological implements of silver and bronze. The fireplace was wide, its frescoes faded and rather soot-stained; before it, in a huge oak chair carved in the fashion of the last century, sat a man who must be Moggin Aerbaldus.

He was tall—easily Sun Wolf's six-foot height—stoop-shouldered, and had probably been thin even before the siege, with gray-green eyes and flecks of gray beginning in his straight black hair. With the long white hand of a scholar, he was folding up a large leather-bound book, a little awkwardly because it had been sharing his lap with a blond girl of six or seven. A girl of sixteen, also fair, sat on the tufted red-and-blue rug near the fire, beside a woman with a kindly face, who looked to have been plump in better days. They must have had their own stores to live on, the Wolf thought. They all looked far better than the people in the line outside. With the other rich families in the city, it must have been the same.

The little girl's voice came dimly to him through the thick glass. "But why didn't Trastwind marry the Lady Jormelay, Daddy? She loved him—he didn't even hardly *know* that old princess."

"Well, Jormelay was a witch," Moggin pointed out sensibly. "Would you want to be married to someone who might turn you into a toad if you left hairs in the bathtub and didn't refill the water pitchers when you'd drunk all the water?" And the little girl giggled, evidently a candidate for toadhood herself. "And remember, Dannah, the Princess loved Trastwind, too."

"Can you do that, Daddy?" inquired the girl, getting down from his lap. Her mother and sister, sitting near the hearth, were fair, but the child's hair was white-gold, tied back with a ribbon of pink-striped silk and curling down over shoulders far too thin in the white linen nightgown she wore. "Fall in love just looking at somebody? Did you fall in love with Mummy just looking at her?"

Moggin's greenish eyes lifted briefly, to touch the brown ones of the woman by the hearth, and, standing on the terrace, Sun Wolf knew that all the Jormelays in the world wouldn't have stood a chance against what lay between them. Moggin said softly, "Of course."

The mother drew her breath to speak, let it out, then said briskly, "And it's bedtime for all good little princesses in *this* castle. *Come* on . . ."

The older girl lingered as her mother and sister left the room, carrying a stick from the fire because there were neither candles nor oil for lamps. Moggin rose slowly, and went to put his book back in the jammed rosewood cabinet on the opposite wall. "And some philosophers claim that works of fiction are frivolous," he sighed. The firelight threw his moving shadow across their gilded bindings, and made demon faces of the carvings on the great inlaid desk that stood between the bookshelves, littered with papers and quills and the tall, gleaming glass castle of a sander. "I sometimes believe that the ability to survive on the memory of joy—or to transmit it—is the quality that most clearly separates the human from the beast."

Her arms folded, the girl said quietly, "She wakes up crying at night, you know."

Moggin stopped in mid-gesture, book still in hand; then he sighed, put it in its slot, and turned. In his sea-colored eye was the helplessness of words that will do no good if said.

"I'm sorry," said the girl quickly. "It's just that . . . It's so hard to tell her not to be afraid when I'm so scared myself." She stepped quickly across the dim width of the room to him, and threw her arms around his slender waist. His locked around her in return, the faded black wool of his robe sleeve like a bar of shade against the white of her nightgown, her hair the color of sunburned grass falling over both.

For a moment her father rocked her gently, holding her close against him; his voice was a murmur audible to the Wolf only by the use of a wizard's senses. "Don't worry, Rianna," he whispered. "They'll go before the rains come. They have to . . ."

She sounded scared. *As well she might,* the Wolf thought, grimly calculating how much she'd fetch in the brothels of the Street of the Yellow Lanterns. "If they break the wall . . ."

"They won't."

"*Daddy . . .*"

"*They won't.*" He took her thin shoulders between his hands, held her out from him, green eyes looking into brown, willing her to believe. "It'll be all right. I promise you." And he hugged her again, tight, desperate.

Sun Wolf wondered, watching her depart through an arched doorway into the darkness of the rest of the house, whether those pretty girls, that serene-faced wife, knew what Moggin was, and what he had done.

Because it wasn't just a case of protecting his wife and daughters from rape and murder at the hands of mercenaries sacking the town. Looking at that narrow, aescetic face in the dull throb of the dimming fire, the Wolf remembered the hotter blaze of the inn as it collapsed around Starhawk and the children she'd been trying to save, remembered the wavering filigree of lamplight touching Starhawk's face as she lay dying in the house of the Lady Prince, and remembered, too, the hand full of darkness, casting the cold web of runes, and the wild triumphant laughter as his soul began to part company with his screaming flesh. *A wizardling, to be my slave . . .*

His hand touched the miniature ax where it hung from his belt.

Moggin turned his gaze from the door and crossed the room to a locked cabinet on the far side of his cluttered desk. Sun Wolf moved a little to follow him with his eyes and saw him undo the fastenings—not a simple lock, as any merchant or nobleman might keep upon his valuables, but three of them, holding the cabinet shut with silver chains. The doors with their elaborate carvings opened to reveal two shelves of books, as well as other things: a child's skull, eight candles of black wax in silver holders, bunches of dried herbs and human hair, the feet and ears of various small animals, and an assortment of boxes and phials.

For a long time he simply stood there, a tall, thin man in his shabby black scholar's gown. Then, with a sort of sigh, he brought forth chalk, herbs, implements, and a black book which he propped open on the desk and turned to roll back the study carpets.

Very quietly, the Wolf slipped away from the window to the door which gave from the terrace into the house. It was latched from within, and he knew better than to use magic this close to a wizard as powerful as he was now sure Moggin was, but Dogbreath had taught him other ways of forcing simple latches with a minimum of sound. He stood for a time in the half-open door, beyond which he could see the darkness of the hall and the ruddy glow from the door of the study, listening to the faint, reassuring scrape of chalk on red-tiled floor.

The throwing ax ready in his hand, he ghosted over the threshhold.

From the dark of the hall he watched Moggin, on his knees now, marking the Circles of Power on the study floor. Smudges of chalk and a phantom latticework of old stains showed where other circles had been marked before, but the Wolf barely saw them. The pattern taking shape under those long, white hands was one he recognized from the oldest of the Wenshar demonaries, an ancient spell, alien and ringed with warnings scribbled in the unreadable shirdar tongue. It was the spell for the summoning of the magic of the earth, the eldritch power that lay in the dark of the world's bones, the very curve of the lines and grid of the runes anomalous to any sorcery of which he had heard.

The fire in the hearth was dying, but Moggin had illuminated the eight candles, burning in their queer, asymmetrical shape. The whisper of his chanting rose, in some unknown tongue that was neither the shirdar nor the common speech of Gwenth. He could see the sweat of concentration on the man's pale face, the candle shadow curved and fragile on the lashes of the shut eyes. The Wolf threw one quick glance at the still-open cabinet and thought, *He'll have books of healing there* . . . and moved forward with his ax.

It would have to be quick, while all Moggin's concentration was focused, riveted on the summoning of that unhallowed power . . .

*This is too easy* . . .

*"DADDY!"*

Sun Wolf lunged sideways and back into the hall behind him, catching only the briefest glimpse of the child Dannah standing horrified in the room's other door, her hands raised in terror to her mouth. Moggin spun, green eyes wide with shock, but the Wolf was already out the rear door of the house. A stride took him to the edge of the terrace . . .

The hoe on which he stepped slammed up and hit him with unbelievable force in the side of the head, dropping him to his knees among the rakes, flowerpots, and baled thornbushes waiting their turn for the fire. Torchlight blazed over the garden wall; a voice yelled "There he is, lads!" and half a dozen archers appeared along its top, bows bent. Sun Wolf turned, stumbling, and made a run through the frenzied shadows for the opposite wall, leaped, grabbed, and found himself looking down into the street where the line for the grain store was.

Only the line wasn't passively waiting along the wall anymore. They were grouped beneath him in a seething mob, more running up to join them, even as he heaved himself up to the top of the garden wall. They stood with makeshift weapons of kitchen knives and cleavers and clubs in their hands and naked murder in their eyes.

"STOP!" shouted a voice from the dark garden below. And then, as the Wolf froze, feeling the eyes of the archers trained on his torchlit figure silhouetted against the black of the sky, it continued tautly, "Or go ahead. Jump. Then you'll find out what happens to people in this city who try to steal grain."

Sun Wolf said, "Pox."

# CHAPTER

## — 8 —

"*F*OR THE LAST TIME, *I DIDN'T COME HERE TO STEAL* your goddam grain."

The Commander of the City Troops who had taken him struck him—not hard, but the man's gold signet ring gouged his lip, bringing a slow trickle of blood. "If you keep insisting that, I may begin to believe you," the Commander said softly. "After all these months, I assure you I know every face in this city, and yours is not familiar. You look too well-fed to have been living on half a measure of corn a day for the last eight weeks." His face was gaunt with starvation, his dark eyes cold and haunted, but the Wolf recognized him—barely—as the young Duke of Vorsal.

Diffidently, Moggin spoke from near the doorway that led from his firelit study into the rest of the house. "I believe the men who tried to go over my wall to the granary two nights ago were from this city, your Grace." Beyond him, in the dark of the hall, the Wolf could glimpse the white blur of nightgowns where Moggin's daughters had stolen down the stairs to listen.

"Then shame on them," snapped the Duke bitterly. His glance cut back to Sun Wolf. "And shame on you, for robbing women and children of the only food they'll get to make us give up our freedom all the quicker. How did you get into the city?''

"I have a magic rope," Sun Wolf said thickly. "It let me down from the sky."

One of the men who surrounded him—angry skeletons in shabby rags—raised his hand to strike, but the Duke shook his head. "We'll hoist you back to the sky soon enough," he said, and the Wolf could see the gaps where malnutrition had begun to claim his teeth. "But our rope isn't magic. Who . . . ?"

"Then why don't you ask him for a magic rope?" the Wolf demanded deliberately and jerked his head at Moggin. "He'll have one."

Moggin went white as the Duke's cold glance slewed to him, narrow with sudden suspicion. "What do you mean?"

"That's—that's absurd," the philosopher stammered. "This man doesn't know what he's talking about . . ."

"Don't I?" the Wolf said, realizing he'd guessed right about the local feeling regarding hoodoos in the besieged town. Need wizards they might—need anything to help them they certainly did—but the Law of the Triple God was adamant and these were Their lands.

Moggin wet his lips uncertainly. By the way the Duke and the scarecrow-ragged men of the watch were looking at him, it wasn't the first time the idea had crossed someone's mind. "Drosis—Drosis left me his books and medical implements, of course," he said finally, his voice regaining its steadiness. "But Drosis was never a real wizard, either, you know, and you can't deny how many lives he saved with his . . ." He visibly bit back the word "powers" and substituted ". . . his learning and skill. But he never used magic."

"No?" the Wolf said, shifting his arms against the ropes that twisted them so painfully around the shafts of the guards' spears. When they'd dragged him back to the study he'd seen at once that the rugs had been hastily pulled down to cover the half-made patterns of power on the floor, the implements and the black book bundled away, the cabinet locked. That, if nothing else, had told him what he needed to know. "Then haul up the rugs."

The guards looked at each other, paranoia in their hollow eyes. One of them stepped to obey, and Moggin in-

terposed himself quickly in front of the man. "This is
ridiculous," he stated in his quiet voice. At first glance
a mildly retiring man, still he had a kind of quiet authority to him that stopped the guard in his tracks. "I'll
answer any accusation this man cares to make when I can
be sure he isn't simply trying to keep you all busy while
his confederates escape."

"He's right," the Duke said, as the guards hesitated.
"Attis, Rangin—take four men and search the neighborhood. I take it you have no objection to our using your
wine cellar as a jail until we return from doing a circuit
of the walls?"

"Not at all," Moggin said, inclining his head deeply
so that the young Duke would not see the pleased gleam
in his eye.

Sun Wolf saw it, however. With a bellowed oath he
wrenched at the ropes that bound him, lunged toward the
door again, dragging three of the half-starved guards,
like a bear dragging a hunter's dogs. Anything was better
than that, he thought; to be bound in darkness, waiting
for those silver ruins to glimmer into being again around
him; to hear that triumphant laughter . . .

He was almost to the door when the rest of the guards
brought him down. He had a foggy glimpse of the young
Duke of Vorsal, standing with arms folded across the
gilded cuirass that was now far too large for him, dark
eyes fixed speculatively on Moggin's carefully expressionless face. Then lights exploded in his skull, followed
by roaring darkness.

He wasn't out for long. The damp cold of the wine
cellar brought him to while the guards were still tying
his wrists to the dusty racks that had once contained bottles of the household vintage. They were muttering to
themselves as they ascended the stairs; he heard the name
Drosis, and an uneasy whisper of witchery. Then the slits
of light around the locked cellar door faded, and he was
in darkness again.

He wouldn't have long, he knew. It was good odds
Moggin had never expected to be holding prisoners in
his cellar and hadn't laid magic guards upon the place.
He could sense no spells at work in the black air around
him. Though his head ached—his face was swelling too,
where that damn hoe had connected—the spells to loosen

the knots and stretch the fibers of the ropes came easily
to him this time. *At least there's no ants,* he thought,
giving his mind over to them, feeling the slow tingle of
power shivering against his skin. *And you're not groggy
with poison and trying not to think about how badly
you're going to die.* All he needed was time.

But he saw the fulvid slits of light outlining the heavy
door long before he was able to free his hands.

*Gutter-nosed festering goddam rope-spells,* he thought
viciously, the spells themselves flicking away as anger
and frustration broke his concentration and he braced
himself to meet the enemy wizard. *I will not become his
slave. I will not . . .* His breath came fast with dread.

But the light dimmed around the door, as if the lamp
that made it were carried a door or two past the small
room in which he was bound. The clack of a lock, loud
in the darkness as a headsman's ax, was not from the
door before him, but from another. Then came a scraping
and a furtive rustle; the lamp brightened again, then
dimmed away as it was carried back from whence it had
come.

*He's hiding the books,* thought the Wolf, *before the
guards come back.*

So Moggin's fear was real. The Duke wouldn't protect
him if he knew. Madness, yes, but then the Triple God
was very strong in these parts, and there might be other
factors as well, anything from local politics to some ancient grudge in operation.

His ancestors really were listening tonight.

There were two solid shelves of books, plus various
implements, adding up to half a dozen trips' worth down
the hall from the study, through who knew how many
rooms and passages—he cursed the guards for stunning
him to bring him here, forgetting it was he who'd tried
to flee. By the pleased look in Moggin's eyes, the wizard
very likely knew who he was, but this unexpected result
of his accusation bought him time. *How much time?*

He was distantly aware that Moggin's feet had passed
the door three more times, before the ropes around his
wrists slacked away. Counting, he found each trip took
slightly less than four minutes.

The lock on the door itself was candy. He counted
Moggin's retreating footsteps up the stairs, then slipped

out into the low-ceilinged passage which connected the cellar's various storage rooms and paused, listening, stretching his senses out through the pitch-black house.

Muffled by the earth of the walls and floor, the girl Rianna's voice came soft to him from somewhere above: "Daddy, what is it? Who was that man? Why are you moving Drosis' books . . ."

*Keep him talking, honey,* the Wolf thought, and ducked through the half-open door into the next rock-cut, earth-smelling chamber. It held the family food stores, a few half-empty sacks of flour and corn looking pitifully small in the bottoms of the big, tin-lined wooden bins. One of the bins had been pulled aside to reveal a sort of safe set into the floor underneath. The flagstone that concealed it lay by the side of its square entry hole. Kneeling, Sun Wolf could see twenty or more books stacked neatly at the bottom, and with them, a small basket containing boxes, phials, chalk, and one or two pieces of equipment that he recognized as medical.

*Medical implements,* Moggin had said. Drosis had been a healer.

Straining for the sound of Moggin's returning footfalls, Sun Wolf reached down into the hole.

Three books were all he could carry, shoved into his doublet against his body and belted tight—two books of medicine and what looked like a casebook of notes. Into the purse at his belt—cursing because he hadn't brought a larger one—he shoved a phial half-full of what he recognized as auligar powder, and the smallest, most delicately balanced bronze trephine he'd ever seen. Stretching out his mageborn senses, he could hear Moggin still making excuses, reasoning with both of his daughters now and his wife and, by the sound of it, two or three servants as well.

He hadn't told them, then. They didn't know. The man must have been living a double life for years. Well, if the local feeling against hookum was such that at this point in the siege they'd kill a mage instead of ask his help, that made sense, Sun Wolf reflected as he glided sound-lessly up the cellar steps. For years past, Altiokis had killed every wizard he could find. Or perhaps they merely knew Moggin well enough to see through that scholarly gentleness and the respectable and orthodox philosophical treatises.

*How many other wizards,* he wondered, slipping through the kitchen door and across the dark garden, *were doing that and had done that down the years?* How many had made a living of dissimulation, gone to Church, and faked humility, deliberate chameleons as opposed to those, like himself, who had refused to admit at all what the mad intensity of those visions might mean.

If there was one, there were probably others. If he could find one . . .

*Another like Moggin?* He shivered as he stepped through the narrow gate and into the alley once more. *Who'll try to snare your soul in silver runes for some purpose of his own?*

He drew the shadows around him still more thickly, his boots making no sound on the cobbled streets that led to the city wall.

It was past midnight when he reached the House of Stratus. The house, like the city around it, blazed with torches and lamps. Riding swiftly up the narrow lanes of the University Quarter, the Wolf hadn't been so naive as to suppose that the oil burning behind all those luminous golden squares of window parchment, the lantern-light streaming from taverns where gray-robed students argued metaphysics at the top of their voices, and the firefly cressets darting along in the hands of hundreds of blue-uniformed linkboys had anything to do with the assault on Vorsal at tomorrow's dawn. It was the shank of the evening; nobles of the ancient landed families had parties to attend, reclining masked behind the curtains of their sedan chairs as their slaves bore them up and down the slanted streets; the wives and sons and brothers of the great merchant houses were still abroad, surrounded by battalions of liveried bravos as they, too, moved from card parties to balls to rounds of delicious gossip about the nobles through whose front doors they were not permitted to pass. Costermongers were shouting their wares at half price to empty their barrows of herring or pies; whores in red and gold with their fantastic purple head-dresses strolled the lanes, masked also or smiling behind elaborate feather fans, their own slaves in front of them sometimes, carrying their night lamps and cosmetics; young clerks with tinted lovelocks curling down over their shoulders promenaded with giggling shopgirls, out to see the sights.

Guiding his horse through the press, the Wolf wasn't sure why he felt such anger at them. It might have sprung from his own fear that he'd return to find Starhawk already dead and what remained of his life echoing empty before him—a fear that had ridden beside him, with hoof-beats almost audible, all the way from Vorsal. It might have been his own frustrated despair as he'd come to realize that finding a master wizard who would freely teach him and not try to enslave or use him—or destroy him, perhaps—might not be as easy as he'd so innocently hoped; and all this riotous bourgeois joy around him irritated him by its contrast.

But mostly, he thought, it was because, for these people, it wasn't war. The man who'd died of cold creeping out in the night to line up for half a cup of corn, whose neighbors had pushed his body into the gutter rather than lose their own places in line; the ten-year-old whore he'd passed, hawking her emaciated and shivering body outside a tavern for the price of enough dreamsugar to forget where she was and what would become of her; the old women patiently digging through the garbage in the streets in search of food; those were all nothing to these people. They made enough money to hire their soldiering done. They voted into city office the nobles who owned the land they lived on; the nobles obeyed the merchant houses who had supported them in their ancient style for the last two generations; the merchant houses needed corn lands, or a wool monopoly, or a deep-water harbor; and so there was war.

Renaeka Strata was cagey enough not to let the war inconvenience her supporters.

Except, of course, people like Starhawk, who'd simply been in the wrong place at the wrong time.

Ari was waiting for him in the lambent blaze of the courtyard lights. He was in his battle armor already, leather plated with steel, the joints of his elbows and shoulders bristling with savage spikes whose edges glittered where the black paint that kept it from rusting had been chipped off in battle, and the ax that was his primary weapon strapped already to his back. His black hair hung to his shoulders, and the gold emblem of the Triple God, a child's medal, glinted in the pit of his throat with the rise and fall of his breath. In the delicate marble and fragile archways of the court, he looked alien and savage, and the grooms who came to take the Wolf's horse gave him wide berth as he came striding across, holding out his hands.

"Don't tell me you beat him up in an alley!" he grinned, with forced lightness, nodding at the bruises and cuts that mottled Sun Wolf's face like an overripe fruit. Sun Wolf, pulling down the saddlebag that contained the three stolen books, the phials and powders and the trephine, didn't answer, and Ari's smile faded, his hazel eyes hard. "You skrag him?"

"No."

The Wolf had already begun to stride toward the colonnade that led around to Starhawk's rooms by the terrace; Ari's grip in his plated glove was like an iron band, forcing him to stop. Their eyes met.

Quietly, Ari said, "The siege engines are already on the road to Vorsal; that's why I'm here. Zane's back at the camp getting the men into final formation. In three hours we're going to be under that wall, with that wizard on top of us." By his tone he already guessed what the Wolf was going to say.

Their eyes held; it was a long time before the Wolf could speak. "I'm sorry."

"They're gonna be killed, Chief. 'Sorry' doesn't cut it."

*Ari*, thought the Wolf. *Penpusher, Dogbreath, Zane, Firecat* . . . all his friends. This young man whose clear hazel eyes were so furious, so desperate, glaring into his. The dark hand reaching out of the storm's darkness, the wild laughter of triumph shaking the skies . . . He remembered the eldritch horror of the patterns on that tiled study floor, the strength he'd felt on the night of the weather-witching as the spells closed around him.

They'd be slaughtered.

He drew a deep breath, everything in him hurting, as if he'd been caught in the twisting of a ship's cable that can sever a man in half.

"They're volunteers. She isn't."

"Horseshit!" His voice, normally very soft and husky, rose suddenly to a commander's cutting lash. "She's one person, Chief, and you're talking about a thousand of us! A thousand, and we might lose five, six hundred, charging into a damned hoodoo like a bunch of kids trying to save Mommy from a gang of bandits! You got no right to leave us to that! You got no right to put your woman's life over ours and the Hawk would be the first person to tell you so!"

"She would if I'd still been the goddam captain, but I'm not!" roared the Wolf back at him. "You are!"

"Then it's a damn good thing you aren't! You're a puking coward! Yeah, you stay back here where it's safe, where you won't have to meet him . . . where you won't have to see if these pox-rotted powers you've been telling us about will cut it in battle!"

Blind with rage, Sun Wolf's hand came back to strike; Ari caught it, his own face, hard as a steel mask, inches from the Wolf's own.

His voice was low again, low and hard as flint. "You haven't got the right to leave us ditched, Chief. They're waiting for you."

He lowered his arm. "No."

"She'll keep. The battle won't. Head wounds . . ."

"Head wounds change fast," the Wolf said softly. "Yeah, she could stay unconscious for days, or she could go. I don't know how long it'll take, or how long I'll have to stay with her afterwards, until I know she's safe. I'm not losing her, Ari."

"It'll all be over by noon. Dammit, with a hoodoo there, defending the city . . ."

"Noon if we break the wall fast. But if we get thrown back? If there's street fighting? That can last for hours— God knows how long, with a wizard in it."

"And you're afraid of him, aren't you?" Ari spat the words at him, and he did not reply. "You know he's better than you, is that it?" He jerked his arm away, breathing hard, his face bitter in the dull burnish of the torchlight. Sun Wolf thought about the siege engines, even now lumbering through the still, unnatural blackness toward Vorsal's walls, remembered his private nightmare of having the bridge of the siege tower collapse beneath him, remembered the thousands of things that could go wrong in an assault, and knew that his men, the men he'd trained and led, the men to whom he'd been captain, friend, and god, were walking into all of them and more. Ari was right. Afraid or not—and he was afraid—a year ago when he'd still been captain, he'd never have chosen the life of any single person—certainly not the life of any of those sweet-scented girls who'd been his bedmates over the years—over going into even the most ordinary, the easiest, the surest battle with his men, let alone one against the dark specter of evil wizardry. Not even Starhawk's.

It was different now, more different than he'd realized. More different than he'd been prepared to face. He was no longer captain. And he wasn't going to lose Starhawk—not to Opium, not to the curse, not to his own stupidity, and not to what others considered his duty.

"Chief," said Ari softly, "I'm begging. Don't let us down."

He whispered, "I can't."

The words "I'm sorry" were on his tongue, but he did not utter them. Goaded, confused, angry, and hurting more than he'd ever thought possible, he watched Ari turn on his heel and walk away.

The din of battle came to him, with the slow watering of the leaden darkness beyond the window lattices. He was aware of both dawn and tumult distantly, like the sky above water beneath whose surface he hovered. But he could not break the healing trance to sniff the air to see whether rain was on its way and could not lessen his desperate concentration to think about his friends piling across the bridges from the siege towers to meet the wizard on the walls of Vorsal. The part of him that had been a soldier for thirty years identified the sound of battle, and the fact that Renaeka Strata's servants had fallen silent to listen. Then his mind slipped down again, calling Starhawk's name, slowly, thread by thread, spell by spell, weaving her spirit to her flesh until the flesh could sustain it alone.

All the magic he could marshal, all the strength of his own flesh, he poured through the channel of old Drosis' spells, healing, cleansing, infusing with warmth and life. Once the magic had shown him where to bore, the trephining had been easy. The spells he'd found in Drosis' grimoires were brighter, surer, more flexible than Yirth's, though it had taken Yirth's training to make sense of them. Even in his inexperience, he could recognize the fine-tuned exactness of them, the greater knowledge of the body's workings and the body's needs. He could feel life, like a plasmic light, going from his palms into the cold flesh he touched, to kindle the faded light there.

When he came out of the trance it was fully day.

Servants had taken away the blood-filled basin, the scraps of bandages, lint, rags, the water, and the poultices and herbs. All around the bed their feet had scuffed the chalked circles of power and protection to cloudy mare's-tails on the tessellated floor. The lamps that had burned all around him during the operation and his subsequent vigil had guttered out. The latticed doors of the terrace arch stood half-opened, against all medical advice, to let in the morning air, but the bronze silk curtains hung down straight.

Outside, the air was absolutely still. There was no smell of rain, though the sky was gray and heavy, as it had been for weeks. The noise of battle seemed oddly clear.

On the terrace wall a bronze sundial stood shadowless, mute. Below it, under its ornamental stone shelter, the waterclock's gilded triton figure pointed to the second hour of the morning. Sun Wolf shivered. Moggin could have summoned rain. The fact that he hadn't meant only one thing—that he wasn't gambling that the storms would break the siege. He was, instead, doing exactly what the Wolf would have done in his place. He was setting up a trap. The fact that he was holding the rains at bay himself could only mean that the trap was a large one, and must involve fire.

Sun Wolf shut his eyes, sick with self-hating despair. For a few minutes he considered getting a horse, riding out, hoping he'd reach Vorsal in time . . .

*In time to do what?* He knew already that the greater efficiency of Drosis' healing magic had drained his powers as well as his physical strength. Even at the best of times he hadn't the skill to withstand the might of that shadow hand. While Moggin lived, the curse was still at its full strength, and he had no way to tell whether it would affect Starhawk now or not. It was two hours' hard riding to Vorsal in any case—far too late to save them.

Nauseated, exhausted, he got to his feet and nearly fell, catching at the arms of the blackwood chair beside the bed. He sank into it, lowering his throbbing head to his hands, his whole body hurting.

*Fine,* he thought ironically. *I've discovered a more efficient way to drain my strength. Just the thing I was always looking for . . .*

But Starhawk was alive.

With the battle din came all the smells of the murky day and the city around him—privies, dye vats, fuller's earth, spices, horses, the thick stench of waiting rain and the psychic miasma of petty politics, religious backbiting, and cutthroat squabbling for money.

He reached out toward the south with the hyperacute senses of wizardry, and even that effort abraded him like haircloth galling an open wound. From the memories of a score of years, he could almost see the swaying engines through thick clouds of yellow dust, the flash of weapons, fire arrows cutting pale streaks in the lightless forenoon. The stinks of blood, sweat, excrement, old leather, dirt, and smoke—the hot stench of boiling oil, molten lead, and heated sand poured down from the walls, the sizzle of charring flesh. He felt weak, ill, as if he saw all this from afar, unable to help them. And above it all the dark hand of the Vorsal mage would be reaching out . . . *What else could I have done?* he demanded desperately. *There was no time! If I'd gone back to kill him, he or the Duke's guards would have killed me! They'd still die, I'd die, she'd die . . .*

Or had he just been afraid?

But his ancestors, if they had any answers, kept their silence.

*Boozy drunken bastards,* he thought.

Then far off, he heard the noise of the fighting change. A triumphant roar, drifting in the still air. Opening his eyes he staggered to the archway, pushed aside the curtains to lean on the cold marble pillar and look southward over the garden trees to where white smoke rose against the dun underbelly of the clouds.

*Fire,* he thought, wrung with horror and grief and frustrated rage. *Moggin's trap.* And another part of him cursed the man, knowing what the trap had to be, knowing there could be no escape.

The acanthus leaves carved in the marble cut into the flesh of his forehead as he leaned it against the pillar's capital, suffocated with helpless despair. *What else could I have done?*

As if in answer, another sound came to him, shriller, higher, a distant keening.

He knew instantly what it was.

It was women and children screaming.

The besieging forces had been victorious, not the defenders. The wizard had not, after all, been triumphant. The fires whose smoke he saw were inside Vorsal's walls. The city was being sacked.

"You couldn't hardly blame them, Chief." Dogbreath set down the two battered saddlebags near the foot of the curtained bed, and shook back his long braids. "It had been one festering bastard of a siege." He shrugged, dismissing it with that, as if his boots and the baggy breeches he'd confiscated from the hapless shepherd some days ago weren't stained to the thighs with blood.

Because they were in a city that legitimately owed them money, Dogbreath still wore his armor. He'd cleaned it with a fast plunge into a horse trough and a wipe with straw, which was still snagged in the bits of chain mail and plate working their way at the edges through the blackened leather. Over it he'd draped a dagged surcoat of a terrifying shade of yellow—yellow that only could have come from the dye vats of Kwest Mralwe itself— and through its ripped sleeve and the parti-colored confusion of Dogbreath's ragged shirt, a bandage could be seen on his arm. The ribbons in his hair were fresh. One of them, pink silk striped with white, Sun Wolf recognized, and it turned him sick.

But he knew his men, and knew what it was like, to breach a city's walls after a festering bastard of a siege that nobody had hoped to live through. He said, "I know," the words bile in his mouth.

"And we didn't kill *everybody*," Dogbreath temporized. "Most of the women and kids weren't worth keeping—you'd spend more feeding them up to strength than you'd get for them as slaves. That went for the men, too. We didn't have any orders one way or the other.''

''I know,'' the Wolf said again, remembering the skinny little girls outside the taverns, the old women digging garbage with arthritic fingers. He and Dogbreath had both mounted sieges where they had had orders to kill everyone, and had done so without a second thought. Remembering that didn't help. Then he asked, steeling himself to hear the worst: ''What about the wizard?''

''Zero about the wizard.'' Dogbreath shrugged, spreading his enormous hands. ''No hide, no hair, not the tassel of his little pink tail. I figure he must have been on the walls waiting for us and got plugged by an arrow in the first volley. Hell,'' he added, seeing the sudden narrowing of disbelief in Sun Wolf's eye, ''it happens, you know.''

''Yeah,'' the Wolf said. ''But it doesn't happen to wizards very goddam often.'' *God's grandmother,* he thought dizzily, *the Duke didn't lock Moggin up because of what I said, did he?* It seemed inconceivable, even for what he knew of Trinitarians; inconceivable that Moggin hadn't either escaped or talked his way out of it in time. For all his scholarly quiet, the man obviously kept his head in emergencies . . .

''All I know is, the attack went slick as slime, like corn through a goose. So I figure whoever it was, he must have bought the farm on the first shot. It wasn't that Moggin grut, anyway, that's for sure.''

''Why 'for sure'?'' He threw a quick glance into the shadows of the bed, where Starhawk still slept, her face white as the fresh linen the servants had brought. Taking his friend's unwounded arm, he led him out the door and onto the terrace. The sun had set, but the garden below them was a fairyland of torches and lanterns, shadows dancing in the naked trees. From the windows of the dining hall at the far end of the terrace, thousands of lamps threw moving shadows on the gravel and the muted riot of hautboys and viols could be detected from that direction, vying with the jangle of hurdy-gurdies in the streets, drunken celebration, and a whore's shrill laughter. There was free wine in every fountain in the city tonight.

Dogbreath shrugged again. ''That was pretty nasty,''

he said. "I guess the King remembered the talk about it in the Council, and was still after getting a tame wizard all for his own. There hadn't been much fighting up in that end of the city, but the pickings were rich. A bunch of us were going through old Moggin's house when his Royal Etcetera showed up, with a gang of his own boys. Some of the guys had done the woman and the older girl before we showed up, but this Moggin pook and the little girl had barricaded themselves in the cellar. We figured, hell, they could stay there—neither would be any use as a slave and we were going to torch the house when we were done—but the King and his bravos hauled 'em out into the yard.''

Dogbreath was quiet for a moment, his wide mouth flexing with distaste. "Hell, I don't know why it was worse. We'd have croaked 'em both anyway. Maybe because it was done in cold blood. You're sacking a town, you kill somebody who gets in your way, it's like battle, you know? But the King gets this Moggin—he looked like a pretty harmless old pook to me, and God knows, if he'd had any magic, he'd have used it to keep the goons from snuffing his wife when they were done with her—down in the yard, and he says to him, 'I want you to do magic for me.' Oh, first he said, 'Are you Moggin Aerbaldus,' and that's when we found out that was the grut you'd thought was the hookum.

"So Moggin says, 'There must be some mistake, I'm not a wizard.' He was pretty steady about it, though he was shook up bad. He had the little girl hangin' onto his coat like it was her last hope of dinner. So him and the King do this yes-you-are, no-I'm-not routine for a little bit, and finally the King says, 'I'll protect you from the Church if you'll work for me, and we'll rule the Middle Kingdoms together and so on and so forth.' And Moggin says, 'I swear I'm not a wizard.' And the King says, 'We'll see about that.'

"So he gets his men to haul the little girl over to the other side of the courtyard—it took two of 'em to get her away from Moggin. Then he takes one of the books from the study, and rips out a couple of pages for tinder and puts them in a heap on the pavement, and says, 'If you don't light that, they'll slit her throat.' Figuring I suppose that if he could get Moggin to admit he's a wizard, it's the first step. It was pretty raw. The little girl was sobbing, 'Daddy, Daddy,' and Moggin fought the guards holding him for a minute, then begs the King to let her go, goes on his knees, cries, pleads, the whole parade, says he can't do it, swears he isn't a wizard . . .''

Dogbreath shrugged. "So they slit her throat. That's when I left. And while all that was going on, damned if Zane hadn't been going through the house while everyone else was out in the courtyard, watching to see if he'd really be able to make a fire to save the kid's life, and bagged all the loot worth having. So I guess we were wrong. But it was damn ugly all the same.''

From the darkness of a near-by colonnade, a voice called out Dogbreath's name. He glanced down the terrace in that direction, where a confusion of musicians and acrobats were preparing to go into the dining room among a mill of servants. Then he turned back and regarded the Wolf with beady black eyes. "Ari asked me to ask you, Chief . . . Can you work the weather for about six days more? Long enough for us to get through the badlands around the Khivas and the Gore? We'll be moving fast now.''

Baffled and sickened at the scene of the child's murder, Sun Wolf pulled his mind back from the desperate puzzle of why Moggin would allow it, what it was that he feared. He'd been drawing the spell-wheels on the study floor, dammit . . . "Yeah,'' he sighed, though the marrow of his bones ached already at the thought of turning aside the storms that he could feel, even now, drifting in from the Inner Sea. "He couldn't ask me himself?''

The squad-leader's brown, simian face grew taut, and the dark eyes shifted. "He doesn't want to see you, Chief.''

Rage stirred in him, like a surge of heat, only to trickle away almost at once, leaving a bleached weariness behind. He glanced up at Dogbreath, to meet the deep concern in his eyes when there was no explosion, no tirade of curses, no bellowed threats. But Sun Wolf had made his choice. Starhawk was alive, and there was very little to say.

"Pox rot it'' was all he whispered.

"Hey . . .'' The quiet seemed to bother Dogbreath, who patted his arm with curious gentleness, as if realiz-

ing that his Chief was very far gone indeed. "He's not
gonna die of it," he said cheerfully. "I'd probably feel
different if the wizard—whoever it was—had been up on
that wall throwin' fire-breathing elephants at us, but as
it is, I'm glad you stayed here and took care of the
Hawk." His eyes, bright and a bit inhuman, warmed
somewhat. "She's a damn good lady, Chief. I'm glad
she'll be around awhile longer."

"Thanks." He leaned against the archway behind him,
his head bowed and his long, thinning hair hanging down
around his scarred face, feeling drained and bitter and
very alone. Part of him hated Dogbreath, with his bloody
boots and the dead child's pink ribbon tied in his straight
black braid—hated him the way he hated himself for what
he had been. He knew that Dogbreath could be no different from what he was—what he, Sun Wolf, had made
him. They had seen combat together, had put their lives
on the iron altar for the gods of war to take if they wanted,
and he knew that what was done in war was done as in
a different life, tainted with terror and the battle rush that
was the only way to survive.

Starhawk was right, he thought wearily. He should have
let nothing drag him back to the way life was lived in
war. He had gone for his friends, his troop, and for the
captain who was like a son to him. And they'd turned
their backs on him, when he'd chosen . . . what? A single
woman's life over theirs? Or life over death?

"Yeah," he said slowly. "Tell him I'll work the
weather for him. I'll give him a week, if I can."

"Thanks. You watch your blind side, Chief." Dogbreath clasped his hand briefly, then strode jauntily away
down the evening-dark corridor, the pink bow on the end
of his braid a jogging blur in the gloom.

Sun Wolf turned back, weary beyond speaking, to the
darkness of Starhawk's room. The place smelled of old
blood, dressings, herbs, and smoke, a sickroom smell he
hated. He wanted to leave the place, to find a tavern, get
roaring drunk and resoundingly laid, and forget that he
was a wizard now, forget that he had responsibilities,
forget everything he was and knew. The troop would be
celebrating tonight, as he had celebrated with them a
score of times, in the torchlight and smoke beneath a
city's broken walls. The memory came back vivid and

bloody-golden; rowdy obscenities and violent horseplay blurred behind a rosy-gold screen of drunken well-being, the crazy elation of being alive when others were dead, the heat of alcohol in his veins and the joy of being with friends who understood him, who looked up to him, who had survived hell and fire with him—his fellow killers, Ari, Zane, Dogbreath, Penpusher, and Hawk . . .

If he turned back and listened, stretching out his wizard's senses in the louring night, he could probably hear the noise of the camp over the cheap carnival clamor of the town.

He slumped back into the carved chair in the shadows of the bed curtains. He saw the drinking contests, the food fights, the wrestling matches, the nights when they'd bring in and rape all the prettier girls among those taken in the sack, the games of making the captive city fathers run humiliating gauntlets of thrown garbage or grovel for coppers in the muddy dirt of the tent floors, and saw them for what they were—the cruel and abusive sports of victors, hysterical with delight and relief that they were not dead, were not maimed, and were able to do these things to those who had opposed them.

But still he missed the gay violence of celebration and missed the closeness, like a pack-dog missing the smell and warmth and fleas of his pack.

They had left him, and he was alone. He had never before been so aware of what seizing his magic, following the path of his destiny, had done to him. He was no longer what he had been. He could not go back.

Cold fingers touched his hand, then closed around it, firm for all their lightness. Lonely, hurting, he squeezed them in return and, looking down in the dimness, met Starhawk's sleepy gray eyes.

# CHAPTER

## —— 9 ——

*T*HEY SPENT ALMOST THREE WEEKS IN KWEST Mralwe, in a grace-and-favor house near the city wall on the edge of the University Quarter. It belonged to the Stratii and, Sun Wolf guessed, was close enough to the great House of Stratus for guards to be sent if there was trouble . . . if, for instance, the King or any other member of the King-Council decided to make a bid at acquiring a tame wizard. The house itself had been built by one of the old noble families, who had ruled the land from the time of the Empire. In Kwest Mralwe these ancient clans had mostly married into the great houses of the merchant bankers, though there were some that held aloof, selling the wool from such ancestral lands as remained to them, going formally masked to one another's parties, and brooding on the injustices of the modern world. Modest by merchant standards and ruinously old, the house was nevertheless perfectly proportioned, quiet, and filled with an antique peace. Its garden was badly overgrown, and Sun Wolf spent a number of afternoons clearing it of weeds, coaxing its tiny artificial springs to run again, and rearranging the rocks that were its bones.

It was a quiet time.

Starhawk recovered quickly, sleeping much, eating

well if little—the despair of Renaeka Strata's second-best cook, who had been lent to them, with two or three other servants, by the Lady Prince. For the first week or so, she had violent headaches, but, once Sun Wolf got her to admit the fact, they yielded to what little healing magic he was by that time again able to work. For the rest, the weather consumed his strength.

Daily at first, then twice, and latterly, three and four times a day and far into the nights he performed the spells and rites. With an obscure caution, he still dared not sink into the deep trance, dared not seek the winds in their own wild quarters, but instead concentrated on holding the dead heaviness of the warm air where it was, over Kwest Mralwe and the long coastline of the north. This took far more of his own energy than guiding the winds did, and, as the pressure of the seasons and of the turning earth built up, left him with a constant, gnawing headache that wore still further at his strength.

Moreover, for each spell, each rite, he had to make anew the full panoply of protective circles, leaving no crack through which evil might come. As the days went by, he grew weary of the tedious ritual of cleansing the long, tile-floored summer dining room and writing the runes of aversion and guard, of light and darkness, in each corner, across each crevice and doorsill and window, knowing that they must all be scrubbed out afterward and all to do again. It was servants' work, patient and pointless and dull, and the warrior in him raged bitterly against it, as his body had raged at his choice not to take the woman Opium when she stood in his arms.

The gray cloud cover, the dense and louring pressure, held, but he could feel it draining his strength day by day of that first week. There were nights when, working alone in the leaden stillness, the strength of the storms seemed to crush him; dawns when he would emerge, sweat-soaked and shaky, knowing he would have to return to his task within hours and wanting nothing so much as to beat to death the first servant who crossed his path.

This, he supposed, was what it was to be a wizard.

He ate little, for the exertion made him sick. In spite of his weariness, he forced himself to exercise, hacking at a striking post he'd set up in the overgrown garden or throwing the knife or the ax, right-handed, then left-handed, at the far wall of the empty upstairs gallery. He meditated in the crumbling summer house, the thick stillness of the air prickling at his skin, or catnapped on top of the bed's coverlet at Starhawk's side, prey to uneasy dreams.

He had abandoned Ari to face the Vorsal mage alone. Protection from the killing storms was the least he could offer by way of amends. There were times when, knees aching from the uneven tiles of the floor, back aching from bending to call forth in chalk and silver and auligar powder the great sweeping lines of strength, the stars of defense, and the closing rings of the vortex of power, he was obliged to remind himself of this fact at intervals of five minutes or less.

On the seventh night, he let the rains begin. Sitting in the window embrasure with Starhawk, their arms locked around one another's waists, he felt the cold ferocity of the air beat his face and listened to the waters pouring down in the blackness outside. The great bedroom where they sat was in the front of the house, its windows looking out into the street; by the glimmer of oil lamps in scores of windows up and down the rocky hill, they watched the waters churn over the cobblestones in a hurly-burly of brown silk, the air alive with blown rain.

Starhawk's voice was barely audible in the darkness. "You gave me this night. If it wasn't for you I wouldn't be here. Thank you."

"If it wasn't for you," the Wolf replied in his rusted growl, "I wouldn't have the brains to be here either."

Ari would be somewhere in the Silver Hills by this time, he thought, staring out into the storm; backside-deep in any of the hundred streams and sour ponds that pockmarked that broken land. The memory of the bitter north returned like the recollection of a voice or a face: eroded valleys that had once held the Empire's farms, now black with standing pines; hillsides that would support nothing but heather; reefs of lichened granite and basalt and rotting lava; and here and there a broken farmhouse, or the crumbling subsidences that marked where ancient mine-workings had been. And back of it all, on the crest of a harsh gray hill that dominated the countryside for a hundred miles around, lay the walled and broken fortress that had once ruled the north.

He wondered if Ari was up to it.

Probably, he thought. *If he could hold that band of bastards together through the siege, when every mother's son of 'em was scared spitless, waiting to see where the curse would land next, he's sure as hell got the juice to lead them back to Wrynde alive.*

And despite what had been said the night before the assault, he smiled, loving that man who was the closest thing to a son he'd ever known.

After that he and the Hawk took some days to explore the city: the wealthier quarters up the mountain where the rain murmured on the pink-tiled roofs just visible above the high walls; the moneyed bustle of the Wool Market and the dye yards behind; and street after steep street of markets under sheets of oiled canvas—whole lanes devoted to silversmiths, or jewelers, or merchants of silk, rare viands, and wine. Sun Wolf bought the Hawk a moonstone earring that stunned her to stammering silence; what she bought for him, in a discreet shop whose clientele was mostly expensive courtesans, delighted and disconcerted him even more. One day they spent wandering the city produce market amid piles of shining melons or fruit imported by caravan from the south, eating buns hot from the baker's ovens with colorless winter butter dripping down their fingers. On another day, they rode out to the ancient tombs that lay in the hills to the northeast, tombs dating from the years when Gwenth was still the capital of most of the world and not a schism-haunted religious snake pit where a titular emperor's courtiers engaged in blossom-viewing expeditions in the imperial garden mazes, comparing poems about the moon. Some of the antique tombs had been looted years ago, their melting sandstone doorways gaping like sad mouths. Others, open also, showed the bright chips of recent damage.

"Could that have been it?" the Hawk wondered, picking her way through lakes of gray puddles to the eroded lintel of a small door into the hill. "At a guess some of our boys did this. Here where the chisels went it hasn't been weathered at all." She touched with gloved fingers the bright broken place on the lintel and glanced back at the Wolf, holding the horses in the little valley among the crowding barrows, bronze-roofed shrines, and faceless statues of saints. "I've heard some emperors used to keep court hoodoos, and gave them tombs in the teeth of the Church. If Zane or Dogbreath were brainless enough to loot one, might they have taken something into the camp that had an ancient curse?"

Sun Wolf frowned, coming to her side to touch the stone, feeling through it for whatever resonances might linger—old griefs, old pride, old hate. But he felt nothing, though whether this was due to lack of skill on his part, the lingering exhaustion of working the weather, or because there was nothing to feel, he could not tell. "It's a chance," he said thoughtfully. "The shadow hand I saw might have been an ancient curse, but the voice sure as hell wasn't. And Moggin was worried enough about the Duke's suspicion to risk me escaping while he stashed his books."

Starhawk raised her dark, level brows. "Doesn't seem to have worked," she said mildly, "does it?"

On the day after the breaking of Vorsal, before the job of working the weather had turned into an all-devouring vocation, Sun Wolf rode out to the shattered town with a packhorse and empty saddlebags to see what was left of Moggin's house and in particular Moggin's library. The house had been burned. In the garden he saw the remains of the child Dannah, her throat cut to the neckbone, and, on what had been the brick terrace, her mother's nude and battered body sprawled, squirming with rats. The other bodies in the house—Moggin's, Sun Wolf guessed, and the older daughter as well as the servants—had been burned beyond recognition. Of that old-fashioned frescoed study, with its tufted blue-and-red rugs and the smudgy lines of the half-finished circles of unholy power, only ashes remained.

*Why?* he wondered, picking his way through the still-warm piles of blackened brick to where he guessed the kitchen wing lay. *Moggin was a wizard, dammit!* By the way the soldiers of the watch had acted, everyone in town guessed it. Even given the Trinitarians' well-known antipathy, stupid and useless as the King might be, his offer of protection was something no father would have turned down.

*What had Moggin feared that much?*

Gingerly, Sun Wolf picked his way down the wet, dirt-smelling flight of what had been the cellar steps to their turning, and stopped. In the darkness, a sheet of filthy brown water lay beneath him, bobbing with wet, shapeless things—pieces of broken chests, rotted apples from the bottom of some storage bin, and the swollen body of a servant with his nose eaten off. The water shuddered with swimming rats, and Sun Wolf backed up hastily, nauseated by the smell, guessing that the sewer had broken. Disgust and disappointment filled him . . . and at that moment he heard his horse in the garden let out a whinny of fear. There was a rushing overhead—turning, he saw all the crows and ravens that had been clustered over the bodies burst wildly into the air.

He ran up a few steps and looked around. The rats, too, were forsaking their meal, streaming in a gray-brown carpet toward the shadows of the ruined house.

Among the piled shadows of the broken grain-store next door something moved. He wasn't sure, but thought he saw the cold glint of daylight on dark metal.

He didn't wait to see more. He made a dash down the garden, hands fumbling with the reins as he untied the horses, glancing repeatedly over his shoulder toward the black carcass of the house. Remembering the deadly speed with which the *djerkas* moved, he urged the horse to as fast a canter as possible down the winding streets of the stinking town, trampling corpses in the narrow ways, leaping the half-burned barricades of broken furniture and fallen house beams where the street fighting had been, and brushing past startled looters and those who sought for who knew what among the ruins.

Once he hit the open ground, he spurred to a gallop. He glanced behind him seven or eight times on his way back to Kwest Mralwe, but never saw anything.

But that fact made it no easier for him to fall asleep after he had worked the weather that night.

"You gonna tell me what the problem is, Chief, or you going to worry yourself bald-headed on your own?"

"Worry doesn't make you bald," Sun Wolf retorted defensively, running a hand unconsciously over the increasing acreage of open pasture at the crown of his head. "And, anyway, it's not something I can do anything about."

Starhawk shoved herself away from where she leaned in the study door and came across to the desk where he sat, put her arms around his shoulders and bent to kiss the three-inch circle of bare pink skin. He cocked his one eye up at her suspiciously as she pushed aside the moldering books and perched tailor-fashion on a corner of the desk. "What isn't?"

"The *djerkas*." He sighed, and leaned back in the great pickled-oak chair. He had been at the desk since after dinner, reading the books of the Witches, as he had every night since the rains began. His hoarse voice was weary. "Moggin. The hex. The fact that even though Moggin's dead I'm not sure I'm out of danger."

"From the *djerkas*?" She leaned an elbow on the stack of books, her white hands lying lightly on the smooth black wool of her gentlemanly hose. A dressing still covered the X-shaped wound and the healing skull beneath it; her cropped-off hair was growing back, a glitter of pale stubble, fine as silk velvet in the alabaster lamplight. "Sounds like it's just wandering around the city like a stray dog. Nobody took the paper out of its mouth, or however those things are motivated. It senses you and says, 'Hmmm . . . I remember something about him . . .' Obviously there's some kind of thaumaturgical spancel keeping it around Vorsal, which should make for a pretty entertaining spring once Renaeka Strata's engineers start building their new wharves."

"Maybe." The Wolf's fingers toyed with tarnished gold on the bindings of a crumbling grimoire. "But the more I think about it, the harder it is to believe old Moggy would sit there and let the King's bravos skrag his little girl, rather than admit he was a wizard. He was afraid of something, so afraid that at the suggestion his cover was blown, he wouldn't even carry through the final phase of the curse and turn his magic against the army when it hit the walls. I think there was a second wizard in Vorsal."

"The one who tried to enslave you?"

"Yeah. There's times I feel I'm being watched . . ."

"You are," Starhawk pointed out reasonably. "The cook sends reports regularly to Renaeka, and I think that new scullery maid is a double agent for the Bishop."

He laughed briefly. "I hope they all enjoyed the report about what we did last night. But no, it's more than that.

Old Master Drosis could have had more than one student in Vorsal. If that wasn't Moggin trying to enslave me—and at this point I don't think it was—I can't blame the poor bastard for being scared. I'm not sure what I'd do, rather than put myself back in that power."

"You think our Hoodoo Secundus might have been behind the curse as well?"

"N—No," he said slowly. "For the simple reason that if the curse was the work of a second hoodoo, he'd have gone through stitch with it and the assault would never have succeeded. I don't think the *djerkas* was Moggin's—if it had been, it would have come to the rescue that last day . . ."

"If it could," the Hawk put in. "He might have locked it up or put it to sleep when you blew him to the Duke."

"Maybe." The Wolf grunted. "But remember that according to Purcell, Moggin wasn't the only man in the city suspected of witchery. There was the woman Skinshab, and there might have been others. They were interested enough in keeping anyone from sneaking into Vorsal, but obviously didn't give two hoots about their neighbors—and considering how wizards get treated in these parts, I don't blame 'em. Wizards have a way of surviving sacks, if they keep their heads down, and coming out of them damn rich, if they're smart."

"So it wasn't your blowing Moggy to the Duke that kept him from fighting off the final assault," the Hawk said thoughtfully. "It was fear of this other wizard, whoever it was."

Sun Wolf nodded, chewing on the corner of his mustache. "I think so, yeah. If the shadow hand can find you, trap you, when you work in deep trance, it could account for why he'd just slap a curse on the troop and hope for the best . . . And it damn near worked, at that. You know Krayth of Kilpithie's men mutinied the night before the assault? Krayth was killed . . ."

"Damn," the Hawk said briefly. She, too, had known and liked the cynical Easterner. "So this second wizard—that woman Skinshab or somebody else—is still out there someplace with the *djerkas*?"

Sun Wolf nodded. Outside the rain made a soft, steady rushing against the plastered house walls, and purled faintly in the garden streams. A chill draft made the lamp flames curtsy in their bowls, and the flicker of it danced like chain lightning down the small silver buckles of Starhawk's doublet. "Why do you think I spent half my time putting every spell and circle of guard around me before I touched the weather?" he asked softly. "Why do you think for the last two weeks I've kept damn close to town?"

"Hence the books?" she asked, waving at the stack beneath her elbow, and the others strewn around the tabletop at her back.

He whispered, "Yeah." He touched the grimoires and demonaries beside his hand, crumbling tomes he had stolen from the wizard Kaletha's snake pit, books which she had stolen in her turn. Like the heat of banked coals, he could feel the spells within them, a shimmering mixture of power, beauty, and evil whose stink turned his stomach. Starhawk, seated casually among them, didn't seem to notice.

"Some of the things in those books are evil, Hawk—medicine of the worst possible kind." He used the word from the barbarian tongue of his childhood, which translated equally as medicine, magic, spirit, God, and madness. "And there's some spells in them . . . I don't understand them as I should. I don't know if they're safe to work or not. Safe for me, for my spirit, my mind. And there's nobody to tell me whether I'm being a wise man or a coward. I know that difference in battle, in a fight, and in a siege. I know what's safe and what's stupid. I don't know it here."

"And I take it," she said, two steps ahead of him as usual, "that the spell you've found that'll show you this wizard is one of those?"

He sighed resignedly. "Yeah, pox rot it."

They had to wait three days, for the dark of the moon, which in itself made the Wolf vaguely uneasy, for several of the moon-spells Yirth had taught him had contained warnings of hidden peril. The ritual was an odd one, from the most ancient of the Wenshar grimoires, its faded instructions jotted in a curious book hand characteristic of the court of that accursed matriarchy which lay open to several interpretations. All the magic in that volume had a different feel to it from those of the other books, different as the "hand" of silk is different from that of wool, and it required some odd things, including straw plaited in certain ways and the skulls of seven children, though two hours' ride and a little searching were all that were needed for that. In eighteen days the rats and ravens had done their work. Setting those pitiful bones in place on the ritually cleansed and protected tiles of the long summer dining room, Sun Wolf felt an obscure desire to apologize to their parents for what he had done.

Starhawk settled herself, drawn sword across her knees, in the center of the small Circle of Protection at the far end of the hall, the tiny lamp beside her casting its upside-down shadows over the gaunt bones of her face. Sun Wolf, book open in his hand, knelt before the empty divining bowl and took himself carefully down into the state of dark and moving meditation in which magic begins, reaching with his mind for the signs of power visible only in the moon's veiled dark.

But in the bowl's darkness he saw nothing, and felt no magic touch him.

It took them four tries before they got any result at all.

"Dammit, it's one of those spells that works from assumptions they don't bother to tell you!" the Wolf raged, scrubbing out all the laboriously written signs. "It could be one of those spells that won't work if you're not a virgin, or won't work if you're a man . . ."

"Well," Starhawk said promptly, "I vote against doing anything about that right now. Why don't we get rid of all the iron in the room and try again?"

Cursing his own lack of training—cursing the dead Wizard-King, for murdering anyone who could have taught him things like this—Sun Wolf began the ritual again, again with no result. Next Starhawk left, much against Sun Wolf's better judgment—he felt an obscure sense of danger in the night, and wanted her firstly in his sight, so he could protect her, and secondly at his back, so she could protect him. But the result was again nil.

It was not until he had ritually cleansed the room again, and set up the skull circle without tracing the glimmering hedges of the runes of ward and guard around the room, that the empty bowl before him seemed to fill with darkness, that strange, clear darkness in which his wizard's sight saw vividly as in day.

With a cry he struck the bowl aside. It skated across the floor, knocking one of the skulls spinning so that the stub of candle fell out of it and rolled. The other little skulls, candles still burning within, seemed to watch with intent demonic gaze. The clay bowl smashed against the wall with a shocking clatter; Sun Wolf whirled on his knees as a dark shadow loomed over him, then settled back as he realized it was Starhawk, drawn sword in her hand.

"What is it?" She set the candle upright again on the tiles. The dance of its light seemed to put eyes in the empty sockets of the little skull, where it lay on its side some distance away and caught a glint like a sword blade on the glassy red of the pottery shards. Beyond the archways, the garden lay invisible, the rain's steady growling filling the night. "What did you see?"

"Only the hand," he whispered, his breathing still unsteady.

It had been tracing silver runes.

That night he dreamed about the empty pottery bowl filled with darkness. The cracks where it had been smashed to pieces against the wall showed clearly, and darkness leaked through them like smoke, to crawl out along the floor tiles of the empty dining room and seep around the seven little skulls with the candles burning inside. Dimly, Sun Wolf knew that couldn't be. He'd thrown the bits of the bowl into the kitchen midden, had put those seven skulls in one of the potting sheds and drawn the Circles around them, Light side inward, just in case. *I should have checked,* he thought vaguely. *I knew I should have checked.*

But what it was that he should have checked he wasn't sure.

He woke shivering, a sense of panic struggling in his chest, perfectly aware that the dream was only a dream, but terrified that, if he should get up now and go to the dining room, he'd see the bowl there, the darkness pouring from it to cover the floor like ground fog, the little skulls grinning their accusation at him with their glowing candle-flame eyes.

It was still dark. He had heard the bells of the Trinitarian cathedral chiming midnight just before he'd started the ritual for the last time, and it must still be an hour before dawn. Moving carefully so as not to wake Star-

hawk—who slept more soundly since her illness, anyway—he slipped from beneath the bedcovers and collected a wide, fur-lined robe from the lid of the chest
next to the bed. It billowed gently around his naked body
as he moved on bare and silent feet down the worn oak
of the corridor, his eye seeing, as a wizard's do in the
dark, all things in a queer violet shadowlessness—the
graceful wall niches with their spare statuary which, to
his barbarian tastes, looked so insipid, the delicate shap-
ing of door arches, and what little furniture there was.
Outside the rain had eased. The sense of having forgotten
something, of having known what to check and passed it
by, lingered naggingly in his thoughts. For some reason
he had the impression of a smell of straw in the air . . .
coming from the dining room downstairs, he thought,
faint but very clear . . .

He was two steps down the wide curve of the stairs
when he slipped. It was something anyone could have
done, descending stairs in the dark, even a night-sighted
wizard with the preternatural reflexes of a lifelong ath-
lete. It was only his reflexes which saved him. Afterward, he wasn't sure how his feet happened to jerk out
from under him, though the sensation was exactly as if
one ankle had been seized from below at the same time
someone had thrust him hard between the shoulders. His
body was thinking, even as he fell, twisting in the air to
grab for the banister. He was moving with such force
that his torso swung sideways, colliding with the steps
hard enough to leave him breathless and bruised as he
caught the polished beechwood of the posts. It was his
swearing as much as the thud of the fall that brought
Starhawk running to the top of the stairs.

"Stop!" he yelled, hearing the barely detectable pat
of her bare feet above him. She halted, trained to instant
obedience of his voice in battle.

"You okay, Chief?"

For answer he expressed himself at some length, while
climbing painfully to his feet and pulling the robe around
him again. He saw her in the dark, naked and beautiful
as the death goddess, sword in one hand and knife in the
other, a few feet from the top of stairs. The bandages
made a pale slash in the gloom. "And no, I'm not okay."

He limped up to her, pushing his thinning tawny hair back from his face. "I fell down the goddam stairs."

They looked at one another for a long time in silence.

"You feel all right to travel in this weather?" Sun Wolf glanced sidelong down at the woman jostling through the crowds in the Steel Market by his side. Except for being thinner—and the close cut of the black doublet and hose she wore these days disguised that for the most part—and the cropped hair, which at the moment was mostly hidden by a tall-crowned hat with a cocky feather, Starhawk looked pretty much as she always had, like a killing weapon wrought of peeled bone and alabaster. He knew she still tired easily, though today, wandering through the stalls of the smiths and scissor grinders and weapon makers, some of the cool golden pinkness had returned to her cheekbones.

"Well, naturally I'd like to stay here and nurse my rheumatism all winter by the fire." She shrugged and glanced up between the crowding houses and tenements at the gray millrace of the sky. It wasn't raining for once, but, by the smell of the wind, it would be by nightfall. "But since, if you got killed, there'd be nobody to make coffee the way I like it, I guess I'll force myself." They split to pass on either side of a fat woman selling wheat-straw amulets and Saint's Eyes from a blanket in the middle of the street, the bright-colored tangles of yarn and bead and bone like primitive flowers against the drab gray-yellow of the street and the buildings. Though officially disapproving of such holdovers from the days of the local sorceress-gods, the Church knew better than to try and root out such things. "Let's not go back to Wenshar, though," she added, putting a languid hand to her brow. "The desert air's *so* hard on my complexion."

"I didn't mind the desert air so much as the ants," Sun Wolf remarked. "We could head east over the mountains or up to the Marches. Grishka of Rhu owes me some favors, and the Goshawk should still be hiding out in Mallincore, if you don't mind garlic and heresy for five months . . ."

"Chief," said the Hawk softly, "we're being followed."

Sun Wolf stopped at a knife seller's stand and held a shining bodice dagger up for inspection and to look at the crowd behind him in the mirror of its blade. "Which one?" The relative niceness of the morning had brought citizens, virtually house-bound for the past two weeks by the unstinting storms, out in droves, and the Steel Market was crowded with servants in livery, beggars in rags, students in their gray gowns, and bourgeois gentlemen in the familiar black, white ruffs of varying width and extravagance nodding like dandelion puffs around their strangulated throats. But before the Hawk could reply, he spotted their shadow, cloaked in black and disguised in a blue leather carnival mask, lurking ineptly behind the ornate iron pillars of a public urinal. The cheap rings and the ancient opal signet were visible even in the chancy surface of the knife blade, and the Wolf swore under his breath.

"Right," he muttered, thanked the knife seller, and jostled on his way, turning out of the Steel Market and down a narrow lane that led back toward the river. Starhawk, tilting her hat at a casual angle and fingering her sword hilt, strolled at his heels. The lane, one of the hundreds that crisscrossed Kwest Mralwe's lower quarter like ant tunnels, ran between the high wall of a merchant palace and the grounds of an ancient chapel built, it was obvious, to honor the Mother and later taken over and refurbished when the Trinitarians had ceased to be regarded as heretics, began to be called the New Religion, and started persecuting heretics on their own. The inhabitants of the tenements of both sides had taken over the tiny square of waste ground before its crumbling porch as a drying yard and pasturage for their pigs, and Starhawk stepped deftly behind a tree full of patched sheets to wait while the Wolf strolled farther down the lane.

The black-cloaked man ducked around the end of the lane and tiptoed swiftly along it, hugging the wall and obviously hoping the Wolf wouldn't turn his head at an inopportune moment. Casually oblivious, Sun Wolf stepped around a corner and flattened to the moss-stained wall. The King of Kwest Mralwe emerged at a high-speed skulk a moment later and was seized, slammed against the wall, and unmasked before he had time to so much as gasp for breath. Starhawk materialized a moment later, effectively blocking his flight.

"There something you want to say to me?"

"I . . ." the King gasped, and then, a moment after

the Wolf released the bunched shirtfront he held, commanded, "Unhand me!" That already having been done, he straightened his sorry ruffles and looked from one to the other with resentment in his watery eyes. "It was necessary to meet you away from That Woman's spies," he declared, pushing back the dark hood from his face. "They are everywhere, even in your own household . . ."

"Yeah, the cook and the scullery maid." Sun Wolf folded his heavy arms and regarded the King narrowly.

The King cleared his throat. "Oh, so you know," he said lamely. Then, regaining his dramatic tone, "Then you know that you only exist here on her sufferance, that whenever she chooses, she can place you under arrest, have you imprisoned, or murdered, as she has others before you."

The Wolf glanced sidelong at Starhawk, though neither's expression changed.

"I sought you out to offer you my protection again, against her, against her servants, and against the Church that she carries like a bauble in her reticule. Can't you see the evil of That Woman? She rules this city! Now that we've conquered Vorsal, she'll have more power, and more, as other cities come under our sway. It's only a matter of time before she offers you a choice—servitude to her, or death . . ."

"Like the choice you offered Moggin Aerbaldus?" the Wolf asked quietly.

The weak eyes shifted under his and the pettish mouth grew spiteful. "A useless liar," he spat irritably. "Cowardly, whining—I told him I'd protect him! He wouldn't even light a fire, wouldn't even admit that he could! Just like that filthy old hag in the Gatehouse Quarter . . ."

"Skinshab?" the Wolf asked, and the pettish gaze darted back to him.

"Worthless bitch! Claimed she wasn't a witch, either, though all the neighbors knew she was. She'd witched their children during the siege, so they all died . . . She even admitted it! They told me so, after the old harridan had locked herself up in that hovel of hers . . ."

"And did you kill her," the Wolf asked softly, "as well?"

"She deserved it," the King flared. "We torched the house—gave her a taste of the hellfire she'd go to when she refused to come out! I thought it would drive her out," he added, with a little sigh, the viciousness fading from his eyes and leaving them again slack and a little puzzled. "Or that she'd use her magic to put the fire out. So you see," he added, reaching out one limp hand to touch the Wolf's crimson leather sleeve, "you're the only ones. And believe me, it will be only a matter of time before that poisonous virago Renaeka the Bastard turns her attention to you."

"Interesting," said the Wolf, as they made their way back up the hill toward the comfortable little house with its faithful troop of servant-spies.

"Last night could have been an accident, you know."

"You care to place a small wager on that?"

She said nothing, and they walked in silence for a time, the first, faint patterings of rain beginning to spot the leather of the Wolf's doublet, and catch like jewels in the frail white feather of her hat.

After a time the Wolf went on, "We've got twelve silver pieces and about six strat worth of copper and bits; we might be able to get another fifteen or twenty from Renaeka if we guarantee we're leaving her lands."

"You want to risk that?"

"Not really."

"There's always that bronze mermaid in the front hall," the Hawk pointed out practically. "And the mechanical clock in the study. We could get ten or twelve apiece for them. Would that be enough to keep us through the winter?" Like most mercs, Starhawk hadn't the slightest idea what household expenses ran.

"No," said the Wolf. "But we'll find something."

Her voice was calmly conversational. "I can hardly wait to learn what."

But the decision was taken out of their hands.

The rain thickened as evening drew on, beating heavily on the windows of the study where Sun Wolf sat, branches of candles blazing on either side of him, reading slowly, carefully through the Lesser Demonary. Its later chapters covered quasi-demons, *golems*, constructs, and elementals, including those which contained spirits—either human or demonic—trapped or drawn into them as their motivating force. It was an ugly magic, and reading it made him glance up half a dozen times at the

faded tapestry window curtains to make sure they were
indeed shut. He found references to the *djerkas* there and
other, more disturbing things as well, hinted at in shapeless terms that made him curse whatever careless goon
had tossed a torch into Moggin's library. In spite of the
fur-lined robe he wore over his clothes, he felt cold; as
the night deepened, every sound in the quiet house caught
his attention like the stealthy creak of floorboards at his
back. When someone pounded on the great front door
shortly after the Cathedral bells spoke the fifth hour of
the night, he almost jumped out of his boots.

Cocking an ear to listen, he heard a servant's voice and
then, muffled by distance and weariness, another that
twitched at his stomach with a sinking premonition of dread.

". . . Of course I know what time it is, I had to get
in the goddam pox-festering city gates, didn't I? Now let
me see the Chief and quit arguing before I burn down
your outhouse."

Sun Wolf was on his feet and striding swiftly down the
tiled hall toward the two figures that stood, framed in a
double ring of lamplight from the sconces by the doors,
in the dense shadows of the hall. He was peripherally
aware of the light tread and tomcat shadow on the stairs
that would be Starhawk, but most of his attention was
drawn to the butler's stiff-backed shape, and, half-hidden
behind it, the bedraggled form whose battered jerkin,
ruinous sleeve dags, and sopping braids were dripping
puddles of water onto the tiled floor.

"Dogbreath!"

"Chief!" The squad-leader brushed past the scandalized butler and strode toward him, delight beaming from
squirrel eyes in a face almost unrecognizable with filth,
a week's growth of black beard, and the last extremities
of hardship.

"What the hell . . . ?" Starhawk's voice said from the
stairs.

"Chief, I hate to do this to you," Dogbreath said.
"It's a bastard of a thing to ask you after everything that
went on, but we're up against it for real. We need you.
We need you now, fast. That curse is still on the troop."

# CHAPTER

## —— 10 ——

"I DON'T UNDERSTAND IT, CHIEF." ARI GOT UP AND poured full the cups that stood on the camp table of inlaid ebony—the cups of green lacquer and gold, which, like the table, the tent, the gold-bound staghorn chair to which the young captain returned to slouch, had all been Sun Wolf's once. Starhawk, sitting quietly on the X-shaped black-oak seat which had customarily been hers, noted how slowly Ari was moving, like a man forced to work at the stretch of his endurance at some hard physical labor, day in and day out and far into the night—a man whose strength is fast running out. In his eyes under the heavy brows she saw he knew it. Outside, rain pounded in whirling frenzy on the canvas tent. Inside, it dripped drearily through a dozen flaws and leaks and faulty seams, making hard little splatting noises on the sodden, carpetless mud underfoot. The braziers filled the air with smoke without warming it one whit.

"Things went from bad to worse after the sack. We got the hell out of there the morning after we were paid. We didn't even wait to divvy the take, just counted it and pulled stakes. But I've never seen so many things go wrong in my life."

The liquid in the cups wasn't wine. It was White Death,

163

the cheapest grade of gin mixed with hot water. The wine, Starhawk gathered, had all gone rancid in its skins a day or two out of Kwest Mralwe. So had most of the flour they'd bought for the journey to Wrynde, a journey intended to be accomplished in record time and which had, instead, been plagued by every delay known to equipment, beast, or humankind. "I swear, Chief, we broke seven axles in one day!" Ari gestured with one bandaged hand, a wound received in the sack and still unhealed. "After the third one, I personally went through every wagon and cart in the train, and by the Three Gods' witness, they were all sound! I've never been that close to crying and kicking my heels on the ground in my life! And three the next day, and all the time the men fighting over whose fault it was, stealing liquor and bread from each other . . . Even the slaves we took from the sack of the town are fighting each other! EACH OTHER for Gods' sakes! Horses and oxen going sick like they'd been poisoned—which I'll take oath they weren't—trees falling in our path, bridges out, a bad lot of beer that kept everybody puking for two days . . . We never even made it over the Narewitch Bridge before the rains began."

Sun Wolf was silent, his single eyelid drooping in speculative thought.

For herself, the Hawk recalled well the inner sigh she always heaved when the troop had passed northbound over the three stone arches of that half-ruined bridge. The Narewitch marked the northern bounds of the Middle Kingdoms. In the twisted lava gorges of the badlands of the Gniss River and its tributaries, the going was harder—swollen streams, broken roads, rockslides—but at least the troop was out of danger of delay by some last-minute permutation of Middle Kingdom religious politics. To her, the bridge had always meant freedom— freedom to rest, to meditate, to train, to be what she was for a winter season before the summer required her to go back to her job as killer again. It was the first familiar landmark on the road home.

The thunder of the rain increased. Starhawk's practiced ear picked up the river's booming—the Gore, not the Khivas, which was the worst of the western tributaries. She and the Wolf had nearly been killed crossing that one yesterday.

The camp had been set at the high end of a bay in the red-black cliffs, where the brutal chasm of the Gore widened over a rocky ford. The shepherds of the Gore Thane's Fort pastured their sheep here in the spring, until the herdboys reported the yearly approach of the mercenaries on their way south. The Gore Thane—nominal lord of this barren corner of the badlands—left them alone, and they, in turn, forbore to molest such stray shepherds or merchants as they might encounter. In the spring, they'd be hurrying south or east to whatever war they were fighting that summer. In the fall, when this sheltered hillock was bare of the spring's grass and the Gore ran low and snarling in the rocky tangle of its ford, they'd be heading north as fast as they could to reach Wrynde before the rains began.

Once, she remembered, they'd been caught late and had to ford in the first of the floods. Oxen, horses, baggage wagons had been swept away in the white riptide; a man who lost his footing would be pulped against the boulders and washed downstream like a bug in a gutter. No one went after them to see if they survived. Any delay in the crossing would only mean the next river—the Black—would be that much more swollen.

According to Ari they had been trapped here on the bank of the Gore for the last six days.

"The storms in the mountains have got to let up sometime." Ari sipped at his liquor with a tentativeness Starhawk readily understood after an experimental taste of her own cup. "The river rises and falls. It slacked yesterday enough to try a crossing, though it was still higher than I've ever seen it. Zane tried going across with a rope to haul rafts. He turned back. There's seven feet of water over the highest of the midstream rocks and it's going like an avalanche. We've even been thinking about crossing back over the Khivas and heading south again . . ."

"Don't," the Wolf said, and moved his heavy shoulders against the mildewing canvas back of his camp chair. Beyond the dividing curtain, Starhawk could hear Raven Girl moving quietly about on the creaking bits of planking set up over the general muck. "The Khivas slacked off a little, too, or the Hawk and I couldn't have gotten across at all, but it was rising already when we were doing it. It'll be a millrace now. I don't think you could have taken wagons over it, even at its lowest.''

"Pox." Ari sat quiet for a moment, staring down into his cup, wet, dark hair falling forward around his haggard face. Above the drumming of the rain and the rush of the river, Starhawk could hear quite clearly the voices in the other tents packed so closely around this one— voices arguing tiredly, and somewhere a woman crying with the bitter, jagged weariness of one who has been weeping on and off for days. It made her feel stifled and irrationally angry, wanting to strike out at random. By the smell, the latrines were far too close to the tents, which were themselves jammed together, a higgledy-piggledy mass of canvas and rope, wagons and mule lines on the pebbly hillock, with the river foaming greedily at their feet.

She asked, "Who're the others in the camp?"

Ari shrugged. "About two hundred of Krayth's boys joined us. They said it was too far back to Kilpithie. I don't know whether these were the ones who mutinied or who were just sick of the whole thing. Their leader's a man named Louth."

"I know him." Sun Wolf grunted, setting aside his untasted cup after one sniff. "And if he's leading them, I'd bet money these were the mutineers."

Ari said nothing for a moment, but nodded to himself, as if adding this piece of information to others in his mind, and the lines in his face seemed to settle in a little deeper in the dim flicker of the ridgepole lamps. The Wolf had told her Ari looked bad, but Starhawk was shocked to see how her friend had aged. He'd lost flesh, and there was a tautness to him now, the feverish look of a man living on his nerves. He went on, "There's singletons and little groups with us, too, some of them from the siege, some of them just freebooters, bandits. Good men, some of them. They don't make trouble."

"Doesn't mean they couldn't." Sun Wolf's tawny eye glinted feral in the candlelight.

"Doesn't mean they will, either," Ari replied, running one hand over his unshaven face. "And if the river falls back enough to use rafts we're going to need all the help on this we can get."

"You still talking rafts?" a voice demanded from the

tent doorway. Looking up, Starhawk saw Zane framed against the darkness, all his modish yellow puffs and slashes oozing rainwater like a drowned cock pheasant. ''Give it up, Ari, that river's not coming down till spring. There isn't enough timber in this whole camp to float everything over, if it did.''

''Not all at once, no,'' Ari replied quietly. ''But there's enough wagons to run a ferry, if people like your pal Sugarman give them up.'' From the cant name and the bite of contempt and loathing in Ari's voice—and from her earlier acquaintance with Zane—Starhawk guessed that Sugarman must be one of the dreamsugar dealers who were as much a fixture in the train of the mercenary armies as were pimps. Two or three of them had luxurious winter residences in the town of Wrynde, at a discreet distance from Sun Wolf's camp. The Wolf, though holding them in considerable scorn, had never been fool enough to tell his men what they could and could not do on their own time, but most of the troop knew better than to come to his sessions on weapons training or go into battle under the influence of either drugs or the various sorts of alcohol peddled by the army's hangers-on. Those who didn't learned otherwise very quickly, or else ceased to be an issue.

''He's no pal of mine,'' Zane hastened to say. ''But you'd be asking for trouble to try and take his wagon from him. He's got his own hired boys to guard him.'' With a gesture curiously boyish he flipped his wet curls back from his eyes. ''Face it, pal, we're stuck, and the smartest thing we can do is to go with what we got.''

''No,'' said Ari, with a dogged quiet that echoed a dozen prior discussions.

Zane turned to Sun Wolf. ''What about the Gore Thane's fort upriver?'' he asked bluntly. ''I've been trying to tell this grut for days that we're stuck and we're running out of food sitting here in the rain, when the Gore Thane has got a good fort, good defensive position, and a winter's worth of food and women holed up five miles from here . . .''

''. . . on the side of a cliff,'' Ari pointed out, ''that we'd lose a third to a half of our men trying to take in the rain.''

''Maybe we would have,'' Zane said, his blue eyes

sparkling. "But now we've got an edge. We've got a hoo-doo on our side . . ." He grinned at Sun Wolf. "Don't we, Wolf?"

Starhawk cringed inside at the arrogant brightness of his voice. In the fretted lamplight she could almost see Sun Wolf's hair bristle. "No," the Wolf said softly, "you don't. And that 'grut' is your commanding officer."

"Aah, come on, Wolf, we're up against it, we don't have time for that kind of candy-mouthed hairsplitting now!" Zane protested, though Starhawk saw his glance shift. "We're all friends, we've all drunk out of the same bottle and puked in the same ditch . . ."

"That doesn't make you commander of this troop," Ari said quietly. He didn't rise from the staghorn chair, but Starhawk wouldn't have wanted him to be watching her that way.

"Wolf . . ." Zane turned to Sun Wolf again, and met only a stony yellow gaze.

*"And it doesn't make him commander,"* Ari gritted, the harshness of his voice dragging Zane's attention back to him as if Ari had taken him by the hair. "He gave it up and walked away from it. It's mine, now, and I'll tear the face off any man who tries to take it from me. All right?" His brown eyes were hard, drilling into Zane's. *"All right?"*

"Yeah, yeah, all right," the lieutenant agreed, but there was an ugly flare to his cupid-bow lips. Starhawk saw him sip in his breath to make another remark—at a guess, she thought, something along the lines of *Pardon me for letting my humble shadow fall across your path, your Majesty,* but wisdom or caution—rare indeed for Zane—intervened, and he turned and strode from the tent, every line of his back and the swirl of his crimson cloak insolent, as if he had spat upon the threshold.

"Aaah, hell, Hawk, I wasn't trying to undermine his goddam authority!" Zane took a long pull on his tankard—White Death containing, by the smell of it, far less water than her own. Evidently the beer had blown up several days ago as well. "I trained with him, dammit! I've fought beside him. I've saved his goddam life, if you want to get technical about it! And then to have him come off with this 'It's my troop so don't ask questions . . .' '' He made a gesture of impatience and disgust, with only a little stiffness, a little mistiming, giving away that it had been calculated and rehearsed.

But then, thought the Hawk, she had never quite figured out how much of Zane's speech and behavior was ever spontaneous.

She had tracked him down in Bron's tavern, whose dozen or so lamps shining through the stained calico linings of its canvas walls turned it, from the outside, into a dim ruby box. Inside, the air was clouded with smoke, the ground underfoot, the benches, the few crude tables, and the plank bar wet, the reek of the unwashed bodies and unwashed clothing of the hundred or so men and women packed shoulder-to-steaming-shoulder unbelievable. Fastidious herself, Starhawk had long grown used to the stench of soldiers on campaign, but this surpassed most of her previous experience.

It was also noisy, and there was a quality to the sound, a belligerent edge, that made her hackles lift and caused her to be uneasily conscious of how far she sat from the door. Usually Bron opened out the sides of the tent, the tables spilling over into the outside under an assortment of makeshift marquees and awnings. Crowded together like this, Starhawk felt again her nervous loathing of crowds, the irrational desire to find the nearest sword and start hacking, and guessed she wasn't the only one in the room prey to those sentiments. In the overraucous voices of the soldiers, the shrill, petulant whines of the whores, she sensed the pulse of helplessness and frustrated rage that only looked for an outlet into armed violence. At the cardtables nearby she glimpsed some of her friends—Dogbreath, Firecat, Battlesow, the Goddess, Hog with the notorious Helmpiddle panting happily at his feet. Nobody seemed to be winning much, but they were all taking it worse than usual. Even Bron, pouring gin at the plank bar, seemed sullen and nervous. As Sun Wolf had warned her, the bard—gap-toothed, unshaven, and clearly drunk already—was comprehensively awful.

"Come on, Zane," she said placatingly, "you know you can't decide things by committee in battle."

"We're not in a goddam battle."

"No." Starhawk turned the wooden cup in her hands. It hadn't been washed. Bron, like everyone else, must be reaching the stage of weariness where nothing mattered very much. "But we're in worse danger than any battle I've ever seen. If that river rises much more we're going to be wading."

"That's just what I'm saying!" he protested angrily, and refilled his cup from the leather pitcher he'd brought over from the bar. "We can take that fort! Hell, it's only a bunch of shepherds, some Mother-worshiping farmers and a two-bit thane . . ."

"Who'll be fighting for their lives, on territory they know," she pointed out. "In the pouring-down rain."

"Rot the rain! We can still take it! Dammit, Hawk, is Ari's damn chickenheartedness catching? You're the Wolf's main jig these days—can't you talk him into lending us a hand with it?"

"Probably not." The rest of the remark she let pass, having learned long ago that taking issue with Zane's attitudes would only lead to arguments as time-consuming as they were pointless.

He made a face. Across the room, the bard had mercifully finished—Penpusher had evidently bought him several drinks as payment for doing so—and was now helping Bron move benches back and toss down extra bits of timber and canvas on the soggy ground. Starhawk saw a woman coming forward, a dancer, shedding back the rain-flecked sheet of oiled black silk that had protected her crimson dress and the raven masses of her hair from the damp. After a quick glance at the mirror she wore at her belt the woman stooped a little, and with a gesture incredibly intimate, incredibly graceful, raised one foot to take off her shoes. From the poker game Dogbreath yelled, "You need help with that, Opium?"

"Not from you, Puppylove," she smiled sweetly, the gold bells of her earrings clinking as she straightened. "You give 'em back all sticky."

Penpusher tuned a mandolin, which also seemed to have been affected by the curse, and the woman Opium stretched like a cat, as if settling bone, muscle, and flesh into easiness. She began to dance.

"Yeah," Zane said bitterly, but he wasn't looking at Starhawk now; his eyes were following the woman in red. "He managed not to be there when we went into Vorsal, didn't he?" A sourness tightened his expression, different from his pets and pouts and rages of former days. The hot light in his eyes as he watched the dancer was like fever. "What the hell's got into him these days, Hawk? He's not the man he was."

"No," she replied, quite calmly, knowing that in one sense the statement was absolutely factual, though not the sense in which Zane spoke. "And he wasn't there at Vorsal because he was taking care of me."

That broke into his hostile silence. He glanced back at her, with a look of comical apology, and for a moment he was the man she had known. "See the Amazing Foot Swallower in Action." He grinned and patted her hand. "But still, he could have . . . I don't know. Two years ago he'd have figured out some way to save you *and* be there for us."

Starhawk said nothing. She wasn't about to argue over events during which she'd been unconscious, but she was familiar enough with Zane's view of the world to know that the man habitually spoke without facts or evidence, only from his wishes, and his instinctive knowledge of what would sting. *Ten* years ago Sun Wolf *might* have tried to do two things of the sort in too short a time, but she was willing to bet that one, or perhaps both, would have failed.

Instead she said, "You made it through Vorsal, didn't you?"

He made a dismissive sputter, his gaze locked on the dancer again, his lips half-parted under the golden mustache which, like many of Sun Wolf's inner circle, he had grown in imitation of his Chief. He wasn't the only one staring as if he'd never seen a bosom in his life, either. The dancer was good, moving easily within herself, sensual rather than lewd as she flirted with her gold-embroidered veil. Across the room even Curly Bear, a notorious fancier of boys, was watching; the two or three bravos guarding the dry little man Starhawk guessed must be this year's camp drug dealer, Sugarman, were frankly admiring, and even Sugarman himself had quit counting his money and his little paper screws of powder. Beside her, the Hawk could hear Zane's breathing quicken and sensed anger as well as the sexual tension rising from him, almost as visible as the faint curl of steam that drifted from his red cloak and brass-studded daffodil sleeves as the heat of the room dried them.

When the woman finished and gathered the copper and silver bits thrown to her, Zane rose, pushing his way through the crowd toward the doorway, with scarcely a good-by to the Hawk, who remained, moodily turning her barely touched cup in her hands, thinking about that handsome and arrogant young man.

She'd known him for three years, fought training matches against him, her skills sharpened out of desperate necessity because he was one of those men who felt his manhood threatened by a woman bearing arms. Off the training floor, he was an amiable companion, generous in buying drinks and scrupulous in his treatment of her, though she had never decided whether this was from genuine respect, fear, or some angle in a game of his own. Once when they were both very drunk he'd asked her to join him in bed, something she hadn't the slightest desire to do; she'd laughed it off and the matter had passed. An excellent fighter, he'd risen fast to squad-leader and she'd guessed he'd take her place as lieutenant when Ari took over the troop.

But she'd never quite trusted him.

Across the room, furious voices rose. Her head came up sharply at the sound. A clumsy-looking, pasty-faced man whom she didn't recognize—one of Krayth's old troop?—was waving a helmet under Hog's nose and yelling. A moment later he drew a knife and reached down to where Helmpiddle lurked guiltily behind his master's legs. This proved to be a mistake. Hog shoved him back, rising to his full six-foot-three of burly black fur . . .

Starhawk got to her feet and began to slip through the crowds for the door.

She didn't make it. There was a bellowed oath in the crowd behind her, the sound of boards breaking, and a whore's scream. Then, like milk too long on the fire, the whole room suddenly erupted into a boiling froth of violence.

Starhawk swore, ducked a bench one of the dice players swung at Dogbreath's head, and sprang back to avoid a locked pair of combatants who came tumbling over the top of the crowd at her like mating cats rolling off a roof. A thrown tankard thwacked her between the shoulder blades, the hard-boiled leather bouncing harmlessly off her sheepskin doublet but dousing her in a rain of White Death; Dogbreath's erstwhile assailant nearly fell on top of her, with Firecat locked onto his back, all her jeweled bracelets flashing, screaming oaths and pounding his head with her doubled fists. Up near the bar, the bard had begun to sing again, a smile of inebriated delight on his gap-toothed mouth, off-key voice skirling into a song of battle while he thumped a foot on Opium's makeshift dance floor half a measure out of time.

The noise was incredible. Someone slugged at her, a punch she slipped more from instinct than from thought and returned as hard as she could with a knee in her unknown assailant's groin. The man doubled up with a grunt. His buddy—such men always had buddies—took a swing at her with an incoherent shout, and she smashed his fist aside and elbowed him, hooked his foot, and dumped him down on top of his friend with an efficiency born of a desire to get out of the situation *fast*. Then she dived for the door, only to be blocked by a struggling mass of warriors—one or two women, but mostly men, many of them soaking wet from the outside, who had come on the run, drawn by the noise of the fracas.

She got a peripheral glimpse of three of the camp followers crowding up behind the minimal protection of the up-tipped bar; of Bron grabbing the lamps as Penpusher and a woman named Nails, who was easily as big as he, locked in mortal combat, slammed into the tent pole, making the whole structure shudder; of Sugarman backed into a corner while his hired thugs struggled with what Starhawk could only assume were dissatisfied customers, stuffing his moneybags and little packets of dreamsugar into the front of his robe. *Rot this*, she thought, and flicked from her boot one of the knives she kept there in defiance of Bron's primary rule about weapons check. *The place'll be in flames in two minutes, and I for one don't want to stay for the barbecue.*

She cut a neat slit in the calico lining of the wall nearest her, sliced the canvas underneath, and slipped out just as another jarring wallop to one of the tent poles dumped several gallons of collected rainwater down onto her head.

*At least it washed off the gin.* Her boots squishing in the mud, she picked her way over tent ropes and around shelters, the rain pouring over her like a river. There was, of course, no question of going back for her cloak. On her way through the tight-packed maze she passed Helmpiddle, the cause of it all, sniffing interestedly at someone's armor, propped up to air in the shelter of a marquee. It was not, she suspected, going to be anyone's night.

Nor was it. Edging sidelong between two pavilions and ducking yet another guy rope, she heard a woman's voice raised in anger and a man's vicious whisper, which she recognized as Zane's. She hesitated, aware that it was none of her business. Between the tents, she could see what might be two figures struggling in the shelter of someone's dilapidated marquee. The night was pitch black, but a sliver of lamplight from a near-by tent caught the streaming sparkle of the rain, the glint of the woman's jeweled plastron, and the gold of Zane's long, curly hair. Above the drumming roar of water of tent hides, she caught his voice. "You're damn choosy for a slave whore . . ."

Then the sound of ripping cloth, and the woman's cry.

Starhawk had gone two strides in that direction when a voice from within the tent protested, "Sir!" The flap opened to reveal the ragged silhouette of one of the camp slaves. Zane's head whipped around, and the woman Opium took her chance, wrenching free one hand from his slackened grip and elbowing him with all her strength in the face. Zane yelled, taken off guard; Opium kicked him viciously in the side of the kneecap and took to her heels like a gazelle, leaving her black silk cloak lying in the puddles at Zane's feet. With an oath, the golden man whirled on the slave who had distracted him, seized him by the back of the neck and kicked him, hard and deliberately, first in the groin, then, when he doubled over with a sobbing cry, in the ribs, and proceeded to administer one of the most vicious and deliberate beatings Starhawk had ever seen.

She watched from the rope-webbed shadows, knowing it was none of her business, until it became obvious to her that Zane wasn't going to stop. Then she ducked the rope and walked forward into the relative open, her boots sloshing in the mud.

"Come on, Zane, don't be a bigger yammerhead than

you are." Weapons being forbidden at Bron's, she'd left her sword back at Ari's, but stood ready, nevertheless, to go for any of her knives. The look on Zane's face when he turned to her was one of berserk rage, and, for a moment, she thought that she would, in fact, have to kill this man.

He mouthed "You . . ." at her, then stopped, half-crouched like a beast. He was as tall as she and much heavier, but in the camp no one had ever gone after Star-hawk without careful thought. She stood on the edge of the lamplight, curtained in the rain, wet streaming down the cropped sparkle of her shorn hair and darkening the sheepskin of her doublet, her gray eyes impersonal and lethal as plague. She seldom fought for the pleasure of it, but she was known through the camp as a quick, vicious, and absolutely efficient killer who would not back off.

Zane screamed in a voice hardly his own, "You bitches all stick together!" After one final, brutal kick to his victim's ribs, he turned and stormed into the tent.

Starhawk did a certain amount of thinking about Zane as she lugged the half-unconscious slave to the medic's tent.

Butcher greeted their advent with a stream of profanity, beginning with, "Not another one!" and ending with suggestions which, as an anatomist, she should have known were impracticable without careful limbering up.

"My heart bleeds for you," Starhawk remarked calmly, looking around her at the tent—leaky, smoke-filled, and crowded already with the still-bellicose casualties of the riot at Bron's. She deduced immediately that she had not been the only one to disregard Bron's weapons policy.

"Well, put a towel around it and keep it to yourself," Butcher retorted, tying a bandage around Penpusher's arm and shoving him unceremoniously out the door. Like a cook skinning a rabbit she ripped the ragged shirt from the back of Zane's slave, and swore again at the sight of the suppurating mess of old bruises, abrasions, and whip marks of at least four recent beatings.

"If it isn't half the women in the camp down with the clap, or pregnant and miscarrying, it's broken noses and broken heads from the men fighting over the rest of 'em," she muttered, gently feeling for broken ribs. She glanced up at Starhawk with sharp blue eyes. "*And* women—Firecat broke that bruiser Nails' nose over some little tart last week. But it isn't only that. The troops fight all the time, but usually it doesn't go beyond fists and maybe a chair. Now it's serious, in hate or rage. We've had more cuttings, more killings—we've lost a dozen men since the siege ended, and four more to accidents, stupid things like not bracing a wagon's wheels before you go in to repair the axle, or not checking the girths on a saddle. And the cuts aren't healing properly. I've never seen anything like it."

She turned the slave over gently and dried his face. His eyes were closed under a soaked tangle of black hair thickly streaked with gray, his forehead corrugated with pain. By the black ring of bruises under the steel slave collar, the chain had been used repeatedly to choke him.

"If there is a curse," Butcher added quietly as she worked, "you'd better keep your wits about you, Hawk, and clear off the first time you get a headache."

"Clear off where? The Khivas is up behind us. There's no going back." She hooked her hands in her sword belt and looked down at the man on the bed. Tears of exhaustion and wretchedness crawled slowly down either side of the delicate aquiline nose, and Starhawk thought she had seldom seem such abject misery on a human face. "Will he be all right?"

"No," Butcher retorted, dousing a rag with White Death to mop at the pulpy abrasions on his arms. "Not till Zane gets that woman to haul his ashes for him or somebody manages to kill him. He had two slaves out of the loot from Vorsal, you know. Most of us did. The other one, an old woman—half-starved by the look of her, like most of 'em—died already. And she wasn't the only slave to have been killed in a rage in this camp." She cocked an eye up at Starhawk. "It's crossed my mind to wonder if the mage who put the curse on us at Vorsal is doing this out of revenge. Maybe he—or she—is still here in the camp as a slave, helpless to get out, maybe, but not helpless to take what vengeance she can."

"Interesting that you should say so."

Butcher had turned away to fetch a dressing, so the soft, rasping voice from the entryway did not reach her.

Nor, thought the Hawk, identifying the bare-wire brokenness of it before she turned her head, was it intended to. Glancing back she saw that Sun Wolf had entered the hospital tent, silent as a tomcat, and stood leaning one shoulder against the tent pole behind her, looking down at the man on the bed. The Wolf had clearly been to Bron's. One cheekbone was cut, and his face and his chest, where it showed through his ripped shirt, bore the marks of fingernails, teeth, and of various makeshift weapons. His eye patch, hair, mustache, and clothes were stained all over with mud and blood and gin. "I was beginning to wonder myself whether he was killed after all, or whether we'd find him here."

"Who?" asked Starhawk, puzzled.

Sun Wolf nodded down to the man on the cot. "Moggin," he said.

# CHAPTER

## —— 11 ——

"I'M NOT A WIZARD," MOGGIN WHISPERED WRETCH-edly. "I swear I'm not." But he didn't sound as if he expected to be believed.

His hands, long and delicate where they weren't blistered raw and swollen with unaccustomed work, shook as he pressed them over his mouth, as if to hide its unsteadiness. For a long time he didn't look up, the filthy curtain of his hair hiding gray-green eyes sunken with fatigue. Ari's tent, to which they'd brought him, was quiet, save for the drumming of the rain and its steady, irritating drip in the puddles beneath the leaks. Around them, the camp had calmed down. The mercs grouped around the chair—Starhawk, Dogbreath, Ari—with their scratched faces and flinty gaze looked as savage a bunch of killers as could be found from the northern wastes to the jungles of the south, but when Moggin raised his head and looked at them, the Wolf saw no terror in his eyes, only numbed exhaustion and misery.

More composedly, Moggin went on, "I realize that's a charge it's almost impossible to disprove, but it really isn't true. Drosis left me his books, and some of his medical things, when he died a few years ago, that's all. All I can say in my own defense is that if I'd had power—

178

*any* power—I'd have used it to save my daughter. The—
the King of Kwest Mralwe . . .''

"We know about the King of Kwest Mralwe,'' Sun
Wolf said, as the scholar's voice faltered suddenly. "I
figured you were lying out of fear.''

The sea-colored eyes snapped wide. "Fear of *what*?!
Anything the Church could do to me couldn't *possibly* be
as bad as . . . ''

"Fear of another wizard,'' the Wolf said, his scraped,
rumbling voice low. "A soul stealer. He tried to enslave
me while I worked one of my own spells. I'm not sure I
wouldn't have let a child of mine die rather than go
through that again, since it was good odds they'd kill her
anyway. And there was always the chance you might have
known something I didn't.''

The chain around Moggin's neck clinked faintly as he
looked up, a frown twitching between the dark brows. It
was as if, for the first time since the taking of the town,
he was emerging from a state of bludgeoned semiconsciousness. "You're the man who tried to kill me that
night, aren't you?'' he asked. "You're a mage yourself,
then?''

Sun Wolf nodded. After a moment Moggin seemed to
remember what he'd been doing when the trouble had
started, dropped his head to his hands again, and sighed,
defeated. "Oh, God.''

"And if you're not a mage,'' the Wolf went on, "you
want to explain those circles you were drawing on the
floor?''

"Do we need this?'' Ari said quietly. He glanced
across the slave's bowed head at the Wolf, his gray-brown
eyes cold and very tired. "It's not a question of whether
he is or isn't, but of how much we can afford to risk
letting him live. And with things as they are, Chief, we
can't.''

Moggin flinched a little, but didn't look up or speak.
Looking down at that bowed head, Sun Wolf guessed that
things couldn't get much worse for him, no matter what
was decided. He knew Ari was right. The troop stood on
the brink of disaster, and it was clear to him now that
the curse, whatever its cause, was far from spent.

But if this man was a wizard—if he wasn't the mage

whose dark shadow hand had tried to enslave him in its sticky nets of silver runes—he couldn't let him die.

And that, too, he saw reflected in Ari's eyes. It was one thing to refuse to help his men because Starhawk's life was in danger. His parting from Ari had not been mentioned between them when the young captain, rain streaming down his long black hair, had met him by the horse lines with a bear hug of genuine delight. In a way, both of them knew it hadn't really mattered.

This was another question entirely.

And he knew that whatever he said, Moggin was going to die.

The worst of it was that Ari was perfectly right. Trapped between the floods, the mutiny that he could feel through his skin brewing in the violence of the tavern and the horrifying plethora of possible misfortunes, they couldn't risk it. If he were still commander he wouldn't even be asking the question.

But he wasn't commander. He was a wizard unschooled, facing an enemy he knew was beyond him, and this man was a teacher.

If, that is, he wasn't the enemy himself.

Quietly, he turned back to Moggin. "What were you doing the night I came in to kill you, if you aren't a mage?"

The scholar sighed, and ran his hand over the lower part of his face again, aged by two days' growth of gray stubble and disfigured by a swollen lip under which a side tooth could be seen to be missing. In a low, beaten voice he said, "Trying to raise magic." He lifted his eyes to the Wolf's again, wry and hopeless but with a kind of ironic amusement at himself. "I knew it was stupid. Drosis had told me hundreds of times I hadn't the smallest glimmering of it and that all the spells in the world weren't going to work if I did them, but . . . I don't know. The spells were there, in his books. For weeks, I'd been working the weather-spells, trying to summon storms—anything to end the siege. I knew what was coming . . . or I thought that I knew. I'm not sure what I would have done if I'd realized then . . ."

He fell silent, staring down at his swollen hands. Sun Wolf knew what he himself would have done, had he known in advance that the woman he loved and children he cherished would die as Moggin's had. The scholar was, he guessed, his own age and, in those forty years, had lived in the contented comfort of his inherited riches. Without a doubt, he had never killed anyone and wouldn't know how to go about it painlessly.

After a time, Moggin sighed and pushed back his greasy hair. "Well, I had to try—with what success you could see, because of course it didn't rain a drop. And I must say I felt extremely foolish, standing there in the study in the middle of the night, muttering incantations with candles all around me—besides the fact that, if I was seen by anyone, it would cost me my life. Two or three people in town had already been lynched for witchcraft, and, of course, since I was Drosis' friend, there'd been talk about me for years. Rianna . . ." He broke off, his jaw and his blistered hands clenching tight. "My daughters used to be teased about it at school. But before the siege, it wasn't a serious matter."

"That wasn't weather-witching you were doing," the Wolf said softly.

"No." He shook his head. "It was—was a spell to raise power out of the bones of the earth, to add to a wizard's power in time of extreme need. In Drosis' books, it was surrounded by warnings, but by then I—I could see our defenses weren't going to last." He looked over at Ari. "It wasn't to turn against your men, you know, Captain. I—I don't think I could do that—even now I don't think I could. It was just to get my family to safety. In any case I doubt it would have worked . . ."

"It wouldn't have," the Wolf said. "Not if you weren't mageborn to start with."

Moggin made a rueful, broken sound that might have been a laugh. "Even if I had been, you scotched that pretty effectively by telling the Duke—I barely got the marks rubbed out before his men returned. I was going to try it again the following night . . ." He broke off suddenly, turning his face aside as it contorted again with grief, horror, and the effort not to weep. In bitter silence, he hugged himself, fighting not to remember the events of that last night with his family and their murders on the morrow.

Sun Wolf looked away, remembering the bodies on the terrace, and met Ari's stony gaze.

"If he's not mageborn he's no threat to you," he said quietly.

"And no use to you," Ari replied softly. "So you shouldn't mind, should you? Unless you've got a real good way of proving he isn't lying."

*Don't say it*, his eyes said, cold and hard as agate. Sun Wolf was silent, remembering the smothering heat of the King of Wenshar's dungeons, and his own desperate awareness of the utter impossibility of disproving such a charge. He looked down at the man he had once thought he'd feared and hated, stripped of shadow and mystery and revealed as a pathetic, broken creature, too ill-equipped by a wealthy upbringing to make even a decent slave. The desolation he had glimpsed in almost losing Starhawk and the horror of his own near-enslavement by the unknown wizard smote him with understanding and pity far beyond his own need of a potential teacher.

But he knew how far Ari could be pushed. Moreover, he knew that as a commander, Ari was right. *It isn't fair, dammit!* he thought, but he knew in his bones that the fact that he didn't think the man was lying didn't prove that he wasn't. For a moment he felt that he looked across a chasm of darkness, not at Ari, but at himself.

Ari signed to Dogbreath. Both of them drew their swords, and went to help Moggin to his feet.

For the first time, Starhawk spoke up. "Who was it you said tried to swim in the ford with a rope a day or two ago, to set up some kind of ferry?"

"Zane," said Ari, pausing with his hand on Moggin's shoulder to look back at her, a little startled by the *non sequitur*. "He's the strongest swimmer, the toughest . . ."

With casual grace, Starhawk stepped between them to Moggin, pushed him a quarter turn on the stool where he hunched, and pulled down his ragged and blood-stained smock, making him flinch where the dried blood stuck it to his back. "How old would you say some of those marks are?"

"Ten days," said Ari after a moment. "Two weeks."

"And Zane didn't drown?" She jerked the smock back up again, covering the stooped, bruise-mottled shoulders with surprising lightness of touch. "You've got the wrong man. And I'd also say—and since I'm stuck here in the same danger as you are, that makes it at least partly my business—that you probably ought to think twice about snuffing one of your sources of information about hexes and hoodoos and whatnot, if, as he says, mageborn or not, he at least read all those books.''

''Thank you,'' Moggin said weakly, as Sun Wolf helped him into one of the several makeshift camp beds jammed into Dogbreath's lopsided chaos of a tent. One or two of these were already occupied—by Penpusher, from the look of the ferocious riot of curls visible above one blanket, and Firecat, by the grimy leather armor and strings of mud-crusted jewels thrown over the foot of another. Dogbreath's random assortment of broken totems and holy relics was mostly packed away for travel, but a few dangling ribbons and a woman's white glove still remained pinned to the inside of the tent, a rotting jungle that would eventually be replaced as it decayed. Dogbreath himself found another cot and fell asleep immediately and fully clothed, still in the garish yellow surcoat he'd taken from the siege, one tippet sticking out from beneath the blankets like the leg of a squashed bug under a brick. Sun Wolf called a faint pin of bluish light into the air above his head as he sat on the end of the cot Dogbreath offhandedly offered to Moggin. It was typical of Dogbreath, Sun Wolf reflected, that he'd been equally willing to kill the man or sleep in the same tent with him after the affair was over. On the road, the men usually slept in hammocks, but a little consideration made him realize why *those* had been abandoned. There were just too many things that could go wrong under the influence of so thoroughgoing a hex.

''It was the Hawk's idea,'' Sun Wolf said, as the dim phosphorescence settled itself among the dangling garlic and rags, edging all things in its pallid blue glow. ''And anyhow, I owe you.'' From inside his doublet he produced the bronze trephine, holding it up to the light between blunt and clumsy fingers. The bronze seemed softly radiant to his touch, warmed by ancient spells of healing and life. ''I pinched this, some powders and gewgaws, and three of your friend's books before I left that night—''

''I would have let you out, you know.'' Moggin pushed his matted gray hair back from his forehead. ''I'm not

just saying that—I truly would have. I was terrified the
Duke would put you in the lockup in the town hall, where
you could give evidence against me, though I couldn't
imagine where you'd gotten your information. My one
thought was to hide the books, then 'accidentally' leave
the door open . . .''

Sun Wolf sniffed. ''And I thought you looked so
pleased because you had me in your power. But I remembered they said Drosis was a healer. That's the only reason the Hawk's alive today. So we both owe you.''

Moggin breathed a sound that might have been a laugh
and whispered, ''I'll remember to mention this to the
Elteraic philosophers the next time they contend there's
no God.''

Sun Wolf tucked the tiny drill away again, and folded
his massive arms. ''Did Drosis have a student?''

Moggin nodded, gathering about him the dirty silk
quilt Starhawk handed him. Though the tent was warm
with the frowst of body heat, he was shivering. He fin-
gered the chain on his neck in its ring of bruises as he
spoke. ''A girl named Kori, a laundress' daughter, I
think. That was nearly twenty years ago, when I first
knew him. She died in an accident—fell off the city walls.
He never took another.''

The Wolf and Starhawk exchanged glances. The Hawk
said, ''Altiokis, at a bet.''

''No odds.'' He turned back to Moggin. ''He ever
mention his master?''

''I'm sure he did, but I simply don't recall it.'' With
everything that had happened to him, Sun Wolf wasn't
surprised. What *did* surprise him slightly was that Moggin could be as coherent as he was, but then, even in the
face of an unexpected accusation of wizardry, he had
kept his head. ''I think most of the books originally belonged to him, but Drosis cut or inked his name out of
them so he wouldn't be traced. Drosis lived in fear of
Altiokis, far more than of the Church. I must have known
him for three years before I even realized he was truly a
wizard at all. He was a sort of cousin of ours—Myla's—
my wife's—and mine.'' His voice stumbled on the unthinking habit, when there was, in fact, no more ''ours,''
but he steadied himself, and went on. ''He was a physician. The local bishop was always suspicious of him, but

never could prove anything. I just thought it was gossip, myself, like that wretched woman Skinshab down by the Gatehouse who was supposed to be a witch.''

"Was she?''

He shook his head. ''I asked him that once. He said no. She was just a nasty-tempered old hag who hated children and was always telling them she'd put the Eye on them. I was surprised no one lynched her during the siege—surprised no one lynched her years ago, in fact. It was only a matter of time, I suppose . . .''

*One point for the King,* Sun Wolf thought ironically.

Thoughtfully, Starhawk said, ''You know, if she *was* a witch, she might very well be one of the camp slaves. The King's account of killing her didn't sound very efficient. She could have survived. Would you recognize her, Moggin?''

''Oh, yes. But I haven't seen her among the slaves . . .''

''If she was enough of a witch to put a hex this strong on the troop,'' Sun Wolf said, ''you wouldn't see her.''

''You mean—she could be here all the time, invisible?'' Moggin cast a nervous glance around the witchy, dripping darkness of the tent.

Starhawk propped one muddy boot on the end of the cot. ''Don't let *that* one get around.''

''Not invisible, no. If you were really looking for her, knew already what she looked like, yeah, you might be able to recognize her. But if not, you'd know you'd seen someone, but you'd have the impression you'd never seen her before, or that it really didn't matter. Your mind would just gloss on past her. That's how those things work.''

''Fascinating,'' Moggin said. ''I knew about nonvisibility from the books, you see, but it never explained *how* it worked.''

''This is getting better all the time.''

''That hoodoo doesn't need to be in the camp, you know. All he'd need to do is mark something . . .'' From his pocket Sun Wolf pulled the glass phial he'd taken from Moggin's cellar, three-quarters full of auligar powder. Uncorking it, he dipped his fingertips in, and rubbed the tiniest speck of the powder on his skin. Then he reached out and lightly brushed the nearest sagging tent pole.

He hadn't quite known what to expect; in the almost-darkness the sticky film of greenish ectoplasmic slime showed very clearly, gumming to his fingers as he brought them away. Disgusted, he wiped them on his breeches before he thought about it and they left a faint, gluey residue, like foxfire.

*That's fine,* he thought, annoyed with himself. *Let's wash our hands before we unlace our codpiece, shall we?* He looked around, and wiped them on a corner of Moggin's quilt, but the residue still clung, a ghostly skin of dirty light.

He was aware that both Starhawk and Moggin were staring at him, wearing the expressions of people trying to be polite while watching a lunatic converse with a tree.

"Can't you see it?"

Moggin shook his head, baffled. Starhawk said, "See what? You mean you've found the Eye already?"

"Not the Eye. But the hex itself shows in a kind of glow, like rotten wood. It's probably everywhere in the camp. Every time someone touches the hex mark—or marks, because I'm willing to bet there's more than one . . ."

"It isn't just by touch," Moggin put in diffidently. The two mercs looked at him, and faint color tinged the white cheeks under the grime and bruises. "Maybe it's incriminating myself to know what was in those books, but . . . I did read them. I read everything, you know, and my memory's always been good. The influence of the hex spreads from the marks, you see. Without the marks it would eventually be worn away by the friction of the life-energies of the people in the camp. But as long as the marks—and it's the usual practice to put a number of Eyes in the victim's house—are there, it keeps renewing itself."

"Sound like a case of the clap," muttered Starhawk.

"It is, as you so elegantly put it, very like a case of the clap. Or like lice, or roaches . . ." Sun Wolf had already seen that both Ari's and Dogbreath's tents—and probably every other tent in the tight-packed camp, wildly uncharacteristically for winter—were infested. "It has to be tracked to all its sources and stamped out."

"Well, we can use the auligar powder tomorrow and see what we can find," the Wolf said, shifting to another cot and pulling off his boots. The ground squelched nastily underfoot; outside, rain continued to thunder on the leaky, compacted tents. "If the river doesn't rise another two feet in the night and wash us out."

"Don't give God ideas," Starhawk cautioned, beginning to undo the buckles of her doublet. "What about Zane, by the way? He's going to want his slave back."

"Stuff Zane," the Wolf said. "We'll deal with that in the morning."

But in the morning Zane had organized a mutiny, and the camp was in armed revolt.

In the deeps of the night Sun Wolf heard the rain ease and a few hours later, still in the wet and freezing dark, he woke, wondering what had roused him. Starhawk, since her injury, had slept more heavily than formerly, but either that, too, was passing, or the atmosphere of nameless peril in the camp was more conducive to wakefulness than had been the soothing restfulness of a town house and servants. In any case, her soft, husky voice came out of the darkness. "The river's going down."

"Aces." He was already groping for his breeches.

Her breath was a drift of murk, even in the relative warmth of the tent. "The Mother only knows how much time we'll have. You roll Ari out. I'll wake the others and get packing."

In the black scag end of the night, the camp began to break. "It could begin to rise again any time," Ari said, as he and the Wolf stood on the yard-wide band of shoal pebbles beyond the first of the tight-packed shelters, pebbles which four hours ago had been under a foot of racing white froth. In the dark across the river, the striated cliffs could just be seen, thin tortuous bays, columns, and talus slopes flattened to a single darkness. Overhead, the late-riding moon made a muzzy smear on the clouds. The cold took away Sun Wolf's breath.

"Damn! It's at least a couple of hours till sunrise. The water could start up again by that time . . . Even with torches it's too dangerous to get a line across . . ."

"I can see." The Wolf squinted out over the water, not liking it much. Though falling, the river was going like a riptide, the rocks below the ford stabbing like broken teeth through a mad froth of black in the darkness.

"You start breaking down the wagons into ferries. Get a couple of the men here with a cable, some grease, and torches, and I'll take it across. I need a bath anyway."

"Your year up?"

Sun Wolf shoved him. "And double-check that damn cable!" he added, as Ari turned and began to pick his way back through the dense snarl of tents, pegs, and guy ropes. "This isn't the time to find out that hex was written on *it*!"

In the event, taking the cable across the river was less dangerous and exhausting than fording the Khivas on their way to the camp from Kwest Mralwe the day before yesterday. Even upriver the canyon of the Gore was shallower and wider-spread, and whatever storm had fed this latest flood in the chewed uplands to the west had evidently exhausted its fury. Moving from boulder to boulder, Sun Wolf was able to keep his head just above the water most of the time, though the undercurrent twice knocked him off his feet. He reached the far shore battered and freezing in his loincloth, eye patch, and coat of grease, made the cable fast and double-fast to the small stand of oaks and boulders clinging to the foot of a talus slope they frequently used when the river was high, and, holding to it, swam back with nothing worse than the conviction that he'd never be warm or dry again.

But there was no half-assembled ferry waiting for him on the pebbles, no piled stores, or hastily bundled tents—only an uneasy mob of men, milling about in the waning flicker of yellow torchlight, and the bass rumble of voices that spoke of trouble more loudly than the noise of the river grinding over its stones. Half a dozen of those who stood nearest the cable were armed. His mind registered this at the same moment he heard Zane's clear, cutting battle voice slice through the murky grumbling of the crowd.

"And I say to hell with trying to ford it! We've got clearing weather and a clean shot at the Gore Thane's fort upriver—*this* side of the river! That river could start rising again any minute! We've seen it go down a couple feet a dozen times since we been here, eating up the supplies that should have taken us north while *you* tried to make up your goddam mind! I say, why bet on what's going to happen once we cross the river—*if* we can get across—when we can hole up for the winter in a strong fort and make a living raiding the countryside?''

"We bet on it," Ari said, as Sun Wolf—shivering violently with his long hair water-slicked to his naked shoulders—pushed his way through the crowding backs of the men between him and the halo of the torches, "because we couldn't take that fort if it was a sunny day in April, and we'd never survive a winter with the countryside against us."

"So you think a bunch of bumpkin farmers can beat us—pansy boy?''

There was little room on the wet strand of rocks and puddles that was now the only clear ground around the camp, but it was jammed with mercs, mostly men, but a sprinkling of women under arms. Across the cleared space around Ari and Zane, the Wolf glimpsed Starhawk with Ari's supporters. She was in the plated metal jerkin of the King of Wenshar's guards, a chain coif over her cropped head and her sword in her hand. The mutineers stood in huddled knots, with the man Louth at their head—heavyset, sullen, his hairless eunuch's face like a floured potato. There were a lot of them: the men who'd left Krayth's troops; the free-lance mercs and bandits who'd joined the troop on its way north; and a generous dollop of members of the troop itself. Standing in the torchlight before them, Zane seemed to glow in his gilded armor, his parti-colored crimson breeches, and his gold-stamped boots, his sword already in his hand. Ari, his frayed shirt unlaced as he dropped his cloak, unarmed save for his sheathed knife, watched him with the eyes of a calculating stranger.

"Don't be a yammerhead, Zane."

"I'd be a yammerhead to . . ."

And Ari struck—neat, fast, gauging Zane's unshakable need to have the last word. He smashed the sword from Zane's hand with the back of his bandaged fist, elbowed him across the face at the same moment he swept his foot from under him, and dumped him to the wet cobble of pebbles like a fallen meteor of red and gold.

Zane swept his legs, knocking him backward and rolling for his sword, neat, catlike, and deadly. Ari was before him, kicking it out of the way; someone flung him a blade from the crowd. Zane came up off the ground to meet him, a knife glinting in his hand. Ari parried, twisted, and struck it aside, every move succinct and sure, as they had fought hundreds of times on the training floor under Sun Wolf's barked directions, like dancers who feel one another's minds, each knowing what the other will do.

Beside Sun Wolf, Dogbreath said cheerily, "Six bits on Ari."

"No odds," said the Wolf, and accepted from him a rather grubby plaid cloak, since he was still soaking wet and all but naked from the river. He was beyond noticing the cold, however. Though Ari might lack Dogbreath's lunatic savagery or Starhawk's cold killer instinct—there had been times when the Wolf had despaired of making the young man mean enough to be a true warrior—Sun Wolf knew him to be strong, coolheaded, and technically perfect. Having trained Zane, sparred with him, and led him in battle, he knew quite well that at heart, in a one-on-one fight, Zane was a coward.

The ground was uneven, sloping sharply and slippery with puddled water and mud. *Cod-proud fools,* the Wolf thought bitterly, *frittering away what could be only hours of low water!* But his instincts told him now that if he bellowed at them to stop, only Ari would obey. The troop was no longer his to command. Ari's foot slipped, and Zane ducked in, ripping the young captain's sword arm from shoulder to elbow—not a deep wound, but bloody; the crowd exploded with yells and oaths. The Wolf had a momentary, hideous vision of a general riot erupting, as had taken place at Bron's. But Ari rolled back as Zane pressed in on him with knife raised to kill and lashed at Zane's legs with precise timing. Zane staggered, slipping in precisely the same wet patch that had felled Ari, and Ari dove upward inside his reach, hurling the sword aside and twisting the knife from Zane's hand.

He flung the blade away into the crowd, caught Zane by the front of his armor, and threw him down into the fist-sized stones on his back.

Then, deliberately, Ari finished the beating with his fists, brutally, calmly, like an older boy trouncing a younger, and kicked him aside when done.

"Now get out," he said, his voice steady and quiet

despite the blood running down his arm. "You take the Gore Thane's fort yourself if you want it so bad."

Zane, half-unconscious, crouched a little at the sound, covering his face. His gilded armor had been half torn off him and his face was slimed with mud, snot, and blood—Ari's and his own, from a broken nose and a split lip beneath which two of his front teeth were missing. His bare arms were purpling where the stones had bruised them.

Ari turned to the others. "Hog, Bron, get your wagons down here in ten minutes. Somebody find that sniveling little pimp Sugarman and tell him we'll need his wagon, too. We're crossing as soon as it's light enough to see."

# CHAPTER

## —— 12 ——

*T*HERE WERE TIMES IN THE ENSUING THREE WEEKS that Starhawk wondered mildly why she, Sun Wolf, and the others had once been so exercised over minor matters like ballistas misfiring, siege towers collapsing, and tunnels flooding. Those, she realized now, were relatively minor matters compared to the unrelenting sleepless hell of the journey to Wrynde in winter.

Knee-deep in half-frozen bogs with cold rain running down her face, half-starved and half-nauseated from bad food, her chapped hands bleeding as she dragged with cracking muscles at the harnesses of the wagons that stuck in what two years ago had been firm ground, she had to admire the wizard capable of producing such an unbroken run of bad luck. Much of her time was spent mentally devising lingering deaths for the aforesaid wizard, but she had to admire him all the same.

Without Sun Wolf, she suspected, they would all have been dead before they crossed the Gore.

The mistake Ari had made in not killing Zane had become evident within the hour. The camp had split, rumor flashing around that Ari had won only because, as Louth had spat at her at some point in the ensuing chaos, "He had a Mother-worshiping hoodoo on his side." By

that time, even killing Zane wouldn't have stemmed the
mutiny, and Ari, sustained against shock and blood loss
by massive quantities of gin, had been unable to prevent
nearly three hundred men from breaking off with the in-
tention of storming the Gore Thane's fort while the
weather held good.

Ari had managed to keep most of the wagons, though
there'd been a fight about it. There had been fights about
everything: the division of the food; the chestful of Stratus-
weight silver coins that had been their final payment for the
rape of Vorsal; Hog's portable forge and, for that matter,
Hog himself, for good cooks were rare and armorers rarer;
Bron's still; Butcher and the medical tent; Sugarman the drug
merchant and his wares; oxen and mules, liquor and whetstones; and, most of all, the women.

By first light, when the broken-down wagons-cum-
ferries began their painful hauls across the river, it was
raining, thin gray rain that fell steadily in spite of everything Sun Wolf could do to delay the oncoming storm.
From where she sat on the money chest in the doorway
of Ari's tent, naked sword across her knees, Starhawk
could hear the croaking mutter of his broken voice from
the shadows within. He'd been meticulous in setting up
his defenses, as he had in the house in Kwest Mralwe;
still, she held herself ready to spring up and go to him
at the slightest faltering in that whispered chant. He had
said it was difficult to work weather against its own inclination in any case. Unable to put his whole spirit into
it, unable to release himself for fear of being trapped in
the strange trance state by the shadow hand, she doubted
he'd hold off the river's rise for more than a few hours.

*Which*, she thought, listening to the savage hubbub of
yet another argument in the insane mill of the camp,
*might not be enough.*

"Goddam it, I don't care what she wants! She's my
woman and she goes with me . . . !"

"You heretical bastard, you're taking all the good
swords . . ."

"We're gonna need those mules . . ."

Then Ari's voice, not loud but cutting as carbon steel,
slicing through the hysterical maelstrom as it could
through the noise of battle.

Two of the camp's three pimps, as well as Sugarman, had

elected to stay with Zane, but a number of their whores, both women and boys, were trying to join Ari; and, as if there weren't enough arguments already, assorted slaves and concubines of men on each side were trying to join the other. *More of the curse?* Starhawk thought, glancing at the cliffs where the canyon of the Gore narrowed upstream and where she thought she'd seen the brown, watching shadows of the Gore Thane's men.

Then Zane had come from the direction of the barges, dragging the dancer Opium by the hair.

He had hold of her wrists in one hand. She was struggling, half bent-over and unable to straighten from the pain of his grip; by the bruise on her face, he'd struck her already. His own face was so swollen and scabbed from his beating by Ari it was hard to tell whether she'd gotten him with her nails or not. She was sobbing "NO! NO!" Tears of fury were running down her cheeks. Penpusher and Dogbreath, hurrying past with a couple of mules on lead, checked their stride a moment, but then went on toward the ferries as fast as they could. Women, after all, do not pull wagons. Starhawk was starting to rise, sword in hand, when she felt Sun Wolf's bulk shadow the doorway at her back.

"Let her go, Zane."

Zane started to drag her in another direction. Starhawk easily headed him off. He swung back toward the Wolf, his face a mask of purpled, puffy rage. "The hell I will! You and your nancy-boy Ari aren't going to take *all* the skirts around here worth lifting . . ."

Men started at once to gather—Louth and a mutineer named Pinky, the Big Thurg, Goddess, Cat-Dirt, and another man whose affiliation she didn't remember . . . There was a mutter of assent. Sun Wolf stepped forward out of the tent.

"She's a free woman, Zane." His face had a drawn look to it in the faded frame of his lion-colored hair. Even in a few hours, fatigue-lines had printed themselves like chisel cuts in the corner of his single eye. "She's got the right to choose."

"Rot that and rot you!" Zane's voice was thick with rage and with sinuses swollen shut. "We need women, not just those scabby sluts you're leaving us with! We have a right to take them!"

Sun Wolf covered the distance between them with no evidence of hurry, arms at his sides, his bite-scarred, gold-furred hands empty. "Why?" he asked mildly. "You thinking you're not going to take that fort after all and have the women from it?"

Zane stepped back from him, twisting brutally at the glossy tangle of Opium's curls and keeping an effortless grip on both slim brown wrists. Blood and spit flecked from his broken teeth as he spoke. "We'll take it, all right. You let it be, Wolf." He moved to turn away, but Sun Wolf was before him, again stepping easily while Zane's movements were hampered by the woman he held.

"Zane," the Wolf said affably, though his eye glittered with dangerous fire, "if you had any brains, I'd suspect you were stalling until the river could rise so Ari would have no choice but to join you in that witless attack."

The blue eyes shifted, the puffed lips pulled back like an animal's.

"I'm not sure you're smart enough to think of something like that, but if you did, I'm telling you now it'd be a stupid trick to pull."

"Not as stupid as the trick you're pulling!" Shrillness skinned Zane's voice. "This is twice you've left us in the lurch, with all your big talk about magic! I have yet to see you charm warts, O Mighty Sorcerer! What's the matter, you want this bitch yourself, as a change from Ari?" He twisted her hair again, smiling just a little at her sobbing cry.

Ari had just come up, the Little Thurg and Battlesow at his heels; Starhawk saw the twitch of his hand toward his sword hilt, but too many of Zane's men were in the increasing mob around them. If Ari attacked this time it would not be single combat.

"What?" the Wolf said, with deadly geniality in his cracked voice. "Don't think you can take the fort yourselves? Think you need a little magic to help you out?"

"NO!" Zane spat instantly. "We can take anything, win anything, without any goddam hoodoos using magic for what they haven't got the juice to do like real men! You're the one who needs magic, old man, to make up for what you haven't got any more on your own! Go on, take your boy and whoever else you can get to follow you for old time's sake and go die in the wastelands! We'll send a couple of sutlers out to look for your bones in the spring! Go on, get out!'' He grinned crookedly through swollen lips. "Or you gonna do a little hocus-pocus on us before you leave, just to teach us a lesson?''

''Zane.'' Sun Wolf sighed patiently. ''You couldn't learn a lesson—you couldn't learn your own name if Helmpiddle wrote it on your back.''

Rage flared the blue eyes and Zane's hands went for his sword, exactly, Starhawk suspected, as the Wolf had intended. Released, Opium twisted and was gone into the crowd. Zane took a step after her, but Starhawk and the Goddess—who must have weighed one-eighty without armor—were suddenly blocking his way.

Later, loading the ferries in the slanting rain, Starhawk got a glimpse of Opium's striped silk dress under Gully the Bard's filthy green coat and hood, being loaded by Bron into the barge. Bron, a slender, unobtrusive man with prematurely gray hair, was nobody's idea of a knight errant, but, the Hawk supposed, damsels in distress had to take it where they could. She knew the tavern keeper well enough to know he wasn't going to exact payment for his protection in kind. *However much he might want to,* she added to herself, catching a glimpse of a slim brown leg.

She and Sun Wolf were among the last to cross, guarding the dwindling piles of supplies against the possibility of Zane changing his mind. The river was rising fast, white and vicious over the drowned black rocks as their barge was hauled across. Dun and blue, the twisted sandstone cliffs reared over them like the potholed scales of a monster's corpse, clouds mantling their broken sky line—water the color of wheat hulls churned and tore at their feet. Clinging to the gunwales and hearing the scrape of those rocks on the wood beneath her feet, Starhawk wondered abstractly if, after all this trouble, she was simply going to be drowned.

*That would be typical,* she thought dourly, glancing up at Sun Wolf's set face, drenched with spray and rain, and fought the childish impulse to cling to him instead of to the side of the boat. She wondered academically whether the curse would divide itself, or remain with one group or the other.

But if the curse had divided, its strength was undiminished; and if it had selected one group, it speedily became obvious which.

Flayed by bitter rain that was never quite cold enough to freeze the sticky yellow-gray mud that seemed to be everywhere in the low ground, lashed by the winds, if they climbed to the bony ridges from which all fertility had long since eroded away, the troop had slowed to a crawl. What had once been the main road from Gwenth to its northern capital at Wrynde had been in decay for years, but now only a rutted track remained, new gullies cutting it every mile or so in the drowning rains. Brambles and the broken-off spears of seedling pine filled these crevasses, tangling wheels and the feet of men and beasts or covering over gaps and potholes until it was too late to avoid them. Twice wolves and once bandits emerged from the dark knots of forest and thicket to attack the train, taking their toll in livestock, injuries, and sheer exhaustion. Mold and spoilage cut rations still further, even as a thousand delays, great and small, stretched what should have been ten days' journey into nearly a month, and what food there was, despite Hog's best efforts, could be termed edible only by comparison. No wonder, Starhawk thought, huddling by night over a smoky brazier of damp coals in Bron's tavern, people have been ready to kill each other after a summer of this. She was ready to garrote Gully, if he sang the Lay of Naxis and Salopina one more time.

Across the table from her, Dogbreath was dispiritedly laying out a hand of solitaire. Few people had the energy to play poker these days, even had anybody been able to win more than a few bits at it. During the siege, Bron had forbidden the game in his tavern as the cause of too many fights; but, looking around her at the weary men, muddy to the eyebrows and too exhausted even to avoid the rain dripping on them from the sagging tent roof, the Hawk doubted many of them had the spunk to fight these days.

*Probably just as well.*

A sharp riffle of voices broke into the numbed buzz of the general noise, and she saw men crowding in a jostling knot by the entrance, gesturing in anger and disgust. The noise level of the benches all around her was such that she couldn't hear what the problem was. She was almost afraid to guess.

A moment later, she saw Moggin detach himself from the press and edge his way cautiously toward her, a boiled-leather mug of skink-water—hot gin and tea—in either hand. A week or so ago, some of the men might have moved away in sullen distrust, but by now no one cared whether he'd been a wizard or a slave.

"Yo, Moggy," she greeted him in mercenary cant.

"And a pleasant yo to yourself, Warlady." He handed her the mug.

Moggin looked tired—worse, in some ways, than he had the night they'd taken him away from Zane. Without complaint, he did his share of the work in setting and striking Dogbreath's overcrowded tent, in loading mules, or levering wagons from slime holes; though he still wore the slave chain, none of the others in the tent—Dogbreath, Firecat, Penpusher, Sun Wolf, Starhawk—regarded him as other than a partner in the hellish business of getting out of the current mess alive. But looking at him now, Starhawk could see how badly the exertion was telling on him.

He was not, as they were, a trained warrior, inured to hardship. Beneath the baggy assortment of borrowed garments—a pair of Starhawk's spare breeches, Bron's second-best jerkin, and shirts taken by Butcher from the bodies of the dead—he was losing flesh; under his unfailing gentle courtesy, she sensed exhaustion and the strain of merely keeping on his feet and keeping up with the train from day to day.

She nodded toward the door. "Dare I ask?"

"The scouting party is back from the Buttonwillow settlement where Ari meant to restock . . ." Moggin broke off in a fit of coughing, deep and ropy and harsh, from the bottom of his lungs. Then he went on, "They found it burned out and deserted, evidently by bandits."

"Why am I not surprised?" Starhawk took a sip of the liquescent nastiness in the cup. At least it was warming, which the coals in the brazier nearby definitely were not. "I'm really *not* surprised," she added, without irony this time. "That settlement and its farms have been hanging on by their teeth and toenails for the last forty years. Ari tells me the land was exhausted, and I know for a fact they got raided about twice a year, once by us and once by bandits . . . But it *would* be now that the ax falls."

"The scouts said it appeared to have happened six weeks ago."

"That counts as 'now.' "

A few tables away, amid whoops of audience laughter, Gully was on his knees attempting to lick out the gin Curly Bear had poured into the hole of his mandolin. Though Starhawk had a good deal of sympathy for Curly Bear's feelings—she was ready to kill the little bard if he whined at her for a drink again—she sighed disgustedly, and called out, "Oh, come on, you want that thing to sound even worse than it does already?" She pitched a copper at Gully's feet. "Get yourself some gin and drink it *real* slow in that corner over there and don't make a sound." She'd planned to have a second round herself, but, she thought, what the hell? In any case the stuff was vile enough to engender a certain amount of pity for anyone who *had* to have it, as Gully did.

The bard bowed to her with a flourish, gin dripping from his mandolin. "Warlady, I shall commemorate your generosity with a ballad in your honor . . ."

With a shudder, she turned back to Moggin, while the Bear and his boyfriends fell on each other laughing and improvised on the theme of Gully's commemorative ballads. "I don't know whether that poor little sap being here is his bad luck or ours. For that matter . . ." She paused while Moggin coughed again and sipped gingerly at his drink. ". . . *could* the hoodoo be someone in the camp? Not one of the slaves from Vorsal, but someone who's been here all along? Someone who came in with last summer's campaign, maybe . . ."

"Nix." Dogbreath looked up from his solitaire with bright, demented eyes. "First week under the walls, I won fifty bits strat off Zane at poker. Now, you know what? I've been dealing poker hands and shooting dice against myself for two weeks, and have gotten zipperoonie, zero—hell, the only way I've been able to win at solitaire is to cheat."

"Which seems to indicate," Moggin said thoughtfully, "that what's operating is completely automatic. If the curse were placed on the troop for vengeance, as I suspect it was, there would be no need for the wizard to follow and see it done."

"Vengeance for *what*?" demanded Dogbreath, genuinely indignant, and Starhawk kicked him under the table. "Wait a minute, it isn't *us* who start the wars. That's like putting a knife on trial for murder." And, when Starhawk raised one dark brow ironically: "Or a knife on trial for being a knife."

"You have a point," Moggin agreed, evidently willing to argue the matter on philosophical grounds. "But just because a man—or woman—is a wizard, doesn't mean he or she is a determinist philosopher, or even particularly rational. Men kill not only the messenger who brings them bad news, but also the horse he rode in on. It may not be fair, but it does relieve one's feelings."

"But by the same token," Starhawk said, "slapping a curse on the camp might do the job; but, if I was out for vengeance, I'd sure as hell want to relieve *my* feelings by coming along to spit on the last man as he died. The Chief's been all over this camp with that auligar of Drosis'. He says he's found the slime, the touch, of the hex everywhere, but not so much as a single Eye on any wagon, tent, box, or bale. And don't forget that someone tried to enslave him back in Vorsal and, when that didn't work, sent the *djerkas* to skrag him. Does that sound like straight vengeance?"

"It might," Moggin said quietly, "if it is vengeance against *him* that this other mage seeks. Where is he, by the way?"

"At Butcher's," the Hawk said, her voice suddenly very small, turning her face away to look into the dull glow of the brazier's coals.

Sun Wolf came out of the hospital tent moving slowly, stiffly, like an old man. And like an old man or like a University doctor or scholar, he wore a long robe thrown on over the red pig-leather of his doublet—a robe mostly in rags, but fur-lined and the warmest thing he could find—and it billowed heavily around him with the cold gusts that snatched at his hair as he stood, arms folded, staring out into the wet hell of darkness and pattering rain. Was he old? he wondered, with the detached disinterest he had frequently experienced in his times of greatest peril. He certainly felt old. Old, and very helpless.

He understood that working the weather in winter was a futile task at best. In putting forth all his strength to turn aside wind and rain, he never knew whether the storms that drenched them, the winds that scoured them, the cold that deepened nightly, were less cruel than they would otherwise have been. He could only repeat the spells, evening after evening when the train stopped after sometimes as little as five miles, and hope.

No rest, no time, not even time to quiz Moggin on the contents of Drosis' spell books beyond what was absolutely necessary for this endless, hated round of healing and weather-weaving. After two weeks, the drain on his overstretched powers was beginning to nauseate him, as if the power that he put out to save them was cut from his own flesh, drained from his veins.

He closed his right eye, feeling the leather patch twitch with the drawing-down of the long, curled shelf of his brow. Clouds moved swiftly in a low roof overhead, surging around the swell of the moor on all sides in the leaden dark. The heart-piercing wildness of the rain smell filled him, the rising cold must of earth, and the scents of wind and freedom and stone. They were all but buried in the stink of the camp, the stench of privies and sweat and, from the tent behind him, clinging to the folds of his patched mantle and the leather of his sleeves, the other stinks he hated—mortifying flesh in wounds that refused to heal, scorched herbs, draughts that had no effect on the nameless fevers that had begun to wander the camp like the Gray Women of fireside legend, carrying off whom they would.

Dimly he could hear Ari talking to Butcher in the deeps of the tent while she bandaged, once again, the still-open wound Zane had left on his arm. *Dammit, that arm should be smooth as a baby's bottom by this time!* He had worked healing spells over it daily, putting his powers into it as he had put them into the mule-wrangler's boy who had died last night of fever, the sutler's slave whose arm, severed in a freak accident with one of the wagons, had mortified in spite of all he could do, and the camp follower who had died tonight bearing a son who would have to be drowned, for it could not survive the journey yet ahead of them to Wrynde. He could feel the power draining out of him, knowing that tonight's brief rest would be no more sufficient to restore it than last night's had been, or the night before.

But having saved Starhawk, he could not turn his back on these others. Every time he touched Ari's arm to work the healing-magic that seemed to have no effect, he could feel the rot there, gangrene waiting like a black syrup just beneath the skin. The day he quit pouring his strength into those spells, the wound would turn like fruit in the tropic summer.

And everywhere he felt the hex. With his eyes closed, it was as if he could see the camp still in the darkness, glowing under the rain like putrid fish.

Feet plashed softly in the puddles. Too late, he smelled a familiar perfume. *Not now*, he thought, blindly, wearily. *God's grandmother, I'm too tired to deal with this now. Go away, damn you, woman . . .*

But in spite of his weariness his palms warmed with the memory of her flesh.

"You've been avoiding me."

In a train of two thousand people it hadn't been easy. Opening his eye, he saw her where the shadows lay blackest, her cloak belling like smoke in the fitful wind, and the edge of the tent's grimy light catching a flame echo of orange from her striped dress beneath. Rain whispered unnoticed around them like the murmur of wind in the coarse heather.

"Yeah," he said quietly. "I have."

She took a step nearer to him and he backed a step away, ducking behind a guy rope, not wanting to come near enough to her to touch her, for fear that he might. "Aren't you going to let me thank you for rescuing me from Zane?" From beneath her cloak her hands, small and brown like a little orange seller's, emerged to rest on the rope that stretched between them. Poor food and physical strain brought out the fragile wildness of her face, deepening his own need to protect and shield. It would be so easy to cup that delicate chin, touch the childish hollow beneath the cheekbone . . . The rain sprinkled her magnificent hair with diamonds in the frame of her hood; for a moment, his hands shaped the thought of warmed gold and the prickle of the jewels that decorated her bodice clasps.

He took a deep breath, and carefully steadied his hoarse voice. "I'd have rescued you if you were forty and ugly, Opium," he said. "I did that for you, not for me."

Though she did not move from where she stood, he sensed the lifted readiness of her muscles settle, as if she had drawn back from him a little, and something changed in the shadowy pools of her eyes. "Really?" She could have made the question a seduction, but she didn't. She sounded, if anything, a little taken aback, not truly able to believe that he had not taken her from Zane because he wanted her himself.

*Really?* To tell the truth, he *wasn't* sure he'd have given a damn if the woman Zane wanted to rape had weighed twice what he did, or had had a birthmark the size of a raspberry on her nose.

*Now that WOULD have gotten a laugh out of the men.*

He nodded. "Really," he said, knowing that it was true—or mostly true—now, though it probably hadn't been then. "I'm sorry if you thought different."

She looked away. Against the dark, he saw only the outline of her nose, small and tip-tilted and perfect, beyond the edge of her cloak hood, but anger and hurt were lambent in the draw of her breath. He felt tongue-tied and vaguely angry himself, at himself, at Starhawk, and at the fate that made him understand what it would cost him to seize this woman and rattle her stupid against the nearest tent. Angry that he knew the cost and couldn't plead ignorance later when faced with the consequences.

Then the hard line of her shoulders relaxed, the cloak's soft vibration like an echo of an inner defeat. "I'm sorry." She took a deep breath, and looked back at him, for a moment as clumsy, as uncertain as he. The soft redness of her mouth twisted, wry. "Mistress Wyse—our madam, back at the house in Kedwyr—used to say you got what you prayed for. All my life I've hoped there was some man in the world a woman could believe when he said, 'Nobody else.' Just my luck he said it to some other woman." And she turned to go.

"Opium . . ."

She stopped, turning back, like a bird on the edge of flight as the wind lifted back her cloak from the orange striped silk of her dress, and he saw the question in her eyes. Resolutely ignoring the part of his mind that screamed, *Take her fast, you lummox! What are you, gelded?* he said, "There's others around—if that's what you really want."

And she relaxed again and chuckled, warm and lazy and rueful. "If I'd ever been able to figure out what I really want," she said, "I wouldn't have so much trouble." Her smile was soft, and for the first time he saw her not as a beautiful woman he desired, but as a person like himself, skilled in love's arts but not in loving itself. "I'm sorry I was angry at you, that night back at the engineering park. It's just that . . ." She hesitated, trying to frame the source of her hurt without sounding conceited, without saying, *It was the first time someone had said no.*

"My fault. That was the first time I'd ever pushed anyone away. I'm new at this. I didn't do it very well."

The teasing light came back into her eyes as she found her footing with him again and her pride. "You'll improve with practice," she said and added with a teasing grin, "If that's what you really want." And turning, she gave him one swing of her hips and faded into the darkness.

He found himself hoping fervently that the curse would not choose to fall upon her next.

"Chief?" Part of his mind had already registered Ari's footsteps approaching the tent door at his back. He ducked back under the guy rope, turning his good eye as the young captain's head emerged through the flap. For a moment, seeing the look in Ari's eyes, Sun Wolf felt a throb of bitter resentment—at Ari, at the hex, at Opium, at his ancestors, and at the men and women dying in the tent and at whatever ill tidings Ari was obviously about to impart. In the greasy yellowish glare, his friend looked beaten, worn down by the redoubled weight of command and the ceaseless gnaw of the pain in his arm. He hadn't rolled back the frayed shirtsleeve or jacket over the dressings, which were weathered, despite a dozen washings, to the color of his flesh. In his paranoid moments, the Wolf sometimes suspected him of deliberately doing something to undo his efforts at healing his arm.

He forced his voice calm. "What is it?"

"Butcher wants you to have a look at that grut they brought in last night with a fever. He's broken out in boils. Butcher says it looks like plague."

A few hours before dawn, Starhawk woke, when Sun Wolf crawled frozen and shivering and depleted into her.

blankets in the pitchy darkness of the crowded tent. The cot was small, but, in this cold, that was an advantage. Even through the clothes they both still wore, his flesh felt icy.

"You should let them die, you know," she whispered, scarcely louder than the hoarse, nasal breathing all around them in the smelly dark. "You're putting out your strength, your magic, to save their lives, but when you've run out of strength, run out of magic, they're going to die anyway. We're making less than ten miles a day. It's a hell of a long way to Wrynde."

He whispered, "Shut up," and turned from her, shaking as if with ague himself. She was right, and she sensed that he knew it as well. The magic in him was sunk to an ember, the magic that had called her back to him from the shadowlands of death, the magic that was now the only thing that stood between the troop and disaster. Whoever had placed it, whyever and however it had been placed, the curse was eating it and him alive.

This was wizardry. This was what he'd traded the troop for, his friends for, and his former life for.

She had nothing to give him but her touch, feeling the coarse hair on his back through the threadbare linen shirt. He turned, suddenly and convulsively, and caught her in his arms, holding her desperately, his head buried in her breast.

They reached Wrynde eight days later; in those eight days, they lost nearly a hundred men to the plague. Sun Wolf—bludgeoned, aching, physically and emotionally drained—had long since ceased to speculate on who might have placed the curse upon the troop or what it was in the camp that was marked; it was enough to work the healing-magic, to weave the weather, to drag and lever straining wagon teams out of mudholes and to fill in as Ari's second-in-command on the day-to-day business of the train. When Butcher was taken with the plague five days out of Wrynde, he took over the running of the hospital as well, assisted by Big Nin, the madam who'd stayed with Ari's half of the troop, and by Moggin, whose copious readings in Drosis' medical books had given him at least a theoretical knowledge of what he was supposed to be doing.

As commander, he had understood that his life was forfeit for his followers when he led them into battle. This slow bleeding away of his strength, of his time, and of his spirit was something different. It was responsibility without glory, and he ceased even to hate it, knowing it only as something which had to be done and which only he, as a wizard, could do. He began to perceive that the curse would destroy them.

They reached Wrynde in the rain, a vast, crumbling corpse of a town whose scattered limbs of walls, churches, and villas had long since, like a leper's, dropped off from lack of circulation and sunk rotting back into the broken landscape of flint-colored stream cuts, granite, and marsh. On the high ground between the cold silver becks that now webbed the remains of the city stood the village, sturdily walled against bandits and offering protection to the farmers, small merchants, and mule breeders who were able to eke a living from what had once been the fertile heartland of the north. A small delegation of them met the train, led by Xanchus, mayor of the town and breeder of most of the troop's stock, to inform them that most of the population of the town had been laid low by a debilitating flux. By this time, Sun Wolf and Ari scarcely cared.

They camped in the ruins of an old convent outside Wrynde's walls and, the following day, labored the last ten miles to the old garrison-citadel which had once defended the town and its mines, perched like a sullen and crusted dragon on its heather-bristling hillside—the Camp. Home!

Sun Wolf crawled to the three-room wooden house that had been his for years, feeling like a very old dog dragging itself into a swamp to die. He slept like a dead man for over twelve hours. When he was wakened by shouts and cries and informed that the camp had caught fire, all he could do was sit on the brick steps of the terrace and laugh until he cried.

The damage wasn't severe, owing to the thoroughness with which everything had been soaked by the rain. But returning, sodden with exhaustion, to stir up the hearth fire in the iron-black hour between moonset and first light, he had a sense of *déjà vu*, of having come full circle from the bitter dawn in the house of the innkeeper's sister, on the slopes of the Dragon's Backbone, hundreds of miles to the south.

On the white sand of the hearth, raised within an open square of brick benches, the fire wickered softly. He could hear Starhawk's light tread on the wooden steps that led down into the overgrown garden where the bathhouse was. Cold as the night had been, the first thing she'd done after the flames in the stables and hospital were quenched had been to heat water for a bath. A moment later he heard the heavy cedar door close, and the creak of the oak floor as she crossed at a respectful distance behind him, in case he was asleep.

He turned his head to glance at her as she folded herself down neatly cross-legged on the hearth at his side.

"Here." She tossed him something silver, which landed with a bright, cold clatter on the bricks. "It's an ill wind that blows nobody good—I remember thinking that some time ago."

"What is it?" He looked down. A stratus-weight silver piece lay beside him.

"Dogbreath and I had a bet on about what would happen next. I bet on a fire."

"I always knew you were a coldhearted bitch."

Moggin's quiet tread murmured on the smooth planking from the direction of the tiny lean-to kitchen. "Thank your esteemed ancestors Dogbreath didn't win. I believe *his* money was on a blizzard." He almost fell onto the brick bench, gray-lipped with shock and exhaustion, and held out chapped and wasted hands to the warmth of the flames. "One can, at least, put out a fire."

"Good," grumbled Sun Wolf dourly. "We've got something to look forward to tomorrow."

In the rough jumble of furs and padded silk quilts from K'Chin that covered their pine-pole bed that night, he dreamed of Opium. He saw her as he'd seen her first, moving through the harlequin shadows of the burned siege tower with her hands full of the rustling bitter-sweetness of hellebore, the golden chain of slavery winking on her throat and her cloak parting to show the blood-crimson silk of the gown that had been her man's last present to her. He saw the Lady Prince like a fever-dream orchid in daffodil sarcenet and pearls, laughing as she held out her crystal vinaigrette to him, and behind her like a shadow, a sloe-eyed woman with long black hair, a woman they had said was a witch . . .

Then Starhawk woke him, and he returned to the hospital in the sodden dawn, to kneel in the wet drafts whistling through the canvas patches on the charred walls, digging the last vestiges of magic from the marrow of his bones to help the dying.

And hating it.

The rain poured down like a misdirected river, dripping steadily through the tenting that patched the roof. Sun Wolf's hands shook with weariness as he traced the runes of healing upon mortifying flesh, his mind reducing the constellations of power to gibberish with endless repetition. He wondered why he had ever thought becoming a wizard was anything he wanted to do, and wished that everyone in the hospital would die so he could go back to his house and sleep.

Near sunset, he stumbled out, starving, sick, and light-headed with fatigue. For a time, he hadn't even the energy to stumble down the plank steps to the morass of the camp's wide central square. He could only stand in the gloom of the sheltered colonnade that fronted the length of the hospital, staring numbly out into the damp grayness of the afternoon.

Across the square, Ari's long brick house, formerly the quarters of the garrison governor and adorned with a colonnade of broken and obscenely defaced caryatids, was dark. Raven Girl lay in the low-roofed cave of the hospital ward behind him, blistered lips muttering feverish words. To his left, the tall, square bulk of the Armory tower reared itself against the dove-colored sky, surrounded by its confusion of galleries, stone huts, lofts, and walls, with the great, slant-roofed training floor and Hog's forge half-seen at its rear. Under the faint whisper of misting rain, it looked half-ruinous, decaying, like the ruins that surrounded Wrynde, like the scattered stone villas, chapels, and old mine works that dotted the countryside near the ancient town, or like the world itself, coming to pieces under the pressure of cold and war, schism, and decay.

He leaned his head against a pillar. *Some wizard you are,* he thought bitterly. He had put forth all his strength, all his magic, to save Firecat's life as he had saved Starhawk's weeks ago, as he had been able to save others', and ten minutes ago Firecat had died under his hands. They were already dividing up her weapons, her armor, and the garish jewels she had worn into battle. He'd have to tell Starhawk, when she came off guard duty on the walls.

Whoever wanted them destroyed was going to succeed, in spite of all he could do.

Across the court Ari emerged from the shadows beneath the defaced carving of the lintel, looking worse than many of the patients Sun Wolf had just attended. His arm was still bandaged, the wound still unhealed. Penpusher followed him, cadaverous in his ruinous black suit, and beside him walked Xanchus the Mayor, a fussy, middle-aged man in a long green mantle trimmed with squirrel fur who, in spite of a poor harvest, hadn't managed to lose his paunch. Xanchus' voice floated fruitily in the bitter air: ". . . may have all the spears, Captain, but you'd be in sorry shape without our mules, our farms . . ." A stray snatch of wind carried the rest of his words away, but Sun Wolf knew that the next ones were going to be: ". . . our forges and our brew houses . . ." He'd heard the whole speech before, times without counting, when he had commanded the troop.

A flash of red caught his eye and a flash of gold. Turning his head he saw Opium crossing the court, the same skiff of wind tossing wide the darkness of her cloak to reveal the crimson silk. Walking beside her, Big Nin was wearing a gown of the identical daffodil sarcenet the Lady Prince had worn. The madam's dress was cut narrower, partly to show off the delicacy of her shape and partly because anything that color was literally worth its weight in gold. But, Sun Wolf, supposed, if one owned . . .

And his thought paused, like a rising bird pinned suddenly through with an arrow.

Shutters covered the latticed parchment in most of the windows of his house. In the queer brown dimness, the books of the Witches seemed to glow a little, as they sometimes did with the bluish psychic miasma of what they contained. From the little wash-leather bag beside them, Sun Wolf took the phial containing what little was left of the auligar powder. He dipped his fingertips in it and crossed to the hearth.

The coin Starhawk had flipped to him last night still lay on the warmed bricks. He picked it up and rubbed it gently, glad that the powder itself held magic; in his exhaustion, even the tiny effort of a simple spell was agony.

The Eye was written on the coin.

He fished in his jerkin pocket and found another stratus-weight silver piece, part of the Vorsal front money he'd picked up in one of those rare poker games in which more than a few coppers had changed hands. Faint and greenish, the mark glowed to life across the emblem of the Pierced Heart.

Standing like a statue beside the banked embers of the sleeping hearth, he felt the rage rise through him like the heat of brandy. *If it had been revenge,* he thought, in some calm corner of his heart, *I would understand. If it had been to keep from happening what did happen— Moggin's wife and daughters raped and murdered, the city sacked and burned—by my ancestors, I wouldn't hold it against them.*

But it wasn't. Part of him was so angry he was shaking, but in his heart lay the cold burn of icy fury, fury that kills calmly and does not feel. Very quietly he put on his ragged mantle again, pulled its hood up over his damp and straggly hair. From behind the door he took a pole arm, seven feet long and tipped with a spear blade and crescent guards, and stepped out once more into the rain.

He found what he sought very quickly. He'd always known the place was there. They all had: a grubby and sodden complex of pits, trenches, mine shafts and subsidences a few miles due north of Wrynde, among which the stone foundations of sheds and furnaces could still be traced. The rain had eased; clouds lay over the tops of the rolling purple-brown swells of the land like rancid milk. Cold bit Sun Wolf's face as he left his horse tied, picking his way afoot among the crumbled reefs of broken rock at the bottom of the pit-shaped depression to poke in the corners of what had once been sheds with the end of the pole arm, listening behind him, wary and half expecting at any moment the *djerkas* to make its appearance again.

He only found what he sought because he knew what to look for. Beside the round, sunken pit of what had been a brick-walled kiln was a pile of rock chips, with which he could gouge the brick and even some of the sandstone of the foundation walls. In what had been another shed, after a bit of searching, he found buried under years' worth of mold and filth a few whitish lumps of calcined substance which, smashed open with a lump of granite, left a faint, bitter-sweet taste on his dampened finger.

''Bastard,'' he whispered, more angry than he remembered ever being in his life. ''Stinking, codless, murdering bastard.''

Behind him, on the other side of the dell, his horse flung up its head with a warning shriek.

Sun Wolf jerked to his feet, pole arm ready, and flung himself with his back to the nearest wall. If he could flip the thing on its back, he thought grimly, it would buy him time to make it to his horse . . .

But the scuttering thing of metal and spikes that flashed forth in the gloom from the darkness of the half-collapsed mine entrance didn't come at him. It went for the horse.

Maddened, the beast flung its head up again, breaking the tether, wheeled on its hind legs and bolted. His back to the lichenous rubble of the old shed, the Wolf watched in horror as the *djerkas* whipped over the stones in pursuit, springing with greater and greater bounds until one final leap put it on the frenzied animal's rump, its hooked razor claws burying themselves in the shoulders. The horse screamed and fell, rolling, hooves threshing, but could not shake off the lead-colored metal shape. Unconcerned, the *djerkas* pulled its way almost leisurely along the convulsing body to rip the throat.

As blood fountained quickly out to splatter the colorless landscape with red, Sun Wolf understood what was going to happen—understood, and knew there wasn't a damn thing he could do. There was no time to make any kind of protective circle or rite. In any case his magic was spent, ground away to exhaustion by his endless battle against the weather, the plague, the curse. As the vicious, bounding thing of black metal wheeled and scurried toward him like a monstrous roach, he knew that he couldn't spare a second's concentration from it anyway. Hopeless, he braced the butt of the pole arm against the rock behind him, readying himself as he would for boar and knowing either way he was doomed.

It stopped inches short of the pike, slashed at him with twelve-inch crescents of bloodied steel. As he whipped the halberd blade to catch and pivot the claws, he glimpsed a darkness, a kind of smoke, emerging from the mine shaft which had hidden the *djerkas*. It snagged at his attention—a shadow hand floating in the twilight, reaching out to him . . .

Then that hand was in his mind, pouring like smoke through his one remaining eye, through his skull, through his nerves. As with an inner vision, he saw it flow into his body, the dark hand's skeletal fingers tracing silver runes as it went, runes that streamed like silver liquid down the screaming fibers of his nerves, freezing to them in tendrils of quicksilver ice. He was barely aware of the *djerkas* ripping the pike from his nerveless grip; in his numbed, dreaming horror, he could raise no hand against it, nor did he need to. His mind bellowing, twisting in despair against the absolute lassitude of his flesh, a detached part of him thought, *No. It won't be that easy.* The *djerkas* didn't move—slow and soft, the chuckle of triumph whispered all around him and grew.

He felt the dark hand flex, curling its fingers around his brain. The whisper of laughter swelled to the roll of summer thunder as the hand stretched and coiled, a black worm now tightening its evil strength like thick and living rope around the fibers of his spine, the silver runes becoming tendrils that lodged, stuck, and clung to bones, bowels, heart.

The *djerkas* stepped aside.

"So, wizardling," whispered a voice he knew, "now you are mine."

Slowly, numbly, in spite of the bonfire rage tearing him to pieces, he dropped to his knees. He fought to scream, to curse, to bellow at the gray form emerging from the dark of the mine shaft, walking toward him with calm deliberation, the silver darkness of runes and power like a halo around it, the shadow hand almost visible, binding him to his new master's mind and will.

# CHAPTER

## —— 13 ——

"Y OU SEEN THE CHIEF?" STARHAWK HAD TO YELL the question at Dogbreath, her hands cupped around her mouth to make herself heard over the screaming of the wind. The freezing storm had swept down from the northern hills a few hours after sunset, turning the rain to sleet, the mud underfoot to bitter slush. Looking down into the square from the lee of the gate tower, she could see shadows moving back and forth across the chinks of light below, where men still worked at repairing the hospital and the barns. It made her uneasy. True, there wasn't much likelihood of an attack under these conditions, but Dogbreath was the only other guard she'd met on her circuit of the wall walk's dozen stumpy towers.

"He was in the Armory earlier!" Dogbreath yelled back, the ends of his braids whipping crazily where they stuck out from beneath the several colored woolen scarves wrapped around his neck. "Went there when he came in around sunset. Gods know where he is now!"

She frowned, peering through the swirling dark at that blind and massive tower. Sun Wolf could, she supposed, be on the trail of some clue as to the hex's origins, for most of the campaign gear was now stored in the tangled complex of galleries and lofts. Or he could simply be seeking solitude.

For the last four years of her tenure in the troop, Starhawk herself had lived in one of the Armory lofts. That was after the last of her brief and uneasy love affairs had terminated with her partner's death in the siege of Laedden. Sleeping there, she'd been aware that men and women, warriors and camp hangers-on, had frequently gone to simply sit in one of those dim little rooms, among crowded shelves and racks, working alone on some project—new straps on a cuirass, sharpening a knife, or throwing a hand ax at a target in the long main gallery— for hours at a time in the quiet.

But the memory of what had happened in the pink stone house in Kwest Mralwe came back to her, and she felt uneasy at the thought of the Wolf being too long alone.

Thus, when she came off duty at midnight, she descended the slippery twist of battlement stair and worked her way around the square in the lee of the wall. Leaving the shelter of the crumbling old colonnade, she fought her way against the wind across open ground to the Armory. The only door into the square stone tower and its mazes was ten feet off the ground, low and narrow enough that big men like Penpusher and the Big Thurg had to snake in sideways, and reached by a narrow flight of rickety wooden stairs that shook and swayed under her with the blasts of the arctic gale.

Inside, the air was still and very cold. The moaning of the wind through the rafters of the lofts overhead was eerily reminiscent of the stone halls of the haunted city of Wenshar, when demons walked in the season of storms. Starhawk pushed the green leather hood back from her cropped hair, and raised the small bronze lantern she'd brought with her to shed stronger light. The Chief, she guessed, carried nothing of the kind. Once you would never have found him without flint and tinder or more commonly a little horn fire carrier filled with smoldering tinder and a couple of coals. He'd been slipping out of that habit as the senses of a wizard had grown in him.

Metallic glints answered the movement of her light— racks of swords, halberds, pole arms, and the locks of chests and bins. The Armory contained not only weapons and the campaign gear, but most of the fort's supplies of hardware: nails bought in the south, or salvaged with meticulous care from the beams of anything in the fort that was torn down; rusted chains and scrap that could be loaded into the ballistas; and vast coils of rope like somnolent snakes. In inner rooms, she knew hides were stacked—if they hadn't rotted, which, given their current run of luck, was more than likely. Near them were rivets, hammers, tongs, cutters, and buckles looted from every city they'd sacked and every merchant they'd robbed, bits of chain mail which Hog—whose forge nestled round on the west side—could patch in to repair larger hauberks and coifs. Elsewhere there were targets of wood and straw, quintains and striking bags, and all the leather and metal needed for their repair; pack frames, wheel rims, and vast, dark tangles of pulley and cable.

The muddied scuff of crusted tracks led through the small anteroom to a narrow inner door. Starhawk followed them down a half-dozen creaky plank steps to the great gallery, a long room curtained in shadow where the hacking-posts and targets loomed in shadow like deformed and mindless sentinels. The smell of mildew breathed upon her as she held the lantern high. "Chief?"

Movement in the darkness brought her heart to her throat. She saw a massive shape in the dark arch at the room's far end and the flash of one yellow eye. For an instant it was as if she had encountered a stranger lurking in these dark chambers which had but one exit. Her pulse froze, lurched, and slammed. But then she saw that it was, in fact, Sun Wolf, tawny hair hanging in damp strings over his craggy face, eye gleaming strangely beneath the curled grove of brow.

His voice was slow, its rhythm halting, almost stammering, as if against some strangling impediment in his throat.

"I'm here, Starhawk."

She made a move in his direction, but he threw his hand up and stepped back. "NO!" For a moment she thought he flinched. Then he pulled a dragging breath. "I just—need to be alone." He rubbed at his eye patch, and went on more easily, "I wanted to have another look

at some of the gear, that's all. I've been over every motherless inch of it with mercury, auligar, hyssop and fire,
and there isn't a mark on it I can find. I may be late.
Don't wait for me.''

''You want some company?'' Scared as she had momentarily been—and the uneasiness was already vanishing from her mind—she didn't like the idea of his being
here alone.

He shook his head again. ''Not just now.''

She hesitated. He was shivering, very slightly—she
could see the vibration in all the hanging rags of the robe
he wore over his doublet. True, the room was deadly
cold; his breath and hers made puffs of frail steam in the
amber lamp beams. But white gleamed all around the
topaz pupil of his eye; pain and tension there were all at
odds with the easiness of his voice. ''You be careful,
okay?'' she said cautiously, and turned away. As she did
so she faked dropping the lamp, and stumbled as she
grabbed for it, falling to one knee. Cursing, she bent to
pick it up and used the movement as a cover to slip a
metal-backed mirror from the purse at her belt, angling
it toward him as she rose.

But the reflection showed her only Sun Wolf, standing
in the black maw of the arch.

Troubled, she turned to face him again. More clearly
than before, she saw the pain in his eye, grief and horror
and a haunted look she had never seen. In spite of the
cold that made his breath smoke from his lips, sweat
stood out on his high forehead. She started to speak and
he shook his head impatiently, and waved her away.

''I'm fine, dammit.'' His hoarse voice grew curt. ''It's
just that . . . I'm fine.''

For a moment she wondered if he could be covering
something to keep her out of danger. That wasn't terribly
like him, but then, who could tell what he might have
discovered?

She decided to trust him and slowly walked back down
the length of the gallery, her boots creaking on the worn
boards and the echoes mingling with the groaning of the
wind overhead.

The hospital was quiet when she entered it. Men were
still working down at one end, mostly those camp slaves

who had survived the march north. They were stuffing rags around the patches and caulking them with clay, but the bulk of the work was done. It was warmer here. Braziers dotted the intense gloom with fitful domes of ochre light that fluttered now and again with the sneering drafts, and there were more water buckets around the walls than she'd ever seen. Ari was taking no chances. Down at one end of the room, Big Nin and two of her girls were scraping soiled straw out from under the worse-off patients and replacing it with more-or-less fresh. Earlier that evening, Dogbreath had broken the news to her about Firecat. She glanced over at the bed where she'd spent an hour earlier that day, sitting by her friend. Firecat hadn't known her. The younger woman's death was no real surprise to her—still, she felt a bitter pang to see the cot occupied by someone else. Though she hadn't seen the Cat for nearly a year before they'd met in the dry foothills of the Dragon's Backbone, for a while it had seemed that they'd never been apart.

Pushing back the hood from her hair, she walked with instinctive quiet between the aisles of stinking cots.

Halfway down, Ari was sitting on the edge of Raven Girl's bed, holding her hand and trying awkwardly to spoon some gruel between her pustuled lips. The dark-haired girl, seventeen and always skinny, was gaunt and wasted as an old woman now, her long hair cut off because of the hospital lice, her face, bereft of it, naked and tiny on the pillow. For a moment, Starhawk stood watching, while the girl dribbled the gruel away and Ari, with infinite patience, blotted up the mess with a rag and spooned up a little more.

She waited until he finished and had put the basin and spoon aside. He sat blindly staring at nothing for a time in the grimy mottling of the shadows. Then she asked softly, "How is she?"

He looked up, startled, and instinctively hid rag and spoon under a corner of the sheet. "Better, I think," he said. "I just came in to see how she's doing." He hadn't known she'd been watching him. "Old Moggy lanced the boils today. It seemed to help."

*It hadn't helped Firecat,* she thought resentfully, then let the thought go. It could have happened in battle, any of the last six summers. "Have the men turned in?"

His eyelids creased in annoyance. "Hawk, in case you weren't noticing, everybody's had their backsides run ragged . . ."

"I think there's something wrong."

An edge of exhausted anger flicked on his voice. "I think there's gonna be something wrong if I haul a full watch out of their sacks because you *think* . . ." He hesitated, then shook his head, rubbed his big hand over the black stubble of his face. "Like what?"

"I don't know. The Chief . . . He's shut up in the Armory—he knows something he's not telling, I think. Maybe he feels something on its way."

At the mention of Sun Wolf's name something changed indefinably in Ari's eyes. "When it gets close enough, I'm sure he'll tell us."

"He may want to keep us out of it." Then, seeing the stubborn dismissiveness in his face, she added, "Ari, don't be a cheesebrain. If we lose him Mother knows what'll happen, to you, to her . . ." She gestured to the sleeping girl on the bed. "To this whole troop. We haven't figured out what's behind this hex and I for one don't want to take chances."

"Fine." Ari jerked to his feet, shaking back his long hair. In the lamplight, his face was still smutted with soot from last night's disastrous fire, his chest, bared by the torn-out points of his faded shirt, blistered in places from the flames. "I'll tell that to the men when I haul them out of bed, shall I? Hawk, I haven't slept more than three hours in as many days and neither have they. You're getting as bad as he is with this business of looking out for each other, no matter what it costs everybody else."

Starhawk studied him for a moment in silence, angry and at the same time aware that they were both far too tired to be having this discussion. She, too, had only had a few hours of sleep between bathing and going back on guard duty. The burns on her own arms and neck smarted damnably beneath the sheepskin and iron of her doublet and the several shirts she had layered on underneath. Her eyeballs felt as if they'd been rolled in sand, her bones as if the marrow in them had all been sucked out, leaving only hollowed straws.

But the animal prickle of warning at her nape remained.

Ari sighed, his compact body relaxing a little. "All right," he said quietly. "I'll see who I can round up. I'll get another man on the main gate, and whoever else I can on the walls. But I'm gonna let them know they have you to thank for it tomorrow at breakfast."

"Suits me fine if we're all able to sit down and eat it," the Hawk returned, hearing under the weariness the anger go out of his tone.

He grinned under his singed mustache and made her a half salute, both of which she returned. She picked up her lantern beside the door, cursing herself mildly for the wolflike paranoia that would now force her to miss a night's sleep over something which might not exist.

And from the darkness of the colonnade, she saw Sun Wolf cross the court.

She saw him in only the dimmest possible way, for the night was pitch black, the torches that sometimes burned under shelter around the camp long ago put out and the raging sky invisible under a Götterdämmerung of cloud. But the brief stab of her lantern beam and the dim brownish light from the hospital door outlined the massive figure as it made its way from the Armory to the covered colonnade in front of Ari's house, leaning into the wind, headed toward the main gate. He was muffled in his fur-lined robe with a scarf around his face, but, from the first moment she had seen him, she had never mistaken any man's walk for his.

With the clarity of lightning it came to her what must have happened. He had had some sign from the other wizard, some portent, some challenge. He was going to meet him, and had gotten rid of her to keep her out of danger. He was going to meet him alone.

*You gaum-snatched blockhead, after a week fighting the plague you don't have the magic to light a candle!* Furious, Starhawk pulled her own hood up over her head and ran down the pillared terrace of the hospital to intercept him at the gate. The scene in the Armory returned to her. Of course he would have gone there to make his conjuration, some other dark spell from the Witches' books . . . He hadn't wanted her or Moggin to know. *Damn cod-proud pigheaded clodhopper . . .*

Wind buffeted the lantern from her hand as she left the sheltered colonnade. She cursed perfunctorily, whirled

around and half blinded by the sleety gusts. She struggled on, followed the hospital wall by touch toward the
thin slip of the gatehouse light. If the Wolf got out onto
the moors before she reached him, she'd never find him
until it was too late. *Wait for me, you brainless barbarian
oaf* . . .

She reached the Gatehouse just in time to see him slit
the guard's throat.

The man had obviously been totally unprepared. He'd
risen, leaving his weapons—sword, crossbow, and
throwing ax—on the bench with his cup of White Death
to greet with a grin the man whom they all still half
regarded as their Chief. Sun Wolf had grabbed his hair
with one hand and slashed his throat to the neckbone
with the dagger he'd held in the other; from the blackness
of the gateway shadows Starhawk could see, through the
burst of flying blood, the nacreous white of the spine.
The Wolf threw the spasming body down casually and
went to unbar the gate.

"Chief!" Starhawk yelled.

For the first confused instant she had the impossible,
irrational impression he was going out and wanted no
one to know. But when he turned, caught up the guard's
ax and flung it at her straight and hard, she knew. The
reflexes he'd trained into her were the only thing that
saved her—that, and her paranoid readiness. The ax
whizzed close enough to her chest to snag her metal
shoulder plates as it went clattering into the dark beyond
the squat arch of the inner gate. Then the sword was in
Sun Wolf's hand and he was coming for her, cold murder
in his eye.

Her body, her instincts, thought for her. She ducked
through the gate into the square behind her, the wind
ripping at her as she jerked her sword into her hand. But
he didn't come through the arch at her heels.

The next instant she heard the scrape of the great gate
bolt, and the echo of men's voices in the low barrel
vaults.

There was no time to stop and figure out what was
going on, and she didn't try. She raced back up the pitch
black of the colonnade, yelling Ari's name at the top of
her lungs, but the howl of the sleety wind tore the sound
from her lips and whirled it away into the darkness. Men

were running after her from the gatehouse, racing along the walls in all directions. And she saw then that Ari and his supporters, exhausted, ill, debilitated by plague and hunger and the most incredible chain of misfortunes ever strung together, stood not a snowball's chance in hell.

She smashed through the hospital doors a few scant minutes before the first of the attackers did, yelling for Ari, but he was already gone. At the same moment shouts began from the jumbled barracks quarters, the shrieks men might make when their throats were cut in their beds mingling with battle yells and screams. Footsteps pounded the terrace bricks behind her and she flung herself down in the nearest vacant bed, rolling the pestilent covers, the stained and gummy sheet, up over her head as half a dozen men slammed through the door.

Sun Wolf was with them, sword in hand and nothing in his eye. The guard's blood covered him, even his face—his eye stared through it, yellow within red, his teeth white as a beast's under the gore dripping from his mustache.

Beside him was Zane, crooked-nosed, gap-toothed, panting and grinning through an ice-covered golden beard, and Louth and Nails.

And with them was the gray-cloaked form of the drug dealer Sugarman, his fur-lined hood flung back and his face in its frame of wispy gray hair calm and prim and naggingly familiar.

She'd seen him before, in Bron's mess tent the night of the riot. And it wasn't, she realized now, the first time she'd seen him, either. She wondered why on earth she hadn't recognized him then as Renaeka Strata's treasurer Purcell.

Then, with an almost audible click, many things fell into place in her mind.

*Of course you wouldn't recognize him if he was a wizard, you dummy.*

*And of course no one in his right mind, using Zane as a tool, would do so without coming along to make sure he didn't go off on some witless scheme of his own.*

*Oh, Chief.*

Because it was obvious to her now, from the glazed, unseeing coldness of his berserker eye, that what he had feared had happened. The dark hand had seized him—Purcell's hand. He was its slave.

"Check the other room," Zane ordered briefly. Louth and Nails ran off between the beds, swords in their hands. From outside, over the howling of the wind, the yells of battle skreeled against the shriek of wind and sleet. Starhawk hoped Ari had managed to rouse most of his supporters in the few minutes between her speech with him and now. "What about them?" He jerked a hand casually at the figures in the beds.

Purcell shrugged. "They're helpless for the moment," he said in his crisp voice. He peered down at the deliriously tossing Big Thurg, his expression that of a buyer gauging an ox at market. "When we start the alumstone mines again, we're going to need slaves to work them—with the negotiations with the King-Council in secret, it'll be nearly a year until we'll have money to buy workers, let alone the power to protect ourselves. Later we can decide who's worth keeping."

*Alumstone?* she thought. *What the . . . ?*

She'd been debating about passing herself off as a plague victim—it would be disgusting, but, having had a milder form of the disease in her childhood, not particularly dangerous—but that decided her. As soon as Zane and his party left, Sun Wolf following docilely at the imperious snap of Purcell's fingers, she slipped silently from the bed, pried aside one of the makeshift canvas patches over the ward's walls, and, hugging the walls in the sightless chaos of wind and struggling forms, crept through the darkness behind the hospital toward the Armory, circled toward the training floor and Sun Wolf's house behind. In the swirled glare of cressets, she could see fighting on the Armory's rickety steps, Sun Wolf and Zane like gods of blood and gold hacking at the defenders.

There was nothing of any strategic importance at the training floor; when she reached it, the vast, barnlike building was silent. Only wind echoed between its high roof and the crisscrossing lattice of rafters that filled the tall spaces beneath.

There were no grapples there, but there were ropes—thin ones, for jumping over or ducking under or learning various forms of escape. Starhawk tied a dagger at one end to give it enough weight for a throw over the lowest beam. She had pulled off her boots, hood, breeches, and doublet, which were all soaking wet from the rain and sleet, in the porch, and now shoved them deep into the cedarwood chest from which she'd taken the rope. She might freeze, she thought grimly, but she wasn't about to be betrayed by water dripping down from her hiding place; she thanked the Mother she didn't have enough hair yet to worry about. The rope looped over the beam gave her purchase enough to walk herself up one of the four freestanding master pillars, weapons belts draped around her shirted form. Coiling the rope neatly, she hauled it up after her, and thought again, *Alumstone.*

Alum was the foundation of Kwest Mralwe's economic power and of Renaeka Strata's fabulous wealth. It was the monopoly the Lady Prince's mother had given her life to control and that any other member of the King-Council would give a lot of other people's lives—if they were cheap, like those of the citizens of Vorsal or the members of the troop—to break.

*So THAT'S what they used to mine at Wrynde!*

Like most of the men, she'd thought—when she'd thought about it at all—in terms of gold, silver, or gems, not in terms of economic advantage, of politics, or of trade. But she knew Sun Wolf did.

Up under the slates, it was warmer than she'd thought, and the rats kept their distance from her smell, though she could see them in the darkness under the other beams, glaring at her with hateful red eyes.

*Pox rot you lousy rodents,* she thought. *If I live through this I'm buying a cat.*

She lay stretched out on the two-foot beam, listening to the chaos outside.

It didn't last long, not nearly as long as the sacking of some cities she'd participated in. *Ari had a few minutes,* she told herself, with a kind of chilled desperation. *He has to have waked some of them. They had to have some kind of chance.*

But Zane, she knew, would never let Ari or his closest supporters survive, no matter how much Purcell wanted slaves for his new alum-digging enterprise.

She spent a good portion of her time on the beam reviewing every oath she had ever learned.

The Mother loved her children, Sister Kentannis used to say. But the Mother did not consider pain and death as things to be avoided and so, out of that love, she never spared her children those experiences. *Sun Wolf must have been under Purcell's power already in the Armory.* Her thoughts raced, sorting through possibilities. Could he be freed of the spell that held him? Or had it eaten out his brain, never to be restored?

She did not even think, *I will kill Purcell.* It was a thing which went without saying that, as far as she was concerned, Purcell and Zane were dead men.

It was to the training floor that they came, when the camp was taken.

Zane, bloodied to the elbows, wet and filthy, was grinning with such spiteful triumph that Starhawk guessed he had caught and raped Opium sometime during the fighting. Louth, Nails, and the other bandits and mutineers were ragged and dirty, blood in their hair and in their beards, those that had them. Purcell, though demure and quiet, had shed completely the air of frightened subservience under which he must for years have concealed his powers from Renaeka Strata and the other members of the King-Council. There was something ugly about that primness now, something cold and self-righteous and absolutely amoral, as if he could not conceive what was wrong with provoking a declaration of war in the Council in order to lure an inconveniently placed mercenary army into his trap. His slim body had every bit of Zane's air of pleased smugness, blood and mud saturating the hem of his warm robe where his gray cloak had not covered.

Sun Wolf walked at his heels. The rain had washed most of the blood off him and replaced it with mud and filth. He didn't seem to notice. In his grimed face, his one yellow eye burned cold and calm as an animal's, and the straps of his eye patch left white stripes on the dirty flesh. There was nothing mechanical about his stride, nothing of the brainless nuuwa or the shambling *gim*—the zombies of northern legend. He looked pretty much as he did after any siege, alert and deadly, like some big, restless animal ready to kill.

Only he was dirty, where he usually got himself clean as quickly as possible after a fight, and he did not look around him to see who and what was behind.

". . . killed along the walls above the gatehouse," Louth was saying, scratching his beardless chin. "Damned if I know who did that. We didn't, that's for sure. Cut to hell, like they'd been carved up with razors . . ."

*The djerkas*, thought the Hawk, even as Purcell said, "Don't worry about that. It scarcely matters, so long as they're dead. What about the others?"

"Got away," Zane snarled, and added several obscenities for good measure. "There was more of 'em than we'd thought, and they were awake, too. I thought you said they'd be asleep or sick or fagged out for sure . . ." The familiar whining tone of blame was back in his voice.

"I doubt they'll make us much trouble." The Councillor tucked slender hands, gloved exquisitely in goldbeaded purple, into the squirrel lining of his sleeves. "In this weather they won't last long. But their escape means that we'll have to take the village immediately, tomorrow morning, and not wait for night again. Are your men up to it?"

Zane grinned. "Granddad, for the kind of money you say we'll make once we get those diggings going, they're up to shoveling enough elephant dung to fill the Gniss River gorge."

"Good." Purcell rationed himself a wafer-thin smile. "Remember not to kill the villagers. Every pair of arms will count until the money begins to come in. We won't be able to rebuild the kilns until spring, of course; but, in my investigations of the last few days, I've ascertained that two of the shafts are still workable, or will be when they've been pumped out."

He looked about him at the shadowy hall, filled with torchlight, the stink of crowded bodies, and new-shed blood. "Not a bad place," he added judiciously. "I shall take the big house across the square for my own. It looks the most weather-tight. As soon as spring opens the roads, I will be returning to Kwest Mralwe, to allay suspicions and set up imports on that end. It wouldn't do for the other members of the Council to know where the alum is coming from until my position is stronger, but that should not take long. There are a number of the merchant houses, to say nothing of the old nobility, who would sooner buy alum at my prices than Renaeka Strata's." His colorless eyes flicked to the men around them, dirty, beastlike, a gleam of knife blades and teeth in the guttering torchlight. The thin line of his little smile altered, but his voice remained affable. "I'm sure your excellent troops will find tomorrow's battle considerably easier than tonight's."

"Poxy better be," Nails snarled, twisting the water from her lank brown hair. "That's the last pox-festering time I want to march through the goddam snow and fight in the goddam rain. That mother-eating alum mine better pay off like you say it will, pook."

Purcell regarded her with the expression of a sober and wealthy bishop contemplating a drunk puking in a gutter, and replied smoothly, "My dear Nails, I assure you it will. And I promise you, you shall receive all that's coming to you when it does."

Zane's voice dropped, and his eyes shifted toward Sun Wolf. "What about him?"

"Oh, we'll need him for the attack on Wrynde, of course." Purcell's cold smile widened, and a thin gleam of spiteful triumph slid into his voice. "We have seen the usefulness of having a man they trust. Fortuitous that he came out to the mine, though I'm a little surprised he guessed that it was behind my plan. Still, with his magic weakened to the extent it was, I could have set the *geas* on him at a distance, or called him to me to do it."

Zane glanced uneasily from the Wolf's impassive face to Purcell's prim, wrinkled smile. "Can he hear us?"

"What if he can? There isn't much he can do about it. Sun Wolf . . ." With fussy care, Purcell removed one of his purple-dyed gloves and, after a moment's thought, flung it into the far corner of the shadowy room. Men stepped aside from it, much as they gave the old man himself as wide a berth as the crowding of the great floor permitted. "Fetch it."

The Wolf turned and walked quietly after the glove.

"No." Purcell's voice was a hard little rap, like an auctioneer's gavel. The Wolf stopped in his tracks. "Properly. In your teeth."

For a moment Starhawk, lying on the beam, thought she saw the big man's muscles bunch in anger. Then he flinched and made a thin sound, barely more than a stifled gasp in his throat. Slowly he got down on his hands and knees, picked up the glove in his teeth, and crawled the width of the great room back to Purcell.

Around them, the men said nothing aloud, but there was a curious, whispering murmur all around the back of the room, which Purcell did not hear.

"If I told him to swallow it whole he would, you know." The Councillor removed the glove from Sun Wolf's mouth and shook it fastidiously. "But purple dye is so expensive. Up on your knees."

The Wolf raised himself from all fours to a kneeling position. Someone in the back made a lewd jest, but on the whole, the room was uneasily quiet.

Purcell struck him twice across the face with the glove, the sound of the wet leather like the swat of a whip on wood. The gold beading left a score of little welts on his cheek under the stubble and grime. "Here." He handed the glove to Zane. "Be my guest."

Hesitantly, Zane struck. Then, gaining confidence, he laughed and struck again and again.

Someone laughed; Louth shouted an unprintable suggestion about what to do next; but on the whole the men were quiet. Starhawk, though not able to gauge the feelings of mobs as well as Sun Wolf, could feel their uneasiness in the face of magic, their hostility toward this humiliation of another man. Neither Purcell nor Zane seemed to notice.

As for Sun Wolf, he never moved. But, looking down into his upraised face, Starhawk could see in his eye the pain, the rage, and the haunted agony of shame and knew that, however strong was the magic holding his will in check, the will was still there. It only remained for her— *evading a wizard, a hex, an army, and a metallic monster,* she reminded herself wryly—to get him out.

# CHAPTER

## —— 14 ——

*I*T WAS NEARLY DAWN BEFORE THE NOISE IN THE CAMP died down. Stretched flat on the beam, shivering with cold in the various layers of shirts she wore, Starhawk had time to do a deal of thinking. The rats kept their distance—she'd swat at them when nobody was in the hall below to hear—but the roaches and spiders didn't. After all the other events of the night, she barely noticed. Now and then her ears would tell her when Zane's men had found some other holdout loyal to Ari, or one of the women or boys who belonged to them. She guessed that, once Ari was clearly defeated, most of his supporters simply switched to the winning side, to be accepted but not trusted by the victors. And who could blame them? But Ari's close friends would never convince Zane they had forsaken the man they'd chosen.

And she, of course, was dead meat as soon as they found her.

She wondered how many of their friends knew it had been Sun Wolf who'd opened the gate.

At dawn she heard the furious half-drunken clamor of the expeditionary force leaving for Wrynde. Reducing the town wouldn't take them long. It was too far away to have heard last night's battle over the noise of the storm, and its inhabitants would be unprepared.

The rain had ceased almost as soon as the fort was taken, and by the smell of the air that leaked in whenever anyone entered or left the training hall she could tell that soupy mist lay over the barren uplands, enough to hide advancing men until it was far too late in the ruin of old walls and crumbing stream cuts that surrounded the town. The mist warmed the air a little—if it hadn't, she thought, she would have frozen. Whatever else his abilities, Pur-cell was a superb weather-witch.

Zane, Starhawk guessed, would leave a fairly strong force to guard the camp, for in the unlikely event Ari *had* managed to rally his scattered forces—or even find them, hiding as they must be all over the moors—now would be the time to attack. And it was odds on that the camp guards would be either bandits or Louth's muti-neers, since Zane wouldn't have had time to figure out which of Ari's turncoats really were sleepers and would therefore send them out to do something safe.

That gave her the core of a plan.

She let herself down from the beam as soon as she judged Zane's troops were out the gate and crossed to the chest in which she'd hidden her clothes. Her bare legs were crimson with gooseflesh—it was colder down here at floor level than it had been up under the rafters—and she put on her soaked leather breeches and boots, wish-ing it were possible to do so without touching the insides.

The camp had been her home for eight years, and she knew its every angle and wall. It was tricky slipping across the open ground to the barracks, but the mist helped her, that and the fact that the men, as they typi-cally did in her experience, lingered around the gate to talk and grumble for a time after the main force marched away. She slipped into the back door of Big Nin's house without trouble.

The diminutive prostitute wasn't there; none of the women who lived in this part of the barracks seemed to be. Starhawk could guess why, and it didn't bode partic-ularly well for her scheme, but there was no time to come up with another. She stripped quickly and pulled on whatever she could find that would fit her—a low-cut bodice of dust-pink silk, a confection of gold-shot skirts, a startling petticoat, sequined turquoise gloves, an assortment of tasseled sashes and scarves. Her boots she left on. She'd be doing rough walking soon, and besides, there was no question of Big Nin's tiny slippers fitting her feet.

There were cosmetics on the dressing table and, best of all, several wigs in varying shades and lengths. She selected a red one and arranged it with a sequined scarf in a kind of turban over her cropped head so that they more or less covered the scar on her cheek. With a certain amount of trepidation—since, though she'd seen women do this, she'd never tried it on herself—she painted her eyes and lips and covered with makeup as much of the scar as still showed. The result wasn't reassuring. The woman staring at her from the warped brass mirror certainly didn't look like herself, but neither did she look capable of earning so much as a copper by getting men to sleep with her.

On the other hand, she reflected, neither Filthy Girt nor the Glutton seemed to have the least trouble finding customers. Reassured, she slipped three daggers and her knuckle-spikes into her belt and boots, found a silk scarf that would double excellently as a garrote, slid a little bodkin dagger down her bosom, added all the jewelry she could find, and put a purple cloak of oiled taffeta garishly lined with yellow-dyed fur over the whole business.

She eyed her tawdry reflection once more and thought, *The things one does for love.*

Rancid gray daylight filled the sky now that the fog was burning off. She wondered whether this was because Purcell no longer needed it—once they got to fighting in among the houses in Wrynde, fog would work for the defenders rather than the attackers—or because there was a limit to how long even a skilled mage could hold weather not suitable to the place and season. Through a crack in the window shutter she could see that the camp was returning very quickly to normal. It looked better, in fact, than she'd seen it since their return, with more guards on the walls and more men and women moving about between the buildings. So instead of gliding by stealth, she moved with purposeful unobtrusiveness across the blood-patched wallow of the west end of the square to the kitchen, where white smoke signaled the first meal of the day being doled out to all comers, warrior, camp follower, and slave alike.

Two of Zane's guards stood by the door, but neither glanced at her when she went inside. The eating hall, a long, low, rather smoky room, was half-filled with people sitting at the rough benches, mostly camp slaves under the eye of another man she didn't recognize—who must therefore be one of Louth's—and a tawdry gaggle of camp followers sitting chattering together at one table. More warriors were up around the swill pots where Hog and Gully were handing out beans and bread and thinned-out gin. Hog was expressionless, the set of his shoulders almost shouting, "I don't give a rat's mess who runs the damn troop, but stay out of my kitchen." Gully's nose was swollen and his sad eyes both blacked. His fingers, wrapped in bandages, had all been broken. The Hawk gritted her teeth. As often as she'd wished while he was singing that someone would do something of the kind, it had never been more than a facetious remark. Of Bron there was no sign, and she wondered if he'd tried to defend Opium against Zane.

*One thing at a time,* she told herself. *If you try to help everyone, you're going to end up caught yourself.* Feeling hopelessly conspicuous, she walked up to the front of the room, keeping her eyes down, and got a bowl. If Hog recognized her, he gave no sign of it, and Gully murmured casually, "Hi, Angelcakes," as he handed her a mug of wretched tea with clumsy, splinted hands. She took her food into a deserted corner of the big, damp room, and rapidly deduced that whatever else was going on, the curse still reigned in Hog's kitchen.

There she waited, watching people come and go, until another group of slaves entered to be fed, among whom she recognized Moggin.

He was thinly clad against the cold, coughing heavily in a way she deeply misliked. He must have slipped himself into one of the camp slave gangs, as he had, he'd told her, in the confusion of the sack of Vorsal. His bare arms, like those of the others of his group, were plastered with mud and sawdust, from which Starhawk guessed they'd been put to work repairing the burned section of the barracks for the benefit of the newly come conquerors. She waited until he'd gotten his food and walked to another deserted table to eat it, moving slowly, as if in pain. Then she got up, fetched a second dollop of swill from Gully, and went to sit beside him. He gave her a polite glance and turned his face away, closed in his own thoughts.

"Don't be so choosy about your company, pook; you're worm food yourself, once Purcell recognizes you." His head snapped around at that. Their eyes met, his still uncomprehending, frightened. "We have to stop meeting this way," she said softly, and mimed a kiss at him. "Sun Wolf is getting suspicious."

He gulped, stammered, then quickly returned his concentration to his bowl. "I saw him with them," he said softly.

"He's under a spell of some kind, a *geas,* Purcell called it."

Moggin nodded. "Yes, that would stand to reason if they needed him to fight or work magic." He coughed again; she saw the muscles of his sides and back brace in a vain attempt to stifle it. In the gray shadows of the mess hall, he looked awful.

She sipped her tea. It was dreadful. "There a way of breaking it?"

"A bypass morphological rune tree is supposed to work," the philosopher said thoughtfully, "but it would take another wizard to set one up." He paused, cradling the dirty wooden bowl of porridge between grimy, blistered hands, contemplating middle distance with scholarly absorption from behind a graying curtain of filth-streaked hair, and Starhawk marveled at the wonders of the pedagogical mind. "Now, the Sishak Ritual is supposed to offer protection, but again, we'd need a wizard to draw the Signs and construct an aetheric shelter before Sun Wolf could utilize them. We seem to be alternating between having one mage too many or one too few . . ."

"Never mind that now," the Hawk said. "Where are you working? On the barracks?"

Moggin nodded, returning to scooping the tacky globs of porridge from bowl to mouth with fingers that shook. He paused, coughing again. He'd be little help, the Hawk reflected methodically, in terms of slugging guards, stealing books, or pilfering horses or weapons; she'd be lucky if she didn't have to lug him physically out of the camp. But at least he could be counted on to do what he was told.

"Listen. Get away from the work party as soon as you can, into any of the rooms near the burned section of the barracks. All of them vent into the old hypocaust. It's flooded and pretty nasty, but you can crawl along it as far as the ruined furnace at the far end near the stables. Wait for me there. With this *geas* thing, how much of his own volition does the Wolf have? Is Purcell *in* his mind, seeing what he sees, or does he just control it like a puppet?"

"A bit of both," Moggin said softly, with a wary glance at a nearby guard, who was busy flirting with Big Nin. "As I understand it, theoretically the *geas* is an aether-fiber extension of Purcell's own being, wrapped around Sun Wolf's consciousness and nervous system. It's partially astral-submaterialized but at least partly physical; it depends on conscious commands, not subconscious volition. Drosis' books contained instructions for the *geas* master linking with the slave's perceptions in a mediumistic trance, so it doesn't sound as if a sensory link is automatic."

"On your feet!" yelled an overseer. "Come on, Wimpy, that puke you're eating ain't good enough to linger over!"

Moggin rose at once, putting aside his unfinished bowl. Talking instead of eating had cost him a good half of what was probably the only food he'd receive that day. The overseer cuffed him, sending him stumbling after the other slaves through the door. Starhawk sat with her head bowed, not daring to look after him for fear of drawing the guard's attention to herself. She'd had years of watching how men treat women in the elation of victory, and the fear she felt now was a new thing to her. In her current guise, she couldn't very well kill a would-be suitor or even—dressed as she was, as any man's property—imply that she would. She had killed literally hundreds of men, usually for business reasons, but had never learned to deal with them in a one-sided amatory situation. Her heart beat faster when she heard a man's footsteps behind her. Trying to pretend she was unaware of them, she rose quickly to go.

"Not so fast, Angelcakes," Gully's voice said behind her. She froze at the touch of his bandaged hand on the cloak she held so close around her. "You forgot your laundry."

"Hunh?" She turned to face him and met those sad, bruise-ringed eyes. He held out his hand. The broken fingers had just enough mobility to support a small cloth bundle that did, indeed, look like laundry, but as she took it she could feel by the texture that there was bread, at least, and probably cheese and raisins wrapped inside.

"Uh—thank you," she said, floored by this evidence of the little soak's wits. And then, conscious of the idly watching guards, she stepped close and gave him a wholly unpracticed-looking kiss. "I owe you a drink, Gully."

He shook his head. "You bought me plenty on the road."

The guard by the mess hall door called an obscenity to her as she passed. She felt a twinge of an unfamiliar panic, wondering what she'd do if he came after her; totally aside from her disguise of implied willingness, she was badly outnumbered, if it came to a fight. Though no trooper was fool enough to rape a woman trooper—if she didn't get him herself, the next time they went over a city wall her women friends or Butcher undoubtedly would—but the female soldiers generally looked upon the whores as a different matter.

But the man only laughed at his own wit and remained where he was. The fog outside was burning off, the day growing colder. Her sodden skirts slapped wetly at her boots as she crossed the square and climbed the rough brick steps to the door of Sun Wolf's little house.

As she'd feared, the books were gone. *Ari's place,* she thought, collecting the coil of rope the Chief habitually hid under the bed, and a heavily quilted coat for Moggin. Of course Purcell, as a wizard, would have taken them.

Tying the food bundle to the back of her belt beneath the cloak, she crossed the strip of waste ground that backed both Sun Wolf's house and Ari's. Sun Wolf had formed his rock garden in part of it, but behind Ari's was only an empty plot of heather, rubble, and weeds in which the ruins of broken furniture and garbage had been left to decay. From it, she identified Ari's bedroom window and, after listening and hearing nothing, scrambled up a half-ruined buttress to look in.

She stopped, frozen with her knee upon the sill.

The *djerkas* crouched in the middle of the room.

If she hadn't known from Sun Wolf's description what it was, she'd probably have gone straight in, for she had no sense of the thing's being alive at all. It looked like nothing more than a big piece of steel machinery, a loom or an experiment with pulleys, dully gleaming in the cool daylight, its razor claws tucked neatly out of sight behind the maze of cables and counterweights. Beyond it, on the low table that stood near the opulent, gilded fantasy of Ari's curtained bed, she could see Sun Wolf's books.

She swore, with considerable vividness, and swung herself back down the broken granite into the stony garden again. There she continued to swear for some moments.

"All right, you want to play the game that way, we'll play it that way."

Keeping to the garden, the waste ground, and the walls as much as possible, she made her way to the old furnace where Moggin was to meet her later and stowed the rope and the coat. The food bundle she kept tied to her belt, with an instictive regard for priorities in the event of unexpected flight. From the midden behind the kitchen, she abstracted rags and wet straw; from Sun Wolf's house a flask of gin and a horn fire carrier, in which she placed a few glowing coals from the hearth and enough dried moss from the tinderbox to ensure they'd keep going for some hours. She tried to locate a projectile weapon of some kind—bow, crossbow or throwing ax—but everything along those lines had been confiscated, not much to her surprise. It remained only to slip back into the waste ground near the corner of Ari's house, settle herself behind a broken wall, and wait.

It wasn't even noon when she heard the din of the returning company. All day the cold had been increasing, the blowing gray cloud ceiling rising to a sullen roof high overhead, and in the sharp air it was possible to detect them at a great distance. By the sound she knew at once that their conquest had been successful. Not, she reflected dourly, that it was likely that the folk of Wrynde could have put up much of a fight, even after they realized that Sun Wolf had betrayed them.

She took a pull on the gin and held her half-frozen fingers around the heated horn, trying not to think of all the excellent reasons Purcell would have for disposing of the Wolf immediately after the taking of the town, always supposing the Chief had survived the fighting. From the brief glance she'd had of him during the battle in the camp, it didn't seem that the *geas* had impaired his fighting skills. Listening, she couldn't hear the deep, gravelly bellow of his voice rising above the general clamor—but then it had changed drastically since last she'd heard him returning with his troops from battle.

Still, the leaden fear inside her did not ease until she leaned cautiously around the corner of the broken colonnade and saw him, standing behind Purcell, a little apart from the boisterous mob that surged in through the gate.

The men were laughing, bussing the prostitutes who'd gathered to meet them, waving the sacks of food, bottles of liquor and beer, and cloaks of fur and wool they'd looted from the town. Some of them had women with them, too, beaten and exhausted, their clothes torn and their skirts bloodied. Louth pulled a girl of eighteen or so whom Starhawk knew slightly out of the crowd and thrust her at Zane, who laughed nastily and shook his head. Then Purcell and Zane started across the square for Ari's house. At a snap of Purcell's fingers, Sun Wolf followed, trailed by four of Zane's guards.

As they approached, Starhawk could hear Purcell saying, ". . . of course not. I had picked you out as a possible partner all the way along, Zane. It was obvious that I needed a trusted confederate within the band and equally obvious that you were the only one strong enough to hold them together and dispose of Ari.''

*Yeah?* Starhawk thought cynically. *Next you're going to tell us you didn't mean for anyone to be hurt.* As they drew nearer, she could see that Sun Wolf had been wounded in one arm, though he didn't seem to notice it himself. He moved more slowly than he had after the battle in the camp, and stumbled once on the slippery goo of the square's mud. His clothing was covered with blood and filth, and his head swayed unsteadily.

*Was Moggin wrong?* she wondered, suddenly panicked, not liking the way he moved. *Did the geas eat out his mind after all? Did it just take time . . . ?*

"You could have contacted me earlier, you know," Zane said, a hint of sulkiness in his voice. "I mean, *I* could have got killed anytime during the siege, or the journey up to the Gore, or . . ."

"Zane." There was a father's tolerant patience in Purcell's voice, gentle amusement in his smile. They had come around the corner of the colonnade, not more than a dozen yards from Starhawk's hiding place. But Zane's guards, loitering at a little distance in the colonnade's shadows, were armed with crossbows—it was clear Zane still worried about sleepers among the turncoats of the troop. Moving carefully, Starhawk slipped back around the rear of the house and into the shelter of the ruined buttress. Purcell's voice drifted to her ears as she kindled a few dried twigs from the horn at her belt, dripped gin onto the ball of rags and straw . . . "Do you think I wasn't watching out for you? Why do you think you *didn't* come to harm?"

"Really?" There was boyish gratification and wonder in Zane's voice; Starhawk wanted to slap him for such gullibility. Only Zane was conceited enough to believe he'd have been excepted from the general disaster because of who he was. She lit a corner of the rag ball, which proceeded to smoke and burn fitfully, and scrambled up the ragged stone projection to lob it through the window. It rolled easily across the tile floor, past the *djerkas*, who had clearly been set to guard against human intruders and nothing else, and came to rest against the gilt-embroidered, jewel-stitched curtains of that ridiculous bed Ari had looted from the Duke of Warshing's palace five years ago. "I never guessed that," Zane was saying, even as she did so. "You picked me all along, hunh?"

"Please forgive me the deception," Purcell was saying, obsequious with years of practice on the King-Council, as the Hawk slipped down into the weeds again and made her cautious way back toward them. At a guess, she thought, Purcell had approached Zane as soon as the band had split, before Zane could carry out the suicide of an attack on the Gore Thane's Fort—as soon, in fact, as it had become clear to Purcell that he'd need military assistance to get rid of the band that currently controlled the immediate vicinity of the alumstone diggings, instead of simply waiting for the curse to do its work. "Men are stubborn, Zane, especially about men who've been their teachers. You're wise enough to know that. They'd never have followed you until they were absolutely fed up, absolutely convinced of the uselessness of Ari's weak leadership . . . for *his* sake." And he nodded toward Sun Wolf, standing, swaying slightly on his feet, staring sightlessly into the twisted laurel trees that half hid the rocks of the stone garden he had made in earlier winters.

"You want to get him fixed up," Zane said, with a jerk of his thumb. "I guess crocking him up with dream-sugar before the battle wasn't such a good idea after all, hunh?"

"On the contrary, it was quite necessary," the wizard replied, with a hint of sharpness that the man who stood like a golden cock pheasant beside him would dare criticize his judgment of the situation. A far cry, the Hawk thought interestedly, from Renaeka Strata's rabbity yes-man, for all the fawning voice. In spite of his business-like patience, how he must hate the Lady Prince—how he must look forward to crushing her power.

Purcell lowered his voice to exclude the guards in the colonnade. "As his powers recuperate, now that they're not being expended on healing and weather-witching, he would become unruly if he weren't drugged. I wasn't about to enter into a battle of wills with him when we had the town to take."

"You mean he might break out of this—this *geas* you've got on him?" Zane threw a sudden, worried glance at his former teacher.

"Of course not!" Purcell snapped. "He hasn't the skill or the training. But he does have the strength to make him unpredictable and difficult to control."

"So you're gonna have to keep him under sugar?" Zane had stepped a pace toward the Wolf, studying him as he would study some remarkable statue. But with hatred in her heart, the Hawk saw in the set of his broad shoulders and graceful back that he was nervous, afraid even now of what the Wolf might do, like a boy walking in front of a chained bear, before he quite gets up his nerve to begin teasing.

"No," Purcell said thinly. "I'm going to kill him." He reached under his vast, fur-lined mantle, and drew out a dagger. He held it out to Zane. "Or you may do it, if you'd like."

Twenty feet away, under cover of the broken buttresses, Starhawk's heart froze. The distance was too great—she'd be dead the minute she broke cover. Strain her senses though she might, she could smell no smoke from the inside of the house. *Dammit,* she wondered desperately, *it can't have gone out!*

A queer, bright gleam flared into Zane's eyes, an adolescent expression, like a boy attending gladiatorial games for the first time or witnessing public execution by torture. "No," he said softly. "I want to see you make him do it."

In Purcell's smile Starhawk saw him mentally noting other ways of holding Zane's interest.

"Very well," he said. "Sun Wolf . . ."

Starhawk threw a fast glance back at Ari's window; a little whitish smoke had begun to leak out, but hung motionless in the still air. *Damn,* she thought. *Damn, damn, damn . . .*

Sun Wolf looked down at the dagger Purcell held out to him. His hand flinched, then balled tight into a fist. She could hear the ragged tear of his breath.

"Take it," said the wizard softly.

Sun Wolf's head twitched, as if he fought to look away from those cold gray eyes and could not. Despite the cloudy vapor of his breath in the air, a film of sweat had sprung to his face. Against the blood and grime, his eye, flared wide and almost black with the dilation of the drugs he'd been given, showed white all around the pupil. His hand jerked, reached out, drew back. The smell of smoke stung Starhawk's nostrils—it was curling thinly out of the house now, but Purcell's concentration was locked in the struggle with his victim's clouded will, and Zane and all four guards were too absorbed in watching to notice much else. *You cheese-brained fools!* Starhawk screamed silently at them, *can't you smell a fire under your noses! If you guarded my house that way, I'd have you trimmed and flogged . . .*

"Take it," Purcell whispered, and Sun Wolf gasped, his body buckling as if with the twisting rip of inner pain. A thin, desperate sound escaped his clenched teeth; the hand that reached out was shaking as if with palsy.

*Fight him!* willed the Hawk desperately. *Buy us some time, damn you! They've got to smell the smoke sometime* . . . The shaking stopped as his fingers closed around the dagger's hilt.

Sun Wolf was panting, tears of exertion, rage, and despair mixing with the sweat that tracked his filth-streaked face as he raised the knife toward his neck. White smoke was billowing from the house now, drifting on the few vagrant breezes, but no one noticed . . . They would notice, however, Starhawk thought grimly, if she broke cover to attack Purcell. She braced herself, gauging the time of her streak over the twenty feet or so of open ground that separated them, the largest of her knives ready in her hand. Sun Wolf tried to twist his face away from Purcell's glacial gaze, his breath coming in sobs, his teeth clamped so hard on his lower lip that blood ran down in a thin trickle over his chin. Mouth parted, Zane's face blazed with an almost sexual eagerness. The razor metal glinted as it touched Sun Wolf's throat . . .

*Purcell dies first* . . .

"FIRE!!!"

Zane's head snapped around. For that first, fleeting second, there was only annoyance in his eyes at being interrupted. Purcell flinched, not, Starhawk thought, at the shout from someone in the square—the stupid guards still hadn't noticed anything amiss—but at the smell of the smoke. He whipped around, still half-lost in the icy grip of his own concentration, like a man broken from a dream, and it took him a second to react to the white smoke billowing now from Ari's house. The look on his face, of startlement passing at once into enlightenment and then to fury, was almost funny, as he realized that the *djerkas* was neither going to put out the fire to protect the books, *nor let anyone else enter the room to do it*. With a wordless yell he flung himself toward the house, followed by Zane and his guards.

Starhawk broke cover before they were out of sight, plunged across the uneven stones to where Sun Wolf stood, dagger edge pressed to his jugular, eye closed, gasping with the effort of the strain.

She wrenched at his arm, bringing it down, though she couldn't force the dagger from his hand. His eye stared at her blindly, black with the dilation of the pupil. She didn't think he recognized her—*Small wonder,* she reflected, as she dragged him violently along the path. The skirts and petticoats tangled at her legs, hanks of hair from the wig got in her mouth, and Sun Wolf lagged and twisted at her grip like an unwilling child. From all directions men were racing toward Ari's house, barely noticing them as they jostled past. Starhawk wondered how long it would take Purcell to realize that the fire had to be a diversion.

Moggin was waiting for her by the old brick cone of the ancient furnace, already wearing Sun Wolf's quilted black coat and with the rope over his narrow shoulders. Grabbing Sun Wolf's other arm he followed her, coughing heavily as he shoved and manhandled him up the broken stair that had once led to the battlements and over the uneven wall walk to the shell of a ruined turret. The rope didn't reach all the way to the ground from here, but the final drop was less than six feet. ''Thank God the place is designed to keep people out instead of in,'' the Hawk muttered viciously. ''Chief, get down the rope . . . The rope, pox rot your eye!'' He swayed blindly on his feet, still deep in the grip of the dreamsugar and the *geas,* the dagger clutched in his hand. Men were milling like ants around Ari's house down below; by the color of the smoke the fire was out already. Purcell would find the remains of the smoke ball and guess . . .

She pushed a bight of the rope into Sun Wolf's nerveless grip, then, with a quick foot sweep and shoulder block, shoved him over the battlement. Moggin gave a yelp of horror, but Sun Wolf, as she'd suspected he might, reacted without benefit of his numbed brain, dropping the dagger to catch himself on the rope. She thrust Moggin down the rope after him immediately, forcing the Wolf to go down instead of trying to climb back up; the uneven surface of the wall was rough enough to give even a weak and inexperienced climber little trouble.

*Some rescue,* she thought wryly, hitching up her wind-ruffled turquoise skirts to follow. *Two big strong men and who is it who gets to do all the work?* Then something metallic flashed among the broken crenelations of the walls to her left, something moving with a fast, sidelong, crablike gait. Her stomach curled.

She swung down the wall FAST, the jolt of the final drop jarring heavily in her half-healed skull.

"The *djerkas*," she gasped as she caught Sun Wolf's arm in one hand, Moggin's in the other, shoving them both into a run. "Can it follow him, track him? If Purcell commands both . . ."

"Blindfold him."

Starhawk stopped long enough to tear off one of her several gaudy sashes to tie over the Wolf's eye. Then they were running again, stumbling down the jagged granite of the rocky fortress hill. She knew every foot of the moor that surrounded on three sides the little valley in which Wrynde, its mines, and its guardian garrison had been built and the jumble of ruins that had once been its attendant villas and farms, every rock and pit and crevice, every swollen stream and wind-crippled stand of trees.

She had intended to go to ground somewhere nearer, but with the *djerkas* on their heels there was only one place she could think of.

It was three miles off. It had once been a villa, the country abode of some imperial governor, in a dell below Cold Tor which had once been fertile. Of the topsoil which had grown its rye and oats and apples, nothing was left between the roaring beck and the nearby sour swamp; of the house itself, little enough. But wine cellars had been cut into the hillside behind it, and there was a small quadrangle of what had been garden where half a dozen black elms still grew, incongruous in the wasted northlands. It was the only place where they'd have a hope, the Hawk thought, as she dragged her male impedimenta into the rocky cover of a knee-deep stream cut—provided the *djerkas*, or Zane's men, didn't catch them first.

By the time they reached the place, Moggin was reeling with fatigue. For rough-and-tumble work, he was a nearly useless ally, soft-raised and suffering from the effects of prolonged malnutrition and physical abuse. Moreover, Sun Wolf, though he moved with his old enduring strength in spite of the blindfold, kept trying to stop, as if every minute it reoccurred to him that he ought to go back. Long before they reached the villa Starhawk was ready to strangle them both.

"Moggin!" She thrust Sun Wolf ahead of her into the narrow shaft that led to the old storage cellar, caught Moggin's arm as he sank, face chalky under the grime, to his knees on the ice-skinned rock. "Moggin, dammit, don't faint on me now! Moggy!" She dragged him by the back of his filthy coat to the nearest rain pool, shoved his head under and dragged him up, sobbing with fatigue, freezing water running in streams from his hair. "Listen to me, damn you! Tell me about the *djerkas*. How do you stop them? What gives them life? Dammit, it'll track us here . . ."

"Crystal," he whispered. ". . . mage meditates on it . . . spells . . . his own blood . . ."

His eyes closed, his body doubling over with coughs. *Dear Mother,* she thought, *he's dying.* She shook him again, hard.

"That thing has a kind of metal turret on its back. Would this crystal be there?"

He nodded feebly. She hauled him to his feet and slammed him back against the nearest elm trunk, holding him upright with fists nearly numb from cold. "Look, you faint later, all right? You die later. Right now I'm going to need your help. We need wood, bricks, rocks, anything about so big . . ." She let him go, to indicate something about the size of a loaf of bread. A little to her surprise, he stayed upright. "Take them into the cellar in there, put them on either side of the door and HURRY. That thing'll be after us and this is our one chance." Her face was white in the red frame of wig and veils, her voice cool and biting, a soldier's voice. It seemed to reach him, for he stumbled off, catching himself for balance on the slender saplings that clustered all around the parent elms. Part of Starhawk felt a stab of pity for him, but most of her was concentrated on speed and efficiency, only stopping to think, *He'll be no help, dammit.* Pulling the largest of her daggers from her belt, she began cutting the saplings. The cellar wasn't large, but it would have to do—it was enclosed, and had only one entrance.

As she dragged the saplings down the narrow hall to the dim little chamber she wondered how heavy the *djerkas* was. The *golems* of legend had been stone, able to crush a man, but, as she'd reasoned before, they had to be impossibly heavy and difficult to maneuver. The *djerkas* had clearly been built to sacrifice this impenetrable power to speed and surprise. *Who fabricated that deadly metal body?* she asked herself, piling up the largest of the bricks and chunks of stone to the immediate left of the chamber's inner arch. *And how long did Purcell let that craftsman survive after it was done?*

*Poor bastard probably died the day after Purcell got the first dunning letter for the fee.*

She glanced at the Wolf, crouched where she'd shoved him, his face to the inner wall, the gaudy orange scarf still bound around his head. Through his ripped sleeve, the wound in his arm looked clotted and ugly—that would have to be seen to soon—and the bruised flesh around it nearly fuchsia with cold. He was shuddering from cold and reaction to the horrors of the last eighteen hours; she fought the urge to go over to him, circle those wide, bowed shoulders with her arms and try to let him know he was safe.

He wasn't, of course, the practical portion of her thoughts replied. At this point, time would be better spent making sure the longest saplings she'd cut would work as levers with the makeshift fulcrum to the left of the door.

*One of these days I'll figure out how to be a tender and loving woman,* the Hawk thought, helping Moggin to stack yet another armload of broken bricks and bits of old window sills and cornices ready to hand. *Till then, I'll just work on getting us to sunset alive.*

As she doused another gauze scarf with gin and wrapped a stick with it to form a makeshift torch, she outlined her plan to the scholar.

"Oh, we don't have to wait for it," Moggin pointed out. Muddy, soaked, and shivering, he looked infinitely wretched, but somehow his voice managed to retain its old pedagogical calm. "If you remove Sun Wolf's blindfold he'll recognize where he is, and the *djerkas* will be drawn to us."

"Well, that's something." She unbuckled the Wolf's leather jerkin, stripped it off him and tossed it onto the smaller of the two piles of debris. "If we had to wait any kind of time for the thing to attack, we'd freeze to death. I need that coat of yours." He gave it up without demur, though, under it, his canvas smock and breeches were threadbare and torn. She added her own heavy cloak and, pulling up her frothy skirt, threw in most of her petticoats as well. It was astonishingly cold without them, colder still once she'd pulled off the wig and veils to add to the pile. Only then did she cross the cellar to pull the garish blindfold from Sun Wolf's eyes.

He moved his head, blinked at her painfully. The run from the fortress had cleared his mind of most of the dreamsugar, but there was still an odd look in his eye of pain and stress and horror. "Hawk?" His hand groped for hers—she took it and squeezed it briefly.

"Stay here. Stay here against this wall and whatever happens, don't move. You're in the cellar of the old villa under Cold Tor."

He nodded, his teeth gritting hard. "He's calling me, Hawk." His grip crushed tight on her frozen hands. "He wants me to come back . . ."

"Can you hold against him?"

Again he managed to nod, though he looked sick. "It's Purcell," he said thickly. "He . . ."

"Yeah," Starhawk said. "We figured that one out." She squeezed his hands again, then drew away. "Just stay here. You'll be all right."

"That is the most appallingly optimistic untruth I've heard since the Duke of Vorsal assured the Senate we couldn't lose the war," Moggin remarked, as she came back to where he waited, shivering uncontrollably beside the levers.

"Haven't you ever heard of a social lie?"

He started to reply, but she gestured him silent. Minutes passed in bitter and deepening cold. Outside, the wind screamed across the gray land; Starhawk wondered if they had time to collect wood for a fire, then dismissed the thought. If one of them went out and was killed, the other could never cope with the *djerkas* alone.

Then, barely audible in the stillness, she heard the light, swift clatter and whir, almost unrecognizable had she not been ready and listening. "There . . ."

It came fast, a grate of razor claws in the short stone passage; she and Moggin flung themselves down on the sapling levers by instinct, before the thing was halfway through the door. It took all their weight, in a single jerking flip, to upend the *djerkas* like a turtle. The next second Starhawk rammed one of the levers like a pole against the thing's underbelly, jamming it, still sideways, against the cellar wall. For all its relative lightness of construction the creature was incredibly heavy; Moggin

threw himself in with a pole the next second, the thing
writhing to regain its balance as Starhawk seized a shorter
sapling and twisted it into the nearest of the leg cables,
tangling its movement. Moggin followed suit, jamming
another pole into one of the swivel joints, his white face
almost unrecognizable with rage and determination.

Two limbs jammed, the creature slashed its razor claws
at Starhawk. One of them ripped through the thick silk
covering her back as she sprang in on top of it, wedging
half a brick into one of the counterweight housings. She
leaped aside, caught up another pole, and thrust in again,
this time tangling the cable that controlled the claw.
Moggin flung Sun Wolf's leather doublet over the claws
to give the Hawk time to jam her discarded petticoats
into more of the joints, the thing bucking and heaving
under her, flipping, jerking spasmodically as it flailed her
with its steel limbs. Her numb hands clawed at the low
metal grille she'd seen before in its center, twisting and
tearing; joints dug at her belly and her sides, and a razor
claw sliced her calf. Head down, she scrabbled at the
hollow under the grille, the startling warmth of the cavity
almost burning. Her fingers clawed something hard and
slick, closed and twisted . . .

Without even a final heave the *djerkas* collapsed, like
a folding chair whose joints Dogbreath might have loos-
ened for a joke. The jerk of it was like falling onto a
heap of cobblestones. Starhawk lay across it, crystal
clenched in bleeding fingers, heedless of the points and
lumps of steel digging into her flesh through the thin
fabric of bodice and chemise. She became gradually
aware of the burning trickle of blood on her back and
legs, startling against flesh that was freezing cold.

Then a slim hand took her arm, gently got her to her
feet. The aftermath of adrenaline and the pain of a truly
awful hammering made her knees weak, and she held
onto Moggin's shoulders for support, his arm circling her
waist with surprising firmness. She had tangled with men
before, but only now she let herself realize how insane
it had been to go after this creature of metal and magic.

Moggin coughed, then said judiciously, "That was
very nice. Have you ever thought of going into the hero
business full time?"

# CHAPTER

## —— 15 ——

*V*OICES. *VOICES CALLING HIS NAME.*

Demons? he wondered. The demons of Wenshar? Bodiless blue shapes whispering to him from the vibrating darkness of another dreamsugar hallucination?

Or Purcell?

*Not again,* he thought, closing his eye as he had closed his mind, burying himself in the black pit of his inner darkness. *Please, by all the gods of hell, not again.*

"Chief, can you hear me? Can you hear me?"

*No. No, no, no.*

But wherever he turned in the black refuge of his mind were the runes, tangling silver tendrils binding him to Purcell. They tore at him, drinking of his strength, twisting tighter and tighter around his bones and brain and heart. And in the darkness between them waited the memory of what he had done.

"I'm not getting to him . . ."

Starhawk's voice? Or only one that sounded like hers, as the demons used the voices of friends? Clouded, twisted with pain and horror and dreamsugar, he half remembered her wind-burned face framed in the darkness of the doorway, damp, fair hair sticking all ways like an urchin child's; he remembered flinging the ax at

247

her heart. He didn't remember whether it had struck or not.

There were too many other memories, too many other men he had seen, shoulders bowing forward, heads snapping down as that flower of blood burst from around the thrown ax's blade. It was too easy to see her face on them, to see the shock in those wide gray eyes . . .

The pain tightened on him again, dragging at him, hurting in a way he had no name for, and he curled himself tighter against it. A measure of his power had come back, like earth-water seeping into a dry well. But it wasn't enough, wasn't nearly enough. His mind was clouded, a fragmented chaos of pictures: Ari's shocked eyes when they had met face-to-face before the torchlit bulk of the Armory, cutting the throats of Rubberface, the gate guard, and that harmless militiaman in Wrynde who used to sell mules to the troop, horrified and trying to stop himself, as he'd tried to stop his hand from taking Purcell's dagger and raising it to his own neck. But clearest of all was the memory of Purcell's will forcing its way past his defenses, of the breathless paralysis of his limbs, the agony compressing and burning all his organs, the horror of watching his own hands move without his volition, in spite of his desperate efforts to stop them . . .

His whole being felt befouled by this rape, and he understood why women killed themselves after they'd been passed around among the troop. And he understood, for the first time, the hatred they bore afterward to any who had the power to do that to them again.

He squeezed his mind shut, trying to sink down further into darkness, where the voices would not reach. But always there were those silver threads of power tangling his mind, pulling and twisting, murmuring to him that there was no hope of escape.

"Don't go down, Chief," the Hawk's voice said. "Come up." Then there was an aside: "Is that right?"

"Yes." That voice barely impinged on his consciousness, vaguely familiar, but he pushed it aside. *Purcell's?*

All voices sounded a little like Purcell's.

Fearing that it was, he tried to sink down still further, but her voice followed him, echoing in the blackness of his fogged mind. "Follow my voice, Chief. Try to—to see light if you can, but follow my voice. Come up, don't go down. You can make a shelter for yourself, make it out of the—'' Indistinct muttering . . . ''—the second and seventh signs of the Sishak Rites. They're written here—open your eye, look . . .''

He'd never heard of the Sishak Rites and didn't want to. He wanted only darkness, and peace where gnawing pain and the blind horror of remorse couldn't touch him. It was a trick, he thought bitterly, a trick to trap him, to make him do things still worse than he had done . . .

"Open your eye, pox rot you, and look at the goddam signs, you barbarian ape!"

*Starhawk?*

His tongue felt thick and swollen upon the word. "Starhawk?" He was conscious of her touch on his wrists.

"Open your pox-festering eye, Chief, or I'll damn well poke that one out, too, damn you!"

He opened his eye. He saw her face, weirdly distinct, as if in some new and beautiful angle of light, but meaningless as something dreamed. And perhaps it was all only dreamed. He thought he should know the man with her . . . thought he should be wearing a black scholar's robe with a shagged silk collar, not that vaguely familiar, mud-crusted black coat . . . younger . . . his hair should be black, not gray . . . he didn't know why. As in a dream, he had no sense of heat or cold, though the Hawk's breath made a faint steam in the dim glow of the tiny fire. A rude shelter of elm poles and heather caught the flickering light, inches beyond the tips of her cropped hair. Looking down, he saw incomprehensible signs scratched in the muddy dirt before his knees.

The other man—the man he didn't recognize—said something he barely heard, a vague distorted murmuring, as most voices were. Hesitantly, Starhawk said, "Can you see the signs, Chief? Their names are Enyas and Ssa—the Nothing-Cloak and the Strength of Air. You can make a shelter of them, you can protect yourself with them against the runes, but you have to put your magic into them. Can you do that?"

*Magic.* The *geas* made it hard for him to remember that he had magic. His mind moved toward them and at once the pain of the *geas* tightened, crushing his brain, his heart, his genitals. He gasped, dropping back for the

darkness within him, but her hands closed hard on his
collar and she jerked him into a brutal slap across the
face.

"Come on, you gutless weakling, there were nuns at
the pox-festering Convent tougher than you! Look at
them, damn you!"

Bands of iron were crushing him, swords ripping into
his lungs. He gasped, tried to cry out, impotent rage
filling him, rage at Purcell, at Starhawk, at his father . . .
He saw how the signs could be linked together into a
shield, how the sounds of them could be used. Twisting,
scraping inwardly at the marrow of his bones, he traced
them with his fingers, and they glowed to life with a
shivering plasmic light in the smoky gloom. The ghostly
glow seemed to feed back into his fingers, drawing out
more. The silver runes within his mind stuck and pulled,
like a badly healed wound, cutting, crushing . . .

With a sob he woke, and opened his eye. He didn't
know when he'd shut it again, or if it had ever been open.

He was in a shelter built in a sort of dip in the ground
near boulders he recognized from their striations of
quartz as those on Pulvren Tor—a shelter built of elm
poles and heather, just as he'd dreamed. It was freezing
cold, even with the tiny fire, and outside it would be
killing cold. Through the blinding smoke—he wondered
that it hadn't stung like this before—he could dimly make
out Starhawk and Moggin crouched before him, and the
wide scratch-work of signs crisscrossing the damp dirt.
His arm hurt like the devil; he was unshaven and stank
like a civet cat in heat.

"Purcell," he whispered, his lips feeling as if he'd
borrowed them from Gully. "It's Purcell. Those mines
north of the village . . ."

"Alum, we know," the Hawk said, with her old, fleet
grin. "Old news. Purcell must have found the ancient
records of it somewhere, though back in those days they
must have kept it as much a secret as they would now.
He figured all he had to do was get rid of the troop. He
didn't count on you."

"I'm sorry." And for a moment it seemed to him that
the shame of what he had done—tried to kill her, betrayed his friends, given over the village to Zane's men—
was beyond what he could endure and live.

"I'll beat the innards out of you when we've got time," she promised.

Then they embraced, crushing one another, the shudder of her breath going through his body like lightning.

"Ari and some of his boys got out," she said, after several minutes during which Moggin politely pretended he wasn't there—not easy in a shelter five feet by five feet. "I saw you in the Armory and thought there was something weird about you—Ari was rousting up the men already when the trouble hit. It's my guess they'll be regrouping at the mines, since those are the only places that could be held, now Zane's taken the village."

"Huh." Sun Wolf scratched a corner of his filthy mustache. For the first time he realized that the Hawk must have gotten out of the camp dressed as one of the whores. Kohl smudged her eyes as if she'd been slugged, and the cloak over her shoulders was a color he'd never seen her wear in his life, the few bits of tawdry jewelry still clinging to it incongruous against the cropped bristle of her skull and the jagged red X of the scar over her left ear. "Whether he knows it or not, he'll be damn safe there— Purcell'll never cave those in. I guessed what was going on and went out there to have a look at those things we always thought were smelting furnaces. They were really kilns to bake the raw stone into alum for shipping."

"How'd you guess it was him?"

"I found the Eyes. They were written on the front money he paid Ari—and more on the final payment, the stingy bastard. As treasurer he was the only one, beside Renaeka Strata, who had access to the money for long enough to mark it—and Renaeka had no reason to get rid of us and no need to use a curse if she did. From the money, the hex spread all over camp like a case of the clap."

"Proving that Sister Kentannis was right when she told me that money is a curse." The Hawk grinned. "Bastard must have been a wizard all the way along."

"Looking back, I'm astounded I never guessed." Moggin edged nearer to them, holding out grimy hands to the feeble warmth of the fire. "I did occasionally suspect Drosis might have had another student he never told me about, from fear of Altiokis. I remember his saying once how he felt obliged—compelled, almost—to pass his skills on to another mageborn so they would not die with him . . .'' He broke off, fighting hard not to cough, his face turning an unhealthy gray with the strain. The spasm, when it came, was bad, leaving him retching and weak.

After a long minute he continued, ''And thinking about it, the House of Cronesme, which was quite minor fifteen years ago, has had some fairly consistent strokes of luck— like a rival's ship springing a plank and letting Purcell's cargo reach the markets first, which is really the sort of thing that can happen to anyone—or that time the entire season's dye lots of the Greambii turned sour in the vats and nearly ruined them. Purcell's brother always had the reputation as the ruthless one. Until the brother's death, Purcell himself was just the head clerk at the Vorsal branch.''

''Where he met Drosis,'' Sun Wolf said thoughtfully. ''And I've got a feeling what happened to his brother.'' A merchant of sedentary habit, as old as Purcell's older brother would have to have been, would never have the reflexes to save himself. ''Wonder if he was beginning to suspect? After Purcell returned to Kwest Mralwe, he could have kept up the connection easy enough. Since they burn witches in Kwest Mralwe, he wouldn't have dared take Drosis' books, not if his trade rivals were keeping spies in his house. But my guess is he made coded copies over the years, long before Drosis bought it. I would have, anyway.''

He fell silent then, staring into the grimy seed of the fire and listening to the screaming of the wind in the rocks. He felt queerly lightheaded, as if he had a fever. Holding the makeshift protection which the Signs of Sishak afforded drained and pulled at what power he had, and he sensed they'd give him no protection against a determined attempt to reassert the *geas'* strength. Maybe they would, if he knew the entire Rite, or how the Signs worked . . . He didn't know. The *geas* was still inside him, curled like leeches around the fabric of his mind, the deadly net of runes dark now but still waiting, still binding him to Purcell.

''Given what things would be like in the Middle Kingdoms, if our pal the King could hire tame hookums,'' Starhawk remarked, adding another chunk of elm wood to the fire, "I can see why they'd have a down on the mageborn. It makes sense even that they burned Renaeka's mother. I don't blame Purcell for hiding behind that rabbit facade all these years."

"I expect Drosis kept an eye on him, too," Moggin said softly. "Purcell went very carefully while Drosis lived—partly from fear of Altiokis, who certainly killed Drosis' other student, but partly from fear of Drosis himself. Drosis couldn't have been his teacher without guessing at least somewhat the kind of man he would turn into, if he weren't watched. The real power of the Cronesmae has only showed itself in the five years since Drosis' death. At the time, I didn't connect the two events, but looking back, I wonder that I was so blind."

"What a hell of a thing," Sun Wolf said softly. "To have the power and the learning that could only be passed on to the mageborn, only understood by one who had the power . . . and to have that one be a greedy whore. Wonder where he got the *djerkas*?" His curling eyebrows pulled down into a frown as a disjointed image floated back to him from the patchy dark of his mind, an image of Starhawk with a pole in her hand, slamming it into a nightmare tangle of metal claws. There were bruises on her face, but in their fighting days she'd always had those. She did not appear to have been hurt in the taking of the camp, and he knew better than to ask how she had fared with a third party present. "Did it come after us?" he asked uncertainly. "You blindfolded me . . ."

She nodded. "We pulverized the crystal that motivated it," she said. "The body was too heavy to haul, and we had to get out of that cellar fast, since Zane knows all the good hiding places as well as we do. But we unhitched all its leg cables, threw them in the streams, and flattened out all those little joints with rocks. Even if Purcell has a spare crystal, it'll take awhile to fix."

Sun Wolf sighed and ran big, clumsy hands through his stringy hair. Somewhere inside him, the *geas* shifted, pulled. He put forth his strength, almost afraid to try for fear of the pain, and it darkened away once again. But he knew it was still there.

"You know how many boys got out with Ari?"

She shook her head. "I know Purcell will be hunting the moors for 'em, though. Even if there aren't enough loose to make real trouble, they'll need all the slaves they can get to start the mines running. But I warn you, Chief—they know it was you who betrayed them.''

''I know.'' The shame of it stabbed him again, searing and soul-deep, and for an instant he wanted to kill himself, to cauterize it out of his memory as he'd once burned the burrowing fire of a *gaum* out of his eye . . .

And the next instant, as the shame and helpless anger broke his concentration, the cold crystal grip of the *geas* clutched at his mind, dragging it toward easy darkness. With a gasp, he fought free of it, but the pain shocked him, zipping like a burning trail of blasting powder along his nerves . . .

''Chief?'' He opened his eye to see Starhawk and Moggin close beside him, concern in their faces. He shook his head, trying to force aside the memory of the pain, the dark hurt of the shame that made him vulnerable again.

''I'm all right,'' he whispered, aware that his lips, his fingers, and feet were icy cold with shock. ''It's just . . . It can't wait. Not for them—not for me. We've got to retake the camp—we've got to kill Purcell. Now, soon. Or it's death for all of us.''


''And you expect us to believe this?'' Arms folded under the ragged cloak of his black bearskin, Ari regarded Sun Wolf with bitter fury in his hazel eyes.

Sun Wolf, who would have infinitely preferred being sold naked on the eunuch's block of the Genshan slave market to facing his friends again, said quietly, ''Not really.''

If Starhawk hadn't been with him, standing unobtrusively in the background with Moggin at her side, he doubted he'd have had the courage to enter the dripping dark of the mine shaft at all. He also doubted that any of the men gathered around the tiny fires in the old pit-head chamber would have listened to him, had not the Hawk had her usual quiet air of being ready to rip off the head of the first man who spoke and spit down his neck.

Penpusher said, ''C-can Purcell see through your eyes? See where we are, how few of us there are?''

''No,'' said the Wolf. Of that, at least, he was sure.

Ari asked, ''Can you prove that?''

"No." The pain of seeing what was in their eyes and on their faces was like a spear blade in his guts. But as a warrior, he'd gone on fighting with weapons in him and only let himself hurt afterward.

Dogbreath spoke up. "Does he know you've pulled free of him?"

"*If* he's pulled free of him," growled the Goddess under her breath, patting her palm with a naked sword.

"Yeah," the Wolf said, ignoring her. "He'll try to bring me under his will again when we meet. He may succeed. If that happens while we're fighting for the camp I want the nearest person to kill me. That includes you, Hawk."

"Don't worry about that," someone else muttered, unseen in the inky shadows. The pit-head chamber was large, hewn from the hill and several inches deep in a revolting stew of dirt, foxes' mess, old leaves, and seeped water that ran down the walls from above. They'd had to pile rocks to build a heather fire a man could have covered with his cupped hands. The flickering blaze splashed random patches of gilding on the haggard faces of the troopers grouped around them, the brass buckles of Penpusher's sheepskin jacket, and the jeweled rings snagged in the tangled jungle of Dogbreath's hair; it outlined in shadow the Goddess' scars and gleamed with a silvery shine in Curly Bear's eyes. All together there were, the Wolf guessed, ninety warriors who had fled with Ari and taken his side—eighty-three men and seven women, not counting himself and the Hawk.

"Considering he knows you *can* break away from him," Ari said, his voice calm despite the gall in his eyes, "he'll probably kill you himself."

The Wolf said steadily, "I know he will. But I'd rather have it from friends."

"Join the club, pook," muttered someone. "*We* already got it from a friend."

Ari moved his head a little, eyes glinting dangerously under the curtain of his tangled black hair, and the man silenced. Bitter wind moaned across the shaft entrance nearby, calling up a deeper groan from the black depths, where the seam of alum-bearing rock plunged downward into the hill. There was no other sound. "Anyone who wants to is welcome to leave," Ari said quietly into that hush. "If you think you can keep away from Purcell and Zane and if you've got someplace else to go."

He scanned them, meeting now one man's eyes, now another's, challenging them to speak. "Let me point out to you that Purcell isn't just out to catch all the slaves he can and that he knows as well as we do that the best way to keep a mine slave from running is to hack off one foot. He's not gonna let *anyone* out of the wastelands who'll peach to the King-Council about him being a hoodoo." After a moment he turned back to Sun Wolf, his eyes, behind the hard wariness and the desperation of twenty-four hours of sleepless fatigue, saying plainly, *Hurt me again and I'll kill you.*

Around them, the men gathered in, the raw smells of drying blood, filth, sweat, and dirty hair rank in the unventilated room, smells Sun Wolf knew from a childhood in the camps of war. Like a dog in his pack, he felt warmed by them, aware of the support once more of those iron bonds that looked so casual to those who had never felt them—bonds that didn't ask questions and didn't care and didn't think what a man thought or felt, only that he was one of the pack and was there when needed.

Home, he thought, and for an instant understood the raw physicality of the bond that achieved through the wordless contact of violence what dancers achieve through dance, what lovers—sometimes—achieve through sex. But at the same time, he saw the burning walls, the carrion crows eating dead women in the streets, Moggin's daughter with her throat slit to the neckbone only because she lived in the wrong place at the wrong time, and disgust and horror sickened him, both at it and at himself for never having seen it before.

The realization passed in an instant, as his concentration went back to what Ari was saying, Ari, who was commander now. But having seen what the bond had sprung from, he finally understood in his heart that this was his home no more.

"The damn thing is that they know the territory as well as we do, Chief," Ari went on. "Zane's got nearly two hundred of the original troop on his side, plus Louth's boys, and every postern, well shaft and low place in the walls are gonna be guarded. We thought about getting help from the village; but, if what you say is true, the men there'll be locked up under guard.''

"C-candy," grunted Penpusher. "Two people c-could bust 'em out of the town hall jail, easy."

Ari nodded. "Yeah, standard stuff. Routine Three—riot, diversion, Zane sends out a troop, we ambush them at Dingle Creek because they'll be ready for it at Crow Rocks, steal their horses and arms, and so on. But there's still ninety of us riding back into a camp of damn near five hundred of them, plus a goddam hoodoo. I don't see how we can do it."

"The same way they did us," said Sun Wolf quietly. "Didn't your mama ever tell you that curses fly home to roost? I know where those Eyes are now, and I know what they look like. I'm gonna take and shove that hex down their goddam throats."

Quietly, Dogbreath asked, "And the wizard?"

The wizard. Purcell. Sun Wolf had a momentary vision of those colorless eyes, devoid even of cruelty, and of the knife outstretched in his hand. Cold, clinging, like nooses of glowing wire, the *geas* whispered of its presence as the growing strain of holding it from him twitched at his every thought, like the pain of the wound in his arm. He knew the time was short, that he dared not even sleep now until it was done. "I'll have to meet him." His voice sounded smaller than he intended.

He glanced across at Moggin, standing next to Starhawk, as if for protection, in the thick shadows near the door. "I'll need your help, Moggy."

"I thought you said he was a fake," protested the Goddess, and Moggin shut his eyes with a kind of weary, ironic patience at this interpretation of his nonpowers.

Ari's eyes flicked from the white-faced and bedraggled philosopher to the Wolf, worried—not as a commander gauging a potentially weak link, which was what, the Wolf thought tiredly, should have been his concern, but as a son anxious for the overstretched strength of the man he most cared for. The anger between them, the quarrels, even the betrayal, Sun Wolf realized, were largely peripheral to that care. In spite of the fatigue, in spite of the pain of his arm and the cold dread of what he knew was yet to come, he felt warmed. "Can you do that?"

He shook his head. "I guess we'll all find that out."

# CHAPTER

## —— 16 ——

"Y*OU KNOW THE ONE WE NEED." MOIST ECHOES* carried the Wolf's words away into the claustrophobic darkness. Moggin paused in the act of fixing the torch into an old socket cut in the rock of the mine's walls, his bowed shoulders stiffening.

Then Moggin sighed, and all the tension seemed to go out of him, taking with it what little strength he had left. He whispered ironically, "Of course." Then he leaned his forehead against the slimy rock face, and Sun Wolf saw the whole gaunt body shiver. "What else would we use?"

At the cracked, sobbing note in Moggin's voice the Wolf crossed the distance between them, a matter of a stride or two between the rock face and the edge of the slimy water which drowned the remainder of the mine tunnel as it turned down, seeking still further darkness. The Keep-Awakes Sun Wolf had gotten from Ari—drugs on which most of the men had been living for the last twenty-four hours—filled him with a tinsely restlessness under the growing pain of the *geas*, but didn't impair the bone-bred instincts of a commander who hears one of his men breaking under prolonged fatigue and exhaustion.

He caught Moggin's shoulders in his big hands as the other man began to laugh hysterically.

Had it been one of the troop, the Wolf would have shaken him, struck him, and cursed back the wave of broken sobs following hard upon that uncontrolled laughter. They hadn't time for it—that much Sun Wolf knew. He could feel the *geas* growing in him, and knew it would get worse when Purcell woke up again and started working it consciously. It was getting harder and harder to cling to the half-understood protection of the Sishak Rites. When the Keep-Awakes wore off he would, he knew, sleep like the dead, and the *geas* would devour him in his sleep. There wasn't time for any of this.

But he only held Moggin tight against him, while the other man wept.

Because, as they both knew, the ritual he would have to work was the one he had seen Moggin working the last night Moggin had spent with his family before their murders, the spell that had convinced him, and everyone else, that Moggin was indeed the mage who had raised the curse—the spell of the summoning of power from the bones of the earth.

Gently, gradually he sank down to his knees, bringing Moggin down with him, to sit with their backs to the wet surface of the alum-bearing rock. All the while, Moggin sobbed as the tight controlled hardness of everything he had endured broke to pieces at once: the flight from the camp before the *djerkas*; Zane's sadism; and the rape and murder of his wife and daughters before his eyes. Sun Wolf remembered their voices drifting down the kitchen stairs while he himself stood in the dark of the cellar, frantic with fear for Starhawk's life and for his own enslavement. He knew that was in Moggin's mind now—the two fair-haired girls and the woman whose smile had still been sweetly serene after five months of siege, all in their white nightdresses in the dark kitchen while Moggin did some fast explaining about why everyone suddenly seemed to think he was a wizard.

Without quite knowing how, the Wolf knew it had been the last time he'd spoken with them.

He'd seen men come to pieces like this under the stress of combat or prolonged physical hardship, and Moggin didn't have either the physical or emotional toughness of the troops. Feeling the *geas* stir within him, flexing the terrifying strength of those glittering tendrils, he wondered if he were getting soft, letting the most vital link of his plan break down like this and delaying things who knew how long when his own endurance could be measured in hours.

But having so nearly lost Starhawk, he wasn't about to say to another man, *Suck it in, soldier.* If his ancestors didn't like it, they could go look for another descendant.

*Which they might have to do in any case.*

At length, Moggin's weeping subsided, and the philosopher turned away from him, wiping his bruised face with shaking fingers that merely served to smear the tear-tracked filth into mud. "I'm sorry," he whispered, and coughed, deep and agonized. "It's just that . . ."

"I know," said the Wolf softly. And for the first time in his life, he did know.

"I know I'll get over it." Moggin leaned his shoulder against the wet stone of the wall, his back half-turned to the Wolf, like most men, ashamed to be seen weeping by another man. "I mean, people do." He wiped clumsily at his gray-stubbled cheeks and sniffled loudly. His voice went on, speaking into the darkness beyond the grubby glare of the torch in its socket above their heads. "I did think I was going to die on the journey. I rather hoped I would, in fact. It sounds stupid to say that all this . . ." He gestured around him, not at the dripping dark of the narrow tunnel's end, but, Sun Wolf knew, meaning the hellish journey north, the exhaustion of fatigue and slavery, the killing exertion of escape, the long nightmare of Purcell, the curse, and the strain of living with the point of a sword at his back. "All this has made it easier to go on living." He turned back to face the Wolf, the ghost of his old philosophical detachment back in his eyes. "One doesn't meditate much about dying when one is trying like hell to save one's life, you know."

The Wolf smiled, and said again, "I know."

Moggin sighed, his breath a pained and heavy drag. Then, after a moment of weary stillness, he wiped his face again with his blistered fingers, and pushed back the long, greasy strings of his hair. "I'll draw out the pattern of the circle and tell you the ritual of its making, but you have to do the actual rite yourself, you know. It was different from the other Circles of Power in the books . . .''

"It's different from any that I've ever seen," the Wolf said quietly. "That's one reason I never liked it. It's in the oldest of the Wenshar demonaries, a broken circle, twisted. My guess is its source is some older magic, an alien power. You get a feel for these things, and I never liked the feel of that one."

"I see." Moggin paused, the chalk stub he'd fished from his coat pocket poised in his delicate hand. "So that's why . . . It was surrounded by warnings, you know, in Drosis' book."

The page in the demonary seemed to shape itself in the darkness beyond the sputtering glow of the torch; the dull black lines of common lettering, and around them, the brownish, spidery trail of line after line of faded ink, handwritten notes in the shirdar tongue. He had guessed without being able to read them that these were warnings. It was one of the spells he had resolved to stay well away from. Sun Wolf felt his skin turn cold. "Warnings of what?"

"It said: *The power runs both ways. The mage must be stronger than the pull of the earth.* And Drosis had written, *When the earth magic is spent, all will be gone, and he will go out like a candle snuffed to smoke.*"

Sun Wolf was silent, thinking about that. "Yet you tried it anyway."

Moggin nodded, the pain of that last night and the desperation he had felt coming back into his eyes. "I suspected that, starting out with no power, the ritual itself would kill me. I just wanted power enough to get my family out of the city." He managed a shaky smile. "So even an assassin was met with not unmixed emotions."

Sun Wolf had to chuckle at that, but at the same time he shivered. "And there's no way of guarding against that possibility?"

"If there is," Moggin said, "Drosis never wrote it down."

The Witches of Wenshar might have, but he could not read the shirdané; in any case, Purcell now had the books. The thought of what *he* might get out of them

turned the Wolf even colder. But all he grumbled was,
"Pox rot it."

Moggin rose, and with the chalk began sketching from
memory upon the nearest rock face the shape of the crescent that served in this case for a protective circle, the
swooping lines of power that spread and vanished dis-
turbingly all around it. Drawing it now—and doubtless
when he had drawn it back in his study in Vorsal—Moggin clearly was only reproducing what was in the old
wizard's notes. But Sun Wolf, who had worked a little
with the Circles of Power and Protection, with the lines
that summoned strength and the lines that dispersed it,
felt his skin creep at the sight of a pattern so clearly
rooted in chaos, whose every curve, every shape, whispered of wildness, irrationality, and unpredictability beyond his or any mage's control.

In the demonary, it had specified that the spell must
be raised within the womb of the earth—something Drosis
hadn't mentioned. This tunnel, the farthest extent of the
mines before bandits, land wars, and religious strife had
broken the back of the Empire's trade in the north, was
as deep as they could get. All around them in the listening darkness, Sun Wolf could sense the presence of powers and entities unknown to man in the dripping volcanic
rock, in the leaden and evil waters, and in the weight of
the darkness itself. The perilous lines Moggin showed
him would draw up the black and lambent magic of the
earth, like an enormous beast that must be bridled with
no more than a slip of silver thread and ridden to the
edge of doom.

Moggin went on, his breath a faint mist in the flickering glare, "I suppose that, to make the spell, a wizard
must first decide how badly he needs what the power will
buy him, and if it is worth the risk of ending his life."

Maybe, the Wolf thought, standing to look over Moggin's shoulder, arms folded as he studied the small circle
written on the wall, so that he could draw it, large, about
himself for the summoning of the power. But in addition
to the possibility of killing him, there existed an equal
possibility that it wouldn't—that it would merely strip
away his powers with its passing, and leave him helpless,
the slave of Purcell's *geas*, this time for good.

* * *

"That's the last of them," Ari's voice breathed out of the dark. "They'll shiver for a couple hours, but at least, if Zane sends out a party, he's not going to catch us all in the same room."

Starhawk, standing beneath the black lintel of the mine, nodded. She hadn't the mageborn power to see in darkness, but her night vision was good; the abandoned alumstone diggings stretched around her in grimy and sodden desolation, eroded, half-flooded, and blotched with lichen and twisted, untidy stands of heather and whin. Even in daylight, she was willing to bet, no one would have guessed that ruined landscape concealed a miniature army.

"How many?"

"The last group made a hundred and eighty. We can count on maybe a hundred or more switching sides in the battle, plus camp followers—wranglers, sutlers, that kind of thing—and whatever we can get from the town."

Starhawk's level dark brow tilted a little, but she made no comment. Troopers loyal to Ari had been drifting silently in all night, either drawn by the logic of using the old mine as a headquarters, or, latterly, guided there by small parties sent out to hunt stragglers who might not know the moor so well.

It was the fact that so many of them guessed exactly where to come which had prompted Ari's evacuation—that, and his refusal to tell any of the newcomers the extent of the plan. One of the groups, Starhawk had been interested to note, had contained three of Zane's guards who'd witnessed Sun Wolf's forced attempt at suicide in the garden.

"I mean, hell," one of them had said, when they'd spoken to Ari and the Hawk in the flickering darkness of the pit chamber. "I got nuthin' against Zane, but damned if I'll stay in the same camp with a hoodoo. Holy Three, if he could do that to the Chief, what's to say he wouldn't do that to me the next time he didn't like the way I spit on his terrace?" And the man had spat, as if to illustrate the harmlessness of the act, into a corner of the room, and scratched his crotch.

"Not bad," she murmured now. Many of them, like Hog, with Helmpiddle tucked protectively under his arm, had only been waiting their chance to escape. Others, it was true, had come simply to learn what Ari's plans were—whether they had the strength to attack the camp, or whether they were simply going to disperse and make their own livings as free mercs, having found the thought of Purcell's command more than they could stomach. But when Ari had pointed out to them the unlikelihood of Purcell either passing up cheap slave labor or allowing word to reach his rivals on the King-Council, they had thought again, and most of them, whether they'd liked it or not, had agreed that an attack on the camp was their only choice.

"We can pass the word the minute the Chief gives us the go-ahead," he went on, folding his arms and glancing back over the ruined floor of the ancient diggings. Down here in the open dell, the moor winds were less fierce, only riffling at the heavy black fur of his bearskin collar and turning the braided scalp locks he wore on his shoulders—the hair of the men who'd killed his parents when he was eleven in one of the endless northlands border squabbles over land that was useless to anyone now. Up above them, the wind screamed over the desolation, smelling of rain and sleet. Then he looked back at her in the gloom, his eyes troubled.

"Can we trust him? Can we know if we can trust him?"

Starhawk met his steady gaze, and shook her head. "I don't know. I don't know if we'd be able to tell or not if Purcell gets control over him again. I don't know how we'd be able to be sure we aren't walking slap into a trap." By his expression she could tell that Ari—and probably every other soldier in the troop—had thought of that one or would think of it sooner or later.

The Goddess had already pointed out the alternative of simply selling Sun Wolf to Purcell. If he defeated the master wizard, aces; if not, they could still go ahead with the ambush, diversion, and the rest of Routine Three. "Fine," Ari had said. "Only then, Zane'll know something's up—and the Chief'll be dealing with a whole campful of goons who have nothing else to think about." The Goddess hadn't exactly admitted she was wrong, but had muttered a lot of things about Zane's ancestors and personal habits, and had let it go at that.

However, Starhawk had to concede the woman had a

point. The plan depended on Sun Wolf's being strong enough to defeat Purcell head-to-head—on his being strong enough, at the very least, to prevent the more skilled wizard from forcing his way into his thoughts again and reading there the entire plan. She shrugged. "We'll know when we count the dead. It's trust or die."

"It's always trust or die," Ari said softly, hooking his hands behind the buckle of his sword belt—as Starhawk habitually did, and as most of Sun Wolf's students came to do. His breath blew out in a wry chuckle, the cloudy puff of steam fraying from under his mammoth mustache. He produced a flask of battered tortoise-shell from beneath his cloak and offered it to her, the gin searing, warming her down to her icy toes. "Hell, if it was anyone else, we'd be hitting each other over the head screaming, 'Don't trust him, you lamebrain!' "

The Hawk laughed, loving him—loving them all. In some ways, the year she'd been on the road with Sun Wolf had been a very lonely one. "Aw, hell—if either of us had any brains we'd be in a different line of business. But when you ambush that relief party, for the Mother's sake, kill somebody my size and get me some real clothes! I feel like a female impersonator in this skirt!"

Ari frowned, studying her, with her sword belted on and the froufrou of gold-stitched ruffles kilted up around her knees. "I been meaning to ask you, Hawk—What're you doing dressed like a woman anyway?"

"I *am* a woman, dammit! I couldn't . . ." From the dark of the mine shaft behind her came the soft crunch of feet. She turned, her sword in her hand.

It was Moggin, alone. He was hugging himself for warmth in the Chief's baggy black jacket; against the abyss behind him, his dark form was stooped, as if he were tired beyond description, but when he spoke his voice sounded better than it had since the attack on the camp. "The Chief says to begin. He'll revive the hex the moment the relief party is sent out from the camp to quell the riot in Wrynde. He says he'll meet you on the road back to the camp, once the relief party has been ambushed and taken."

"Is he all right?" the Hawk asked. She, too, remembered the unintelligible warnings written in the ancient demonary, and Sun Wolf's uneasiness about some of those eldritch spells.

Moggin hesitated for a long time before replying. "It's—difficult to tell," he temporized. "He survived the rising of the power, which I gather not everyone does." His voice wavered a little, as if still shaken by what he had seen.

Ari glanced at the sky, slate and charcoal above the broken iron teeth of the rim of the dell. "How long will it last?" he asked softly. "It'll take the Hawk at least two hours to get into Wrynde, skrag the guards, and free the men there to start the riot—say another hour or two for whomever they let get away to reach the camp, depending on whether the chump is smart enough to steal the horse they're going to leave standing around unguarded. By the time the relief party hits our ambush, will he still be able to help us?"

That was the trouble with war, the Hawk thought detachedly: she, too, was considering the Chief in terms of the cold economies of his strength, suppressing the part of her that screamed *To hell with that! Is he going to live through all this?* It was something Moggin wouldn't know anyway, and something that, in a way, didn't matter at this point.

"I think so," Moggin's soft voice said out of the shadows.

"He need more Keep-Awakes?" Ari cared about him, too, the Hawk knew. But at this moment, what he really cared about—what he had to most care about—was his men, and the success of the exercise as a whole. There would be time to grieve afterward, if Sun Wolf's contribution to all this turned out to be his life.

A small part of her still wanted to slap him for the callousness of his tone.

"No," the philosopher said. "No, that's all been . . . eaten up in the power of the spell." He coughed, the sound of it bad, and fell silent for a long moment, while Ari gave the wordless signal to the Little Thurg, the closest of the relay messengers, to start the men for the ambush point.

Then Moggin said, "He asked me to tell you both that he loves you, in case he doesn't see you again."

* * *

Purcell was aware of him now. Somewhere, Sun Wolf knew, the cold little business mage was stretching forth his dark hand, locked in the grip of a magic trance, sitting in the predawn shadows of the half-burned room which had been Ari's, rocking back and forth among the burned curtains of the bed, whispering the words that never quite surfaced in Sun Wolf's consciousness—the words of weakness, of defeat, of subservience to his will. But that Sun Wolf knew only abstractly.

What he knew, what he saw, what he felt, was the darkness all around him, the darkness within his own body and mind—the darkness where the dark hand twisted and clutched and dragged at the strands of spell that cut his every nerve and bone like heated wire. He could feel, could smell almost, Purcell's mind holding on to his, and hated it like an animal hating the smell of death.

And within him, around him, as if he burned in a halo of roaring black flame, the earth magic consumed his mind.

He was only dimly aware that he knelt still on the slime of the mine shaft's floor. His senses were magnified, screaming out of proportion to anything he had known; every pebble was a knife blade, stabbing the flesh of his knees, every crease in the leather of his breeches and fold of his shirt where his doublet pressed it tight to his flesh dragged like a binding rope; Ari's footsteps and Starhawk's, retreating away on the surface overhead, ground through his bones and entrails, and he fought not to scream with pain and blind rage. The earth magic had risen through his hands, through the ground, and through the chalked rings on the tunnel floor, pouring over him and through him like a pounding torrent of blackness, ripping free the guy wires of his soul until he felt his mind flapping like a tent in unnamable winds. Only by clenching his mind like a bunched fist of light on the center of his being could he remember who he was and why he had wanted this power in the first place; and at that center, gripped with the grip of his life, was the *geas*.

The gouge of Moggin's returning stride was agony; the smell of the man—like his own a foul compound of reeking old sweat, unwashed linen, cooking grease, man-

hood, and filth—mixed nauseatingly with the stench of
the guttering torch, the foetor of the stagnant water a few
feet away, and the terrifying breath of the unseen things
that dwelled beneath its surface. Mind screaming, raw,
he lurched to his feet and swung around; Moggin's face
a barely recognized tangle of shapes, flesh, and hair, and
the skull underneath, and the soul beneath that, in the
howling blaze of torchlight and darkness.

Moggin held out his hands, not initiating the shock of
contact; after a second the Wolf reached out and touched
them, the blood scalding under the ridgy squishiness of
the fragile flesh. The rage in him, the barely contained
madness of the earth magic's fire, whispered that he could
rip this man to shreds with his hands, as he could rip
himself or anything else that came near him, and Purcell's *geas* coiled and pressed, like a clutching black
tapeworm, in reply. Moggin whispered, "Can I get you
anything?" as if he were aware how all the world, the
wind overhead, and the faint drip of water shrieked and
dinned and pounded into his senses.

His mouth numb, he only gestured the torch away and,
turning, stumbled toward the water. The thought of the
water and of the things that his senses told him dwelled
deep within it terrified him, but he needed to scry with
something, and the thought of looking into the fire was
more than he could endure.

He could barely stagger; Moggin had to take his arm
and lead him to kneel at the stagnant pool's edge. "Do
you want to be alone?" he whispered.

"NO!" The word came out an inarticulate snarl—Sun
Wolf seized him, crushing his arm in his berserker grip.
Then, forcing back the madness of the pain, forcing back
the howling magic, he eased his grip, and shook his head.
He wanted to say *Stay with me. Please.* But the madness
had rendered him dumb.

In the water he could see Starhawk. Part of him knew
it was nonsense that she could have reached the walls of
Wrynde already, but he could see her, slipping in and out
through the broken ruins of what remained of the larger
town, slipping through the crumbling brick archways of
what had been its sewers and holding to the dense black
shelter of decaying walls where dark pines forced apart
the stones and streams roared sullenly through skeleton

houses. By the light, he could sense that where she was it was approaching the first pallor of dawn, in truth several hours away . . . or was it? Time seemed to have disappeared from his perceptions; he had no idea how long it had taken him to summon her image in the fetid depths. Maybe it *was* nearly dawn.

The walls of Wrynde, looming above her against a wasted sky, looked pathetic and ineffectual. Ari's men could have taken them for sport in an afternoon. He remembered building those shabby turrets and gates, strengthening them and pointing out to the mayor where the weak spots were. Scorn them though they might, the Wolf had always known the value to the troop of the farmers and townsmen—the need for mules, for food, and for a place to go that wasn't the camp. It was he who'd ordered the worst of the ruins that surrounded the walls to be razed, to preclude just what the Hawk was doing now—sneaking up through the stones, stream cuts, and weeds unseen.

The Hawk looked different, seen this way, through the lying medium of the water and the pounding blackness of the fire within—as if he could see both the scarred bony beauty of her, and the cool opal glints of her soul. Later he saw her again, in the earth-smelling lockup under the town hall, with the blood of two different guards— he didn't know how he knew that—splattering the garish flounces of her dress and bodice. He saw the townsmen locked in the cells reaching through the bars to touch her hands, and the stink of their rage that came to him from them, even through the water, was overwhelming, like the crackle of new flames. The vision was silent, but he knew she spoke to them, calm and reasonable; in other days it had always been the Hawk rather than Ari who'd dealt with the Town Council in their endless squabbles with the troop. He saw her reach down to take the key from the body of a dead guard. The men were arming themselves as the image faded to darkness.

He became more aware of Purcell's strength, the *geas* swelling black and fat in his brain; the grip of the dark hand pulled tighter. The earth magic's colorless wildness filled him, holding Purcell's will at bay as he stumbled to his feet. His numb knees gave, the pain of the blood rushing back to circulate again in an unexpected hammer blow. Moggin caught him as he stumbled, but after a moment, with a queer, slow deliberation which seemed to take minutes, he shook loose those steadying hands.

Painfully, slowly, fighting to control the frenzy of madness on the one hand and the agonizing drag of the *geas* on the other, he began to scrape from the wet earth of the floor all the marks of power and protection that he had drawn. The magic flowing into the new circles of power that he drew, the Circles of Light and Darkness, the curves of strength and guard, and the clean powers of the air, frightened him. He felt the momentum of the earth magic behind everything he did, like swinging a weighted weapon only barely within his control. Yet he felt exultant, filled with a wild rage and madness held barely in check; he laughed, and saw Moggin draw back from the staring gold of his eye.

It was just before sunrise when word reached the camp that the men of Wrynde whom they had taken for slaves had broken loose and were slaughtering their guards. Sun Wolf couldn't see it clearly, meditating again on the black waters of the pool, for nothing he could do would enable him to see into the camp itself. As if he stood on a distant hill, he could see the gates and the road that led to them, a twisted skein of yellow-gray mud and glittering silver. He could see the man riding along it full tilt, though it seemed to him no faster than a walk, could see the blood splattered on his hands and clothing and hair. He had been more and more aware of Purcell's strength, dragging at him as the hours had passed. Now it slacked, the relief from the pain as intense as pain itself. He smiled. Someone must have called the mage and broken his concentration. *Time,* he thought grimly. *All I need is time . . .*

In time, he saw the relief party emerge from the gates.

Louth was leading them, huge and chunky on a galled and unkempt bay gelding. They were more numerous than he'd expected, and heavily armed. Evidently Zane wasn't yet aware of how many of the men who'd pledged their loyalty to him had vanished in the ensuing twenty-four hours. Nor, apparently, had it occurred to him that a riot in Wrynde might be a diversion to draw troops into just such a sortie. It would make more work for Ari, he thought distantly, watching as the horses pounded through the churned muck of the road. But it meant less men holding the gates.

Then he turned his mind away. From the bottom of his soul—hollowed, screaming, a black and billowing universe of wildness—he called up the memory of the glowing sign he'd seen written on the money paid for Vorsal's ruin, and gave his whole being to the magic of ill.

Like silk streaming through his hands he felt the power of it, and his ability to turn it here and there as he willed. Not small things this time, he thought. Not a matter of bread unrisen, of a thrown horseshoe or a snapped lute string. There was no time for the slow grinding of a thousand little misfortunes. He saw now, or felt through his skin, that what was needed was the great ills, rising wherever the money was or whatever it had touched within the walls of the camp: fire in straw, in bedding, in roof thatch; a healthy man's bowels loosening in agonizing flux; doors jamming tight; floors that had formerly only creaked collapsing in splintering shards; beams and posts and overhead shelves giving way; horses spooked and running wild; the rage and accusation engendered by one final straw, one last indignity or insult or fancied slight, breaking loose in murder . . .

*Curse you,* he thought, remembering the fair-haired girl dead in the barren garden, Starhawk and the child on her back falling under the crumbling of the burning wall, that boy Miris whom he hadn't even known screaming as he pitched off his frantic horse's back into the seething red-black carpet of ants. *Curse you, curse you, curse you* . . . Like a falcon riding the thermals, he saw from high above the uneven stone circle of the camp, a piebald blot of color in the colorless hills, no bigger than a piece of money. He reached with his hand into the water and picked it up like a piece of money. And on that circle, that piece, he traced the mark he had seen.

As a warrior he had never fought in hate, but he hated now.

The pressure of the *geas* slacked and eased. Purcell, for the moment, had other things to think about.

He got stiffly to his feet. The agony of madness eased for a moment, allowing him to speak, his words thick as a drunkard's.

"Let's go," he said.

# CHAPTER

## —— 17 ——

*H*E MET *ARI ON THE STONY RUIN OF ROAD THAT RAN* between Wrynde and the camp, rising from the heather before them like the mad ghost of a demon bear. The men sent up a cheer when they saw him, the noise of it tearing him, kindling rage again and berserker wildness in the madness of the magic that gripped him, even as did the colorless glare of the overcast daylight and the clawed gash of the wind. He held enough control over his own mind to raise his fist to them in his old gesture of triumph and shut his eye in pain as their cheering re-doubled. Only Ari, in the black-painted mailshirt of one of the bandit mercs, looked askance at the mad gold eye staring from its bruised hollow beneath the tattered hair; and Starhawk, now in hauberk and breeches again and looking as if she'd been skinning men for her living from the age of five, began to dismount, shocked concern in her face.

He could not speak, but waved her violently back. Be-tween the savagery of the earth magic and the brutal drag of the *geas* in him, he dared not try to speak to her, dared not remember that he was glad to see she'd done her part in freeing Wrynde without getting killed. He felt like a man holding two maddened stallions on leading reins,

272

who, at a false step or a break in attention, would rend him to pieces. He tried not to think about how long there was of this yet to go.

Dogbreath brought a horse for him and with Starhawk helped him mount. As in the water and as when he had looked at Moggin in the firelight, neither of them looked quite as they had, as if he could see their bones, their viscera, all surrounded by pale colored fire. Deep down, part of him hoped they'd understand when he did not acknowledge them, hoped they'd all live long enough for him to apologize and explain. He managed to wave to Moggin, left in the desolation of wet bracken and stone, coughing as if his lungs would shred within him as the cavalcade spurred away. Before them, above the hills which hid the camp, white smoke had already begun to rise.

As they passed the broken foundations of the watchtowers which had once guarded the gap in those hills, the Wolf became aware of Ari's men, lying stretched in the heather all around them and waiting the signal to storm the walls. They were hidden, invisible in the landscape as he had taught them to make themselves invisible, but now he smelled them like a beast, the fetid stench of them choking him, and saw the foxfire of their thoughts dancing above the heather which hid their bodies.

And at the same time, as Ari's riders mounted the little rise and saw the stumpy granite knoll with its ragged wall and boxlike turrets, he felt the earth magic in him give and shift, its madness slacking as deep down in the bowels of his soul he felt pain begin.

Some instinct told him that this was the beginning of its end.

*God's Grandmother, not NOW!*

The camp gates were shut when they reached them. Hog—who, without his beard and in Louth's armor, actually did look a little like the now-deceased Louth—bellowed, "Open the goddam gates!"

The man in the turret above yelled back, "The motherless counterweight's jammed! You'll have to come in through the postern!"

"Nice hex," Ari snarled as they dismounted and crowded forward.

The small man-door in the gates was flung open; the

guard there said, "By the Queen of Hell's corset, it seems like everything's gone . . ." His face changed as he registered who was in the gateway with him, but he hadn't time to make a sound before Ari cut his throat with a backhand slash that nearly took off the head. Blood sprayed everyone in the narrow way, and suddenly men were converging on them from all over the square beyond.

With an inarticulate bellow of desperation and rage, Sun Wolf jerked the gate guard's sword free of its scabbard and plunged into the ensuing fray.

Behind him he could hear yelling, as the narrowness of the postern door trapped the attackers or tripped them over its high sill. Ari and Hog drove in after the Wolf, trying to clear the narrow passage of the gate before reinforcements could arrive, but more and more men crowded in from the open square of the camp, all yelling wildly for help. The low stone ceiling groins picked up the roar of the seething, shouting, hacking mob and amplified it to a skull-splitting bellow. The smell of opened flesh and spilled blood, of confusion and rage and fright, flayed Sun Wolf's mind as the dark magic within him transmuted slowly to agony, as if the power in him were clawing holes in his flesh in its efforts to get out. He fought desperately to clear a way into the camp before the earth magic deserted him, howling his battle yell and yet fighting coldly, instinctively, with all the long training and skill of his life.

From beyond the squat arch of the gate toward which he struggled, he could smell burning and hear a chaos of shouts. He had the impression of horses rushing here and there beyond the packed mob that now filled the gate passage, of men breaking off their pursuit of them to get weapons and join the fighting, of other fights everywhere in the camp, and of furious yelling and the crash of falling wood. Even as he parried, thrust, severed hands, and opened the shrieking faces before him, he sensed a vast, boiling chaos all around them in the camp, and his stripped senses, above the immediate storm of fear and stress and battle rage, picked up such a confusion of blind hate and resentful violence that his mind felt torn to pieces, and he found himself screaming like a madman as he fought.

One minute they were being pushed back and trapped. The next, half a dozen men from within the camp itself fell upon the defenders from the rear, all bellowing Ari's name, and through surging confusion the attackers burst out of the choked gateway and into the open spaces of the muddy square. Arrows spattered them, mostly shot at random from the walls and mostly missing, since both bows and arrows were still warped and splitting; a mule raced past, eyes white with spooked terror, scattering men before it. Ari was yelling, "Take the gatehouse! Take the gatehouse!" as more defenders came swarming down the walls.

Then Sun Wolf felt the *geas* clamp on him with killing pain. The cold wrenching in his guts made him think for a moment he had taken a mortal sword thrust; the next second, it was only Dogbreath's fast work that kept him from doing just that, as his arm went limp and a defender's blade drove in on him. He fell back against the wall, breathless and sweating, his vision graying out. For a wild instant, he felt the overwhelming compulsion to turn and begin hacking at those nearest him, Dogbreath, Ari, Penpusher. He clutched at the dimming earth magic, pain now instead of madness, but the agony of the *geas* did not lessen; it was like two crossed ropes straining at one another, with his own flesh caught in between.

He screamed an oath, a hoarse shriek like a disemboweled animal, and his mind cleared a little. The madness was lifting, bit by bit, and the wild dark of the power with it—soon it would be gone. More men shoved past him out of the shadows of the gateway and into the square, swords clashing, the reek of blood and smoke like a knife blade driven up his nose and into his brain. He heard others running along the top of the wall, and saw a body pitch over; the rest of Ari's men, fleshed out with as many fighters as Wrynde was able to field, would be trying to scale the walls. Then the *geas* hit him again, the silver runes swimming visibly in his darkening sight and the rage, the need, to kill Ari and the others almost smothering him. *Purcell*, he thought blindly. *Now, quickly* . . .

Heedless of whether any followed him or not, he plunged across the square toward Ari's house.

There were fear-spells all around the old governor's

quarters, lurking like ghosts in the shadows between the chipped caryatids of the colonnade. Though the Wolf sensed their power objectively, the earth magic still in him brushed them aside like cobwebs. He smelled Purcell before he saw him, smelled the sterile, soapy flabbiness of his flesh and felt the metallic cold of his mind—felt by the pull of the *geas* where he must be found. He turned his head, and caught the flicker of shadow heading across the waste ground toward the Armory.

With a hoarse cry he turned, pointed—only just becoming aware that Dogbreath and Starhawk had followed him and were standing gray-faced with shock just outside the colonnade's protective spells. But when they turned their heads it was clear they didn't see. Still unable to speak, he flung himself in pursuit once more.

The square all around them was a scene of the most appalling chaos, of Zane's men fighting Ari's, Zane's men fighting each other, sutlers frenziedly looting soldiers' quarters, and wranglers wildly chasing horses and mules, which plunged back and forth through the confusion with white-rimmed, staring eyes. Near the barracks row, two camp followers were tearing one anothers' hair and screaming in a circle of their watching sisters, oblivious to the pandemonium around them. Men were fighting along the tops of the walls, without concert or purpose; others were simply running to and fro in unarmed panic.

*This had better be fast,* Sun Wolf thought with the corner of his mind that had once commanded men. *Once Zane rallies them, Ari's going to be swept away.*

Where the hell *was* Zane, anyway?

A squad of guards intercepted them at the Armory door, led by the woman Nails. She was armed with a five-foot halberd, which far outreached Sun Wolf's own sword, and moreover stood above him on the steps. The madness within him and his own desperation drove him forward; he wanted nothing but to end this, finish it or die before his borrowed power waned. Screaming wordlessly, he cut, feinted, and ducked in under her guard, crowding her before she could turn the pole on him as a weapon to knock him off the steps. He killed her when her dagger had half cleared leather; behind him, Starhawk and Dogbreath had turned to guard his back against the half-dozen men pounding up the steps behind.

He flung Nails' body over the edge, ten feet down to the mud of the square, turned, and threw his weight on the door. By the way it jerked, he could tell it had been latched but not bolted. *Maybe the bolt's jammed,* he thought dizzily, slamming his shoulder to the door again. *This is the last goddam time I mess around with a hex. You just can't aim the bastards.*

It might, he reflected through a haze of pain and madness, be the last goddam time he did anything.

Smoke burned his eyes. It was drifting everywhere, thick and white in the damp air; his head was pounding, the raw magic burning up his flesh. *Finish it,* he screamed within himself. *Finish this before it finishes you!* He braced his feet and slammed against the door, which gave at the same moment the rickety staircase under his feet creaked, swayed, and collapsed.

It went down like a sharecropper's shack in a gale, taking them all with it—Starhawk, Dogbreath, their attackers. Sun Wolf, halfway through the narrow door, had the breath knocked out of him as his belly hit the doorsill, but managed to drag himself up and inside. The dark maze of the Armory was filled with smoke, choking and blinding him even as the *geas* filled his brain with a thin, whispering darkness. Pain ate his flesh and clouded his vision. He felt the blind compulsion rising in him again with the urgency of insanity to turn his sword, not on his friends this time, but on himself. He tried to scream again, but only a thin, strangled wailing came from his mouth, like a child trying to make noises in a dream. When he moved forward, drawing on all the earth magic in his crumbling flesh to put one foot before the other, it was like wading through glue.

One dark room—two. He knew the Armory as he knew his own house, but for an instant he felt lost, disoriented, trapped in an unknown place. Black doors and endless voids of empty space yawned on all sides of him, and behind each door silver runes seemed to hang like glowing curtains in the air. Stumbling into the main gallery he could see smoke hanging in the air, bluish in the sickly light that fell through the room's high windows, and across the planks of the floor a sprawling spiral of Circles of Power, curves and patterns he had never seen before,

like the galactic wheel drawing all things into its lambent
heart.

On the far side of the room Purcell stood beneath the
arches of the gallery, a trim, dark shape which no light
seemed to touch. His magic filled the room like the bass
voice of unspoken thunder, vibrating in Sun Wolf's
bones. The dark hand of shadow reached out toward him,
trailing darkness from skeletal fingers. The hated voice
spoke, soft and spiteful and smug, from the gloom.

"Don't come any farther, Sun Wolf."

The rage that surged in him at the cold timbre of those
words was almost nauseating. Shame, fury, and humiliation blazed into lightning in his hands, and he flung that
lightning at the dark form. But the shadow hand gestured, repeating the wave of the soft white fingers emerging from Purcell's furred sleeve. With a shifting crackle
the power dispersed, cold little lightnings running away
into the walls.

Then Purcell gestured again and pain locked around
Sun Wolf's head, like the spiked bands torturers used to
rip off the tops of their victims' skulls. Though he did
not look down he was aware of the silver runes all over
his flesh, clinging stickily to his bones and nerves and
mind, to his life and the very core of his being.

*I've fought on with worse than this in battle,* he told
himself, through blinding agony, though he knew it was
a lie. *I can do it now . . .* He forced himself a step forward; it was like pulling his own bones from his flesh.
Purcell flinched back, for a moment seeming as if he
would run. Then he stepped forward once more. The
smoky light picked out wisps of gray hair under his velvet cap, and the white-silver frostiness of his eyes. "I
see you've been fool enough to tamper with earth
magic," he said coolly. "Good. That will make it easier
for me. I suppose you looked on it as just another convenient drug. You thugs really are all alike. Get down on
your knees—I won't have you standing."

Sun Wolf's knees started to bend in an almost reflexive
obedience. He stopped himself, panting.

"Down, I said! DOWN!"

A shudder passed through him, but he remained on his
feet. In the cold bar of light, he saw Purcell's nostrils
dilate with real anger and that prim upper lip tighten.

"You defiant animal. I see I was right to abandon the thought of making you either slave or ally, with such an intransigent attitude. What a waste of power."

"I wonder—you didn't—seek Altiokis—as an ally," Sun Wolf panted, the sweat of exertion pouring down his face with the effort not to kneel. His tongue felt numb with the long silence of his madness. Panic fought at the edges of his mind, the sense that the world would crumble, that he would die, if he didn't kneel—and what was kneeling, after all? "You're two of a kind."

"We are nothing of the sort!" Purcell retorted, deeply affronted, and some of the agony eased as his attention flickered to his offended pride. "The man was a drunkard and a sensualist, like yourself! He gathered power only to waste it on his perverted pleasures. He was a gangster, not a businessman."

"What the hell do you think businessmen are but gangsters with the bowels cut out of them?" He'd hoped making Purcell angry would have freed him, but with every ounce of strength he could summon, he could neither take another step, nor touch the black whirlwind of pain and insanity that was fading slowly back along the scorched trails of his nerves and bones. As it did, the *geas* tightened, slowly strangling—he was aware he was trembling with exhaustion.

Nevertheless anger washed over him, anger at this cold little man in his neat gray robes and hands that had never wielded more than ledger and quill. "You and your damn King-Council would wipe out Vorsal rather than risk them cutting out your trade; and you'd sooner wipe out my friends than negotiate with them . . ."

"Negotiate?" Purcell spoke the word as if it were a perversion beneath his dignity. "With a pack of barbarians who would trade their influence to the first merchant who offered them dancing girls? If I'm to hold control of the King-Council, I can't be wondering from month to month about alliances with people who haven't the faintest idea what business is about. No—it really was the only way. You must see that. Now . . . draw your sword."

"Eat rats." He was fighting for breath, the pain unbearable. He wondered if, when the last earth magic went, he'd die. Remembering Purcell's dominance of him, the rape of his mind and will, he hoped he would.

Smoke had thickened around them even as they spoke, a fog of choking blackness dimming the light. With a crashing roar something fell behind him, and the heat of fire beat against his back. Trapped, pinned where he stood against the glaring light of the blaze, he could move neither forward nor back. The Armory was burning—or was it only the searing heat of the earth magic consuming him? His scraped voice managed to gasp out the words, "You want to kill me, you come over here and do it with your own lily-white hand!"

"Don't be foolish." The hated voice was calm as if addressing a child.

A shower of sparks whirled through the doorway behind him. One of them lighted on the back of his hand; his other hand jerked to strike it out, but could not move. As the hot needle of pain drilled into his skin and the thin smoke of his searing flesh stung his nose he heard Purcell say, "I know what will happen when the earth magic ebbs—what it will take with it when it goes. It's fading already, is it not? The mere fact that you can speak tells me it is. So I have only to wait . . . ."

Dark madness filled him, swamping the insignificant agony of his hand. With a cry, he tried to lunge for the old man, to kill him as an animal kills; the *geas* seemed to explode in his skull, blinding him, smothering him, holding him fast.

Around him the sparks had kindled little lines of fire across the floor, crawling in blazing threads toward the walls. In another few minutes the place would be in flames. The dark magic surged and thrashed in him, but could not overcome the deadlock of the cold silvery will bound so fast around his mind. He realized in panic Purcell would hold him here until the fire reached him, hold him in it, unable to move . . .

"CHIEF!"

The *geas* slacked infinitesimally as Purcell looked past him into the smoke-filled anteroom. Sun Wolf heard, or felt beneath the greedy crackle of the flames, the light spring of Starhawk's boots. He tried to scream a warning, and the *geas* locked on his throat like a strangler's hand. A moment later, Starhawk was beside him, the wildfire light splashing red over the blade of her lifted throwing ax. Then she gave a cry, doubling over in agony, her knees buckling as she clutched at the X-shaped scar on her head. The ax slipped from her nerveless fingers; she caught at the wall, fighting to stay on her feet.

Purcell smiled.

And Sun Wolf thought, as if the woman sinking sobbing down beside him were as complete a stranger as those he had spent most of his life being paid to kill, *It isn't just business to him. He does enjoy it.*

And the rage of his anger turned cold, collapsing inward, a black star swallowing light.

Deliberately, coldly, he conjured the last of the earth magic into himself, for he could not cast it out past the bonds of the *geas*. But with all the strength of it, with all the strength he possessed, he gathered the *geas* around him, drawing it into his mind, his soul, his life; holding fast to the tendrils that bound him to Purcell's will—and Purcell to him.

"Starhawk," he said quietly, and she looked up at him with eyes streaming with smoke and pain. "Take the ax. Kill me with it."

Purcell had felt the change in the *geas*, the slacking of his resistance; he stumbled forward as if some physical pressure had been released. "What?" he gasped, and Sun Wolf smiled, feeling the strength of the *geas* now from the other side. He held it closer to him, using all the earth magic to bind those silver ropes to his life.

"You want me to die, Purcell, you're coming with me. Now. Do it, Hawk."

Whether she understood what he was doing or not he didn't know, but she had never disobeyed his command. Her hand shaking, she picked up the weapon again, and swaying, forced herself to her feet.

"What are you doing?" screamed Purcell. "I forbid this! I command you to . . . to . . ."

"Release you?" said Sun Wolf softly. Perhaps he did not say it—he couldn't tell. Perhaps the words sounded only in his mind. But he knew the master wizard heard. "No. You release me—or you come with me. Do it, Hawk." He felt the *geas* bite, rip, twist like a terrified bullock on a rope. But its very nature twisted it around his mind and soul, and he held it fast.

Beside him the Hawk drew herself up, her eyes dilated, delirious with the pain gouging at her skull. "You're insane!" Purcell was yelling. "Let me go . . ."

Sun Wolf made no reply, watching the Hawk, willing her to find the strength against the pain in her own head. He had taught her that strength, and taught her obedience to the Cold Hells and beyond. Shadowed black against the flames in the doorway behind her, the Cold Hells of pain and madness were in her eyes. The earth magic was evaporating from his flesh; he could feel his strength going, and tightened his grip still further on Purcell's *geas*, on the silver mind entangling his, to drag it down with him into death.

Wearing her cold, soulless battle face, Starhawk raised the ax. Purcell screamed, "Let me go . . ."

*You let me go, dammit,* he thought, but all he could manage to cry was "Do it, Hawk! NOW! That's an order!"

She screamed her battle yell and swung with all her strength at his skull.

The snapping of the *geas* from his mind was like a rope breaking, disorienting in its suddenness; he barely twisted aside in time. But the Hawk's reflexes, even in pain and madness, were as fast as his own. Her momentum was broken, even as he snatched the ax from her hand. He was turning as he did so, turning and throwing, and even with one eye—if he aimed with his eye, and not by instinct and magic and hate—his aim was true.

The ax took Purcell right where it should, at the base of his spine. He seemed to break at the waist and fold backward, collapsing in the archway where he had first stood; at the same moment there was another crashing, and a beam from an upper floor ploughed down from above, setting the rafters overhead on fire. Sparks rained down, igniting the wooden floor. Sun Wolf caught the Hawk by one arm as she staggered, and together the two of them ran through the falling sparks and choking blur of smoke, through the furnace of the two chambers behind them, to the white rectangle of the outer door.

He knew the stairway outside was gone and was long past caring. He and the Hawk flung themselves through the door, and for endless minutes, it seemed to him, they floated outward and down . . . to land in a tangle of mud, lumber, and the bodies of the slain.

The earth magic left him as he jumped. He hit the waste of struts and boards limp and muscleless as the last of that black torment vanished like vapor, taking even its memory with it. His own magic, the power that had slept in his bones since his childhood, the power to weave the winds and to call back the living from the shadowlands of death, vanished, too. He felt nothing inside him but a vast white hollow, an emptiness that filled the world. Later it would hurt. He knew that even then.

For a long time, he lay on his back, wondering if he would die, and looking up at the smoke pouring up out of the burning Armory into the gray belly of the sky.

Then Starhawk's voice asked, ''You okay, Chief?'' Her hand reached down to help him to his feet; she had to put her shoulder under his arm to help him cross the square to where Ari and his men waited for them beside the gate.

Zane had never made his appearance to rally his men or to give any kind of direction to the fighting in which they so greatly outnumbered their attackers. Without Purcell, Louth, or any other leader, they had given up quickly. Once Ari and his forces had broken through the postern gate, there had been relatively few casualties. A number of these, the Wolf was told later, had been in fights between members of Zane's own forces, over booze or whetstones or fancied thefts, or all the meaningless trivia over which they'd fought all summer—fights which had broken out immediately after the departure of the relief force for Wrynde.

Zane himself they found in his bed. Sun Wolf looked up from the eyeless and sexually mutilated corpse sprawled among the gory welter of the sheets in time to see Ari turn away, gray-lipped and sick. ''I knew Zane was a bastard,'' the young commander said softly. ''But Holy Three, he didn't deserve a death like that from any man.''

Others had crowded into the room to see—Hog, still in Louth's armor with the faithful Helmpiddle waddling behind; Penpusher, with a bandage torn from some corpse's clothing wrapped around his arm, and Dog-

breath, limping, holding onto a halberd to stay on his
feet and grinning like a golliwog through a mask of dirt
and blood. Behind them in the doorway Sun Wolf saw
Opium, clothed in a very plain blue dress that was too
big for her, obviously borrowed from someone else, the
velvet profusion of her hair not quite concealing the livid
brown bruises on her face.

"What makes you think it was . . ." began Starhawk;
but her eyes followed his; after regarding Opium for a
thoughtful moment, she raised her eyebrows, shoved her
hands behind the buckle of her sword belt, and held her
peace.

# CHAPTER

## —— 18 ——

"Tʜᴀᴛ'ʟʟ ʙᴇ ғɪᴠᴇ ᴄᴏᴘᴘᴇʀs."

"Goddam highway robbery, that's what it is," Sun Wolf growled to himself, but watched Opium's backside appreciatively as she reached down the credit book from the shelf behind the bar and marked his page. "Worth it," he added, as she glanced back at him with teasing eyes through the tendrils of her hair, "for a drink of real beer."

"Sure be nice," muttered Dogbreath, raising Penpusher four wood chips at the poker table nearby, "if we could pay for it with real money."

Sun Wolf said nothing. He knew the remark had been directed at him, though not with any particular malice.

Opium folded shut her credit book. "The credit you've been spreading all over camp is more money than you've seen in your life, Puppylove, so make the most of it." She pulled the lever on the keg, loosing a stream of nut-brown silk into the pewter tankard Sun Wolf maintained on the premises, and set the beer on the plank bar before him. For a moment their eyes met. She was still heart-stoppingly beautiful, but he was growing used to that. The fact that she was now living with Bron helped, satisfying some male territorial instinct in him that took

offense at the thought of an unclaimed female. Though
he might toy with the notion of dragging her down and
ravishing her under the bar whenever he walked into the
place, he no longer had to fight to keep from doing so.
At least not much.

It might have been that she was more content with her
life now, happy with Bron and making money—or at least
what would be money when currency became once more
available in the camp—hand over fist. Since Bron and
Opium actually *had* wares to sell, a good portion of the
fund of credit in the camp was slowly making its way
into their ledger books, and the always-active camp gossip had it that Opium was one of the chief investors in
the consortium that would run the alumstone diggings.
Some of the men added that she'd turned bitchy since
she'd gotten rich—meaning that she no longer danced in
the tavern, and the dark flightiness, the vulnerability that
had drawn the Wolf's protective instincts, was gone, replaced by a calm and confident peace. But if Sun Wolf
missed the romance of that hunted helplessness, he at
least did not grudge her what she'd gained instead.

She still moved with a dancer's lightness as she brought
him his beer, pausing for only a moment before the little
mirror back of the bar to adjust the silk flower in her
hair. "And you?" she asked softly. "Is it going better,
Wolf?"

He was silent, staring down at the marble-white froth
in the tankard cupped between his scarred hands. *Was* it
'going better'?

He made himself nod. "Fine," he said. "All right."

Her dark brow puckered with a friend's concern. "Do
you think you'll ever be able to . . ."

"I said I'm fine."

Her breath drew in to apologize, or query, or express
her very genuine worry for him, and he concentrated on
keeping his hands on the tankard and not slapping her
and telling her to shut the hell up. But she let her breath
out unused. After an awkward pause, he drained his beer
and gave her a smile he hoped didn't look manufactured.
"Thank you," he said, and left.

His magic had not returned.

Winter had locked down on the camp. As he crossed
the square, the frozen mud crunched treacherously be-

neath his boots, blotched with trampled and dirty snow. Wind moaned around the fortress' rubble walls, low now, but rising in the nights to dismal shrieking in the high rafters of Sun Wolf's house, in the lofts of Bron's tavern and the makeshift ceilings of the hospital and stables. In the hospital it scarcely mattered. Those who had not died of the plague, no matter how ill they were, had begun recovery almost from the moment Purcell had perished in the burning Armory.

Xanchus, Mayor of Wrynde, had sent two midwives to help with the nursing until Butcher recovered. Neither was mageborn or had the healing power in her hands, but both understood granny magic, and Sun Wolf had humbly boiled water and sorted herbs for them in order to learn whatever they could teach. Moggin had volunteered all the lore he'd accumulated about medicine, but the older of the two grannies confided to the Wolf one day while grinding elfdock that in the main, the Wolf's assistance was by far the most useful. The few men who had laughed at his helping the old ladies had quickly regretted being heard. Later, when Sun Wolf had suggested that they go a few training bouts with him with wooden swords after one of Ari's classes, they had regretted being born. When the weather cleared a little between storms, the Wolf still rode the ten miles into Wrynde to improve his herb lore. He understood now that this and the healing he was studying with Butcher might be the closest he would ever come to magic again.

By day, he understood that he was lucky to have survived the earth magic at all.

Waking in the night was different.

In dreams he returned, again and again, to his first, ancient vision of magic; to the little wooden naos behind the village long-house where the Ancestors dwelled. In the dreams he was a man, not the boy he had been, but the place had not changed. In the shadowy forest of spirit poles on the other side of the stinking blood trench he could still see the faint gleam of the skulls racked along the rear wall and pick out the names of ancestors crudely carved on each stained trunk. The tokens of their mortal lives—usually a knife or helmet, but sometimes only a few scraps of hair, a bit of braided leather, or a tuft of woven straw—seemed to move restlessly with the

leap of the fire on the stone altar, where it blazed as it
did on the Feasts of the Dead. It was higher, hotter,
fiercer than he'd ever seen it in life, blazing wildly up
toward the rafters as if old Many Voices had dumped
powdered birch bark into it from his trailing sleeves.

But the old shaman wasn't there, and the fire poured
upward nevertheless, though the Wolf could not see what
it was that burned.

The core of the fire called him, as it had in his dreams
of childhood, and his hand yearned toward it. In his ancient vision he had grasped the flame, felt the agony of
it searing away his hand's flesh, to leave only the bones
that wielded the fire's glowing core like a sword. A few
nights after the fight with Purcell, when this dream had
first returned to him, he had felt hope leap in him at the
sight, for it was that sword which he'd used in his first
vision to free himself of Purcell's dark hand. Gritting his
teeth, he had reached out and grasped the flame anew.
Searing, excruciating pain cleaved into his loins like a
sword, but what he had taken from the flames was not a
skeleton hand grasping the magical core of his power,
but only a charred and blackened stump.

The training floor was quiet when he reached it. There
had been a class that morning, run by Ari as he himself
had once run them, pushing and bullying and thrusting
the men through the pragmatic intricacies of armed and
unarmed combat, making every reflex, every reaction,
every blow and parry as unthinking as the blink of an
eye against dust. Working at the back of the floor, with
the freezing air of the open veranda cold on his back and
the steam of breath and body heat pouring out under the
eaves, Sun Wolf had remembered how it had been when
he had trained the men and felt the fire of their spirit
moving like a finely balanced weapon in his hand.

The huge room was leaden-colored now, with the whitish reflections off the snow from its wide parchment windows dimly illuminating the dozen or so warriors still
working there on their own, swinging the weighted weapons through training forms, or sparring for timing and
wind.

On the far side of the vast floor he saw Starhawk, patiently instructing Moggin in the first uncertain rudi-

ments of swordplay. The philosopher's cough was responding, slowly, to the grannies' herbs; he'd finally gotten rid of his slave chain, though the scars of it would remain for life on his throat and collarbone. He looked better than he had since the first time Sun Wolf had seen him back in his house in Vorsal. By selling his services as an amateur geologist to Ari and Xanchus—he was the only man in the north with any knowledge of how to set up a kiln to bake alumstone into the white mordant itself—he'd amassed a small amount of credit; he was, moreover, making a reasonably steady living as a storyteller. Now that Gully had found his true métier as a mopper-up in the tavern, Moggin's memory of every romance, play, and poem he'd ever read in his sheltered and bookish life was a moderate godsend during snows and rains that lasted a week at a time.

*We never know,* the Wolf thought ironically, *where we're going to end up.* Probably Moggin would never have believed it a year ago if you'd told him he'd be working as a storyteller in a tavern on the backside of creation. Nor, undoubtedly, would he have believed it a few months ago, if you'd told him he'd live till spring—or want to.

Stripped to a loincloth and shivering in the bitter chill, the Wolf began to warm up in the dark inner corners of the room, where that morning's accumulated heat still lingered. At one time, he'd thought he was going to remain captain of the troop, the richest mercenary in the West and the best teacher of arms in the world.

At another time he'd thought he was going to be a wizard.

He pushed aside the memory of what it had been like to wield the winds in his hands.

He took a weighted sword of split wood from one of the cedar chests and began to work through the ancient training forms, slowly at first, then with deeper and deeper intensity, driving himself like a man possessed. As his body moved, seeking precision and perfection, his mind gradually stilled, and he sank into meditation, as deep as the meditation that Starhawk had taught him all those months upon the road.

"Does he blame me?" he asked Starhawk that night as they lay on the furs they'd dragged down to the warmed bricks of the hearth. Charcoal hissed on its bed of white sand, the flame light losing itself in the woven gloom of the rafters overhead.

She shook her head, knowing of what he spoke. ''You were their teacher,'' she said softly, ''but you weren't the reason they were warriors, killers, in the first place. That wasn't entirely true of me. You didn't make me what I am, Chief—you just made me good enough to survive it.'' The bones of her shoulder, delicate as the horned strength of a compound bow, moved against his pectoral. ''And he knows that, even if he'd been able to use a sword last summer, his family would still have died. It's just that, like me, he's not going to let himself be anyone's victim. He's decided that his philosophic principles against taking life don't extend to letting his life be taken because he's too helpless to prevent it.''

And so months passed.

It was just as well, Sun Wolf thought at times, that among the other effects of the earth magic's passing had been to hypersensitize his system to alcohol. Another time he might have dealt with the loss as he had dealt with loss before—by getting drunk and staying that way— but as it was, more than a single beer made him ill, and he did not share the desperate need that drove Gully to drink long after the puking point was reached. Likewise, he reflected once or twice, it was just as well that Ari had burned Purcell's entire stock of hashish and dream-sugar. Aside from the doses Purcell had given him, he hadn't tried them since his twenties, but he didn't like to think too much about the cozy oblivion they promised.

Coping with loss without something to take the edge off it—booze, drugs, or a dozen casual affairs—was something else he found unexpectedly difficult.

He did not return to teaching, but trained under Ari's command with the others. Mornings and evenings he'd work with Starhawk and Ari, and a few of the others who wanted to understand more about the disciplines of the sword than simply what was necessary to kill other men— Dogbreath, Penpusher, Battlesow, the slow-talking merc named Cat-Dirt and Cat-Dirt's woman Isla who, like Moggin, wasn't even a warrior, and Moggin himself. Some of the men grumbled, but Sun Wolf found, a little to his surprise, that what they thought of him concerned him far less than it had. He hadn't been aware how much it had concerned him before. He found himself far less inclined to the easy camaraderie he'd once had with all his troop, but discovered that his friendships with a few, like Ari and Moggin, deepened.

He read, slowly and thoroughly, all ten of the Witches' books, recovered unharmed from Ari's half-burned quarters; worked in his rock garden until the snows prevented him, arranging and rearranging the stones there, seeking the wordless rightness of a beauty for which he could find no other expression. Far into the nights, he trained and meditated by himself on the training floor, kindling small lights on the pillars because even his ability to see in darkness had left him, or talked away the evenings with his friends over beer and the maddening poker games for wood chips and IOU's that were the sole currency of the camp now that the marked money had been taken out of circulation. Many evenings he and Starhawk spent up in Moggin's rooms, the three low-raftered lofts in the heart of the unburned section of the Armory which had once been Starhawk's; many more, when Starhawk was off with Butcher and Battlesow, he spent there talking to Moggin of magic, of time, and of how things happen and why.

"I don't know." Moggin sighed. "There was so much in Drosis' books which simply made no sense to me. Things which make no sense are far more difficult to remember clearly than things which do." He settled back on the piles of old blankets and fleeces which served as seats, and gathered one of his half-dozen adopted cats onto the lap of his long, dirt-colored robe. His sword— which had once been Firecat's—hung above his narrow bed, and the makeshift table was piled with an astrolabe, a broken orrery, and whatever pieces of astronomical equipment he'd been able to dig from the scrap of years of looting dumped in the Armory's various storerooms. His long hair, hanging on the garish colors of the shawl wrapped around his shoulders, was almost completely gray now, but the pain in his eyes was less harsh than it had been.

"Damn those yammerheads for torching the house." Sun Wolf pushed Drosis' much-thumbed notebook from

him on the cluttered floor between them. ''That whole
motherless library up in smoke . . .''

''I wonder about that.'' Moggin stroked absently at the
flat, red-gold head of the cat in his lap. ''I'd been hit
over the head and they thought I was unconscious—which
I nearly *was*—when they started fighting over the loot
from the house, so my recollection isn't very clear, but
my impression is that the house wasn't burning when I
crawled away and hid among the other captives. A lot of
the city wasn't burned until the following day, you know.
It occurs to me that Purcell would have taken what pains
he could to salvage the library, as he was in a better
position to keep the books hidden than he was when
Drosis died. When spring opens the road it might pay
you to return to Kwest Mralwe and investigate Purcell's
house.''

For a split second the old excitement warmed the Wolf,
the old eagerness he had felt, lying in that far-off chamber in the foothills inn, when Dogbreath had said that
there was a wizard in Vorsal. It hit him like the half-
forgotten illusions of childhood, followed at once by the
bitter bile of disillusionment and the familiar, horrible
emptiness, as if his entire chest had been gouged away,
leaving only a bleeding hole. He turned away. ''What
would be the point?''

Later that night he thought about it, long after Starhawk had fallen asleep in the circle of his arm. It was a
long and tedious journey back to the Middle Kingdoms,
and the thought of dealing once again with Renaeka Strata
and with the King-Council and the King reacted on him
as if he'd bitten into bread and found a chip of metal
grinding at his teeth. He thought about trying to tell them
he had no magic anymore, and about what the King might
think of to coerce him into service.

At one time he'd considered going with the troop again,
not as commander—that was Ari's position now and daily
more unassailable, even if he'd wanted it—but as a sort
of uninvolved elder statesman. But he'd discarded it. The
arts of combat were one thing to him, a meditation, an
art, a need which could not be explained to a non-
warrior. War was another matter. He had seen both sides
of it, loyalty and friendship and the brilliance of life on

the edge of a sword, and like Starhawk, he would never take arms against the innocent again.

But without magic, he thought, looking down at the spare composite of scars and bones that was Starhawk's sleeping face, what was left?

Master-at-arms, either at some pretty southern court or here in Wrynde? In the moonlight, he turned his hand over where it lay on Starhawk's shoulder, seeing heavy muscle and the slowly healing scars of the demon bites, but seeing also the old vision shape of the naked bones that had grasped the fire. He had lost both what he had been and what he could have been. The empty wound of it opened again, and pain flowed out to cover him.

He forced it back, as he had forced back the pain of his many wounds. *At least I'll go see if the books are there*. Better that than let the King get them. And maybe, someday . . .

How long would he go on hoping, before it became obvious that in freeing himself from Purcell he had ripped out the mainspring of his life?

For a moment, the memory of holding the winds in his hands consumed him—as, Moggin had said, there were nights when Moggin woke from sleep overwhelmed with the kinesthetic memory of his wife's plump body nestled at his side.

He stroked the silk-fine skin of Starhawk's shoulder, touched the cockled ridge of an old scar, then the wispy silk of her hair. He'd tell her tomorrow of the plan to ride south, see what she thought of it. At least it would be something to do.

She had said once that to be with him was all she had ever wanted. But he knew that if he died tomorrow, Starhawk would find something else to do—return to her life as a nun, become a master-at-arms herself, or become an assassin. Deprived of his magic, there was nothing to which he could cling, except this woman herself—and that, he knew, would be the death of the love between them as surely as betraying her with Opium would have been.

Lonely, frightened, and more helpless in the face of fate than he had ever been, he lay and looked into the latticed darkness of the rafters until he fell asleep.

He dreamed again of the fire.

It rose before him, casting its gleam back among the
forest of pine poles where the eyes of his ancestors
gleamed, and this time he could see what burned on the
blaze: cities, he thought; cities burning on hills—Vorsal,
Melplith, Laedden, and villages without count; the face
of a woman he had killed in Ganskin, thin as a skeleton's
surrounded by clouds of black hair, when the women and
children of the town were taking the places of the slain
men on the walls; heaped bodies of men, such as they'd
made outside the walls of Noh, to teach them a lesson
for not surrendering promptly, swarming with ravens and
rats; a merchant he and the others had beaten to death
while drunk, for cheating them out of two stallins' worth
of booze; and a child he'd ridden down in street fighting,
he no longer remembered where. They whirled together
in the column of the fire and the crackling of the blaze
was mingled with their laughter.

He wanted Starhawk with him, for, like a seer, she
sometimes understood these things, but Starhawk, too,
was gone.

He was alone and he had failed, not only in the things
that he was good at—the things his father had demanded
that he be good at—but the things he had wanted so desperately—Starhawk's love and the magic that had been
the bones of his soul. From the fire they mocked him,
Opium, the child Dannah with her throat slit like a gaping red mouth, and the dark hand of Purcell, tracing runes
that were consumed in the fire.

The flames burned up higher, the images vanishing
into its white core, the laughter fading into its hiss. Where
he stood, he could feel the heat of it scorching him. His
bones were empty of marrow, hollow like a bird's; at the
touch of the blaze they would shatter and give him for
his agony only the blackened stump, and a world of continued pain.

Nevertheless he reached out, knowing what would
happen but knowing nothing else to do, and grasped the
core of the fire.

Starhawk heard him cry out in his sleep, and jerked
from the depths of her own dreams with a start. Sharing
his bed for the last ten weeks had not been easy. She was
not entirely used to it, even at the best of times, after her
years of sleeping alone; between his ruthless dreams and

bouts of desperate lovemaking in which he tried to forget his loss, his guilt, and his grief, she had been short of rest. But she responded to the crush of his grip on her and held him close against her until the storm of sobs subsided, the thin silk of his hair pressed to her lips, the long, curled tufts of his eyebrows and mustache scratching her neck where they pressed the soft skin, and the hot tears burning, shed by his hollow eye as well as his good. She did not speak—in time, she knew, she would learn.

But he put her aside and rose from their bed, walking naked in the cold moonlight that streamed through the lattice of the windows from the dirty snow outside. He stretched his arms up toward the dark voids above the rafters, furred, heavy-muscled arms crisscrossed with the scars of battle and the hands of a butcher, like big-boned lumps of meat. He cried out again as if the sound were being torn from him by an iron hook; like a clap of silent lightning, fox fire streamed up from his lifted palms to splatter against the rafters overhead and pour in viscous, glowing rivulets down all around him, flickering, dancing, filling the room with its cold blue glow and bathing him in frosty splendor.

Another incoherent cry ripped from his broken throat, and the bedside lamp, the candles beside his books, and the fire on the hearth in the other room all burst into simultaneous flame. In the shuddering frenzy of new light, she could see the pain and wild exultation twisting his upturned face. She sat up, pulled the blanket up over her shoulders—he was a wizard and above such things as warmth, she guessed, besides being a barbarian and damn near covered with fur to boot—and waited, while the light around him faded, and, after a long time of silence, he lowered his arms.

In a disappointed voice she said, "What, no earthquake?"

He came striding back to the bed like a puma, ripped the blanket aside. "You want an earthquake, woman, I'll give you an earthquake . . ."

She was laughing like a schoolgirl when he took her in his arms.

# CHAPTER

## —— 19 ——

THE FOLLOWING MORNING THEY RODE OUT TO THE
ruined cellar of the villa where they'd put the money
chest—Ari, Sun Wolf, Starhawk, Moggin, and at least a
dozen guards. Snow half-blocked its entrance—they'd
hauled away the remains of the *djerkas* for Hog to dis-
mantle weeks ago—but inside, the cave was fairly dry.
For the first week or so, there'd been a guard on it all the
time, until it was remarked that whoever volunteered for
that duty tended to lose in poker, even with wood chips,
for days. Sun Wolf himself didn't care whether the money
got stolen or not, though he promised a flogging on his
own account, in addition to Ari's official one, to the man
or woman who brought one silver strat back into the
camp.

"I got to tell you, Chief," said Ari, holding aloft his
torch as they waded over the slushy snow and into the
short tunnel, "I'm damn glad you got your power back,
if for no other reason than this. It's gonna take us the
rest of the winter to sort out who owes whom what."

"Yeah, well, I hope nobody invested too heavily in
buying up Dogbreath's poker debts." He stood for a moment, looking down at the chest in the mingled gray and
yellow of torchlight and daylight. When he had come

here before, it had only been a chest of money, sitting in the dirty chamber. With the return of his magic, he was aware of the stink of the curse clinging to it like months-old decay.

"I think the Goddess did," Starhawk remarked. "She's taken a hell of a shine to him—says she'll let him take out his debts in trade."

Sun Wolf, well acquainted through camp rumor with the Goddess' tastes, gave a wordless shudder. Moggin edged into the cellar behind him, muffled in the long robes of brownish wool and as many plaids and shawls as he could get in trade for his services as the Mayor's mining engineer, his hands in their shabby mittens holding the wicker baskets containing the two black chickens that were part of the rite for this particular type of curse. His pockets bulged with phials: mercury, the last bits of the auligar powder—of which Sun Wolf, now that he could work spells again, promised himself he'd make more—and whatever else could be identified of Purcell's effects.

Sun Wolf took off his thick sheepskin vest and his gloves, knelt gingerly on the hard-frozen dirt, and began to draw a Circle of Power around the chest.

They were still there six hours later when the daylight faded, and the torchlight flared a jumpy gold with the night drafts that blew in over the moor.

"The bastard won't come off."

"This isn't time to be funny, Chief," Ari said dangerously. He'd ridden back and forth from the camp two or three times, and every time the Wolf had come out of the cellar there'd been more people milling around the shambling ruins of the villa. Bron had lit a fire and was pouring White Death out of a goatskin flask. Opium, bundled in the purple velvet coat someone had looted years ago from an Eastern queen, was sitting on a broken foundation comparing credit records with the mayor of Wrynde, whose boots, unbeknownst to him, Helmpiddle was in the process of desecrating. Even Gully was there, breath streaming in a gold cloud from his gap-toothed smile while he cadged drinks from all and sundry.

"The time to be funny was six hours ago, when I wasn't bone-tired and damn near frozen," the Wolf retorted, rubbing his cold hands together and tucking them under his armpits for warmth. "We've worked every kind of take-off spell either of us could think of, and when we put the last of the auligar powder on a strat piece that hex is still on there like a tattoo on a sailor's arse."

He didn't add the conclusion that he, Starhawk, and Moggin had come to, crouching around the ninth or tenth Circle they'd made in the privacy of the cellar—that it was beyond a doubt the mad strength of the earth magic which had fixed the curse to the money for good. "After all," Starhawk had pointed out when they'd agreed not to break this particular piece of news to Ari, "there's about six more weeks of winter to go."

"You mean now you can't even tell whether the curse is off the money or not," said Ari.

"Sure you can," supplied Dogbreath, who, under the Goddess' watchful blue eye, was the only one looking slightly relieved. "After every try, just play a hand of cards next to it. That'll tell you fast enough how well it worked."

"Well, unless you want to pony up the cost of some more chickens," Sun Wolf growled, "that's out, too." Three of the rituals of cleansing had called for blood sacrifice, and, in the middle of winter, chickens did not come cheap. "I'm telling you, we've tried every method either of us ever heard about. That curse is on that money to stay."

"You let that bastard die too easy," Ari muttered viciously. "So what are we going to do? We owe half the camp to old Xanchus over there."

"Well, you better not pay him with that money if you're planning to operate the mines in partnership with him."

"Let's give it to the Mother's shrine at Peasewig," suggested Dogbreath brightly. "Those heretics deserve it."

"Could we melt it down?" suggested Opium, coming over to the group by the arched tunnel-mouth and delicately readjusting a jeweled comb in her hair. "Melt it down and sell the silver?"

"And let whoever buys it deal with the taint?"

She shrugged. "Melting might take it off."

"And if it doesn't?"

Her voice got defensive. "That isn't our business."

He suddenly found he loved her considerably less than he had.

"Not in my forge, you're not," Hog put in, coming over to them like a polar bear in his great white coat. Helmpiddle, waddling at his heels, sniffed inquiringly at the chest which rested upon the threshold, but backed hastily away and forbore any further attentions.

*Incontinent he may be,* the Wolf thought, the only one who noticed, *but not stupid.*

"All right," Opium said. "When Penpusher goes south to buy mining equipment and set up the initial trade treaties with Kwest Mralwe, that's the money he can use. You said yourself curses go home to roost."

"He'd never make it south," the Wolf pointed out, and there followed another awkward silence as they all digested the fullest implications of the hex.

Ari swore for fifteen minutes.

Then they all rode back to camp.

A bitter northeast wind sprang up later that night, while Ari was explaining to the troops gathered in the training floor that the IOU's they'd been trading all winter were universally worthless, and it started to sleet a few hours later. During the winter this was no great struggle to accomplish; it would have done so by the following afternoon anyway, but Sun Wolf was taking no chances, and wanted a night's sleep. It sleeted all the next day.

The site of the ruined villa, when he and the Hawk returned to it a few hours after sunset, was like an outpost of the Cold Hells, a frozen morass of dirty ice, with a few broken pillars and a granite bench or two barely recognizable where they rose from the crusted muck of old snow and iron-hard mud. By the faint glow of the ball lightning that drifted over Sun Wolf's head, he could see his own breath, Starhawk's, and that of the heavily blanketed pack pony they'd brought, skirling away in white rags. Through the shaggy robe he wore over his jacket and the mantle over that, the cold went through him like a battle lance.

*Good,* he thought. *No competition.* He half wished the Mayor of Wrynde, whom he didn't like, would try stealing it, but the money—and the curse it bore—would filter back to the troop very quickly in that case, besides dev-

astating the entire alum-digging project, which promised
to bring a good deal of wealth to the impoverished north.

Gingerly, using a pewter cup as a scoop, even though
he knew he could now with little trouble take the dim
slime of the hex off his hands, he transferred the money
from the chest to the packs and saddlebags they'd brought,
Starhawk carrying them out to the horse. When he'd told
her what he planned to do, her only comment had been,
"Then we'd better not get caught, because if we do, it's
gonna look like hell."

Thinking about it, he had to agree.

When he was done, he lit the chest on fire, picked up
the last two bags, walked down the short tunnel that led
to the freezing outer air, and stepped out smack into Ari.

"Chief," Sun Wolf's pupil said reproachfully, "I'd
never have thought it of you."

But the rank disapproval in his voice was a caricature,
as was the lofty expression on what the Wolf could see
of his face, muffled by scarves and hood in the dimly
flickering light of the lantern that hung from his staff.

"Yeah? So what are you doing out here? Going to buy
yourself a villa in Dalwirin and retire?"

"I don't even want to *think* about the size of the ter-
mites the place would get," Ari returned with a grin. In
the background, Sun Wolf could see Starhawk standing
near the pack pony, and beside her another, slightly taller
form and one of the transport mules. Then, more soberly, Ari said, "What were you going to do with it?"

"Take it up to the Kammy Bogs and scatter it in the
quicksand. Not all in one place. It's a week's journey,
this time of year, but that should be safe. Nobody would
be unlucky there but the demons."

The winds were fading. Here in the shelter of the hillside the air was nearly still, save for a flinty gust now
and then that stirred the rags of the Wolf's long mantle,
and bit his ears through his hood.

Ari nodded. "I'd figured the river at Amwrest, but the
bogs are better. There's just too many people in the camp
who'd want to risk passing it along to someone else."

Like Opium, the Wolf thought. Getting to know her
over the last two months, he'd come to realize she was
both vain of her beauty—not without cause, certainly—
and rather mercenary. Considering the fact that money

was her protection against the vagaries of fate, this attitude was understandable. But the knowledge had, like the growing confidence that let her stop trying to be all things to all men, eroded his romantic desire for her. A pity, he thought regretfully, but there it was.

"Can you explain my being gone?" he asked. "The Hawk was going to stay and cover for me, but . . ."

"Chief," said Ari reasonably, "if you disappear, and somebody comes out here and looks for the money, and *it's* gone—and it was your word in the first place that the hex wouldn't come off it—no. There's no *way* I could explain that." He shrugged, and gestured . . . Starhawk and the other muffled figure approached, leading the laden mule. "But if Dogbreath disappears for a couple of weeks, with the Goddess beating the camp for him, nobody's gonna be surprised."

In the jumping dimness of the lantern glow, Dogbreath's teeth gleamed in a grin. His black braids blew out from between scarves and hood like raveling bell ropes, the bullion braided into them sparkling faintly. "I'm willing to deal with the hex on the way to the bogs, Chief," he said, "but I tell you, if I get set on by bandits, I'm gonna let them *have* the festering money. Personally, I still think we should donate it to the Mother's shrine at Peasewig."

"That," Starhawk said darkly, "is only because you've never had the Mother sore at you personally. You wouldn't like what happens next."

"You gonna be all right?" the Wolf asked.

Dogbreath shrugged. "My whole life's been one long run of lousy luck. It's nothing I can't cope with. See what you can do about the Goddess by the time I get back." And he disappeared into the sleety darkness, leading the depressed-looking pack mule by the bridle. Sun Wolf had sufficient technique to turn aside a storm's effects from his own immediate area, but not to dismiss one altogether at will, particularly not during the time of storms; he returned with Ari and the Hawk in secret to the camp. By the time he had brought down the winds to a dreary fall of thin show, everyone's tracks were sufficiently covered to prevent whoever in the camp might have been interested from knowing what had taken place.

* * *

"I was damn naive." Sun Wolf settled back on the fur-covered brick of the bench and laid his great arms along the chipped rim of the pit which surrounded the bricks. "All that altruistic hogwash I spent the last year spouting, about how I had to find a teacher because I didn't want to hurt or kill anyone out of ignorance . . . My ancestors must have been laughing themselves into seizures. What I need is a teacher who'll keep me from getting enslaved again, maybe worse next time—maybe for keeps."

"If," Starhawk pointed out, propping herself up on her elbows in the thick furs of the bench, "the next teacher you pick doesn't try to enslave you himself."

Sun Wolf regarded her accusingly and picked up his mug of beer. "You know, I could have gone all night without hearing a remark like that."

Though winter solstice was over two months past, the dark still fell early. The last of the gray daylight was dying outside the few window lattices undefended by shutters, and the small, bare room was nearly dark. Outside, torches were lit along the ruined colonnade and in the training floor, where the remains of that afternoon's class were still bashing one another with wooden swords and poles, their voices penetrating faintly through the western wall. Sun Wolf was peripherally aware of other voices—the slaves packing up after working on the rebuilt Armory, women chatting about the cut of sleeves as they crossed the hard-frozen square toward Hog's mess hall, and two wranglers in front of Ari's longhouse loudly admiring the thick-sinewed bay horse of a messenger from the south who'd ridden into the camp two hours ago. The wind made a little hooning through the rafters and across the cedar tiles of the steep roof and sang through the scaly-backed granite boulders of Sun Wolf's stone garden outside. It was the time of thaw, before March's granny winter that would lead, in turn, to genuine spring.

"It's what I'd do," she commented, rolling over to lie stomach-down, her chin on her hands, her slippered feet protruding from beneath the billowy robe of white wool she'd put on after her bath, "if I were selfish and greedy, and had spells whereby I could enslave other mages. Now that Altiokis isn't out there to make me fall off a wall someplace, I'd start putting the word around that I'm ready to teach all you tender little fledglings.''

"You really are a damn nasty woman.''

She shrugged. "Hey—nine years in a convent makes you tough.'' With her baby-fine quiff of ivory hair falling down over eyes smoke-gray in the shadows, she had never looked less tough. He handed her the beer and turned his head to the soft, familiar clump of Moggin's footfalls on the wood veranda outside.

"Come!'' he said, and a moment later the philosopher entered, huddled in his dirt-colored burnoose and plaid cloak and looking, as usual, like a house plant someone had accidentally left outside during the first snow. He was carrying a weighted wooden training sword, and looked as if he'd definitely gotten the worst from whoever had been sparring with him.

"At my current rate of learning,'' he said with dignity, sinking cross-legged onto the hearth, "I have estimated that by the time I've trained long enough to withstand one of your men, I shall have been dead for forty-three years.''

"At least they'll bury you with a sword in your hand,'' the Wolf said comfortingly.

"Ah, good. Another lifelong wish fulfilled.'' He produced a leather bottle of beer from beneath the plaid, topped off the tankard in Starhawk's hands, and took a morose pull from the flask. "However, I didn't come here to make plans for my funeral, but to tell you that I think I know the name of Drosis' master. The Big Thurg was one of the men who got part of the loot in Zane's quarters at Zane's death. Today he traded the last of it— bits and scraps of silver for their metal content, mostly— to Opium for credit in the tavern, and Penpusher, who was there, recognized some of them as pieces of an astrolabe. Drosis had a silver one, which was among my things—Zane must have looted it from my house.''

As he spoke he dug in the flat leather purse that hung at his belt, and Sun Wolf remembered Dogbreath's voice, in the gloom of Starhawk's room with the carnival riot going on outside . . . *damned if Zane hadn't been going through the house while everyone else was out in the courtyard* . . . From Moggin's voice Sun Wolf could tell he wasn't aware of exactly when Zane had acquired the instrument, and forbore to enlighten him.

The philosopher handed him a bent piece of metal. It was battered and badly tarnished, but Sun Wolf recognized the *rete* of a large astrolabe. On one side, the positions of the stars were vaguely discernible, finely engraved in the soft metal. On the other—the side which would be invisible against the circle of the astrolabe itself when the instrument was assembled—he made out the name *Metchin Mallincoros* in spidery letters.

"You sure that's Drosis' master and not just the maker of the astrolabe?"

Moggin nodded. "Drosis told me his master made the astrolabe, for one thing, and you can see the orthography's the same here on the front where the names of the stars are graven. The joining of the letters 'tch' in 'Metchin' is the same as the star Atchar. It's characteristic of . . ."

"I'll take your word for it," the Wolf said. "Metchin of Mallincore." He stroked his mustache thoughtfully. "We never did make it up to the Mistlands, you know. It's a start . . . if, as the Hawk says, he or his surviving student isn't going to come up with some other type of *geas* to use on fledgling wizards."

"Well," Moggin said uneasily, "I remember there were at least two other types of enslavement spells mentioned in the Ciamfret Grimoire, though not given . . ."

"This gets better all the time."

"If we're going to Mallincore, I hope you like garlic," the Hawk remarked, sitting up. "Chief, I think you're going about this all wrong."

He took the tankard, of which, though brimfull while she snaked from a prone to a sitting position, she hadn't spilled a drop. "Considering the events of the past year, I'm not going to give you an argument," he grumbled. "You got an alternative plan?"

"Why find a teacher at all?" she said slowly. "Why not take time to learn what you have? To study it thoroughly, to work with it . . . to practice what you know you can do. You have Moggy to help you; you have the books of the Witches; you have Drosis' books, the three here and whatever we can loot from Purcell's shanty. Yes, you need teaching—but you also need time to learn. You aren't giving yourself that by haring around the country-side, looking for somebody to make you a better wizard. You need to make yourself a better wizard, Chief. It's got to start with you. Then maybe you'll be a little safer going out looking for a master.''

He was silent for a long time, staring into the heart of the fire and wondering why he felt fear. Fear that if he didn't make it, he would have no reason to give, no excuse? Was that what he had been seeking—someone to take the responsibility for his success or failure? Wizardry, like combat, needed a teacher—one could no more learn to wield power from a book than one could learn to swim. But it needed practice, as well, and unstinting work, solitude, patience, and care.

He remembered his exhaustion on the road north from the Dragon's Backbone to Kwest Mralwe, traveling all day, vowing to himself he'd look in the books for some kind of cure for Starhawk and falling asleep at the end of each day's ride. He remembered the calm peace of the last few months, the reading and study, trying to puzzle truth from the books, and the sense of time being his own. *Not months,* he thought. *Years.*

He glanced up and saw the glowing dots of rose light reflected in Starhawk's eyes. ''Here?''

''Unless you're willing to hire an agent to field job offers in the Middle Kingdoms.''

''We'll have to go back to Kwest Mralwe, at least, to see what's in Purcell's house.''

She nodded. ''And we'll have to do that as soon as the roads are clear, before some other enterprising hoodoo gets the same idea. But . . .''

Footsteps clacked hollow on the veranda again, swift and clipped, and Sun Wolf had barely time to identify who it had to be before she slid open the door. ''Wolf . . .''

She crossed the plank floor with her old, swift grace, holding up the wine-colored velvet of her skirt. To his surprise, Starhawk greeted her as a friend. *Of course,* he thought. *Over the winter in the tavern, they, too, had time to get acquainted.* Opium asked, ''Did you see who came to camp this afternoon?''

''Messenger from Ciselfarge, wasn't it?'' He knew the arms of most of the small merchant cities of the Middle

Kingdoms and the Gwarl Peninsula, and had identified the white castle on the green-and-red checkerboard embroidered on the courier's tabard that afternoon, even through the crusted layers of mud. "That's Ari's business, not mine anymore."

"Guess again." Dim firelight splashed off the barbaric rubies of her gown clasps under the fur-lined cloak—clasps Sun Wolf remembered the Little Thurg having stolen years ago in the Peninsula somewhere. He'd undoubtedly sold them to her this winter when he ran out of credit at the tavern.

"After all that happened through the winter, you know the troop's short—down to six hundred or so, fighting force. Ari's taken Ciselfarge's offer . . ."

"Kedwyr attacking them?" Opium looked startled at this piece of mind-reading. "I've been expecting that since they signed their nonaggression treaty the summer before last. Go ahead."

"Yes," she said, rather shaken; the Wolf did not comment on the fact that Opium was evidently being included in negotiations meetings these days. Considering how Ari and Penpusher had been taken at Kwest Mralwe, it wasn't a bad idea. "Ari wants to, because he owes the cost of the troop twice over to Xanchus and the other tradesmen for food, medicines, and mules for the summer's campaign. It's not a debt he can welch on, either," she added sapiently, "not unless he wants to carry his tents in his pockets from now on. But now Xanchus is saying he wants Ari to take out the debt in trade, and remain here to guard the diggings while they're being set up."

"At a rate of about a third what Ciselfarge is offering," the Wolf guessed, and again Opium looked surprised.

"Half, actually. So, since the Mayor owns most of Ari's debts, they've reached a compromise to leave a hundred men as a security force—and you, to recruit and train a hundred more."

Sun Wolf jerked bolt upright on his bench, his one eye blazing. "ME!?"

Three months ago Opium would have flinched and gazed at him with those liquid eyes; now she folded her hands calmly before her jeweled belt buckle and pointed out, "I can see Xanchus' point. Those diggings are worth not only money—they're power to whoever can control the trade. That's why we're using go-betweens and conducting the negotiations in the south in secret—so we won't get some Middle Kingdom army on our backs."

"That's their goddam problem," Sun Wolf retorted. "I'm not working for that fat little crook . . ."

"But he owns most of your debts," she informed him. "He's been buying debts all winter, as soon as it was known there was no way to pay off the credit with real money."

Sun Wolf's voice cracked into a hoarse roar. "The hell I'll stay here all summer as a—a guard over some festering hole in the ground! I'm no man's poxy debt thrall . . ."

"I shoulda left him locked up," Starhawk remarked to no one in particular.

"Legally, he can take the debts out however he wants, you know," Opium pointed out. "According to him, you set up the precedents on debts and welching yourself . . ."

"I did, goddammit, but that was different!"

It wasn't, he knew, even as he said it. The camp depended too much on the good will of the town to disrupt the economics of good faith.

"He's over there now." She nodded back toward the half-open door, through which, in a narrow bar of bright amber torchlight, figures could be seen between the smoke-stained brick of the corner of Ari's house and the crumbling statues of the colonnade. Ari, the gold rings in his ears and hair glinting softly where the light caught them, was nodding gravely at the inaudible jobations of Xanchus, muffled like a cabbage in a dozen fur-lined robes, gimlet-sharp eyes peeking out from beneath the fur brim of his hat. Penpusher stood by, skewed white ruff lying dead over his black shoulders like a smashed daisy, his account books in hand, and next to him, the messenger from Ciselfarge with his mud-slobbered heraldic tabard pulled on awkwardly over several layers of woolen hose and a sheepskin doublet. "If you want to get away before he can ask you face-to-face, I can hold them."

Her dark eyes met his, and held. "Fair trade," she added, with the ghost of a smile.

"You mean because I *am* forty years old, and ugly?" He took her hands, and bent to kiss her lips lightly.

Her smile broadened with mischief, and the comfort of knowing that he would remain, if not a lover, at least a trusted friend. "Something like that. Over the summer I'll see what I can do about buying your paper back . . ." Then she laughed. "And *not* to take it out in trade, if that's worrying you. Unless you insist, of course . . . Poor Dogbreath's been living in our back room with Gully for weeks. Bron's going to sneak him out in the campaign wagon when the troop leaves, since the Goddess is staying here as commander of the mine guards."

"That'll teach him to bet the same twenty strat five times." He kissed her again, and glanced over at Starhawk, only to see that she'd gone. A moment later, she emerged from the bedroom, buckling her sword belt on over the thick black leather of doublet and jerkin, into which she'd changed with her usual lightning efficiency.

"Now I know why I could never go on the run," Opium laughed, releasing his hands and walking over to the Hawk in a silvery froufrou of swishing skirts. "It never takes me less than an *hour* to get dressed, and that's without makeup . . ." Starhawk laughed, as the two women hugged. "I'll give you as much time as I can." And she was gone, slipping through the rear door into the garden so that Xanchus and the others in negotiation with Ari wouldn't realize where she'd been.

"Hawk, can you get the horses while I pack your gear?" the Wolf said. "I think Little Thurg's on gate duty tonight . . ." He turned back to Moggin, who had risen unnoticed in the gloom of the hearth pit. "You coming?"

The philosopher looked a little surprised that he'd been asked. "If you'll have me."

"It's gonna be rough," Sun Wolf cautioned, gauging with his mind the weather, the cold, and the frailty of that stooped gray form. "And Kwest Mralwe might not be easy for you, considering."

The sensitive mouth flinched a little, then Moggin shook his head. "After four months of the bucolic amenities of Wrynde, believe me, I am willing to go almost any place where books and soap may be purchased at will. I don't suppose anywhere will be easy for me, for a time," he added more quietly. "But I'd really rather be in the company of friends, even if it is on a grossly substandard road, than alone here. I'll try not to be a nuisance."

"Get your sword and your astrolabe, and meet us by the stables, then. And don't let them see you leave." He strode for the kitchen to collect the food they'd need for the journey, his mind already running ahead to the road and to the weather, wondering if he should turn aside the driving rain he sensed not far off or whether it would be of more use to hide their tracks from his own incensed men.

In the gloom beyond the tiny stove, he could just make out Starhawk, a lanky black silhouette against the few inches of open door, the dim torchlight from the colonnade catching blurry reflections on her pale hair and the metal of her jerkin, sword belt, and boot tops. Coming over to her, he saw why she was waiting. Xanchus and the messenger from Ciselfarge were standing at the corner of the colonnade, expostulating and pointing in the direction of the house. Past Ari's shoulder, they would be able to see movement in the bare rocks of the garden.

A moment later Opium emerged from Ari's doorway behind them, said something which caught their attention in her husky, drawling voice. They turned, looking back toward her, and it seemed to Sun Wolf that, in that moment, Ari gave her a querying look, and she replied with the most infinitesimal of nods. The young commander's voice was clearly audible, saying, "Oh, before we present him with your proposition, I did mean to ask you about the terms for buying your mules . . ." And, draping a muscular arm around each man's shoulder, he drew them back into the shadows of his house.

Sun Wolf grinned, put his arm around the Hawk's waist and kissed her hard. "Come on," he said. "We can be ten miles away before they know we're gone."

# ABOUT THE AUTHOR

At various times in her life, Barbara Hambly has been a high school teacher, a model, a waitress, a technical editor, a professional graduate student, an all-night clerk at a liquor store, and a karate instructor. Born in San Diego, she grew up in Southern California, with the exception of one high-school semester spent in New South Wales, Australia. Her interest in fantasy began with reading *The Wizard of Oz* at an early age and has continued ever since.

She attended the University of California, Riverside, specializing in medieval history. In connection with this, she spent a year at the University of Bordeaux in the south of France and worked as a teaching and research assistant at UC Riverside, eventually earning a Master's Degree in the subject. At the university, she also became involved in karate, making Black Belt in 1978 and competing in several national-level tournaments. She now lives in Los Angeles.